LAS

CHOCOLATE SOLSTICE.

CHOCOLATE SOLSTICE

To Demetrius, my summer love.

Thanks yous, Shoutouts & Such

Thank You.

My Lord and Saviour Jesus Christ.

My mom, Julia, and her love of storytelling and vocabulary.

My dad, Robert, (SIP) and his Caribbean idioms.

My husband, Demetrius, for affording me the time, space and finances to conjure up and finally bring this project to completion.

My children, Zion and Zoe, for constantly cheering me on.

My Semper family for their steadfast love and encouragement.

My Alleyne family for their long distance love.

Guerilla Beta Readers: Walili Dailey, Dee Lew & Taunna Fagan.

Shoutouts.

BooCrew. 968210. Sway Collaborative. Positive Sisters. SUNY Farmingdale. Starstudded Dance LLC. Crown Me Brands. Councilman Derek Hamilton. DA Kelley.

In Memory.

Ivy Semper. Robert Alleyne. Dedric Darcelin.

Acknowledgments.

Editor – The Author's Pen.

Photographer – DiezzVisions

Cover Model – Gerald Hamilton

Makeup Artist – Karin Smith Nealy

Far Rock – STAND UP!

I

Q113

Bad & Boujee

Daniel heard his phone buzz as he stepped out the shower. He looked at the screen as Diamond's name popped up on his phone. *Oh shit,* he thought. Today was her birthday, and he hadn't called her all day. He knew she thought he had something planned. He let out a sigh before answering.

"Hello?" he hesitated, as though the screen didn't give full information as to who was calling.

"Bae!" Diamond yelled into the phone.

"What's up?"

"Nigga, it's my birthday! That's what's up! You don't call me all day and when I call, you say *what's up?* Fuck is that bullshit about?!" she continued.

"Diamond, that's not necessary."

"I knew you were gonna forget about my birthday. I knew it!" she cried.

"I didn't forget," Daniel pleaded. His hand slid down his face. He was hoping she bought it. But he didn't forget. He just didn't plan anything. He was getting tired of her and her filthy mouth. She was supermodel beautiful but wore her ghetto badge like a medal of honor.

"Ok, so what we doin' bae?" she asked.

This chick was bipolar, and he knew it. "Imma handle it, Diamond. Just be ready later."

"Yeeeeeah, Zaddy. Make sure you're ready, too," Diamond giggled.

Now that was something he didn't need to plan for. Daniel selected the contact in his phone and hoped his go-to could help him get out of this jam.

"Crane." the voice answered.

"Crane, it's Hersh," Daniel said.

"Hersh, weh you deh?"

"I'm good. I need a table."

"You coulda call de reservation desk fi dat," Crane said annoyed.

"But I need a table tonight."

"Wha kinda business you tink me runnin', my yout?" Crane snarled.

"I know Crane, but I'm in a bind."

"Eeh heeh. A woman?" Crane snickered over the phone.

"A which one dat?"

Daniel sighed with an attitude, "Does it matter?"

"But you fresh eeh? You ring my phone fi favor but nuh wan gimme information."

"It's for Diamond."

"Ahhhhh, yes bredren."

From the day his mother introduced him as her "friend" several years ago, Samuel Crane made himself available to Daniel as a male mentor. He wasn't necessarily a father figure but someone he could look to for aspects of manhood. Early on, Crane observed how Daniel's mother and grandmother coddled him, so he made it his business to lend the boy his brand of stern, Caribbean, abrasive love. But to Daniel, it mostly seemed that Crane just liked to get in his business. Even so, Crane bought him his first suit. Crane taught him how to clean fish and cook oxtails. Crane took him to his first basketball game. Crane taught him how to balance a checkbook and how to cut grass. And even though he was no longer involved with his mom, he was still an important mentor to Daniel.

Over the years, Daniel spent summers in Crane's restaurant bussing tables, mopping, prepping vegetables and any other odd job that needed attending to. And back then, it was just a small dive with a couple of tables. But Crane managed to parlay Crane's Caribbean Cuisine into one of the hottest restaurants in Queens. So, he couldn't shake Crane if he tried. He loved and respected him, but damn if the man wasn't nosey!

Crane's

Diamond came sashaying through the dining floor of Crane's.

"Hey, bae. Were you waiting long?" she asked as she leaned in for a kiss.

"No, you're right on time." Daniel told her.

He learned not to be on time for any dates with Diamond. As she once told Daniel, her public appearance took time and preparation. Daniel, along with some of the other male patrons of the restaurant, eyed her skin-tight dress. She was a personal shopper at a high-end boutique with aspirations of becoming a stylist. She made a decent living but spent most of it on clothes, shoes and bags to look the part. Daniel wasn't exactly sure what "looking the part"really meant.

She knew how to use what she had to get what she wanted. She flung her thousand-dollar hair and batted her eyelash extensions for car note money. Oddly in the next breath, she'd refer to Daniel as her boyfriend. Daniel didn't finance any part of her lifestyle, although, he did pick her dog up from the groomers once— a $40 favor he swallowed in reciprocation. And though he didn't mind the boyfriend title, he still made sure to wear a condom every time.

They met at a video shoot. Daniel was helping out a friend who was an up-and-coming video director. And Diamond was assisting the lead stylist when she spotted Daniel. The way he sat shirtless while being prepped by the makeup squad forced Diamond to assume he was a divo-type model/actor.

"It must've took you months to get a table here!" she screeched.

"I did what I had to do," he answered.

"There's always a celebrity-spotting here. You think we'll see somebody?"

"Somebody like who?"

"I don't know, somebody famous! Then I could give them my business card."

Oh boy, Daniel thought as he did an internal eye-roll.

"You never know," he stated nonchalantly.

She gave him the side-eye. "You acting all cool and shit, like you're a real model or whatever," she fussed.

It was the "whatever" part that made him laugh on the inside. Diamond pretty much knew nothing about him. She assumed Daniel only got occasional work on video shoots and spent the rest of his time working at his uncle's auto shop. She knew nothing of his background, education or interests. She never asked, and he didn't volunteer any information.

Midway into dinner, Daniel could smell Crane's Dunhill cologne from where he was sitting. Crane always made a big production of coming to the table and introducing himself. He did this any time Daniel brought a date to the restaurant. He'd put on his best Yankee-voice and check out his date.

"Good (h)evening, I am Samuel Crane. I hope you are enjoying your dining experience," he announced.

"Oh my God! Crane, like Crane's Caribbean Cuisine? Like this is your restaurant?" Diamond shrieked.

"Yes, my dear. I must say, you are a stunning (h)addition to the décor this (h)evening."

He couldn't drop that inadvertent "h" if you paid him.

"I saw you in the newspaper," Diamond paused, "but you look different. You look much younger in person," Diamond said flirtatiously while she batted those lashes and stroked her hair simultaneously.

Crane laughed, and his mouth revealed several gold crowns and fillings. "Thank you, that warms my heart coming from such a beautiful lady. Please," as he motioned for a server to come over to the table, "(H)Accept this cocktail. Something beautiful and sexy, like yourself. I call it, *The Jewel*, compliments of the house. That is, if your husband doesn't mind."

Daniel picked at his plantains. He wanted to take his eyes out, turn them backward and place them back in his head. This was just to save him the trouble of rolling them. But instead he said, "Nah, B. We're not married,"

Daniel saw the jump in Crane's eyebrow when he said it because Crane hated to be addressed by anything other than his given names.

"I have a special drink on the house for you as well." Crane nodded to Daniel. "(H)Enjoy the rest of your (h)evening and please, come (h)again." Then Crane walked off to another table to greet more guests.

Daniel could tell Diamond was drunk before they left the restaurant. He knew the Jewel drink Crane gave them was something sweet yet strong. If she drank that and that alone, she would've been ok. But she insisted on ordering an additional one plus a shot of Patron. She was gone. He was pretty sure she would be spending the night, and he hated when she spent the night.

He helped her on to the bed and tried to take her shoes off. The 5-inch red bottomed heel scratched his arm. He couldn't figure out which straps and zips were functional and which ones were just for strap and zip's sake.

"Diamond, help me out."

"Bae, the shoes can stay onnnnn," Diamond purred. She then slithered across the bed. He had enough of her for the night. However, his lower region thought otherwise. When she removed her dress, nothing but a G-string was revealed. While tossing her hair over her shoulder, she teased, "I see you lookin'," as she slapped her behind. "Come get it, Zaddy." His annoyance with her took a temporary leave of absence for the next hour, compliments of the herbal roots and rum mixture Crane aptly dubbed *The Iron Man*.

Gooooal

Daniel sat on the sideline of the high school's all-purpose field. The fickle spring weather had changed, and he was cold despite the fact it was the month of May.

He was concerned about the scratch he received during a block. He didn't want to hear his cousin Jeremy, or Germ, as the family nicknamed him, calling him a punk-ass about a little scratch. So instead of obsessing about it, he listened to Germ drone on about his "flavor of the month."

"Yo when Shorty talk that patois shit, that shit is fire," Germ said.

"But you barely understand what she's saying," Daniel answered.

Germ bragged, "I know enough to know that mean I'm killin' her son!" He then motioned with several obscene thrusts.

Daniel laughed, "She probably say that to everybody."

Germ stopped in his tracks, "What?! What you tryna say?"

"She loose," Daniel deadpanned.

Germ's face read wounded. He'd seen her on the arms of a couple neighborhood players, but that was some time ago. He hated when Daniel was right. *Who asked him anyway,* Germ thought. *Pretty motherfucker always adding his two cents.* "Me and her good. I ain't tryna marry her anyway. But I can't help if she like my good looks from my momma and my swag from my daddy," Germ boasted.

"Well somehow, you came out butt ugly and wack," Daniel countered.

"Whatever, man," Germ said and changed the subject.

"Yo these assholes cheated, son." Germ stated.

"Nah, we got our ass beat," Daniel said while taking off his cleats.

They'd been playing in the same soccer club for the past two years. Every time they lost, Germ declared injustice. The VS Auto Group soccer team was comprised mostly of players of Caribbean descent and was the worst team in the soccer club. Most were men of a certain age who were rusty and out of shape. They played for nostalgia and comradery, and not much else.

The team that whipped them today was young and fit. It looked like they were straight out of Central America by way of JFK airport. The winning team's captain approached Daniel and Germ and shook their hands. "We have beer and food, *venga,*" he stuttered. His English was shaky, but he pointed in the direction of the bleachers to show them where to go.

"Good looking. I'll tell my team," Daniel told him.

Germ looked at the opposition in disgust and protested, "Fuck them. I ain't going over there."

Daniel said, "Stop being a dick. I'm going. These hungry negroes will probably go, too." He patted Germ on the back, whistled to the team and shouted, "Sonrisa's team has drinks and food by the bleachers!" The team agreed to the invitation with a chorus of cheers and whoops. He looked at Germ, "You coming?"

Germ waved him off and said, "I'll be in the car."

Daniel and the team were greeted by the sounds of salsa music and the smell of grilled food.

The red-headed Latina watched Daniel rest the aluminum-foiled container of rice and grilled chicken on the bleacher. She continued to watch his over six-foot tall frame while he put on his black skully. When his arms stretched up to his head, the muscles in his upper back flexed visibly through the moisture-wicking synthetic fabric of his shirt.

She sauntered up behind him. "I was hoping you lost," she admitted.

He turned around almost bumping into her top-heavy frame. Daniel scanned her from head to toe while chewing a mouthful of food. She sported a short bob of fire-red hair, a fitted hoodie, tight joggers and red wedge sneakers.

"Oh, yeah? Why's that?"

She grinned and put her hands in her hoodie pockets. "Because we don't invite the winners over to eat." He nodded. "Well, it's a good thing we lost huh?" He leaned against the bleacher.

"What's your name?" she asked.

"I'm Hersh."

"Hersh?" she repeated.

"Yeah," he mumbled with a mouth full of food.

"Like a Hershey bar?"

"Yeah," he continued eating, "you like chocolate, right?"

"What do you think?" she inquired and licked her lips. He laughed at her response.

"I'm Jennifer." Then she reached out her hand and gave him a fingertip handshake.

"Jennifer, you cooked this food?"

"Nah, my aunts and them did. I'm too cute for the kitchen."

"Oh! Word?"

"Fashion is more my thing."

Another Diamond type, he thought.

She asked, "What do you do?" But before he could even answer, she interrupted, "Lemme guess." She looked him up and down. "You look like an office type." He only smiled in return. "What size shoe you wear? Like a 12?" she interrogated while looking down at his Nike slides and socks.

"You would look good in a pair of Allen Edmonds," she suggested.

He gave her a bored look. "I'm partial to Paul Evans," he told her.

"I could get you into a pair of those too, Papi."

Jennifer referring to him as *papi* reeled him in. "What's the hook?" he asked.

"40 percent off."

He looked her up and down again. She was cute. He could get a deal on a pair of shoes and most likely, she would lay down, too. "Who's the connect?" he asked.

"Me." she stepped closer to him. "You should come see me at the store. I'm at Neiman Marcus in the mall."

"Maybe. That's all you offering?" He gently pulled at the zipper of her hoodie.

She playfully slapped his hand away. "Maybe. Gimme your phone." He handed it to her, and she called herself.

"I'm good at fitting size 12s," she flirted.

Before he could answer her, Germ pulled up and beeped his horn.

"We'll see about that," Daniel told Jennifer as he walked backward away from her.

VS Auto Collision Group

Uncle Vince helped cultivate Daniel's interest in cars as early as he could remember. Vincent Semper, the self-proclaimed cost-conscious car connoisseur was good people. Cheap, but good. Daniel had to convince his grand-uncle to renovate the auto collision shop. And with just a few cosmetic changes and updated technology, the shop saw an increase in business over the last year. While Daniel bopped his head to the old-school mix coming through the surround sound speakers, he overheard one of the junior technicians coming on to a client yet again. And although the technician had been with the shop for some time, he was still referred to as a junior tech because of his lazy and shiftless work ethic.

"You stay around here, ma? You got a man?" Junior Tech asked while leaning over the counter.

"Um, I just wanna get my car fixed," the young lady answered. She seemed overdressed in spite of the fickle, May weather Far Rockaway was experiencing at the moment.

Upon hearing this, Daniel stepped up to the counter and shoved Junior Tech aside. "I'm sorry, miss. How can I help you?"

The client explained that the car made a clicking sound when she drove. Daniel lifted the hood and saw that it was a simple problem. He walked her to the service desk and explained how long it would take to finish the job and gave her an estimate. While Daniel checked the computer for the parts needed to fix her car, she removed her shades and began to fill out the paperwork.

She asked, "What's the deposit on this estimate?"

Daniel looked up from the computer, and his breath caught in his throat. She had large, wide-set, sparkling gray eyes with lashes that went on to infinity. They stared intently at him waiting for his response. But he was dumbstruck.

"Like $75?" she asked. Her mouth twisted to the side. It was pouty and perfect.

He'd seen plenty of beautiful women before, but this one had an odd effect on him. *Wait, what did she say about the price?* he thought to himself. But then he recovered, "Yeah. Yeah, $75, that's right."

She signed the form and pulled her credit card from her wallet. When she slid the card toward him, he almost lost his balance. She furrowed her eyebrows and jerked her head back. He felt himself sweating. As the receipt printed, he decided to shake it off and act like a grown man. He'd seen beautiful women before. She was pretty, sure. But her marble eyes were almost hypnotic. He looked down at the receipt and read her name, *Asha Martin*.

Khalil

Asha wiped her forehead. She tried to slide out of bed without much motion. So she felt around with her foot and was able to find her underwear close to the edge of the bed.

"You out?" he asked.

Dammit, she hated when he said ANYTHING afterward.

"I have a lot of errands to run," she stated. But that was a lie.

He got up and sat on the edge of the bed. She wanted so badly to beat him to the bathroom.

"Go 'head, Asha." He motioned with his head towards the bathroom.

Thank goodness, she thought.

She always felt weird afterward. Khalil was a cool dude, but he wasn't boyfriend material. He was a maintenance worker at the nursing home where her best friend worked, and he always seemed to materialize anytime Asha visited. Her best friend regarded him as a straggler and discouraged interaction with him. Even so, Asha thought his rugged handsomeness and borderline thug appeal was worth looking into. But she soon found out that he had no personality. He didn't have much conversation either, no real sense of humor nothing Asha found funny anyway. Nothing to keep her attention, and other than the sex, which he was really good at, he had nothing else going for him.

She quickly grabbed her underwear and small handbag and headed for the bathroom. As she freshened up, she thought about how different it would be if she really liked him instead of just meeting up for boredom sex, because that's all it really was. Nothing to do on a Thursday night? Horny on a Sunday afternoon? Idle on a Tuesday after work? It was better than using her toys and eating Cold Stone, which is what she was doing before she met Khalil.

Unk & AJ

Asha took an Uber back home from the auto shop. As she turned the key in the door, she felt her phone buzzing. Unlocking all three locks, she answered her phone.

"Hello?!"

"Cupcake!"

"Hi Unk."

"You take care of that car yet? I can always take it over to Barry and get it done for you."

"I just came back from the auto repair shop."

"Which one did you go to?"

I should've just let him take the car, she thought. *He won't be satisfied with any place I choose or the cost.*

"I took it to..." she pulled the receipt out of her wallet, "VS Auto, on Central Avenue."

"VS Auto?! How much they charge you?"

"Unk, it's fine. It was a good price. I had the money for it.

"Now what you know bout prices for auto repair?"

Asha sighed and laughed to herself at the same time. Here it comes. "$250, Uncle Rand."

"$250?! Those sons of bitches. Now I told you I would've taken it over to Barry, he would've..."

his voice trailed off. "Yeah I know Jazzy, but I told the girl...naw, she don't listen." Asha heard muffled noises, then her Aunt Jasmine's voice, AJ she called her, came through the phone.

"Hey, baby. Don't worry 'bout your uncle."

"AJ, I can get my car fixed on my own," Asha whined to her aunt.

"Now you know he loves you. He's just trying to help," her aunt soothed.

"Is he still there?"

"No, he went to the den."

"Ok, let me tell you about this guy at the auto shop," Asha gushed to her aunt. "The jerk that was trying to hollah at me was so frustrating that I was about to walk out the shop. But when Daniel appeared at the service desk, my head spun."

"Is that right? I thought you went to fix your car, not check out guys."

"He was foine, AJ. And he was nice, too. Mmmm, he was tall with broad shoulders and chocolatey skin."

"Ooh chile, that sound like your uncle was there," AJ teased.

"Ewww, AJ. First of all, Unk looks nothing like that. Thanks for ruining it for me."

"Girl, your uncle was a real catch back in the day, and honey I caught him," AJ joked. She knew it made Asha uncomfortable when she talked about her uncle that way.

Asha teased in a haughty tone, similar to the ones used by her aunt's church members. "Now Missionary Martin, I do not think the auxiliary board would approve of such language."

"Missionary has several meanings, and I can tell you about more than one. Don't let the white gloves fool you, chile."

"AJ, ew!" Asha rolled her eyes while her aunt cracked up on the other end.

Asha

Asha trashed the salmon and rice Ms. Jeannie gave her yesterday. She entered the living room and looked at her daddy passed out on the couch. She covered him with her rainbow quilt and re-read the small card she pulled out of her bible that morning:

Police Officer Randolph Martin

101st Precinct

555 2026

"That damn Rand," her daddy would say every time they passed the precinct. "Think his shit don't stink."

She always wanted to laugh when he said that because she was almost certain everyone's doo-doo stunk. Even so, Asha liked her uncle Rand. He and his wife Jasmine were really nice to her a couple weeks ago at Thanksgiving. In fact, after pie and ice cream, he pulled her to the side and gave her the small card.

"I have something for you, cupcake."

"AJ already gave me my Christmas gift."

"No, it's not your Christmas gift. I want you to keep this card."

She read it. "Randolph Martin. That's you."

"If you or your dad ever need anything, you call me ok?"

"Ok, Uncle."

She would go see "shit-don't-stink Randy" today. But what would she say to him? She would talk to him nice like she'd seen daddy do with his friends. As she approached the precinct, the door was huge and almost too heavy for her to push. She stumbled as she tried, and an officer pulled the door open from the other side.

"Hello, young lady," he smiled at her.

"Hi," she said. She quickly walked up to the front desk where a large red-faced police officer sat. Her nerves began to take over, so she took a deep breath. "Good morning. I'm looking for Police officer Randolph Martin, please."

"Well, aren't you cute? And who may I say is calling for Police officer Randolph Martin?" the officer laughed.

"I'm Asha Martin," she said, hoping to get this over with quickly. The red-faced officer pressed a button on the desk and barked, "Officer Martin, front desk."

She heard Rand's baritone timber before she saw him. "Man, I lost $50 on that game. Their weak defense did me in." As he approached the front desk, he looked over at Big Red's face and said, "What's up?" The officer looked down at Asha and smiled.

"Asha!" he shouted, as he swept her up in his arms. Once he put her down, he bent down to her level, checked her face and felt her arms and torso. "Are you ok? What are you doing here? Where's your daddy?"

Other than her lop-sided ponytail and wrinkled jeans, she looked fine.

"Heeey, Uncle Rand. How you been? You're looking good today. So here's the thing. I was wondering if you could help me out with a couple dollars." She managed to recite this all in one breath.

For Rand, it was eerie. As if his brother was speaking out of Asha's tiny mouth. "Girl, what you need money for? Your daddy put you up to this? Where is he?"

He stood upright and walked towards the door, ready to curse his brother out for sending his child to beg for money. Asha quickly followed and managed to slide out of the heavy door before it closed behind her uncle.

"He didn't tell me to do this, I just wanted you to help me out."

"I'm walking you home right now. Furthermore, why aren't you in school?"

Asha stared up at him blankly. Rand stopped an officer entering the building, "Hey, I'll be back in an hour or so." He took Asha's hand and led her down the street.

Asha's plan had failed. Why couldn't he just give her the money? She knew how to go to the corner store; she'd done it a couple of times already. She knew her daddy would be upset if she showed up with his younger brother.

"How much did Ashe tell you to ask me for?" Rand huffed. She struggled to keep up with his long strides.

"It wasn't daddy, I wanted to ask you on my own."

"He can't even make sure you get to school every day, but he sends you to ask for money. Wait until I see this stupid mother…"

He stopped himself and looked down at Asha. Her face was so painfully familiar to him, it made him wince. Staring up at him was a tiny version of his mother's face. He wished to God that she was still alive. She would help the poor girl and save her from his dumbass brother. But with his mom gone, he was left to deal with his big brother's bullshit.

"My daddy was tired. That's why he didn't take me to school."

"Well, he should've gotten his behind up. Did you even see him come in last night? —with his triflin ass," he added before she could even answer him. She didn't like the way Uncle Rand was insulting her father—treating him like a perp. At least that's what they said on "Law & Order." The kids in her class didn't watch "Law & Order"—something about it being for grown-ups and airing too late. But her daddy let her stay up late. He was fun like that.

She stopped in front of her building and put her hands on her narrow hips. "My daddy was tired, and he says everybody is tired on Monday because the weekend is the time to do it up! So yesterday I put his pajamas on him, but he smelled stinky. I sprayed the air freshener, and I put some of his shaving perfume on his face. I made toast, but he didn't want it. So I left it there and went to school. When I came home, the roaches were eating the toast and that was the last piece. I didn't want Ms. Jeanie's salmon anymore, I just wanted you to give me some money to get some more bread. You were the one who told me to ask you if I ever need anything!!" She spewed and ran out of breath.

Rand's heart fell.

It's a Date

Daniel looked at the clock one more time. He wasn't sure what time Asha would be there, but he knew she'd be picking up her car today.

"Hersh!" his uncle Vince called to him from the small office of the auto collision shop.

"What's up?"

"What's this invoice about?"

Shit, he forgot to flag her bill before his uncle saw it. Daniel poked his head into the office.

"Oh, that."

"Yeah, that. The price for the parts are at cost. There's no markup! You wanna run us out of business?"

"I'll handle it."

"Mmm. A...Martin. Who's that?"

Daniel sighed.

"A girl, huh?" Vince asked. Daniel looked off into the distance. "Yeah, I figured that much. What's the matter? Them model girls can't pay their own way?"

"She's not a model girl."

"Whosoever she is, if you gonna be giving out discounts, you need to flag these tickets."

"Ok, cool." Daniel turned to leave.

Vince called out smiling while showing off his over-sized dentures, "She fine, huh?"

Daniel laughed, "Yeah Uncle V, she fine."

Daniel felt the hairs on the back of his neck stand up as he stood upright and looked down into those huge, feline gray eyes of Asha's.

"Hey, uh, Martin right?" He said as he wiped his hands on an already filthy towel.

"Actually, its Asha."

"Right. Asha."

He reviewed her button nose and pouty lips. She wasn't as bundled up as the last and first time he saw her. Today's weather allowed for a long sleeve t-shirt, jeans and cowgirl boots. Her hair was pulled into a ponytail, and a fluff of cocoa curls let loose behind her head. She stood a little over five-foot-tall. Curves were in all the right places, particularly in her bra and in her jeans. She was not the statuesque, booty magazine type he was used to, but her features were striking. Her curves were soft and inviting.

"Hersh, is it?" She squinted to read the name on his mechanic's suit.

"Uh, no." He suddenly felt self-conscious about the childhood nickname and covered the name tag. "It's Dan, Daniel."

"Ok, Dan, Daniel." She smiled at him with her eyes. "I want to thank you for giving me a break on the price."

"Giving you a break?"

"Yeah, you gave me a break on the price of the parts. I got estimates from a couple other places. I also looked online and saw that you billed me for the parts at cost. Didn't you?"

Her head tilted to the side.

Daniel smiled. Her eyes were reeling him in. "Maybe."

She laughed. "Maybe doesn't get you asked out for coffee."
"In that case, I gave you a huge discount."

She laughed a big laugh. He didn't expect such a big burst to come out of her small frame. "How about Saturday at four at Peninsula Java?"
"Sounds good."

He dangled her car key by the key fob. She reached out to take them from him, and her fingertips grazed his. He felt an electric shock. And not the kind that comes from walking on carpet. He saw that she felt it too when she blinked unexpectedly.

"See you then, Hersh, Dan, Daniel," she giggled as she walked off.
She caught him off guard. He did not see that coming. But he liked it. And seventy-two hours seemed like forever.

Peninsula Java

Daniel parked his car fifteen minutes before their meeting time. He thought about Diamond and laughed to himself. She wouldn't be caught dead in a coffee shop on a first date.

Asha parked in municipal parking down the block from the coffee shop. She hurried along Mott Avenue with unexpected butterflies in her stomach. She had an outer-body experience when she invited Daniel for coffee. It was her first time asking a guy out. Her friend, Cleo, had staunchly advised against it. But Asha figured, fuck it. What did she have to lose? The worst he could say was no. And it was just coffee. A thank-you coffee at that. It was basically a Starbucks gift card, but in person. With makeup. And perfume.

He stood up when he saw her come in. She immediately spotted him and looked surprised. She wanted to be the first one there.

"Hey," he smiled and gazed down at her.

"Hi!" she looked up at him with those crystal eyes.

He reached out to envelope her in his broad chest and long arms. She found it forward, but it looked so inviting. She figured, *why not*? He. Smelled. Good. She couldn't figure out what the scent was, but she'd never smelled anything like it before. And just when she started to lose herself in the scent, the embrace ended.

He moved to pull out the chair for her. She was impressed. Not because no one had ever done it, but because no one had done it in a long time.

"You're a good hugger. I gotta watch you," she flirted as she sat down.

"You can watch me all day," he said with a twinkle in his eyes.

She smiled back.

"What can I get for you two?" the waitress asked.

"I'll have a chai tea," Asha answered without looking over the menu.

"And for you?" The waitress turned to face Daniel, and instantly, he recognized her.

"Hey, Paula," he said as he stood up.

"Hershey Bar! Oh my God, look at you!" she squealed. She hugged and rocked him left and right despite his size over her.

"How've you been? How's your mom?" he asked her.

"She's great, retired and loving it. But calling me every day because she's bored out of her mind."

Paula caught a glance of Asha. "Oh I'm sorry, honey. I'm Paula, I used to babysit Hersh when he was an itty-bitty thing. We lived next door to each other back in the day."

"Hi, I'm Asha. Nice to meet you."

"Your eyes are incredible, Asha. So beautiful!"

"Thank you," Asha said. She caught Daniel watching her.

"Hersh, mint hot chocolate, right?" Paula guessed.

"Yeah. Thanks, Paula," Hersh answered.

"I'll get your orders out right away. It's so good to see you," Paula said leaving their table.

"You're probably used to the attention you get from those eyes," he said.

In the process of asking, he almost got lost in them himself.

"Yeah, sort of." She was slightly embarrassed and directed the conversation away from her and back to him. "An old babysitter, huh? I bet she's got stories."

"We're only a couple years apart, but she convinced our mothers that she could babysit me. One time, I asked her to make bacon for me and she refused. I snuck into the kitchen, wrapped some bacon in foil and put it in the microwave." Daniel shook his head.

"Noooooooooooooooooooooo." Asha's eyes widened as she laughed.

"When those sparks started flying, I thought the house would blow up. I hid in the cabinet under the sink."

Asha smiled. The impromptu childhood story was so honest and genuine, she found it endearing. Daniel never told that story to anyone. And oddly, it felt natural to share it with her. In fact, they sat in the coffee shop for hours chatting seamlessly about nothing in particular. They discovered they had similar tastes in music, TV, movies and food. They even exchanged social media handles. Asha was hesitant, but he made a boy scout oath not to be a stalker. After two chai teas and an assortment of pastries, Asha was ready to wrap up the date.

"Well, I had good time," she said chin in palms.

"So did I," he said while drinking in her eyes. Their instant and easy going rapport made her feel comfortable. She felt really flirtatious, soft and pink around him. His pheromones jumped at her in a way she hadn't quite experienced before. She did find the not-so-subtle glances he received from other women in the coffee shop quite interesting. But he was hard to miss with his long limbs and rich dark skin. He, on the other hand, appeared to be completely aloof to the attention. Either that, or he was used to a lot of attention himself.

Asha glanced towards the back of the coffee shop. "Is Paula still here? We never received the check.".

"The check?" Daniel asked.

"Yeah, she never came back with the check."

"We're good."

"Excuse me?"

"We're good." Hersh smiled.

"How is that?"

"I took care of it."

"But I invited you out." she said.

She thought it was a nice gesture for him to cover the bill. However, she never saw him pay Paula or approach the cash register. Daniel leaned back in his chair and looked her full in the eyes. Men were usually intimidated or distracted by her piercing gray eyes. But he looked at her as though he wanted to take up residence there.

"I took care of it Asha."

He said her name and the tips of her ears tingled. It was an odd and warm sensation.

"Well," she paused. "Ok." But she was still unsure of what happened.

Asha stood up and grabbed her small handbag. Daniel also stood up, and his motion sent his cologne wafting into her nose. She almost opened her mouth to ask him what it was but thought better of it. Instead, she swallowed the scent to save for later.

Cleo's Coffee Shop Review

Asha sat down at Cleo's breakfast nook. Her best friend of forever had finally moved into her own place. She lived at home with her family until she could afford to purchase her own condo down the beach. And although Asha's apartment was nice, Cleo's had all the bells and whistles that came with new construction.

Cleo was anxious to hear what became of this ridiculous coffee shop date. If you could even call it a "date" in a place like a coffee shop. She wished Asha wasn't so down-to-earth and straggler-friendly.

"Well?" she asked Asha while loading fruit into her Nutri Ninja blender.

"Well, what?"

"Girl, I will slap you." Cleo threatened.

Asha laughed. She liked to get under Cleo's skin. "Well, it was fun." She popped a strawberry into her mouth.

"Mmmm hmmm, I don't know how much fun a coffee date could be, but..." Cleo pursed her lips and pressed the appliance's frozen drink option.

"He was sweet! And funny!" Asha yelled over the loud whizz of the high-speed blender.

"What does he do again?" Cleo questioned after the blender finished its job.

"Cleo." Asha sighed.

"I'm just asking, I forgot!"

"Forgot my ass," Asha said with an attitude. Cleo poured her a glass of the green smoothie. "I wanted a pink one," Asha frowned.

"Oh, bitch drink it. You need some green in you," Cleo scolded.

"He's a mechanic."

"Hmmmm," Cleo replied. "I hope you got your belly full."

"I invited him out, remember?" Asha took a sip of the green concoction. To her surprise, it wasn't half bad.

"Oh yeah, that's right. You don't listen. I told you that's some thirsty shit." Cleo placed a pink swirly straw in Asha's glass. "There's your pink," she added.

"Whatever, I didn't pay for anything."

"You better not had paid, shiiiit," Cleo told her. "And I hope you wasn't impressed by him paying a couple of dollars for coffee..."

"Chai tea," Asha interrupted.

"And some bullshit muffins," Cleo added.

"Blueberry scones," Asha interjected.

"Whatever, bitch. It's not impressive."

"You know, I actually didn't see him pay for anything. I think he has a tab there or something."

"A tab at Peninsula Java? What kinda low budget-baller shit is that? He must take all his dates there then?"

"I took him, Cleo."

"Hmph!"

"All I know is that I had a good time, and I'll probably see him again."

"Where? At the 7-11 this time? Maybe he has an account there, too."

Asha was beginning to get annoyed. "Why don't we talk about what you did yesterday, Cleo?"

"Now you wanna change the subject. Well if you must know, I met up with Crimson."

"I'm gonna need his government name in order to listen to this story."

"That is his real name! His daddy was a Southside Blood!"

"Let me guess, you're impressed by that."

"Whatever, hoe."

"Carry on," Asha prompted her.

"So we went to Karma- a real date venue, I might add. We were vibing, we had good chemistry as usual. I wore that pheromone perfume, the one I bought from HSN, remember? I think that shit really works!"

"Well, it should for $200."

"En-tee-way...so after dinner, we ordered dessert and I gave him a mic check. I ordered the bananas foster you always rave about, it wasn't all that to me..."

"Ok, WAIT. What?!" Asha interjected.

"I didn't like the sauce. It was too sweet."

"NOT the dessert, the blow job!"

"Asha please, don't be a prude."

"Where did all this happen?"

"What do you mean? We were at Karma."

"I mean in the bathroom? In the car?"

"Girl, please. Under the table. We sat at a booth. You know it's dark in there."

"WHAT?!"

"Asha, when's the last time you been on a date? And not that coffee shop bullshit."

"I'll NEVER be on that kind of date."

"Do you want me to finish the story?"

"Cleo, I can't. But go on."

"So, I ended up having some of his milkshake because like I said, the bananas foster was nasty."

"I'm sorry. All I heard was *nasty milkshake*."

"Did I mention the waitress chick had a bad attitude?! Every time we asked her for something, it was like pulling teeth. So I told Crimson, 'Bae don't give her no big tip because she was wack.'"

"He's your bae now?"

"I think he would've given her a good tip too if his card wasn't declined."

"Hol' up."

"Whatever, Asha. Don't act like your card was never declined."

"Not on a date after bustin' off under the table!" Asha doubled over laughing and could hardly catch her breath.

"Whatever. You're too uppity and that's your problem," Cleo told her.

If Cleo deemed a coffee shop date uppity and what she did at Karma normal, then Asha would be the most uppity chick this side of the beach.

"Uppity? Cleo, please."

"You need to get back out there, Asha."

"Out there and do what? Pay to give blowjobs? I'm good."

"Imma let that slide." Cleo warned. "But what I'm saying is that you let your breakup turn you into a prude. Strange, usually women suffer heartbreak, and then let loose. You went in the opposite direction. And nobody likes a prude, Asha."

"I know, everybody likes hoes. Hoes are winning, right?"

"Imma let that slide too 'cause I think you were trying to throw shade, but you missed boo." Cleo popped Asha on the nose. Asha slapped her hand away.

"My goodies are an independent agent," said Cleo.

"Oh, really?" Asha laughed. "That's what they're calling it now? My, times have changed."

"Yeah, get with the times, bitch." Cleo hissed at her best friend.

Boardwalk

Asha walked the festival with AJ and Unk.

"Rand, I shouldn't have had that second funnel cake," AJ paused to rub her stomach.

"Yeah, I told you that right before you told me you was grown and could eat whatever you want."

Asha laughed at her uncle's "I told you so" attitude. "AJ, you want to sit down?" Asha asked. She walked AJ over to an empty bench. The annual boardwalk festival was something that AJ looked forward to. She enjoyed stopping at almost every vendor's table and perusing their wares. Her favorite part of the festival was the food. She would sample a bit of Uncle Rand's and Asha's food, whether it be fish sandwiches, fresh fruit smoothies or in tonight's case, funnel cakes.

Asha's phone buzzed.

Daniel: Hey beautiful

Asha blushed.

Asha: Hey handsome *blush emoji*

Daniel: Are you at the boardwalk festival?

Asha looked around her. Her phone buzzed again.

Daniel: I'm not a stalker, just thought I saw someone who looked like you. *eyeball emoji*

Asha scanned the perimeters but saw no signs of him.

"Cupcake, we're gonna head back home. Your aunt thought she was grown," Unk said rubbing AJ's back.

She sat next to her aunt on the bench, "AJ, do you have ginger ale at home?"

AJ made a face and continued to rub her stomach.

"Yeah, I think we have some. If Rand didn't use it all in his dark and stormies!"

"Uncle Rand!" Asha scolded him about his promise to cut back on his high balls for the sake of his high blood pressure.

"Is this about me or your aunt?" Rand barked. "We got ginger ale at the house. If not, I'll stop and get some. You two always make a big fuss out of nothing," Rand huffed.

"Well, I'm gonna stay and hang out for a little while longer. AJ, I'll come and see you tomorrow," she kissed her aunt.

"Ok love," AJ said. She got up from the bench with the help of Rand's arm.

"She'll be alright, just greedy," Rand teased while kissing Asha on the forehead.

Asha watched them walk off the boardwalk. She sent a text back to Daniel.

Asha: Yeah, I'm here. I'm near the Dred Surfer.

She looked around again and still saw no sign of him. She sent a text to Cleo.

Asha: Bout to meet up with coffee shop at the boardwalk fest.

Cleo: This guy is a real winner, huh?

Asha laughed. She saw nothing wrong with an impromptu meetup. They were at the same place at the same time, why not make the most of it?

The coffee shop was fun. Since then, they'd been texting back and forth and checking out each other's social media. She saw a couple likes from him that made her smile. She was careful not to like too many of his posts, for fear he'd think she was looking at his timelines every day. Which she was. What she did see was the likes and comments from his friends and followers, most of them female.

She'd been busy with work and helping AJ with Unk's retirement party. So that left her with little time to meetup with him again. But tonight, was the perfect opportunity. No pressure or fuss. *Asha: It's not a date, it's just a meetup *fist emoji**

Cleo: Whatever you say.

Cleo: Ooh, is the Gino's mobile pizza there? Bring me back some zeppoles when you're done with your fake date *tongue out emoji*

Asha shook her head at her phone and looked around for him again.

Daniel had been watching her for the last 15 minutes from the passenger seat of the van. She'd been walking and talking with an older couple until the couple left the festival. He watched the rise and fall of her backside in her striped maxi dress as she walked over to a table in front of the Dred Surfer cafe. He saw her tapping on her phone and looking around her surroundings.

Daniel finished up his well-deserved Red Stripe beer. He gave a dap to the driver of the YMCA's van, hopped out, then he walked toward Asha. He'd been at the festival to work his soccer club's booth and also to support the local Y at their membership table. He spent his time between the two booths switching organization t-shirts until ultimately he showed up at the Y's table in his soccer club shirt. When a group of women visiting the Y's table pointed out the t-shirt mix-up, he went shirtless altogether. The female enrollment rate spiked for the two remaining hours he spent taking memberships. Asha was scrolling through her feed when she felt a sudden urge to turn around. When she did, she saw Daniel walking toward her.

His gait was leisurely. As if he had no place to be and would enjoy the scenery while getting there. Long limbs covered the path to her with lengthy strides and a subtle dip. The rhythm of his walk gave stimulus to her swallow reflex. Army fatigue shorts hung low on his waist and shifted with each step in spite of his belt. His white tee draped the muscles in his chocolate shoulders and chest. The low, fitted Yankee cap casted a shadow over his already dark eyes. Shit, she didn't remember him being this fine. She stood up as he got closer and could see the corners of his mouth turning upward. He walked right up to her just short of touching her. If he weren't so

37

fine, he could be accused of invading her personal space.

"Hey," he greeted her.

"Hi," she smiled back and inhaled the mix of his cologne and outside scent.

"I wasn't being a creep. I promise." He smiled down into her face. "I wasn't sure if that was you and just wanted to confirm."

"It's me," she blushed, breathed him in again and gathered herself. "It's good to see you again." She put her phone in her wristlet.

"It's good to see you, too. What have you been up to?"

"The regular. Actually been kinda busy."

"Yeah, me too. You want to take a walk?"

"Sure," Asha agreed.

He placed his hand on the small of her back, gently guiding her toward the boardwalk's path. His light touch gave her goosebumps. Asha was surprised by her physical reaction to him. She'd have to be careful. Or not.

They walked the boardwalk beginning at Beach 17th street enjoying the evening's cooling sea breeze. The saltwater permeated the air as soft waves continuously crashed against the shore. Although the festival was almost over, the boardwalk still buzzed with people. Gaggles of teenagers, elderly couples walking hand-in-hand and families with children and strollers occupied the boardwalk. The locals were enjoying one of the small peninsula's most valuable amenities: the beachfront experience, at night.

Asha and Daniel strolled along making small talk but mostly in a comfortable silence. Several vendors were still posted on the boardwalk trying to hawk the last of their goods.

"Do you mind if I stop over here?" she asked him looking over to a lone vendor's table.

"No problem," Daniel answered as he approached the vendor's table with her.

Beautiful hand-blown glass figurines were lined up on the black felt table. Asha picked up a calla lily shaped paperweight.

"$20," the vendor told her.

"$20?!" Asha repeated.

"Yes, that's a special price for you beautiful lady," the vendor answered while packing up a box of other items.

"Oh, please. That's too much." She put the paperweight down.

"My man," Daniel began. Asha turned to him, "No, it's fine. If he wants to lug all his stuff back to where he came from, that's his problem." She turned away from the table. The vendor looked from Daniel to Asha. Daniel reached in his pocket and pulled out a $20 bill from his money clip.

"Oh no, that's ok. I got it." Asha protested in spite of her first refuse and dug into her wristlet.

The vendor took the money from Daniel and said, "Thank you brother." He wrapped up the piece and handed it to Asha in a small gift bag. Asha wasn't prepared to spend $20 for the paperweight, but he'd paid for it so quickly. She was a little miffed that she hadn't received the bargain she wanted.

Asha took the bag and turned to hand Daniel her $20 bill. He'd since walked away from the table and was waiting for her toward the middle of boardwalk.

"Thanks," she said stretching the $20 toward him. His hands were in his pocket. "So you like calla lilies?" he asked her. She stood there with her hand extended. "Yeah, and I'm saying thank you," she laughed. "You're welcome," he said. His hands remained in his pockets.

"I mean, I appreciate it," she stepped toward him with the bill in her hand. She looked different than he remembered. Maybe it was the glow that the giant streetlights casted. Her gray eyes were bright, and she appeared more youthful. At the coffee shop, she was wearing makeup. Tonight she was natural and more relaxed. Her insistence at paying for the paperweight amused him.

"Consider it a gift," he laughed and put his hands up in surrender.

"Oh," she blushed. "Well, thank you. And I love calla lilies," she added.

"Very feminine," he said.

"That I like flowers?"

"No, the calla lily. It's very feminine."

"Most flowers are metaphorically feminine, I guess," she shrugged.

"True," he nodded. "But that particular flower has..." Daniel thought for a moment. "Crazy yonic symbolism. Or...maybe I'm just a creep," he smirked.

Asha laughed. "Yonic, huh?"

Daniel smiled.

"Yeah, you might be a creep. But one with an impressive vocabulary."

"Thanks," he laughed.

"I don't know a lot of men who walk around using words like yonic."

"Maybe you don't know the right type of men," he raised his eyebrow at her.

She side-eyed him, "You have a point. Still," she continued. "I don't know many mechanics who use that word."

He stopped mid-stride, "What does that mean?"

"I mean, it's not a word that people throw around."

"You mean that grease monkeys throw around?" He leaned on the boardwalk railing. She paused. "I didn't mean to offend you. I know fixing a car isn't just something any idiot could do. And I assume you're good at what you do," she said sincerely.

"Trust me," he looked her straight in the eyes. "When I lift the hood, I know what I'm doing."

"I bet you do," she laughed.

Asha's cheeks warmed at his double entendre. She'd been around enough Jamaicans to get the undertones of his message.

"I don't remember you telling me what you do for a living," he said.

"Oh, I'm a professional escort," she said without missing a beat.

His eyebrows raised and he let out a big laugh. "So you're off duty or nah? Let me know, cuz I might have to run to the ATM." He reached for his pocket.

She smiled. "I'm a paralegal."

"Cool, what type of law?"

She was a little taken aback by his follow up question. "Trusts and Estates," she told him. She then took a seat on a bench next to where he stood.

"Like, probate and wills?" he asked.

She gave him a questioning look.

"What?" he asked her.

"Well, I don't want to risk the chance of offending you again." She put her feet up on the railing next to his legs.

"Risk it. The night is young," he joked.

"What do you know about probate and wills?" she squinted.

"Grease monkey strikes again." He winked at her and something in her fluttered.

"See, I didn't mean it like that." She placed the paperweight next to her and folded her arms.

He stared at her chest. He couldn't tell if she was wearing a bra or not. She might have been wearing one of those bras built into the dress. Whatever the case, her cleavage was on display, and it looked full and bouncy from what he could see.

"Most women don't ask me how I know what I know." He crossed his long legs in front of him. "They're just glad that I know it."

Her eyes glided up from his Nike Foamposites to his dark, lean, hairy legs to the pattern of his camouflage shorts and nonchalantly over his groin.

"Perhaps you don't know the right type of women," she squinted.

He laughed at her quick wit.

"Yeah, your kind doesn't care about Daniel's story," he said in a melodramatic tone.

She pressed her palm to her chest. "Well, I would never treat you like that."

"You're sweet," he smiled.

"Kids?" she asked.

"What about them?"

"How many do you have?"

"Excuse me?" he laughed.

"What? That's a general question," she told him.

"*Do you have kids?* is a general question."

"What are the chances of someone like you..."

"A grease monkey with an impressive vocabulary?" he cut her off.

Asha laughed. He wasn't going to let that go.

"So, do you? Have kids?"

He paused in her eyes. He enjoyed it there.

"Let me guess, none that you 'know of'" she air quoted.

Daniels face crumbled. There was a change in his disposition. "To have a kid and not know or care about it. That's disgusting."

"Well, there's a lot of that out there."

He looked down at his sneakers.

"So?" she pressed.

Daniel looked back up at her. "No, I don't have any kids."

"Really?" she gasped.

He smiled at her reaction. "You think I just sling it to the highest bidder?"

"Highest bidder, longest weave, fattest ass, your choice." Asha said.

"Ohhhh!" He covered his mouth while she tried to contain her smile. "I'm pretty selective, for your information," he lied.

"I'm sure," she pursed her lips. She was interested in the type of women he was used to dealing with. Since he brought up the subject, she wouldn't feel like she was prying. She continued. "Back to these women that don't ask you questions." She leaned forward in pretend interview mode. "What is it that they want from you?"

He moved from his leaning position on the railing and sat next to her, resting his arm along the bench behind her. His body was warm next to hers and his cologne looped around her nostrils again. He seemed really comfortable with his body and hers. She thought back to their embrace at the coffee shop, how warm and tight and firm it was.

"I think you can guess what they want." He gazed out into the dark beach.

"Well, what are you offering to them? Companionship? Loyalty? Protection? Anything other than your...services as a ladies' man?" she inquired.

He turned his head to her. She struggled to see his eyes under the brim of his hat. She dared herself and reached up to remove his hat, expecting him to resist or knock her hand away. But he never flinched. His hair was cut low and tapered up high, in a low mohawk/military cut. His eyes looked a little tired but still maintained their dark intensity.

"Nah, I'm no ladies' man. I just connect with women...on a familiar level."

"So do pimps," she said. He was right about his connectivity. His closeness to Asha made her hyper aware of her own body.

He gave a slow grin. "I use my power for good though," he told her.

The idea of his *power* stirred something inside her. "Let's talk about your power." She turned to face him sitting criss-cross applesauce, her long dress covering her pretzeled legs.

He laughed. "Wait, are you sure you're not a journalist? Or a therapist? Or some other "ist" who asks a lot of questions for a living?"

"No, just curious," she shrugged.

"You know what curiosity did to the pussycat, right?" His eyes combed over her.

She blushed. "I don't recall it being a pussycat, per se."

"Well, in this case it is."

"Can we get back to the topic?" she giggled.

"Sure, go ahead." His eyes twinkled in hers.

"Your power." She looked up into the stars.

"Yeah, what about it?" He spread his legs, stomped his feet and took a sniff of ocean air.

She laughed at his body language. He looked over at her. He waited for her to finish.

"How many women, as of today—" she paused, "have experienced this power of yours?" she put her chin in her palm and waited for his answer.

"Wow, you get straight to the point, huh?"

"It's just a question. You don't have to answer if you don't want to."

"Including potential power recipients sitting on this bench?" he asked her in faux seriousness.

"You're a confident one," she teased him. But hell yeah, she wanted to experience that power. Cleo was right, she needed to get out there. But not just yet, she still had recon to do.

"I'm not comfortable disclosing that information at this time," he told her.

"Wooooooow, curve," she laughed

"Nah, that's not a curve. I just don't know you like that." He gave her a playful snarl with a curl of his upper lip.

"And you won't either, with that type of body count." She unfolded her legs.

This whole time, he pretended that her eyes didn't faze him. Looking into them made him a little lightheaded. He liked it. Her insistence at paying for the paperweight, her surprise at his vocabulary and her line of questioning about his past gave him a window into who she was. Independent, a little stush, somewhat inquisitive with a side of judgmental. But there was something else he picked up about her. An underlying fervor that she fought to keep under wraps. His mind quickly flashed to unwrapping it. Her question wasn't one he was used to answering. He could count on one hand the number of women who inquired about his past. They were usually just content to be in his present.

"What about you?" he asked.

"Excuse me?" she looked surprised.

"Just a question, you don't have to answer," he threw back at her.

"Well," she took a deep breath and exhaled.

"Whoa, whoa," he laughed. "You need extra oxygen for what you're about to say? I don't know if I want to hear it." He ran his hand over his head.

She laughed at his faux stress. "What I'm saying is," she smiled. "To me, emotional connections and physical connections are two different things. But I could just be a creep." She looked at him out the corner of her eye.

He remained silent, and they both looked out onto the now timid waves nudging against the shore.

"It's possible to have two separate connections. But when the connections are connected? It's lit," she said.

He watched her eyes roll and her chest rise and fall with her statement. She'd slashed his function in relationships, if you could call them relationships, down to something base. He'd always considered what he had to offer tantamount to air and water, a necessity. But her palpable reaction to *connecting connections* was enticing. He was interested in experiencing that reaction again.

II

N32

Shore Gallery

Asha tried to balance three crab rangoons in a napkin atop her champagne flute. She noted an annoyed look on the server's face but remained unbothered. She was hungry. Starving even. She'd worked through lunch, only snacking on chips and a bag of M&Ms. She rushed home, showered, changed and ran out the door to make it to the art gallery on time.

She hoped her little black dress and sleek shoulder-length ponytail would do for tonight. The chic pencil dress provided enough lycra for comfort. On top of that, the deep V-neck exposed enough skin to serve up some sexy, just short of thotville. She prayed her monthly shoe club's animal printed stilettos would play nice for the night. Sadly, the walk from her car to the gallery on the unforgiving concrete pavement proved otherwise. Her left pinky toe had begun to stage a coup. She prayed for seating inside the gallery.

She'd never been to one of these artsy fartsy events. Daniel invited her via text a week ago and proposed it would be a fun night. She didn't usually accept text-vites as date offers but made an exception this time. Regardless of what they'd be doing, she looked forward to spending time with him. Firstly, because he was sweet and funny. *No, scratch that*, Asha thought. Firstly, because he was fine as fuck and smelled really good. But he was also sweet and funny in spite of his good looks.

Daniel's friend, an amateur photographer turned social media darling, was premiering his work at the gallery. Before tonight, Asha had no clue there was a local art gallery in the neighborhood. Never mind the fact that she'd lived in the same beachfront neighborhood for most of her life. But since the rediscovery of Far Rockaway by well-to-do millennials, there were a couple of trending venues Asha had yet to visit.

After stuffing her face with appetizers, Asha decided to make her way around the gallery. The former 99 cent store cleaned up well and could pass for an actual Manhattan exhibition space. Some of the art was abstract and hard to decipher. She'd taken art courses in college but barely recalled what she was supposed to be looking for in terms of style. She felt a hand on the small of her back.

"Hey," Daniel smiled when she turned around to face him. "Hi," she said and paused before reaching to greet him. Asha hugged him and felt heady from the combination of his body heat, the smell of his cologne and the bristle of his beard against her cheek. He was wearing the living daylights out of a crisp white dress shirt that she was sure was hand crafted for his broad chest. A pair of expertly tailored black flat front slacks showcased his long legs. And a wealthy looking pair of oxblood chukkas covered his feet. A rather plain ensemble but his rich chocolate skin and athletic physique made it look delicious. Asha's eyes drank him in from the bottom up, making a brief pit stop between inseam street and belt buckle boulevard.

Daniel warmed from her gaze and surveyed her almond skin and curvy frame. "You changed your hair?" He touched her ponytail. She felt her head almost fall backward at his touch. "Um, yeah it's just straightened," she quickly regained her composure. Daniel smized, her subtle reaction gave him goosebumps under his sleeves. "Nice," he said wandering into her eyes.

"Herrsheeee, I thought that was you," a shrill voice called out from behind Asha.

"Ms. Hyacinth, how are you?" Daniel greeted the large woman clad in electric blue lace and chiffon. Ms. Hyacinth practically mowed Asha down in order to get to Daniel. Asha struggled to keep her balance and remembered that she was taught to respect her elders. "Herrsheee, look how you grow so niiiice," Ms. Hyacinth cooed in her Caribbean accent smiling into Daniel's face. She stood inappropriately close to him with her hand resting on his chest. Daniel deftly spun Ms. Hyacinth around to face Asha, "Ms. Hyacinth, this is my date Asha." Ms. Hyacinth James was the hefty, ill-shaped, tackily styled owner of the local West Indian market. A woman in her mid-fifties, she wore too much makeup, too much hair and too much perfume. "Nice to meet you." Asha extended her hand. Ms. Hyacinth offered a dismissive limp hand for Asha to shake, "Yes darling." She turned to face Daniel while giving Asha her back. "Hersheee love, give your mother my regards and keep good, you hear?" Ms. Hyacinth pawed Daniel's arm and leaned in for a kiss on the cheek. "I will, it was good to see you." Daniel kissed the side of her pancake battered face. Ms. Hyacinth floated off into the crowd and Asha's eyes widened.

"That was...interesting," Asha said finally.

"Yeah, she's interesting," Daniel laughed. "But she's a family friend and a patron of the gallery, so I had to oblige her." He explained while lifting two champagne flutes from a server's tray.

"She looked like she wanted to swallow you whole," Asha laughed. Daniel stifled a guffaw and managed to take a sip of his champagne without spitting it out. "I mean, she practically shoved me out of the way. She was in full cougar mode," Asha continued.

Daniel laughed, "Nah, I'm no cougar snack." He crossed his arms across his expansive chest and spoke into Asha's imagination, "I'm a full course dinner."

Asha gulped the rest of her champagne and tried to ignore Daniel's last comment. She didn't want to go there. Well, she did, but not tonight. Not that tonight was a bad night to go there. She had a three-day old wax and a pack of Magnums at the house. She took note of the way Daniel's paw hands engulfed the champagne flute. She also sized up the length of his shoe, about twice the size of her size 8s. Maybe tonight wouldn't be a bad night to go there, after all.

"So, your friend the photographer," Asha said changing the subject. "Yeah, let's head over to the exhibit," Daniel motioned toward the exhibit. They navigated their way through the crowd, stopping every few steps while Daniel greeted guests. Asha took note of how many women tugged at, waved to or called out to Daniel. She considered Ms. Hyacinth a fluke, but now she had second thoughts. A part of her was annoyed but another part felt reassured as his hand never left her waist. They approached a cypher of people buzzing around the roped off exhibit. Daniel walked right up and crossed the velvet rope with Asha in tow.

A short, stocky Latino man dressed in all black waved them over. "You hot in these streets tonight," the man said giving Daniel a brotherman handshake.

"Nah, it's your night bro," Daniel bowed his head and clasped his hands. He turned to Asha and said, "I'd like you to meet Diego Santos, the featured artist tonight."

Diego shook Asha's hand, "Thank you for coming. I hope you enjoy what I've created."

Asha, caught off guard by the introduction found her voice, "Oh, I'm sure I will. It's nice to meet you."

"I appreciate you, man. You always come through in the clutch," Diego said punching his fist into his palm.

"No doubt. You know how we do," Daniel answered and noticed Diego looking behind him into the crowd. Diego's face turned to melodramatic alarm, "Yo D, go 'head before my buela...uh-oh too late."

Daniel turned around directly into an elderly woman fully decked out in a 1920s-styled sparkling flapper dress. "AYYYYYYYEE, DAAAHHHNEEEEE. Aaaye que chulo Daahhneee," Ms. Carmen catcalled. She wrapped her petite arms around Daniel's waist. Asha stepped back from the embrace and into the crowd. This was becoming comical. The younger women, she could understand. But what was it with him and these old bitties?

"Doña Carmen, you look hot! Don't go getting a boyfriend tonight," Daniel joked.

"Daahhhnee, tan fresco!" Ms. Carmen blushed and dismissed him with a wave.

"Ms. Carmen, this my date Asha," he introduced them.

Asha didn't extend her hand this time, she was over these old ladies. "Nice to meet you," she said stepping next to Daniel.

Ms. Carmen gave Asha the once over and a smile of approval "Hiii, nice to meechu, too." She was pleasant enough, but still on the cougar list as far as Asha was concerned. "Dahnee, thank you for helping my precioso," Ms. Carmen cupped Diego's blushing cheeks. "Ju see Daahnee pikchur? Aaaye tan handsome," Ms. Carmen offered to Asha.

Daniel quickly answered, "Uh, no we haven't seen the collection yet Doña, we're gonna walk around now." Daniel gave a final dap to Diego and a hug to Ms. Carmen and led Asha over to the premiere exhibit.

"You have quite a way with the older women," Asha said.

"Ms. Carmen?" Daniel laughed, "She's Diego's grandma. We grew up around the way."

"She seemed nice, but I'm gonna keep my eye on you." Asha teased.

They walked along the wall that showcased Diego's work. He worked mostly in black and white and sepia tones featuring the beach town and its residents. In one photograph, Asha recognized the gates of the local Queens Public library. His back against the gate, a homeless man ate from a foil takeout container while his dog did the same at his side. In another piece, the sun was rising behind a young woman at a bus stop in a party dress, with 5 inch stilettos in hand.

"I love the way he captured the neighborhood," Asha commented.

"Yeah, he's fire. Ms. Carmen bought him an old camera from the pawn shop when we were in middle school. I can count how many times I've seen him without a camera in his hand," he told her. Asha approached the third photograph in the installment. It was

53

the bare back of a man in sweatpants doing pull-ups on the arm of a traffic sign while a dice game was in full swing in the background. His muscular back was a melanin rich paradise of hills and valleys. The gray sweats hung low; his construction Timberlands unlaced. Asha almost tried to peek around the corner to the front of the photograph, confident that a V formed where his lower abdomen met his hip. She was impressed but hid it well. "I wonder who won this dice game," she quipped. "This guy to the left looks like he's losing," she chuckled and pointed, ignoring Daniel's dominance in the photograph.

Daniel laughed. He was just about to tell her who the real winner was when someone approached them from behind. "Oh my God, Danny. You think you the starrah? You not the starrah, love. It's Diego's night, boo," a slim, sharply dressed man with feminine features flamboyantly barked at Daniel.

Asha stepped back from Daniel once again. She quietly observed.

"Alexander, why you always got drama for me," Daniel asked the man who twirled about a dinner-length cigarette holder.

Alexander gave Daniel Hollywood air kisses. "Never drama, always love for you, hun. You know that. But look at all these people out here to see Diego's pictures," he shook his head. "He's living it, honey. I'm happy for him though, no shade," he declared. "Although he didn't ask me to pose, mmm hmm," he added with a hint of shade. "That's ok. At least he finally made something good with that camera. Always with that wretched camera in everybody's face," he said slightly disgusted. Before Daniel could get a word in, Alexander continued. "But, who is this Hershey Pie? Who you tryna hide, on the low, in the foundation, basement and sub cellar?" Alexander ran his mouth like a loud, cheap motor.

Daniel sighed, exhausted from this exchange.

"I'm just asking," Alexander said, craning his neck to get a good look at Asha. Asha looked back at him, slightly annoyed. He was so loud and animated. She wasn't sure what to make of this character, or what his relation was to Daniel.

"Asha," Daniel extended his hand to draw her close to him, "this is my friend Alexander DeVeaux."

Asha's brows raised, "Of DeVeaux's Divine Brows and Lashes?" she asked.

Alexander, impressed by his own notoriety, answered, "Yes, one and the same," he grinned. Alexander's makeup boutique was another hotspot in what her uncle called "the village" of Far Rockaway that Asha heard about but never visited. Cleo, on the other hand, spent tons of money in the Mott Avenue location and raved about how talented Alexander was. "Alexander is also a sponsor of tonight's show," Daniel said still holding on to Asha's hand.

"And an old friend," Alexander added pointing his cigarette holder at them both.

Asha's face remained neutral to the news, or so she thought.

Alexander picked up her unspoken question. "Oh, but not like that. We don't partake of the same meals, love. I prefer beef and he's partial to, well...fish," Alexander made a face as though he smelled something offensive. Then he reviewed her brows and peered into her eyes. "But you are a pretty one." "Thank you," Asha said, somewhat relieved.

"Keep her around Danny, and let loose of those skanks you like to pass the time with," he dramatically advised. "I'll see you both at the afterparty?" Alexander asked Daniel and then gave Asha one final glance and a wink, "Or hopefully you'll be otherwise engaged, mmm hmmm." With a flick of his unlit cigarette, he made his way past the exhibit.

Sandy Cove

Daniel walked Asha out of an emergency exit door that led to a small garden space. He hoped some fresh air would change the mood after that encounter with Alexander.

"Let me guess, you grew up with him too?" Asha asked as she sat down, finally resting her feet at one of the wrought iron bistro sets in the outdoor area illuminated with stringed lights. She was learning a lot about Daniel/Hershey, whatever he was called. It seemed that people naturally clamored toward him. Young, old, male, female, gay, straight. It was as if he was the mayor of this event, yet it was Diego's celebration. Asha felt like she was being sold on him, and it made her uneasy. If people behaved this way with her on his arm, she could only imagine what it was like when he went anywhere by himself.

"Well, yeah," Daniel said sensing her mood change. "Diego is a neighborhood artist, this is a community event. I've lived here my entire life with a lot of these people," he explained while taking a seat next to her.

"You have? Here, in Far Rockaway?" Asha questioned.

"Sure, you seem surprised," he answered. "I've lived here for a long time, too. How is it that you've been here and I've been here," she clasped her hands together, "and we've never run into each other?"

Daniel noted the V-neck on her dress was lower than he originally thought. With all the distractions, maybe he didn't get a good look at her inside the gallery. His eyes combed over her under the illumination of stringed garden lights. The window of dewy cleavage promised C-cups he guesstimated. Full C, chocolate nipples, he visualized. Her dress was fitted but not irrationally tight, and her mid-section folded over into two natural rolls. The iron pedestal chair supported only a small circumference of her ass. The rest spilled over the sides of the chair like a muffin top. His eyes finally made their way back up to hers, where she welcomed them with a squint. He was busted.

Daniel smiled and stood up from where they sat. "Let's get out of here, maybe grab something to eat or get a drink." "Sure," Asha agreed. The appetizers she had earlier were beginning to wear off. Her stomach was just short of grumbling as they exited the garden space into the sidewalk.

"I'm parked in the lot across the street. I'll follow you," she said, thankful that her car was nearby. She felt her shoes expiring.

"We can take my car and I'll bring you back," Daniel suggested. Asha stopped in her tracks. This couldn't be his m.o. She surmised he didn't have to work hard for ass. But the "let's take my car" routine was a bit of a reach. "Will you now, Daniel?" she turned to face him. "Yeah," he said, looking down at her. "Of course, I will. What kind of dude do you think I am?" he said with a serious face. She felt a bit of remorse, maybe she over thought his offer. She was about to apologize when he said, "Tomorrow morning, I'll bring you back."

"What?!" she yelped. His head fell back with laughter. She shoved his arm, "You've got nerve!" She was tickled and a little embarrassed at the same time. "If you feel more comfortable taking your car now, it's fine. But I promise, I'll bring you back here as soon as you're ready," he assured her. They were already halfway to her car, "I'll take my car thank you, sir," she said and remotely unlocked her car.

Daniel put his key in the ignition of his oversized SUV. He wasn't sure how to read her. He was having a good time but didn't want to push too fast. He surprised himself at his offer to have her spend the night with him. He rarely offered sleepovers. If she came home with him, that would be cool. If she didn't, that would be ok too. No, it wouldn't be ok. He wanted to close this deal tonight. Daniel repeatedly checked his rearview mirror to make sure she was still tailing him. He put on his turn signal and turned into the parking lot of an outdoor bar lounge.

Asha pulled her car into the space next to Daniel.

She sent a quick text to Cleo: *At the Sandy Cove on Beach 9th with #CoffeeShop.* She didn't usually extend dates across multiple venues or follow men in cars, but the late spring/early summer night air had her feeling adventurous. Letting Cleo know her whereabouts gave her an illusion of assurance about her actions. Her phone buzzed with Cleo's reply: *Another dive. I hope he has a big dick.* Asha rolled her eyes and put her phone away.

The waitress brought their appetizer platter to the table and Daniel asked, "So what school did you go to?"

"I went to private school," Asha stuffed a cheese nacho into her mouth.

"St. Mary's? You look like a St. Mary's girl." Daniel took a swig of his Guinness.

"No," Asha said.

"Church of God?" Daniel guessed again.

"Nope." She wiped her mouth with her napkin.

Daniel thought for a minute, "St. Rose of Lima."

"Uh-uh." She laughed, knowing he was stumped.

"Well, that's it," Daniel counted on his fingers. "I think those are all the...wait, was it St. Joachim?"

Asha laughed, impressed at his knowledge of local parochial schools. "I went to Kellenberg," she admitted.

"Kellenberg?" Daniel questioned. "In Long Island?"

"Yeah, I guess that explains it," Asha nodded.

"Oh, that's why." He leaned back in his seat and smiled. "You were kept hidden from me."

Asha blushed at his insinuation. "I'm sure that was my uncle's plan. To hide me from the likes of you."

"Your uncle?"

"I was raised by my aunt and uncle."

"And your parents?" he inquired.

"My dad passed when I was young. My mom too," Asha said matter of factly.

"Wow," Daniel exhaled. He sat deflated by her statement. He couldn't imagine growing up without his mom.

"Wow to you," Asha said.

"What?" Daniel asked.

"You were really sensitive to that," Asha smiled into his eyes.

"I mean," he straightened his posture. "that's a sensitive thing. I assume your aunt is great but a mom is, well..." Daniel's voice wandered off.

Asha gushed, "Awww you're a momma's boy?"

Daniel laughed, "That's what they say."

Asha pursed her lips, "I bet. I bet you are."

After another round of drinks and a shared slice of chocolate cake, they headed to the parking lot. "My uncle and aunt are great," Asha picked up their previous conversation. "They did everything and more for me. My uncle is getting ready to retire, and my aunt is afraid of what it'll be like once he's home. He may have to get a security job or something," Asha laughed.

"Security?" Daniel asked.

"Yeah, he's retiring from the force," Asha boasted.

"Your uncle's a cop?" Daniel's eyes narrowed.

"Yeah," Asha paused. "Why? You have something against law enforcement?"

"Nah. But some, apparently have something against me and my kind," Daniel told her.

Asha leaned against her car and folded her arms, "Well, my uncle is not like that, ok?"

Daniel saw her mood shift, "Understood. I'm not trying to offend you, but I'm sure you can understand my point of view."

"Oh, of course." Her nostrils flared. "But I just want you to know that my family does not condone that behavior and it's not like that across the board."

"Got it." Daniel concluded the conversation.

They stood at her car in uncomfortable quietness. "Did you enjoy the exhibit?" Daniel placed his hands in his pockets.

"I did." her face brightened. "Diego is really talented. It's cool to see familiar places through his camera lens," Asha told him.

Daniel remained quiet.

"Or did you mean, did I like seeing your bare back sprawled across the canvas?" she asked.

The corners of Daniel's mouth turned upward.

"Well you're hot, but you know that already." She told him. "What's something that I can tell you that you don't already know?" Asha asked placing her hands on her hip. Daniel stepped in front of her and leaned in to whisper in her ear. "That you'll go out with me again."

Asha looked up to the sky and put an index finger to her chin. "Let me think... maybe."

Daniel faked an incredulous look, "Maybe?!"

"Yeah, perhaps! I have to think it over," Asha giggled.

"That's fair enough. Let me know when you get to that decision."

"I will," Asha said.

"Yeah, keep me posted," Daniel replied, barely able to hide his smile.

"No, that's my answer: yes, I will go out with you again." Her cheeks rose, nearly touching her lashes.

"That was fast," he said to her warm smile. "I wonder what brought on that speedy decision?"

Asha bit her bottom lip. "Your bare back sprawled across the canvas."

Daniel's hearty laugh gave her tingles. "Maybe Diego has more stills. I'll see if he can hook you up."

"Actually, I'm into works of art that feed my other senses. Tasting and touching, along those lines." Asha drunk him in with her eyes. Daniel slowly nodded his head.

Asha felt reckless. She had no idea what she was doing propositioning this man in a parking lot late at night. Aside from the interruptions at the gallery and the slight tension about her uncle, things seemed to flow easily between them. Sure, he was annoyingly popular and women fell all over him, but his attention was focused on her now. He wasn't hard pressed for female company. If she drove off in her car right now, he'd most likely call a bench warmer or a starter even, she concluded. He was fine, he smelled good, he fed her and the night was still young. *Let's just see how this unfolds*, she thought to herself.

Lovin' You Tonight

Daniel didn't necessarily see this coming. Not this fast at least. Especially with all that had gone on at the gallery. It was like a comedy of errors. Almost anyone who could ruin his chances, approached him at the event. Daniel thought for sure that Alexander had put the nail in the coffin. With all that nonsense about "an old friend," he doubted Asha would want any parts of him.

Alexander was lucky that they went so far back, otherwise he might have draped him up in the middle of Diego's show. When they were young, the three of them had gone to summer day camp together for years up until they eventually aged out. And even back then, Daniel sensed there was something different about Alexander, but he could never put his finger on it. On the way home from camp, the summer before they became junior counselors, two boys approached Alexander and confronted him about being a battyman. Daniel wasn't sure what that meant, but he could see the fear in his friend's eyes. He and Diego told them if they wanted to fight Alexander, they'd have to fight all three of them. Outnumbered, the boys ran off and never approached Alexander again.

The following summer while Daniel and Diego enjoyed their junior counselor paychecks, Alexander went to Atlanta to visit relatives. He returned to Far Rockaway as the most fabulous and stylish homosexual or heterosexual the neighborhood had seen. Diego and Daniel questioned him as to what happened during his summer away. Alexander told them, "I found myself this summer and this is who I am. But if you don't want to be associated with the new Alexander,

I understand." Diego and Daniel looked at each other and scoffed. Diego said, "Man, I don't give a fuck about you being a sissy. Are you coming to my birthday party? My grandma wants your moms to make the fried chicken."

Daniel knew a lot of people. That wasn't his fault. Most women were into it. He could see it in their faces when he introduced them to people he knew. Not Asha, she seemed indifferent, if not bothered. But now, she gave the impression of a green light. The change of scenery at the Sandy Cove helped, he was certain. Maybe she would agree to come back to his apartment. He ran down a quick checklist: chilled wine, clean linens, no dishes in the sink, condoms and such in full supply. He was ready.

"I thought you'd be into architectural art," Daniel shrugged.

"Architectural?" Asha questioned. She thought he was smarter than this. She threw out a clear signal, but somehow he missed it. She'd still make the best of the night. Why should all that yummy goodness go to waste?

Daniel leaned against his own car, wide-legged. "Yeah, like pillars, obelisks and towers?"

Asha felt her body reacting to his words. She stood in the space between his legs. "I bet women just fall all over themselves at the offer of your pillar tower, huh? They probably hop on that thing like it's the last express train to Manhattan." she placed her arms around his neck.

Daniel feigned an appalled look, "Yeah, women consent to my offer of sex," he spoke into her face and wrapped his hands around her waist. "But my only offer to you was another date," he smirked.

Asha pushed him back with both hands, he didn't budge. "You know what?!" Asha laughed.

Daniel held on to her, "But I'm not opposed to fast forwarding," he snickered.

Asha couldn't help but laugh. "You're a piece of work," she looked into his eyes.

He pulled her closer to him, "I bet men lose their souls in those eyes," Daniel said, feeling his own soul wander into the grey abyss. He leaned in but paused to gauge her reaction. Her eyes closed and her lips parted; Daniel dove in.

Asha's body sizzled as Daniel's tongue navigated her mouth, and his hands slid down to cup her cheeks. He felt and tasted so good.

She didn't want to cheat herself out of what she was certain was a good slay, but she decided it was too soon. She had come to her senses. Cleo would have to wait until another time to get the eggplant verdict. She finally pulled away from the entangled bliss of their mouths and tongues and gathered her wits about her. His eyes were low, and his hands remained in place as he stared at her mouth while she spoke.

"Mmmm. On that note, I think we can call it a night." She couldn't believe she put herself in such a position. She had to escape before she fell prey to the energy he was giving. He played the game well, but he wasn't getting any ass. Not tonight, not from her.

Daniel was a little disappointed. Actually, he was a lot disappointed. But he enjoyed the cat and mouse play that Asha presented. This deliberate chase was new for him, but his interest was piqued. He never had a woman second-guess sleeping with him. Not that he knew of, or could remember.

She unlocked her car with the remote, and Daniel opened the driver's side door for her.

"I'm gonna follow you home to make sure you get in ok," he offered, as she turned the key to the ignition.

"To make sure you get in, you mean," Asha laughed.

"Asha," he said taking a different approach. "You don't think I have to beg for ass, do you?" Daniel rested his arms atop her car.

Amused by the change of tone in his voice, Asha informed him, "Daniel, I know you're 'selective'" she air quoted. "But, this selection isn't available yet," she smiled. Daniel gave a slow smile. He mentally accepted the challenge and backed away from the car. Asha drove off feeling both relieved—and frustrated.

In fact, Cleo cursed her out about her change of heart the following morning at brunch.

"Bitch, if he as fine as you saying, what the fuck happened?"

"I changed my mind, Cleo. It was kinda soon," Asha confessed.

"Soon? How soon is soon? You waiting for the prom?" Cleo pressed.

"I got cold feet, I guess. Plus, he took for granted that it was happening. I didn't like that," Asha told her. She took a sip of her modified mimosa of orange juice, seltzer and vodka.

"He's a man, Asha. Of course he thought he was getting some," Cleo advised.

"He gets ass all day and night, Cleo. He ain't missing mine. You should have seen the women throwing it in his face."

"Yeah, but he obviously likes you," Cleo reminded her as she cut into her French toast.

"Why? Cuz he took me out? He likes a lot of women, and they like him back."

"And you're mad at that?" Cleo huffed. "Why you ain't let me see him yet? Why you hiding him?"

"I'm not hiding anybody. He's not mine to hide. You can look at him, if you want. Google him."

"Asha, I'm just saying. Live a little. He seem alright. I mean, he did make up for the coffee shop with the art show and dinner."

"Oh, I didn't tell you he was featured in the art show. I'm thinking that's why he invited me."

"But Asha, I want to know why you're upset. If he's fine and he likes you, just go for it."

Cleo had a point. But she had always been more liberal with her goodies. Cleo always seemed to have fun with men, except for that one time she got a venereal disease. It was the one time that made Asha leery.

Retirement Party

Asha and Cleo primped themselves in the mirror.

"I should have worn the yellow dress, Cleo," Asha complained as she adjusted her dress.

"You look fine, Asha. The blue is fire, and you know that's your uncle's favorite color," Cleo glanced over at her in the mirror. Asha always looked stunning, yet she frequently second guessed herself.

"Yeah, but I would be able to eat more in the yellow dress. I can't have cake in this unless I take off these spanks. Help me take off these spanks." Asha leaned against the sink and started to yank up her dress.

"Asha, stop! You don't even need those spanks in the first place." Cleo laughed at her friend.

Asha laughed at herself. "I just don't want to be gassy when I make my speech."

Asha freshened her lipstick.

"You'll be fine. Just don't go up there and start boo-hooing," Cleo warned.

"Ok, I'm gonna need another shot then," Asha said, as she opened the bathroom door.

Asha wrote the speech for her uncle's retirement party months ago when she and AJ booked the venue. She wasn't much of a public speaker but wanted to do something special for her uncle. Had it not been for him and AJ, she couldn't imagine what her life would be like. She was relieved that her uncle was able to retire from the force in good health and unscathed. Several of his buddies never made it to retirement. And some that did, died shortly thereafter. The job sucked the life force out of them and left them with little time in civilian life. But her uncle looked great to be in his early fifties, enjoying golf, fishing and an occasional game of basketball.

Asha stopped at the bar and took a shot of Patron to steady her nerves for the speech. Heading back to her table, she accidentally bumped into one of the servers. Luckily, he was able to save the bowls of soup before they spilled onto the floor.

"Oh no, I'm so sorry," she said as the server dipped to prevent the spill.

"That's ok, miss…" he spun around and faced Asha.

Both stood frozen.

"Asha?" he said.

"Khalil, what are you doing here? I mean, I see what you're doing but…" She looked around, hoping not to cause a scene.

"I'm working, what do you think I'm doing?" He looked her up and down. "What are you doing at this cop party?" He hadn't heard from her in weeks; his calls and texts went unanswered. Khalil knew that they weren't serious, but they'd been hooking up every now and then. Even if their schedules didn't allow for them to meet up, she usually had the decency to respond to him. Maybe she met someone, which was fine, he just thought it rude that she'd drop him like a hot potato.

"This is my uncle's party," she told him.

"Your uncle is five-o?!" Khalil snarled.

She escorted him off to the side, "Yeah, why are you acting like that? What is your problem?"

Khalil put his tray down. "All this time, you never told me nothing like that? You just said your uncle work for the city!"

Asha was confused, "Well, he did work for the city, what difference does it make?"

Khalil looked at her. "That's why you stopped answering my calls, your uncle didn't want you with somebody like me?"

Asha sighed and crossed her arms. "Khalil, I'm grown. My uncle doesn't have a say over who I do anything with. I just haven't called you because I haven't called you."

Khalil stepped closer to her and was about to give her an earful when two men interrupted them. "Is everything ok here?" a young, bald Latino man in a gray suit asked her. Another man, with locs in a navy suit stood behind Khalil.

"Um, yeah, everything's cool. I was just asking the server if we could get some more bread," Asha said trying to diffuse the situation. The two men stepped back and allowed Khalil and his tray to leave the area. Khalil gave Asha a dirty look as he walked past them.

Just then, Asha's uncle approached them dancing to the beat of the 80's R&B playing softly in the main dining area. "Alright detective, don't hurt 'em," bald, gray suit teased.

Uncle laughed, "Y'all don't know nothing about this here." He shimmied. "Hey Cupcake, you alright?" Uncle wrapped his arm around Asha's shoulder.

"Yeah, I see you're having a good time," she laughed.

The bald, gray suit guy stepped up. "Detective, is this the niece you're always talking about?"

"Yes, this is my beautiful niece, Asha. Asha, this is Officer Santiago." Uncle pointed in bald, grey suit's direction. "And you remember Burnett?" Uncle motioned to locs in the navy suit.

Santiago offered his hand to Asha and held on to it for two seconds past uncomfortable. Santiago looked her in the eyes, "It's a pleasure to meet you. Detective brags about you all the time."

Asha gave a courteous smile but wasn't impressed with Santiago's smooth tactics. He'd been creeping her out since she caught him staring at her during the appetizer hour. He was one of those cops who thought that every woman was a uniform freak. She'd run into that type before, but none ever had the nerve to seriously approach her given who her uncle was.

68

Burnett offered a modest nod in her direction. "Burnett," she turned her attention away from Santiago, "didn't your wife just have a baby?"

Burnett's face lit up. "Yes, she's 4 months now." Then, he took out his phone to show off photos of his baby. Asha oohed and ahhed and turned her back to Santiago. She hoped that sent him a clear message that she wasn't interested.

"Good evening, everyone. I'm Asha Martin and Detective Rand Martin is my uncle." Asha looked over at her beaming uncle from the podium. "I know it would be hard for some of you to think of Detective Martin as a warm, silly, kind-hearted father figure," she began.

An officer yelled out from the crowd, "HELLLL NO!" and the crowd erupted with laughter.

Asha continued, "But he is all of those things and more." Asha took a deep breath, she felt herself getting emotional. She held up an old crinkled business card. "My uncle gave this card to me when I was eight years old." She read from the card, "Officer Randolph Martin, 101st precinct."

Officers yelled and whooped at the mention of their precinct.

"I had to use this card one month later when his brother, my dad, died. Uncle and my aunt Jasmine never hesitated with their decision to take me in and raise me as their own," Asha swallowed tears. Asha saw AJ take a napkin to her delicately beat face. "My uncle gave his best to his family and also to the force. I'm so happy that he has this time to enjoy his golden years."

"Watch it, now," Uncle warned.

Asha laughed, "My uncle exposed me to some of his favorite hobbies like fishing, golf and poker."

AJ pursed her lips at the mention of poker.

"He encouraged me and even coached me in any activity I wanted to do as a kid. Uncle, remember when you helped me with that

choreography for the talent show? You almost threw your back out."
Asha reminded him and the room laughed. "Even now as an adult if
I ask him to hang out with me, he's always game. I even got him to
join me at hot yoga," she added.

"Had me sweating like a whore in church!" Uncle laughed, and AJ
clapped her hands at the memory.

"Uncle, I just want to let you know that I love you. I'm happy for
you, and I'm so proud of you." Asha closed her speech to a standing
ovation and a bear hug from her uncle.

Rooftop

Daniel took a swig of his drink as he surveyed the crowd. Germ was already halfway drunk due to heavy pre-gaming. "A-yooo. Get in this flick, son!" Germ yelled over to Daniel. He posed for the picture with Germ and his group of minions. Then he walked away as soon as the photographer's camera flashed.

"Hersh, one more," Germ slurred.

Daniel hated these dumb party website photos. He knew Germ only took them because he thought it would give him a sense of hood celebrity.

"Oh, you too good for the hood?" Germ asked as if he read Daniel's mind.

"Shut up, man," Daniel replied as he posed for the pic by staring blankly into the camera's lens. The photographer showed them the picture on his camera screen. Daniel's simple outfit consisted of a black V-neck t-shirt, dark denim jeans and black designer loafers. It gave him an unbothered male model look.

On the other hand, Germ was outfitted in an army green t-shirt adorned with gold epaulettes. He had it paired with leather camouflage jeans with a gold usher strip that ran down the sides. The ensemble was bookended with a green Yankee fitted and fresh construction Timbs. He looked like a militant organ grinder's monkey. Daniel knew Germ thought he was stuntin' in his getup. The decorative shoulder hardware and leather jeans were one thing. *But a Yankee fitted in anything other than Yankee blue*, Daniel thought, *was sacrilege.*

Just as Daniel expected, Germ was doing that dumb ape face pose and pointing his finger in Daniel's direction. "Yeah, son!" Germ exclaimed as though he had struck gold with his pose. Germ and Diamond both loved those dumb club photos. He thought back to the last event he went to and bumped into Diamond. He got wasted and only remembered waking up naked in bed with her. Germ sent him some of the club photos from that event later that week. He was definitely drunk, and Diamond took full advantage.

Daniel received free VIP tickets from a promoter friend for this event. He knew Germ lived for this type of crowd, so he invited him along. Usually, Germ would be with his crew in the general population. But because of his VIP status, he was free to roam about the party and return to the VIP section at his leisure. Daniel hoped not to bump into Diamond tonight. Their social circles orbited each other, which made for awkward encounters when they weren't on good terms. He didn't know what terms they were on at this point. He hadn't seen her in weeks.

He went to her profile and saw "Enjoying the sun and sand" with a check-in at Shelter Island. She included a picture of her barely restrained boobs in a nude triangle-cut bikini. *Good*, Daniel thought. No chance of running into her today. Just as Daniel took a seat in the section, he saw a group of women approaching his direction. He recognized one immediately. It was Jennifer. He hadn't been to her store since her invitation at the soccer field. As she was about to pass him by, he reached out and touched her hand.

She snatched her hand and turned in his direction with a scowl that transformed into a Cheshire grin. "Oh hiiii!" she squealed as he stood up. She hugged him and rubbed her hands up and down his back. "Where you been stranger?" she looked up into his face. Jennifer was wearing a silver dress that wrapped her assets like a straightjacket.

"I been around," he said.

Jennifer's friends circled him and sized him up like hungry coyotes. "You need to come by the store," she kissed him on the cheek, "I got something for you."

"Yeah. Imma be up there soon," he said to her. She blew a kiss as she pranced away with her crew. One of the women accompanying Jennifer rubbed past Daniel when there was clearly enough space for her to get by otherwise. She winked at him, and he smiled back.

Daniel laughed. Some of these women were so desperate. He was all for a good time, but they never gave him a chance to pursue them. He enjoyed that about Asha. She allowed herself to be chased. Either that or she didn't care for him much; he wasn't sure at this point. From what he could see of her social media, she had an average amount of male followers. Not many selfies. Minimal party pics. A lot of pics of her cats and plants. Was she a weirdo cat chick? She couldn't be. She was beautiful, smart and funny. She liked some of his posts but never the ones he thought she would. Well, rarely the ones of him bare-chested. Although, she admired his bare back at the gallery, but maybe that was as far as it would go.

Daniel's drinks were working their way through his system. On his way back from the men's room, he ran into a familiar group of men. "Ahhhh damn, look at this nigga here! Ain't givin' the average motherfucker a chance," a cinder block of a man with a canine face yelled out.

Daniel stopped in his tracks and hung his head. The man continued, "That's why I stays in the hood. Motherfuckers like him come to the party and get all the hoes!" Daniel laughed and held his hands up in surrender.

"What's good, my G?" He gave Daniel a brother man handshake and embrace.

"I'm good, dog. Can't complain," Daniel answered.

Lemuel Parker was known as Bulldog because of his harsh re-semblance to well, a bulldog. After returning home from a drug possession bid, Bulldog tarried in his sister's shop, and accidentally worked his way up from follicle cemetery sweeper to master stylist. A convicted felon turned weaveologist.

"I hear you, G. Yo, it's some hoes in here tonight. They acting stuck up and shit though," Bulldog snarled. "Half of them got that low-grade bullshit on they head. I'll call a bitch out in this motherfucker if she try to front on the kid, ya heard?!" Bulldog scanned the crowd with his beady eyes.

Daniel laughed at his threat. As he followed Bulldog's gaze, he did a double take at a familiar face in one of the reserved sections. He spotted Asha. He gave dap to Bulldog, went back to his VIP area and pulled out his phone. He went to a couple of her timelines but saw nothing that hinted she'd be here. Her most recent post was of her cat asleep in her laundry basket last week. She definitely wasn't like the majority of women he'd met who documented every minute of every day. They would definitely post something like VIP status at Long Island's premier rooftop party.

He sent her a text.

Daniel: Hey Beautiful

He could see her from where he was sitting. She looked bored. She sipped from her glass and reached for her phone.

*Asha: Hi Handsome *heart kiss face**

Heart kiss face? Maybe she was tipsy.

Daniel: Whats up?

Asha: I'm good. Whats up with you?

She certainly looked good from where he sat. Her hair was in wild curls and tamed only by a gold silk headband. She was wearing a short khaki belted shirt dress with strappy cognac sandals.

Daniel: Chillin'. What you getting into?

*Asha: I'm about to get you on the dance floor. *winky face**

74

Daniel blinked at his phone and looked up in her direction. She raised her glass in toast toward him.

Asha saw him when he walked in close to an hour ago. She peered into the crowd to see if the mirage was real. It was him. He sauntered through the crowd; his tall frame head above shoulders of most of the partygoers. She thought to text him or mention him but decided to wait. She was seated in an elevated area in the middle of the venue. He was bound to see her. She peeped his green glow in the dark wristband, similar to the orange one she was wearing. She watched as a gaggle of geese descended upon him. One bird hugged him, and another brushed up against him when she thought no one was looking. *Fine bastard*, she laughed. She'd wait. If he didn't see or approach her, she'd reach out to him when she was leaving. Very nonchalantly. As nonchalantly as she could carefully plan. She would make up for back pedaling at the Gallery.

Asha's phone buzzed.

Daniel: Lemme see what you got.

Asha looked in his direction. He got up and walked to the edge of the crowded dance floor and motioned for her to join him. She squeezed through the crowd and met him already in the midst of a two-step bounce. AJ once told her there was a correlation between the vertical and the horizontal dance. Both required rhythm, attention and synchronization with the woman's body. AJ was referring back to a different time. As far as Asha knew, everyone danced the same two-step sway bounce. There was nothing really to detect from dancing with a man these days. But that wouldn't stop her from two-stepping with Daniel.

He stood closely behind her while casually bopping to the beat. Just as they were getting into a friendly groove, the DJ changed the direction of the music to a reggae set. At the sound of the siren drop, the crowd fired imaginary gunshots into the air. *BUP BUP BUP!* Daniel backed away from the crowd taking Asha with him and parked his back against the wall. AJ's words returned to Asha's mind. Reggae was an entirely different animal. Reggae was a near simulation of the horizontal dance.

The acapella introduction of a popular lovers' rock tune got the crowd into a frenzy. Asha was caught up in the high of the music mixed with the effects from her earlier shots of candy apple liquor. She began to sway her hips with her arms raised. The bassline dropped and sent vibrations through the crowd. Daniel pulled Asha close from behind and proctored the movement of her hips with his hands. They moved together in a slow deliberate rhythm over the syncopated beat.

Her loose curls brushed against his chest while she moved with the music. With his knees slightly bent, he slid his hands from her hips and let them rest on the edges of her short dress. His fingertips met the skin of her outer thighs as Asha pressed herself into Daniel's motion. The DJ spun the record back and started another song with the same riddim. Daniel removed his grasp and allowed her to dance freely. He watched her from behind and followed her deep hip movements without missing a beat. Neither separated from the sensual Velcro that held them together for the next 3 songs.

Asha felt warm and soft to his touch. She smelled good. A cocktail of a fruit scented shampoo, perfume, alcohol and mint gum. Daniel felt that the buildup had reached its peak. He whispered in her ear, "You ready to get out of here?" Asha nodded yes.

Asha felt her thighs beginning to sweat. Daniel danced well, but what else did she expect? He wasn't too forward or touchy. He gave her freedom to lose herself in the rhythm. He also led her to change pace and direction with the most subtle movements. Asha hoped this was a foreshadowing of things to come. She turned around to face him, "Let me tell my friends I'm leaving. I'll meet you by the elevators in 10."

Asha spotted Cleo grinding on the wall with a bearded dance

partner. She pulled Cleo out of her twerk session, "Cleo, I'm out. I'm leaving with Coffee Shop," she yelled in Cleo's ear. Cleo nodded and began to dance with Asha. She was drunk. She motioned to another friend who came to the party with them. "I'm leaving. I told Cleo, but she probably won't remember. Get home safe, and I'll call y'all tomorrow." She gave a cheek kiss and left. Asha was finally going to follow Cleo's advice and live a little.

Daniel hadn't seen Asha since the gallery's false start. He was ready to ditch Germ and close the deal with this beautiful creature—a beautiful tipsy creature, he laughed to himself. He was in no terms a creep or used to taking advantage of mildly inebriated women. He figured the drinks would loosen her up a bit, and she'd be more relaxed with him.

He sent Germ a text.

Daniel: Yo, I'm out.

Germ would see the message eventually.

Daniel saw Asha in conversation with one of Germ's minions near the elevator. His first thought was to escort her out of the conversation. Instead, he stood back and watched. Asha touched the guy's arm, smiled and walked away.

Dude called out, "Ok, ma. I see you though." Minion watched Asha walk away from him and into Daniel's embrace. Minion mouthed, "Fuck" and returned to the party.

Asha's phone buzzed.

*Cleo: I hope you leaving me for a good reason. *eggplant emoji**

Asha: Cleo, goodbye.

Cleo: I'm just saying.

Asha: Again, bye.

Cleo: Stop fronting on dude and get you some!

Asha put her phone away. She allowed Cleo to drag her to the party, but really Asha just wasn't in the mood. Which is probably why she drank more than usual. In fact, she was in the mood. She was horny. She'd stopped seeing Khalil since just before her uncle's retirement party, and her toys weren't cutting it anymore. She wasn't the type to bed multiple men at the same time. Not for the sake of being prude, but for the mere task of scheduling. She just didn't have the time management skills. Even though what she had with Khalil was casual, he was the only one she'd been with in the last six months.

"Your boyfriend over there seemed upset," Daniel joked, "Is that him texting you?"

"Funny," Asha answered. "I was texting my friend I came to the party with. She just wants me to get some dick, that's all." Asha shrugged.

Daniel paused, "Tell her I'm on it."

Asha laughed as they stepped into the elevator, and he pressed the button for the garage level. "I've been turning that dude down all night. He would not take the hint."

"It's a game of chance. If they see the slightest opening, they're gonna go for it."

"Oh, so that's what you guys do? Interesting."

"You guys?" Daniel asked. "No. Some men, not me." He set her straight while looking down into her cleavage.

Asha pressed her body against his, "Well, what do you do then?"

The candy apple shots and flutes of champagne were creeping up on her. Maybe she wouldn't be as apprehensive as she was at the Gallery. Everything seemed to bother her that night. Tonight, she was already mellowed out. Almost prepped for the main event.

Daniel felt her softness against his body. He smiled down at her, and the elevator doors opened.

They stepped into the garage, and Daniel handed the valet his ticket.

The drive to his apartment was only about a half hour, but it seemed like forever. Thankfully, the traffic was light on Broadway. This was one of the main strips that connected Far Rockaway and the neighboring Five Towns to civilization. The tension in the air made it difficult for him to focus on driving. She turned sideways, folded her legs under her in the passenger's seat and stared at the side of his face. He briefly glanced at her. "You ok?" he asked. "No, but I will be," she teased. Her marble eyes were at half-mast, and she licked her lips. He was running out of space in his boxer briefs. He had a mind to pull over and slay her right on the side of the road but thought better of it. He squeezed the steering wheel and avoided several near red lights. He didn't look over at her again until he pulled into his parking spot, only to find her slumped over, asleep.

"Fuck," he echoed the Minion's earlier sentiment.

Sleeping Beauty

Daniel gave one final look at her asleep on his bed. He was pissed but somewhat amused. He finally had her in his lair, but she was out cold. Trying to wake her up in the car was a futile effort. Getting her upstairs was a feat.

"Asha." He rubbed her arm. Nothing. "Asha," he said louder, giving her a little shake. Nada. He tried two more times. He sighed. She couldn't be roused from sleep. He looked in her wallet and found her driver's license. She lived in Bayswater, which wasn't that far away. *Fuck that*, he thought. I'm not driving her home. The last thing he needed was to look like a burglar/rapist entering her home. He didn't know her neighbors, but he knew his. They knew he wasn't a creep, although he did look rather suspect carrying her onto the elevator. Luckily, his doorman was away from his station and the lobby was empty. He lived there for two years and rarely brought women back to his place. Diamond had been the only regular. Even then, she'd only been there for a couple of hours, rarely from one day into the next if he could help it.

Logistics got tricky when he arrived at his apartment door. He carried her in his arms from the car into the building. To gain access to the lobby, he used the keycard in his back pocket by pressing his butt against the security pad. She weighed about 150 pounds from his guesstimate. That was fine for curls at the gym but not in drunk girl dead weight. First, he looked up and down the corridor. Then carefully slung her over his left shoulder like a wounded warrior. He prayed none of his neighbors came out of their apartments. Asha's dress rose up, and her cheeks were slightly exposed and flush with his face. He reached for his key in his front pocket and managed to open the door.

He headed straight to his bedroom, laid her on the bed and removed her shoes. "God please don't let her throw up." Daniel whispered. He covered her with a light throw from the leather club chair in the corner and left the room.

Asha stirred and stretched. She opened her eyes but didn't recognize her surroundings. She was alone in a bedroom. She jerked up into a sitting position, and her head spun. The last thing she remembered was...she couldn't remember. *Oh shit*, she thought. She took a deep breath and smelled something familiar. Her memory jogged. She smelled Daniel. It was coming back to her now. She was dancing with Daniel at the rooftop party. How the hell did she get here? She checked her clothing. Her dress was wrinkled and her shoes were off, but everything else was in place. She could see her clutch on the nightstand with help from the light shining in from the hallway. She reached into it for her phone.

Fuck, Asha thought. She had ruined the night. Again! She should have stopped after the third drink. She took another deep breath and exhaled. Her stomach felt ok, thank God. That would have been the pinnacle of embarrassment, had she thrown up. She opened the flashlight on her phone and scanned her surroundings.

The room was painted in charcoal gray and sparsely decorated. A flat screen TV was mounted on the wall, and an oversized chocolate leather armchair sat in the corner.

She sat on a king-sized, cherry wood, four-poster bed. The navy bed linens were soft against her skin. A half dozen various sized pillows lay against the headboard. She sat almost a foot off the ground. She looked down at the floor and saw her shoes.

"Shit," she said into the dark. She didn't want to show her face at this point, but there was no other way to get out of the situation. Asha hopped off the bed and followed the glow of the light from the hallway.

Daniel was sprawled out on a gray leather chesterfield. Asha always wanted one of those tufted couches. It was one of the few things she remembered from the brief time she spent with her father. They had a tattered butterscotch chesterfield that her dad was usually passed out on. He told her it was a classy piece of furniture. Only high post motherfuckers have these, he'd say. How her crackhead father procured one, she never knew.

A wall mounted TV was playing "Law & Order" on low volume. Daniel was laid on his back, his forearm covering his forehead. His muscular chest rose and fell slowly under the black wife beater. Asha took an assessment while he slept. His basketball shorts showed his dark strong legs, the right leg was stretched on the arm of the couch, his left leg stretched onto the ground. His hair had a tight curl pattern to it that if left unattended would morph into beady beads. It was well maintained and disciplined into low cut waves. Asha took in the thick full brows and dark curly lashes that looked like they were crowded into a subway car, fighting for personal space. An airplane nose sat parked on a velvety cocoa blemish free runway between his high cheekbones and above his full lips. His jet-black beard was full and shone in the TV's light. He was beautiful. And seemingly a nice guy, from her brief interactions with him. No wonder women threw it at him. He definitely had no problems getting ass. Entitled and pretty, hmph, she laughed to herself.

He suddenly rolled over and grunted. Asha turned and did a tiptoe run back into the bedroom. What the hell am I doing, she thought when she caught her breath.

Good Morning

Daniel didn't realize he fell asleep until he woke up. He said one last prayer about her throwing up, put his feet in his slides and went to his bedroom. Asha was sitting on the bed looking at her phone in the dark. The glow from her phone screen illuminated her eyes making them look translucent.

"Good morning," he said, standing in the doorway.

She looked up from her phone, "Hi." Her embarrassment filled the room. "Listen, I... I apologize. I'm completely mortified. I don't usually drink that much," she stopped mid-rant, "I know you probably hear that a lot."

Daniel grinned.

"But I really don't," she protested. "I was just chilling with my girls having fun. I would've probably passed out on my girlfriend's couch had I not left with you," Asha sighed.

"Don't worry about it. You feel ok?" he asked her.

Daniel turned on the light and walked into the room and sat next to her on the bed. Her eyes were a bit puffy. Her dress was wrinkled and her headband hung around her neck. She looked pitiful. And vulnerable. And beautiful.

"Yeah, I'm ok. Just a little out of it. Thank God I didn't throw up," she said.

Daniel laughed, "Yeah that's what I was worried about."

She smiled and busied her hands with her phone.

"Do you want something to eat? Come."

"No, I should get going."

"I'll take you home after you eat something," Daniel yelled on his way to the kitchen. Asha jumped down from the bed.

A part of him felt bad for her. She really seemed embarrassed. She didn't seem like the type to get pissy-ass drunk and pass out in a dude's car. But he did think he would finally get her in bed tonight. He thought tonight was the night because of the look on her face as he drove home. On top of that, the way she whined her hips and ass on him at the party was hypnotizing. This was the second false start they'd had. He wasn't sure what this meant, having never experienced it before. Another part of him was annoyed. Maybe she was just a fucking tease. He got her in bed, alright, while he slept on the couch. Daniel made the decision to feed her and take her home. Maybe this was the end of the line for them, and they'd just be friends. His mind flashed back carrying her on his shoulder over the threshold. He'd been so close to that ass. Damn.

Asha sat at his breakfast bar and watched him take a plastic container out of his refrigerator. "Pasta?" he asked with his back turned to her.

"Sure," she answered, watching him move around in his kitchen.

The kitchen was small, and his wingspan was wide. He could pretty much reach everything from where he stood near the sink.

"Do you want coffee?" He spun around to her as he put the pasta in the microwave.

"Um, sure. Pasta and coffee will definitely work for a hangover," Asha laughed. She checked out the stainless-steel appliances, hardwood floors and modern fixtures. "This is a nice apartment. Where am I, by the way?" As soon as she said it, she busted out laughing.

Daniel turned on his Keurig and laughed too. "What if I was The Killer? You'd be fucked up!"

She banged her fist on the counter and held her hand to her chest.

"Oh my God, it's my life's work to not get got by The Killer. And look, I end up passed out in a strange man's bed." She could barely contain her laughter. He laughed at her laughter. He plated the linguine and placed it in front of her. "Ooh," she said. "This smells good. Is this what you give all the drunk girls you bring home...here... or wherever this is?" She dug her fork into the food.

"Wherever this is, is Lawrence," Daniel answered. "I give the other girls beefaroni," he paused, "you're special." He winked at her.

She made fast work of the hangover food while they got swept up in the "Law & Order" episode. Asha was both full and fully awake now. Daniel put the dishes in his dishwasher and asked her, "Ready?"

She looked at him leaning against his refrigerator. He'd been a good sport through the whole thing. At the gallery, he seemed a little cocky but never pushy. He was a gentleman at the Sandy Cove, even though she changed her mind at the last minute. Tonight was a pleasant surprise, seeing him at the party. They had fun and their dance had piqued her curiosity. Asha got up from the bar stool. She walked up to Daniel, reached up to his face and pushed her way into his mouth. Forget about her linguine and coffee breath.

Daniel was caught off guard and pushed her back, "Woah." He held her at arm's-length. He looked down at her. Her lips were bruised pink from her aggressive kiss. She had a hungry look in her eyes, although he had just fed her. "You...ok? I mean, I know you had a crazy night. Are you sure you don't want me to take you home?"

She gave too many mixed signals. He wanted to get a clear answer from her. She turned from him and walked in the direction of the bedroom. Before turning the corner, she paused and her dress fell to the ground. She looked over her shoulder at him and continued into the bedroom.

Daniel exhaled and ran his hand over his face. He didn't understand her, but that would have to wait until later. He turned off the kitchen light and walked toward the bedroom.

The Main Event

Asha removed the headband from around her neck. She almost forgot about it in her attempt to be sexy. She'd seen that move in a foreign film recently and hoped her dress drop translated as sensuously as it did on film. She stood at the bed in only yellow lace underwear. Her heart beat out of her chest as Daniel's frame darkened the doorway. He pulled off his wife beater and walked toward her. Standing in front of her with their bodies barely touching, he felt heat coming off her body.

Daniel reviewed her from the bottom to the top, finally landing in her eyes. The frustration of their game of stop and go coupled with her heightened breathing made him want to thrash her about. A little punishment for stringing him along. He lifted her and seated her on his bed and she spread her legs wide to accommodate the width of his body. She finally kissed the underside of his chin like she'd fantasized about. Daniel undid her front fastening bra hook and slipped the straps off the soft skin of her shoulders. Her breasts bounced out of bondage with caramel nipples at attention. Asha hummed at the touch of his tongue on her breasts. He left her nipples glistening and went to her mouth. She held his face and tried to pull him on to the bed. He climbed on top of her, and she wrapped as much of her legs as she could around his waist.

Daniel's skin felt smooth and taut against hers. She felt the hills and valleys of muscles under her fingertips as she ran her nails up his broad back. Their positioning made her aware of their difference in scale. His torso completely covered her body. Although he supported his weight on his elbows, he felt heavy and hot on top of her.

Daniel looked into the shadows of her face. She offered a grin.

Her eyes moved rapidly about his face in the limited light. She again pushed her way into his mouth, and the space in his shorts completely disappeared. He rolled off of her and removed his shorts and underwear in one motion.

Asha paused at the sight of his power. She had her game face on, she hoped. She got a hint from their dance but didn't anticipate the combination of his length and girth. She prayed she hadn't bitten off more than she could proverbially chew. She blinked, swallowed and reached for it.

He was dark, veiny, stiff and thick. She rubbed her thumb over the tip and it returned a dollop of fluid. Asha glanced at his face only to find him looking directly into hers. "Condoms?" the question came out throatier than she'd expected.

Daniel watched her as she touched him. Her hands were small, warm and soft.

He reached over and opened his nightstand drawer.

Asha watched as the condom made its way down his shaft.

He nodded toward her panties.

She fingered the waistband and laughed, "They're cute, right?" He only blinked in return. Her stall technique failed. She quickly removed her lace thong.

She had to think fast. What would be the best position given their difference in size and his huge schlong? She took one last look at it and decided.

Daniel watched as she got on her knees and slid her arms and shoulders onto the bed, her ass pointed upward. The silhouette of her hips and plump ass presented to him as an offering caused his ears to shift back.

He positioned himself behind her and cupped her ass. He gave it a slap, and it wiggled in response. The scent of her essence, ripe and ready, filled the room.

Asha ached with anticipation as he took hold of her waist. She inhaled and braced herself. Daniel steadied himself and eased the tip into her. She exhaled. He took it back out and gripped her waist even tighter. This time he pushed himself further, and she hissed. She was warm, tight and slippery. He hadn't begun the work yet, and his skin was already coated with a light mist. Her touch, scent and sounds made the hair on his neck prickly. He drove into her. She gasped. He worked her from behind and filled up every inch of her.

Asha welcomed the pummeling, met his rhythm and threw it back at him. She moaned into the linens above the clap of their skin-to-skin collision. Daniel pulled out completely and paused. Asha took this opportunity to change gears.

She turned around and took another look at his power, making sure it was still encapsulated in the tight condom. She rolled over onto her back and lifted her knees to her chest, exposing herself to him.

As he climbed onto her, she flipped him over in one fell swoop, a technique she learned in a self-defense class.

Daniel uncharacteristically yelped. She smiled into his face and perched on top of him. She was limber and strong for her size. Her maneuver caught him off guard, and he liked it.

She climbed her way up his chest until her knees pinned his shoulders.

She had no issue letting him know what she wanted. He hadn't expected to go this route, at least not on the first go round. But he was cornered, her landing strip stared him in the face.

He raised up, flipping her back onto her back. She landed with a thump.

She pulled her knees in again and transformed into a wide-V and licked her lips. Daniel took a mental picture of that image before situating himself between her legs.

Asha shivered at the first touch of his tongue. The visual of his broad shoulders under her thighs made her head spin. He was slow and purposeful in his execution. Licking, kissing and sucking until she was at the brink of release. When she thought she couldn't take any more, he pressed on. He persisted until she gasped and squirmed, holding on to his ears for leverage. At last, he applied perfect pressure to her pearl. She growled. She arched. She gushed.

Daniel looked to her neatly trimmed V, past her navel, up her soft stomach, through the valley of her breasts, beyond her clavicle, past her pink lips, flushed cheeks and closed eyes and finally to her loose curls lying in a whirlwind on his pillow.

His mouth missed her release by centimeters. A bit of her juice dripped as a souvenir on his beard. He moved from under her legs.

She tasted herself on him when he kissed her lips. She was spent. He'd made short work of her. She looked up at him towering over her, even though only on his knees. His power was still at the ready. Seemingly, it never faltered or wavered during his tongue's time in her inner and outer folds. His job was done, but hers wasn't.

She straddled him, and his hands reached up to touch her breasts. She welcomed all of him back into her. Her ears tingled at the sound of his moan. She balanced herself atop of him and had her way with him inside of her. He enjoyed the waves of contractions as she enveloped him in her warm slick. Daniel watched her work, she seemed caught up in her own personal ecstasy. He pulled her down to him and she accepted his tongue once again, as it probed her lips and mouth. Finally, he firmly anchored her ass with his hands and pumped into her. She bounced with each injection, head back, hair tossing, letting out tiny cries of surrender. Daniel felt the end coming. His ears felt hot, his toes curled and his legs stiffened. He exploded. He was finished.

He opened his eyes to meet hers smiling down at him. She felt victorious after their first round and drifted off to sleep for a couple hours. She was awakened by kisses on her neck and a probing hand between her legs. Before she knew it, she was holding on to the bedpost for dear life. She took the thrashing like a champ and was knocked out again.

The Morning After - Asha

Asha opened her eyes and struggled to get her bearings. The weight of his arm was heavy on her chest. She pulled the sheet back to see his paw-like hand full of her right breast. The air smelled of him, her and them. "RONK," he let out a loud snore and shifted his body, freeing her from the embrace.

She sat up on the edge of the bed. Her feet dangled. Gathering up her underwear, she hopped down onto the floor. That is when the remnants of last night's events snuck up on her. She tiptoed to the hallway, feeling every muscle in the lower part of her body vibrate. He had worked her over good. She took a look back at him on the bed. An odd sight in the supine position, like a fallen tree after a storm.

She tiptoed to where she'd dropped her dress and went in search of the bathroom. The first door she opened was a closet. A really neat linen closet. *If my closet could only look like this*, she thought. *He must have a cleaning lady. or a woman.* Her eyebrows furrowed at the latter thought. Asha walked down the hall, and the next door she opened was the bathroom. She opened the medicine cabinet. A medicine cabinet was good for some insight into who a person was. Tweezers, Q-tips, the regular fare. A case with small vials of liquid stared back at her. If she weren't so anxious to get out of there, she would have investigated further.

Asha turned on the shower as quietly as she could. She hoped the Uber she ordered wouldn't take long. She did not have the luxury of an extra pair of underwear in her bag like she usually did when she hooked up with Khalil. *Just jump in the shower and go commando*, she figured. After all, it wasn't her first morning-after going commando, but maybe it would be her last.

The Morning After - Daniel

Daniel turned over in search of the soft, warm body next to him. He patted the sheets only to find a cold mattress. He opened his eyes and looked around the bedroom. There was no trace of her. No shoe, bra, watch, phone. Nothing. He sat up in the bed. Did she leave? *Nah, that couldn't be*, he thought. He never had a woman leave before dawn. Not of her own volition, anyway. He heard a clicking noise. Daniel raced to find his underwear and almost stumbled over his slides. Tumbling out of his room, he made it just in time to see her back as she turned the knob to his apartment door.

"Hey, "Daniel called to her as the door opened.

Asha turned around and smiled. "Oh hey, no need to get up. I'll call you later," she whispered.

He laughed, "What? Where are you going?" He looked over at the cable box, "It's five in the morning."

Asha leaned on the door jamb, "Yeah, I know. I have to be up in a little while. But, you look like you're already up." She glanced at the tent in his underwear and giggled. "But text me later," she winked.

Before he could reply, she was on the other side of the door. *What the fuck just happened?* he thought. Daniel was left standing in his hallway shocked and stiff.

Ashe & Cindy

Uncle Rand had five fishing poles lined up against the wall.

"He doesn't want to save all these, does he?" Asha asked her aunt.

"Well," AJ said as she looked up from a crate of vinyl records, "one of them belongs to you. You want to take it with you?"

"Absolutely not," Asha answered. She had enough junk in her apartment. No sense in adding to it. She promised to help AJ clean out the garage to convert it into Unk's man cave. But almost everything she picked up to throw away, AJ tried to keep or have her take home with her. Asha resigned to be there all day.

Asha picked up a shoebox in the corner and the bottom fell out from under it. The contents spilled on to the floor. She gathered up the contents: letters, cards and photos. She recognized one of the photos instantly, her mom, dad and her at the zoo. The picture was tattered and fuzzy, but it was an image that was blazoned into the recesses of her mind. She didn't know if she owned the memory or if it was repeated to her so many times that she created a memory based on the repetition.

She stared at the picture. AJ approached her, and she knew exactly what the box contained.

"I feel like that was just yesterday." AJ took a seat on the step stool next to Asha. "Ashe told anyone who would listen about how he and Cindy took you to the zoo and how well you behaved. You were about 5 years old there," AJ looked at the picture. "Ashe was fresh out of a program and wanted the three of you to be a family. He was doing so well, until Cindy left."

Asha looked up from the picture and felt her eyes water.

"She loved you, Asha," AJ rubbed her back. "I know she did. But her parents threatened to cut her off completely and this was Ashe's second time in treatment."

Asha felt a wave of emotion come over her. She sat silent for a moment and finally erupted. "She could've taken me with her, AJ. I don't care what anybody says, I wouldn't even leave my cats that way!"

Asha heaved and wept. AJ hugged her. "Oh, honey. I know it hurts, and I'm so sorry. Cindy's parents didn't react well to a..." AJ's voice trailed off. "It wasn't like now, Asha. People weren't as open-minded. Even now, hell, people have issues with mixed race children." AJ ran her hands over Asha's untamed curly hair. "Girl, Cindy used to have mousse and banana clips all up in this head. Poor thing, she didn't know how to handle this nap infused curl pattern." Asha chuckled in the midst of her tears. AJ smiled to see Asha's emotions subsiding.

"Fuck Cindy AND Ashe!" Uncle Rand bellowed from the garage door. "Ashe didn't care about anything but his goddamn pipe." Uncle Rand took a deep breath and continued. "And Cindy, that crack bitch. She went running home to them backwoods the first chance she got."

AJ and Asha were startled by his outburst.

"Rand!" AJ scolded.

Rand turned and left, knocking over a garbage can on his way down the driveway.

"Oh God, AJ. I didn't mean to hurt Unk, or you," Asha sighed.

AJ rubbed her back again, "I know, honey. You know Rand is so sensitive about that whole situation. He knows you love him, and you know he'd do anything for you."

Asha hugged her aunt. Tears she didn't realize she still had began to fall.

AJ comforted her niece. "It's ok, honey. It's ok."

Unannounced

Daniel turned the key to his mother's front door. He could certainly buy or cook his own meals, but he stopped by to have lunch at least once a week. Sometimes she'd be home, sometimes she wouldn't. Regardless, her delicious food would always be there waiting for him. He saw her car out front so that was an added bonus; she would probably pack him three days' worth of food.

"May!" he barked into the foyer. "Mavis Jacobs," he yelled as he walked into the kitchen and dropped his keys on the quartz island.

Mavis came into the kitchen, her kimono-style robe flowing behind her. "Hi, love, I didn't know you were coming over today."

"I was gonna stop by yesterday, but I ended up at Crane's." He removed several plastic containers from the fridge and closed the fridge door with his foot.

He placed the containers on the counter and turned to greet his mother. Something was off. His mom would never wear her robe in the afternoon, unless she wasn't feeling well. She smiled and greeted him with a hug around his waist; his height almost a foot taller than hers. He ended his bear hug and noticed her hair was tousled, and her face was flush. She smelled like Tom Ford Noir.

"May?!" he whispered. His eyes were wide as he held her at a distance for review. "You have somebody in here?!" he asked her in a panicked tone.

"In HERE? Boy, this is my house!" Mavis shrieked as she pulled away from him.

"That's nasty." His face looked like he smelled something foul. "It's Tuesday! It's," he looked at his watch, "it's 2:30!"

"Daniel, whose house is this?" she asked.

He hated when she called him Daniel because it meant she was displeased. "I know, sorry. But who you got in here?" He looked over her shoulder as if to see past the walls into her bedroom in the rear of the house. "You never said you were seeing somebody." He looked around the kitchen for evidence, a car key, a hat, something.

"Do you tell me all about who you're seeing? Rhinestone and whoever else?" Mavis asked him. Daniel opened his mouth to answer and then thought better of it, and closed his mouth. "And stop making all that noise," she admonished and began to prepare a plate of food for him.

"Oh nah, I'm not eating that here," he sulked.

"What? Oh Hersh, don't start." Mavis turned to him.

"I'm good," he told her. "Go ahead with your afternoon delight," he said under his breath.

Mavis reached up to twist Daniel's ear. He dodged her grasp and circled the island. "But who is this you got in here?" he paused, "in your house," he rolled his eyes. "How do you know him? What if he's a killer?" he warned.

"He's not a killer! Calm your nerves."

"So you not gonna tell me who it is?" he pressed on.

Mavis crossed her arms and was about to remind him who her house belonged to when he began to walk toward the rear of the house. Mavis grabbed the tail of his t-shirt and with a yank, he doubled back into the kitchen.

"I'm saying, these old nig..." Mavis shot him a look. "These old men, they be scamming. And they have diseases too," he informed her.

"Excuse me?!" Mavis's hand went to her hip.

Daniel let out a hiss and turned his back to her.

"You losing air, boy?" Mavis said to his back. Regardless of his age or size, he knew she would and could knock him down to size.

"I'm gone." He gave up his questioning and grabbed one of the containers of food.

"Listen, Hersh," Mavis's voice softened. "I am grown, ok? But thank you for your concern. And I love you. Always."

"I know." He pouted and fumbled with the container of food.

"Now come and hug your mother," she offered to him.

He screwed up his face. "I don't know who you been hugging," he teased. She pinched him and he cried out and then laughed. He hugged her and sighed deeply, "I love you, too."

"Alright now, take your food and go,"

She tightened her robe.

"You kicking me out over some dude?!" he challenged her.

"Hersh, don't make me slap you, hear?" Mavis snapped.

Daniel laughed at how swiftly her mood changed. He blew her a kiss, grabbed his keys and backed out the kitchen before she made good on her promise.

Coach Danny

Asha confirmed the movie time on her phone as Cleo climbed into her passenger seat.

"Ok, I have to make one stop. Actually, two stops," Cleo greeted her.

"What?! Come on, you know I like to see the previews!" Asha complained.

"It will take a couple minutes. Girl please." Cleo waved her off.

"Two stops, where?" Asha pulled off from in front of Cleo's house.

"I have to pick my little cousin up from swimming."

"At the Y?! That's in the opposite direction," Asha huffed. Cleo stared straight ahead, ignoring Asha. "Ok, pick her up and then what?"

"I just want to drop her off at my grandmother's." Cleo pleaded.

"On Cornaga?!" Asha's eyes bugged.

"My cousin got stuck at work, Asha. It takes a village, you know?"

"Fine," Asha slid down into the driver's seat, "I didn't know I was the village car service."

Moments later, Asha parked in the Y's parking lot and got out of the car.

"You can wait in the car since you complained the whole ride here." Cleo told her.

"But I have to pee," Asha whined.

Cleo hurried toward the entrance, leaving Asha behind. She quickly found the ladies room and relieved herself of the grande macchiato she had earlier. Exiting the restrooms, she heard splashes of water and children laughing and yelling. Asha could take or leave children. She rarely ooh'd and ahh'd at babies and never had a desire to babysit. She did however, enjoy Cleo's little cousin, Moscata. She was a beautiful, bright and funny kid. It was a shame her mother was allowed to name her.

Asha walked over to the pool area and saw Cleo's neck craning and hand waving. *Oh boy, she's giving some poor soul the business*, she thought.

Cleo hovered over the swim instructor as he bent down to place the pool noodles in the storage racks.

"So you're Moscata's aunt?" he asked from the noodle storage crate.

"No, her mom is my cousin." Cleo told him.

"And are you authorized to sign her out?" He yelled from his hunched position.

"Yes, I just told you that. She's in the 7 to 10-year-old group, and her class ends now. Check her file or whatever you have to do. I'm on there. Cleopatra Jones." Cleo's head bobbled.

The swim instructor stood upright when he heard her name. "You're serious?" he said to her.

Cleo was about to let him have it when he looked past her and said, "Asha?" His face lit up with a hundred-watt smile.

Asha looked up from her phone into Daniel's smiling face. She felt faint.

He walked toward her; his 6 feet 3 inches, 200-pound chocolate frame, glistening. The vision of his broad shoulders, strapping bare chest and long sinewy legs were confirmation. She was definitely going to faint.

Feeling her head swoon and praying her face didn't meet the ground, Asha tried to formulate a sentence in her head.

"Coach Danny, Coach Danny!" Moscata yelled running toward them with her swim bag bouncing on her hip.

"Mo, I was just telling your cousin what a great job you did today,"

Daniel said giving Moscata a double high-five.

"Thank you, Coach! It was my sparkly goggles that made me win," she told them as she waved the shiny goggles in the air. "Coach Danny is the best coach because he lets us race after our lessons!" she announced to Cleo, beaming up at Daniel.

Cleo was so distracted by Asha's reaction to the swim instructor. She didn't hear a word Moscata said.

"So you two know each other?" Cleo asked looking back and forth between the two.

"Yeah," Daniel's eyes lowered onto Asha.

"Yeah um," Asha stumbled. "This is Daniel. We hung out at the coffee shop and stuff."

Cleo's eyes widened, and she tucked her chin. "Ohhhh, so this is coffee shop...and stuff." She looked him up and down.

Asha found her voice, "This is my friend Cleo."

"Patra Jones," Daniel laughed and extended his hand to her.

"You got jokes." Cleo shook his hand.

"So you've heard about me?" He crossed his arms across his broad chest.

Asha, uncomfortable with the topic and Daniel's gaze burning through her, shifted her weight between her legs.

"Yeah, I heard a little somethin' about you." Cleo looked dead into Asha's eyes.

"Cleo, can I get a smoothie, pleeeease?" Moscata begged.

"We'll be at the snack bar," Cleo told Asha. She looked to Daniel, "And I'm taking my cousin, just so you know," her lips pursed.

"You can sign her out at the desk," he laughed.

Cleo gave an attitudinal neck wave to Daniel and followed Moscata to the snack bar.

Daniel smiled at Asha. "What's up?"

"You work here?"

"Yeah, the swim program is an easy workout. And I help out with a couple of the programs as a favor to a family friend," he told her. His words fell on deaf ears while her eyes rode the curve of his pecs.

"So," his eyebrows met, "we good? I mean... because I never... not that I could remember... had someone run outta my place like that," he paused and unfolded his arms. "Did I do something to upset you?" He placed his hands in his swim trunk pockets, pulling the waistband just below his natural waist.

Her eyes landed on the perfectly placed drawstrings of his trunks. *He had done something alright*, she thought. He'd done it really well. She momentarily flashed back to his powerful backshot, and her body fizzed like the opening of a soda bottle. She shook it off and hoped her reaction wasn't visible in her body language.

She ran her eyes up his body.

"Oh, no. I just had a lot going on that weekend." She twirled her phone in her hand.

Daniel didn't buy it but said, "Ok, as long as we good."

"We are," she blushed in spite of herself, "I'll hit you up later this week."

"Cool." He looked over to the snack bar where Moscata and her aunt were waiting. "Cleopatra Jones is waiting for you," he nodded in their direction.

Asha laughed, "Later this week then."

He watched her walk away. *Hit you up*, he replayed the verbiage in his mind. Nonchalant, distant and non-committal was what he heard in "hit you up". He chuckled having used that exact phrase countless times before.

The next day, Daniel sent her a "Hey beautiful" text to which she replied, "Hey what's up?" hours later, at Cleo's insistence.

"Don't text him right back. That's some thirsty shit," Cleo advised.

"What? I'm just replying. He text me first," Asha defended herself.

"You said you felt ways about what happened, so leave it alone."

"I felt in a way because I was passed out Cleo. I was embarrassed. I don't do stuff like that."

"Whore's remorse. Don't worry, it'll pass," Cleo dismissed her.

"What?! I'm not a... never mind Cleo" Asha said.

"Not that you're a whore! It's just when you have regrets about bustin' it open. Everybody has it."

"Cleo, no. That's not what I have. Ew."

"You felt embarrassed but still fucked him." She gave Asha a mean side-eye.

Asha backpedaled, "No, I meeean..." and laughed at herself.

"I knew you had some hoe in there." Cleo said and shook her head. Asha just stared at her phone.

"You like him," Cleo teased.

"He's alright. I mean, he's cool." The words tumbled out of Asha's mouth.

"Yeah, ok." Cleo looked through her friend.

A couple days later, he liked one of her #TBTs. It was a pic of her on her uncle's shoulders at a carnival. That only gave her license to scroll through his profiles, careful not to click or tap. A lightbulb went off in her head. He was probably used to having to drag women kicking and screaming out of his apartment. But her abrupt exit threw him for a loop. What began as awkward embarrassment morphed into something else—Triumph!

Gone Fishin'

Uncle Rand swayed to the soulful sounds of Guy coming from the portable speaker. Asha held on to the rocking boat, "Uncle, I swear."

"Girl, you don't know 'bout good music," he continued his one-man groove session.

"Unk, if this boat turns over..." Asha threatened.

"Cupcake, stop it. You got a lifejacket on."

She looked him dead in the eyes. "I'm gonna tell AJ about that flask you have buried in the tackle box." Uncle Rand stopped swaying and turned down his late '80s R&B. He didn't want to deal with AJ's nagging and whining. Bad enough, he had to hear it from Asha.

"Mmmm hmmm," Asha said admonishing her uncle.

"I didn't think I raised a bully," Uncle tsked.

They sat in the comforting silence of the water. He turned to Asha. "Listen, I want to apologize for the other day in the garage." "Unk, don't," Asha said as she struggled to hook her minnow bait.

"Look now. I want to say this," he insisted. Asha stopped baiting and gave him her full attention. "Now Ashe was my big brother, and I loved him. I just hated..." he looked out onto the bay, "I hated what he did to himself. I know everybody says it's a disease and all this mess." Rand paused. "But I accepted that for other people. Not for my brother. I knew he could beat it if he tried hard enough..."

Asha interrupted her uncle. "Unk, addiction is not that cut and..."

"Let me finish now," Rand said in a voice reserved for discipline. He let out a heavy sigh. "Ashe left us both to fend for ourselves. As your daddy and my big brother, he could've helped us figure this life thing out." Rand fidgeted with his line. "Instead, he smoked his life away." His voice uncharacteristically cracked. "But, we did pretty good for ourselves, huh girl?" He cleared his throat and gave Asha a gentle shove.

"Yeah Unk, we did," she smiled.

"You didn't burn down the house or maim your Aunt Jessie. I didn't leave you in a store or locked in a car."

Asha piped up, "I did fall off your shoulders that time at the precinct carnival. You said AJ started wheezing when she saw me on the ground," Asha busted out laughing, causing a flock of birds to fly off a nearby jetty.

Rand laughed and held his stomach, "Yeah, but she wouldn't let nobody give you CPR, not even the EMTs that were there. 'I don't know where these nasty ass paramedics lips been!'" Rand wiped his face of tears, and Asha cried out and fell over on her side. After they caught their breath Rand added, "Thank God you only had the wind knocked out of you. I don't know what AJ would've done. I don't know what I would've done either. We were so happy to have you," Rand smiled at Asha.

"I love you, Unk. Thank you." Asha reached over and wrapped her arms around her burly uncle and swayed him back and forth.

"Alright, who gon' topple us over now?" Rand laughed holding on to the sides of the small boat.

Booty Text

"Hersh, now listen," Mavis pressed.

"No!" Daniel yelled.

"Don't be that way. She just wants to come by," Mavis pleaded with him.

"For what?" Daniel slammed his hand on the countertop.

Mavis looked out the window. "Love, you can't treat her that way. She did what she thought was best for you." Mavis reasoned with him.

"I don't want to deal with this."

"I love you, you know."

"Mom, stop."

He rarely addressed her as mom, mommy, mother or any other maternal title. He called her May or by her given name, Mavis, in jest. She had no issue with it. They knew who they were to each other. He also addressed his grandmother as Maw. Incidentally, it was a shortened version of her name, not a variation of Grandma.

"You're the best thing that happened to me," Mavis continued.

"I love you too," he told his mother. "But what does she want now?" He felt a headache coming on.

"Just to see you babes. That's all. It will be nice. We'll have a nice dinner and it will be over, ok?" Mavis reassured him.

"Ok," he resigned to his mother's plea.

"Maw will be there."

Daniel's eyebrows raised, "I'm not looking forward to it, but I don't know if it's a good idea to have Maw there."

"She will be ok. I will talk to her beforehand."

"And say what?" Daniel laughed at the thought of his mother reprimanding his grandmother.

"Oh, Hersh. Don't bother with that. I will figure it out. It will be ok, love." Mavis rubbed her son's back.

Daniel hugged his mother. In all actuality, Mavis was his mother. The other woman who popped up every couple of years or so was a woman who got knocked up by a drug dealer and ran off with a con artist. Daniel's stomach started to churn. Why couldn't she just forget him altogether? The last time she "visited" she told him about his "sisters". Sisters? He considered himself an only child. He guessed she visited out of guilt. She could keep it for all he cared. He never wanted to see her, but he did it for his mother.

She trusted Mavis with her son over 20 years ago. What were the periodic checkups for? Anything he ever needed or wanted Mavis and Maw provided with backup from Uncle Vincent and Crane. Mavis and Maw were often criticized for spoiling him rotten. He'd overheard the conversations. But neither cared what their critics thought. He had no use for this woman who birthed him. He only did it to appease Mavis.

Daniel left Mavis's house stressed. His first thought was going to the gym to work it out in sweat. But he wasn't necessarily in the mood for that. His second thought was Diamond. She was always a good distraction. So he began to text her but saw from their previous texts that she would be in LA this week working with her lead stylist. He drove his car in the direction of the nearest liquor store. Then he remembered Jennifer. He would definitely be able to let off some steam with her. But he didn't feel like driving all the way to Washington Heights. It was a late Thursday night, so he would probably end up in the gym. His mind wandered to Asha. She never did hit him up although the week wasn't technically over. Could he call her now? If he called her up now, it would be for stress sex. He didn't want to do that to her. Well, he did want to do it *with* her. But they'd only had sex that one time, and she seemed to be avoiding him ever since. When he ran into her at his swim class, she looked as though she'd seen a ghost. She seemed a bit distant, but he had a good time with her. Fuck it, he texted her.

Daniel: Hey Beautiful

He stepped into the liquor store. He walked toward the back of the third aisle. His phone buzzed.

Asha: Hi *smiley emoji*

He grabbed a fifth of Jack Daniels Honey. He only drank that when he was stressed. It was terrible for his body, but it was one of the only things that helped. Working out would help, but it wouldn't numb the feeling. Jack numbed. Jack and sex.

Daniel: What's up?

He walked to the counter and paid for his liquor. Stepping out of the liquor store, his phone buzzed.

Asha: Nothin'. Whats up with you?

He didn't know how to approach the subject since he wasn't that familiar with her. That never stopped him with other women. He was annoyed that it was an issue now. He second guessed his contacting her. Maybe he should just close out and fake that he was just checking in. No. He was gonna go for it.

Daniel: I'm good. Wyd?

Asha was in the middle of giving herself a pedicure. "Wyd?" she read. It's 10:37 p.m. on a Thursday night, what did he think she was doing?

Asha: Chillin'.

She was short with her answers. But she was answering right away. An unclear read, which he was finding common with her. He suddenly remembered, he had an ace to play.

Daniel: You left your headband at my apartment.

She'd counted the headband collateral damage but was relieved that he mentioned it. But still, she decided to amuse herself and go along with this counterfeit booty call.

Asha: I did?

Daniel winced at his phone. Women usually keep track of their accessory bullshit. One does not simply misplace a designer headband and never look back. Was she being sarcastic? Where else did she think it could have been? It was possible she really didn't remember, given the night's events.

Daniel got into his car. If she wanted it back, he'd swing by his crib and deliver that to her, and more. If not, he would take the L and end the conversation. These texts usually worked in three steps: *Sup? Wyd? Comin' thru.* With her, he found himself plotting and planning. There's no plot and plan for a come through?! In what Bizarro universe did this happen? He took a swig of Jack and leaned his head back on the headrest. His phone buzzed.

Asha: Can you drop it off?

Daniel squinted at his phone. He still wasn't certain. His body was beginning to turn into one big knot.

Daniel: Where?

He knew he was taking a chance and prolonging this dumb torture. He was too quick to text, now he was stuck in this text reply quagmire. What if she said to drop it off where she worked? Or to leave it in her mailbox? Why was he even thinking about all of this? He looked at his phone, no answer. No anticipatory text bubbles. Forget it. He was going home to get ripped on shots of liquor and go to bed. He started his car when his phone buzzed with Asha's address.

Her whore's remorse had subsided, as Cleo said it would.

"Hoe is relative," Cleo reminded her. "Men don't care about the body count, as long as they're included."

And Asha sure wouldn't mind including him again. And again.

111

Initially, she figured it would be fun to climb that tree for climbing's sake. He was fine as fuck. A divine notch in her skinny belt. But after spending a little time with him, she found that she enjoyed his company. He was sweet, smart, hung and had a devil's tongue. He also liked to feed her. She recalled their late-night snack at the Sandy Cove and after party linguine. If not careful, she could easily spend her life chasing the next high of him. Definitely a headache and/or heartache waiting to happen. But the summer was young, and she'd wait and see what unfolded. Hopefully, her toes would be dry before leasing space on his shoulders tonight.

Magic Hands

Daniel: Ok, be there in a half hour.

Asha put her phone down and began her quick tidy ritual. Her place was clean; it just needed a quick spruce for short notice company. She waddled around on the heels of her feet for sake of her pedicure, fluffed sofa cushions and threw junk mail in a drawer. She spritzed the automatic air freshener in the bathroom a couple times and changed the cat litter. She threw the few dishes she had in the sink into her dishwasher and wiped down the counter. Her bed was made, and she had just showered, so those were checked off the list. Hair in a ponytail, white tee, no bra and black leggings. That'll have to do. She looked inside her leggings. Her V looked good. Cleo dragged her to the wax salon last week. Although she had some initial irritation, everything had smoothed itself out. Her doorbell rang.

One of her cats came trotting in from the bedroom. She scooped Biggie up and put him in the bathroom. Tupac, her other cat, had just turned the corner when she grabbed him and put him in his carrier. He meowed and gave her a look that promised revenge.

She looked through the peephole, and he was looking dead into the tiny window.

Asha opened the door.

"Hi," she smiled and invited him in. Daniel felt his face transform into a slow grin. She was scrubbed clean, and her hair was pulled back into a ponytail. Daniel stared at her. Asha felt her skin warm, and she began to blush.

Her welcoming eyes instantly relaxed him. He stepped into her place. It was clean with light neutral colors and lots of greenery. The only bold colors were her red bookshelves crammed with books and the artwork on the wall.

"Thanks for bringing my headband. I was wondering what happened to it." She held her hand out. He handed her a small gift bag.

"You didn't remember where you left it?" he gently probed. Daniel had a feeling he was asking for it, but he was up for the game.

"Well, I knew I left it in some strange man's apartment. I just couldn't remember which one." She shrugged and gave him a fake smile while taking the bag from him.

Daniel nodded. She had a slick mouth. A cute, pouty, slick mouth.

She walked toward the couch, "Come in and have a seat."

He watched her saunter toward the couch; her leggings hid nothing. He took a seat next to her on the couch. He looked tense.

"You ok?" she asked.

"Yeah, I'm good," he cleared his throat, "How you been?"

Asha sat on the couch Indian style. "I've been good. Working and stuff."

She reviewed his grey t-shirt, black joggers and brightly colored basketball sneakers. He looked to have a fresh haircut. The line up of his beard was so sharp that she thought she'd cut her finger if she touched it. And he smelled good, as usual. Something grapefruity with a hint of sandalwood. Again, something she'd never smelled before. She always thought her couch was roomy, but it did nothing to support the length of his thighs. He sat with his palms on his long legs spread wide apart. *So inviting*, she thought. But she had to remain focused. She hadn't decided if she wanted to consummate this booty call or not. She was still on the fence, but slowly climbing over it. Slowly climbing onto him in her mind.

"Are you sure you're ok?" she asked again.

His eyes seemed dull. They lacked the twinkle that was usually there. "Yeah, just stressed," he answered.

"Stress sucks. Stress from what?" she asked.

"Family BS," he told her.

Asha nodded. "Yeah, can't choose family." She always heard that phrase and used it sometimes though it didn't apply to her.

Daniel huffed, "Right." He was also familiar with the phrase but knew it wasn't his truth.

"Do you want to talk about it?" Asha offered.

Daniel stared at his hands on his lap. "I have... a relative. She's not really a relative but well, yeah, whatever. She doesn't know her place. She likes to pop up out of nowhere, and it puts pressure on my family. It's annoying."

"Is she on drugs?" Asha leaned in. Her eyes were wide as she listened attentively.

"If only," Daniel shrugged. "At least that would be an excuse." Daniel exhaled and looked around her apartment. "You have a lot of books." He got up and went over to her bookshelves. The current conversation was killing his vibe. He picked up a book. "Achebe. School?"

"No, just for kicks."

"No one reads Achebe for kicks," he informed her.

"Someone does." She leaned over the back of the couch and watched him peruse the pages of her red shelves.

He picked up another book. "The Secret? Oprah got you caught up, huh?"

She laughed, "It's good information. You can borrow it."

"I got enough secrets, thanks." He placed the book back on the shelf. "Wally Lamb," he nodded.

"Oprah," they said at the same time and laughed.

"How do you know so much about Oprah's reading list anyway?" she asked him.

"My mom and grandma, Oprahnites," he told her. "Langston Hughes." Daniel's face perked up.

"Which one?" Asha squinted to see which book he was holding.

"The Ways of White Folk." He thumbed through the book.

"Classic."

He smiled, "One of my favorites."

"Is that right?" Asha got up to join him.

"There's no rhyme or reason to your bookshelves," he said squatting down to look at the lower shelves.

"I know where everything is. It isn't a public library," she laughed.

"Diane McKinney Whetstone, Bernice McFadden, Martha Southgate, RM Johnson, Stephen L. Carter, Carl Weber, Margaret Johnson-Hodge." His eyes darted through the shelves.

Asha stood next to him in front of her books. He still didn't seem himself. Though she'd only spent relatively a couple hours with him, she never saw him like this. The night wasn't going the way she thought it would. She was getting a different type of vibe from him. She still wanted to jump his bones, but she didn't feel his spirit reaching for her as she had before.

"Can I give you a hug?" Asha said while tilting her head to the side.

"What?" Daniel's head jerked back; he was put off by her question.

"I know it sounds weird, you just seem like you need a hug."

Daniel looked into her earnest eyes. It was an odd request. They'd already slept together, and he'd seen her naked. Odd but endearing.

"Um, sure," he answered.

Asha wrapped her arms around him and hugged him tight, rubbing his back and breathing deeply. Daniel felt the warmth from her hug pull some of the tension from his body. She looked up into his face.

"Hey, you know what's good for stress? Massage therapy." She abruptly ended their embrace and walked toward her bedroom. Daniel blinked rapidly. She walked away just before he succumbed to the vortex of her eyes. He'd blown it. Now she was suggesting he go to a spa. He was so out of sorts he didn't have the presence of mind to orchestrate the evening according to plan.

She felt bad for him. He seemed like a big, sad puppy dog. She could sleep with him because that would do them both some good. Or she could try to selflessly help him and show some self-restraint.

She shuffled toward the living room with what looked to be a giant briefcase. "What is that?" he asked her as she opened and unfolded the contraption.

"A massage table," she informed him.

He looked around the living room confused, "Ok, and? What are you doing with that?"

"Massage therapy really helps," she told him. "Stress has such a crazy effect on the body. Particularly the organs and muscles, you'd be surprised. I took a course but never took the completion exam. But I really learned a lot."

She waxed poetic about the benefits of bodywork as she set up the table. After set-up, she returned to the back of the apartment.

Daniel looked around again. *Was she for real?* He didn't know what to make of the situation. He yelled out, "Um nah. That's ok. I'm good."

She came back with sheets and towels in her arms.

"Asha..." he began.

"Daniel, I promise you it will help. You can change in the bathroom. Or you can take it off right here."

She backed up and looked him up and down. Daniel scratched his head. *Fuck it*, he thought. He was so wound up when he first walked in the door, but something about her space and presence calmed him. It never hurt him to get naked before, so he doubted it would do him harm now. As if she was reading his mind she said, "You can keep your underwear on, sir."

Daniel lay on his back in his boxer briefs. The sheet that covered the mat had a soothing lavender scent. *Never tried it like this before,* he thought. He heard of friends going to kinky massage parlors, but he'd never been. Never had a desire or need to. Watching Asha approach him with two squeeze bottles of oils caused a stirring in his

117

underwear.

Asha looked down at him barely fitting the massage table. She tried to ignore her quickened pulse at the sight of the bulge in his underwear.

"Sir," she said. Her mock reverence excited him even more.

"Comere." His eyes lowered, and he sat up on his elbows.

"Sir," she repeated laughing. "Please lay on your stomach."

Oh, she's really into this, he thought. He was game. He turned over, and she covered the bottom half of his body with the towel. She resisted the urge to smack his ass. Asha dimmed the lights and turned her phone's music app to a soft jazz mix. She warmed the massage oil in her hands. Asha started with long strokes from his neck to his shoulders.

She worked her hands from the top of his broad muscular shoulders, then slowly down his spine. When she reached down to the space just before the curve of his butt, she applied gentle pressure. She heard an unintelligible sound come from Daniel, something between an umph and a whimper. She repeated the long strokes until she felt his body warming up.

She loosened his muscles using her upper body. Applying firm pressure in between his shoulder blades and down his spine was doing the trick. His breathing slowed almost as if he were asleep. She was taken aback by the large, dark canvas that was his back. Not a hair, pimple, scar or blemish in sight. His skin was supple and velvety; she was almost tempted to lick it.

"How is this for you?" she whispered. He moaned. She concentrated on the left side of his back. He was a big bowl of small, crunchy knots. Pressing into the individual knots, she felt the tension releasing. She heard another sound from Daniel. It was more of a grunt this time.

Switching to his right side, she slowly worked the flat parts of her knuckles all the way down to his lower back. She saw and felt Daniel inhale and exhale deeply. The tension was finally leaving his body.

She felt redeemed. She hadn't given a massage in a long time. AJ and Cleo used to let her practice on them when she was taking the massage therapy course. She regretted never taking the completion exam. But with Daniel's massage, she felt a personal gratification in being able to help him feel better outside of sex.

Asha used a deep swaying circular motion into the area where his back dipped and scooped before it reached his ass. She rhythmically rocked him from side to side in an effort to further relax him. As she was about to move back up to his shoulders, she felt his body stiffen and contract. *Shit*, she thought. She was certain that she was using proper technique, in spite of not having massaged in some time. *Lord*, she said to herself. *I hope I didn't displace anything in his back.* All she needed was to have ruined this Adonis.

She went to the head of the table and bent down to see his face. "Daniel? Oh my God! Are you ok? I'm sorry. Did I hurt your back? Wait, don't move ok," she blurted in one breath.

He pushed himself up on his elbows and gave her a blank stare. His face was a little puffy from the pressure of the face holder. He looked like he had just awaken from a nap. His eyes were small.

"Are you ok? You're not in pain?" she asked

"I'm...good," he said.

"But what happened? You kinda tensed up when..." her words drifted off, and her eyes widened.

She remembered her massage instructor bringing this up once. She'd never experienced it before. She was embarrassed for herself and for him. She got a washcloth and dampened it with warm water. She offered it to him.

"Sorry about that," they both said and laughed.

Daniel had since sat up with the sheets and towels covering him.

"I mean, it happens. You know your body is super relaxed and well, it is a mental and physiological release...of sorts," she explained.

"Look, I didn't mean for that to happen. I mean nah," he sighed. "I did come over here for this reason to be honest. I was probably going to pound it out of you," he added with a straight face.

"Damn," she said in mock regret.

He smiled, "My family drama was really laying heavy on me. Heavier than I thought," he paused, "thank you."

"You're welcome. That'll be extra though." She held her hand out for payment.

He took her hand in his.

He looked at her so earnestly, she had to divert her eyes. Daniel stood up and removed his underwear, which left him only in socks. Even in its flaccid state, she couldn't resist a quick glance at it. He caught her eyes direction and gave her a half grin.

"I can throw that in the wash with the linens," she offered.

"Full service," he nodded.

"Um, no," she laughed, "I'm only doing this because you're cute."

He laughed.

When she returned from putting the sullied linens and underwear in her kitchen's compact washing machine, she found Daniel fully dressed and standing near the bookcase again. He had the Langston Hughes book in his hand.

"I thought you said that was your favorite. Surely you have a copy at home," she said, leaning against the bookcase with her arms crossed.

"I do, but I can't find it. So, I'm gonna borrow yours," he told her.

"I bet your neighborhood library has a copy." She raised her eyebrow.

He stepped closer to her, "I wanna borrow it from here. The library has too much rhyme and reason."

"Right," she grinned.

He opened his arms to her and she entered into a long, warm hug that made her light-headed.

Beverly

Beverly watched the video for the third time.

Jada called out to her mom, "What are you still doing on the computer?"

Beverly quickly opened another tab and pretended to focus on Corinthian tile from the overpriced home decor website. "I'm about to shut it down, just looking at these colors. What do you think of this?" she asked.

"Any one you like ma, I don't care. I'm going to bed," Jada sighed.

"Ok, honey. I'll be off in a minute," Beverly said.

She waited for her daughter to leave the room. Beverly quickly switched back to the YouTube tab to resume the music video on mute. Daniel looked so much like her brother, Travis, whom she'd lost to colon cancer earlier that year. He also favored his dad in the way his eyes twinkled when he smiled. Beverly never regretted her decision to give Daniel away but always wondered, what if. The way those hussies were pawing at him made her chuckle. He was playing the role of a hustler in this hip-hop video. Little did those floozies know that he was nothing like that. Thanks to Mavis, she felt as though she knew him. And her heart longed to reconnect with him after more than 10 years.

Daniel

"May, you are a godsend. I don't know what the fuck I'd do without you," Beverly said.

"Bev, you sound crazy," Mavis laughed at her friend. Only Bev could curse and thank God at the same time. "How are the girls? I haven't seen them in weeks." Beverly usually brought the girls with her when she came to pick up Daniel, their little brother.

"They're great. Oscar thinks Karen should take ballet, she's only three but they can start as early as two, he said. And when she gets older, he says Jada would be good at piano because she loves music."

"Don't you think you're moving a little fast with Oscar?"

"Fast like what? It's been close to a year now, I don't see why I should wait." Bev told her. "And don't give me that look May."

"Seems as though you're pushing the girls on him."

"I'm not. He loves them." Beverly insisted.

"You're trying to make him accept them Bev. Meanwhile, you still haven't told him about Daniel," Mavis said as she kissed the sweet brown baby on his fat neck. He patted her cheeks.

"I never met a man like Oscar. I'm telling you. He's different," Beverly announced.

Every man was "different" in Beverly's eyes. Men loved her, and she loved them back. Hard. She already made the mistake of getting knocked up by a neighborhood drug dealer twice. He was also "different" until he got locked up.

Beverly was always coming with some shit. Some outlandish adventure for them to take part of. If not for her stern mother, May would be in a world of hurt running behind Beverly and her antics. But she was her best friend, and May couldn't give up on her. Not after her first, second or third child.

"Mavis Ann." Beverly teased her friend by using her full name.

"I'm serious." May finished changing the baby, gave him one more kiss and placed him in the playpen. Her hands went to her hips.

"What's keeping you from telling Oscar about the baby?"

"I wanted to talk to you about that. Oscar wants to move to Westchester. He has a great job opportunity there, and he thinks it'll be better for me and the girls."

"You and the girls?!?! Bev, did you hear what I just said? What about Daniel? How long do you think this can go on for?" Mavis asked.

"I want you to take him."

"Take him where? He's always with me as it is."

"May," Beverly took a deep breath, "I want you to raise him."

Mavis sat down. "Bev, is what you saying?" Beverly laughed at her friend.

May's Caribbean accent only surfaced when she was angry, excited or caught off guard. "This is your child, Beverly," Mavis pleaded to her.

"Big Danny left you with a beautiful gift, and you want to give it away? I love him Beverly. You know that, but I can't take him permanently."

Beverly took Mavis's hands. "You know how hard it's been for me since Danny passed? I still blame myself."

Beverly looked up into the sky and exhaled.

"Two kids is one thing, but three? Plus, I haven't been that truthful with Oscar," she admitted.

"Oh fuck, Beverly. What did you tell him?" May demanded.

"May, don't start. You know you're the only one I can really talk to, and you're giving me a hard time. I don't need this shit." Tears fell from Beverly's face, and she started to pack up the baby's belongings.

"Wait, just wait." May held up her hand. She could see the hurt and frustration in her friend's eyes. "Calm down." May soothed Beverly, and they both took deep breaths. Then Beverly sat back down.

"Oscar thinks Daniel was the girls' father," Beverly blurted out.

"Oh, Beverly." Mavis covered her face with her hands.

"I know it seems like a dumb lie, but Oscar comes from a good family. If he knew he could be the third man to father children for me—"

"You mean you're pregnant?!"

"No, I'm not pregnant, but I think Oscar wants a child of his own."

Mavis couldn't believe her friend, and her expression said as much.

"Don't give me that look!" Beverly yelled. "Listen, I don't have anybody to support me like you do. Your mother is helping you through nursing school. I barely had enough encouragement to graduate high school. Oscar is my chance to get out of here and start a new life for myself and my girls. I love Daniel, May." Her eyes started to well up. "That's why I know this is the best decision I could make."

Mavis let Beverly's words sink in. A botched abortion a couple years back coupled with fibroid occupation in her womb made pregnancy a scary concept for Mavis. She still hoped for a miracle one day, but not today. They both looked over to the playpen where the baby quietly played with his toys.

"Beverly, I have to think about this. This is a big decision."

"I know Mavis, but I wouldn't trust anyone else with something like this but you."

Hersh

Years later, when Daniel was a toddler, Maw climbed the final flight of stairs of Mavis's three-story walk up. Why this girl would want to live in this God-forsaken structure was beyond her. Granted, it was right off Central Avenue and near transportation but still. She offered her daughter time and time again to move back home with her until she was done with nursing school. That was up until she voluntarily took on Beverly's problem. Beverly was a sweet girl but much too popular with the men in Maw's opinion. A bit of a *sketel* as they said in the Caribbean. So Maw couldn't understand why Mavis would take on someone else's responsibility. It had been about a year, and Maw prayed Beverly would change her mind and come back for Daniel. But she didn't.

Maw rang the bell, and Mavis opened the door frazzled. "Hi, Maw," she said, barely leaving the door open before running back inside.

"May, what is going on?" she asked in disgust and offense.

"I was helping Daniel wash his hands when the doorbell rang, sorry. Mmm, I can smell that stew chicken."

Mavis took the Tupperware container from her mother and kissed her on the cheek. "Thank you so much."

"Oh May, hush. I am your mother, that's what mothers do."

As Maw went to sit down at Mavis's small dinette table, she almost stumbled over Daniel. "Lord, child!" Maw exclaimed. "You need a bell round this boy neck. So he doesn't just sneak up on you."

Maw looked at Daniel who was staring directly back into her eyes.

"Come, Daniel. Come and sit. Grandma bought us dinner." May

stretched her arms to Daniel who allowed himself to be placed in his high chair.

"May, I done tell you already," she covered her mouth, muffling her speech, "me and that child have no relation."

"Maw!" Mavis gasped.

"You know it, May. I don't know why you carrying on so," Maw huffed in dismissal.

"I never knew you to be so cold." Mavis shook her head.

Maw watched Mavis fawn over the boy, and she felt a tiny pang of remorse. It wasn't the child's fault that he added more to her daughter's plate than she deserved. She was so proud of Mavis for pursuing her nursing degree. She only wished she wasn't encumbered with Beverly's burden.

Maw quizzed Mavis as she ate her dinner while picking up the pieces of Daniel's dinner that ended up on the floor. "You doing good, girl. You get 38 of the 40," Maw congratulated her.

"Thanks Maw, but I need to get 40 out of 40. I will get there."

May wiped Daniel down and took him out of his high chair. Daniel went over to his toy box and took out some toy cars. He walked up to Maw and offered her a red pickup truck. "May, this child want something," Maw said uncomfortably.

"He just showing you his toy. And 'this child' has a name." Mavis added. Maw sucked her teeth in reply. "Oh, and the red truck? He never gives that one to anybody. He likes you Maw," Mavis smiled.

Maw looked at him suspiciously as he stood firmly in front of her. "But he ain't talking, May. You check his hearing?"

"He can hear, Maw," Mavis sighed "he's not ready yet. The doctor said he has time to develop. Ooh, I have to get him a costume for Halloween," Mavis suddenly remembered.

"Halloween?"

"Yeah, they're having a party at the daycare."

"Since when you participate in them kinda foolishness?" Maw's

126

nostrils flared.

"It's just a little party at school. He can't be the only one without a costume." Mavis rubbed her hand over his tiny, fluffy afro.

"Hmph." Maw shook her head in judgement. Daniel shook his head too and offered her the truck again. Maw reluctantly opened her hand, and Daniel placed the toy in it. Maw put the toy on the table. Daniel continued giving Maw each of his toy cars while she and May discussed the upcoming nursing exams. Maw lined the cars up on the table. When he was out of cars, he handed her a toy phone.

"May, this child making a mess with all the toys," Maw said as she placed the phone on the table. Daniel picked the phone back up and handed it to her. Maw placed it down again. Daniel went for the phone once more and stepped closer to Maw.

Mavis laughed, "He wants you to talk on the phone."

"What?" Maw barked, "Girl, I ain't got time for foolishness."

"Maw, just talk nuh?" Mavis said in her mother's frustrated, Caribbean lilt.

Maw took the phone from Daniel and held it to her ear. "Hellew?" she said in her best British accent.

Daniel's dark eyes widened, and the corners of his mouth expanded. He let out a belly full laugh; the kind that only amused toddlers could produce.

Mavis and Maw looked at one another. "I never saw him laugh like this." Mavis looked on amazed. His small body shook. Maw looked at him curiously and gave him back the phone once his laughter subsided. He handed it back to her. She answered again, but this time more dramatically. "Hellew? This is Marguerite Jacobs." This time, Daniel laughed so hard that he almost tumbled to the ground. Maw quickly put her arm around his waist and eased him down to the floor. A smile peeked through Maw's face. "May, this child strange, you hear?" Maw regularly referred to him as "the boy" or "child".

But this time, it was with a different tone.

Daniel yawned and began to rub his eyes.

"He tired, and I gone. It's getting late, and I still have lesson plans to review," Maw announced.

Daniel watched intently as Maw got up to put on her jacket and picked up her pocket book. Mavis and Maw exchanged hugs and walked toward the door. Daniel ran in between them and stood with his back to the door.

"Daniel, move out of the way," Mavis told him.

He began to cry.

"May, take this child. He want sleep." Maw advised.

He stared at Maw.

"I don't think he wants you to go," Mavis thought out loud.

Maw exclaimed, "What? Girl, I ain't got time!"

Daniel cried even harder. Maw looked down at his face wet with tears. She bent down to his eye level. "What you crying for child?" she questioned him. He smelled of baby lotion and the coconut oil Mavis used in his hair. His chest heaved. "Alright now, you ain't got to make all that noise." She held his tiny shoulders. "I will come back and visit you, you hear?" She pulled out a handkerchief from her pocketbook and wiped his face.

Daniel stared into Maw's eyes. He seemed satiated by her promise to return. He sniffed and moved away from the door. Maw got up from her bent position to see May smiling. Maw's lips were pursed. "What you grinning for girl? One of you bawling, and the other one grinning. Look, I gone." Maw reached for the door.

"Ok, bye Maw," Mavis said.

"Bye, Maw" Daniel repeated.

Maw froze in her steps, and Mavis's mouth fell open.

"Daniel!" Mavis clapped her hands.

Maw turned around, "What he just say?"

"He said 'Bye, Maw', you didn't hear him?" Mavis asked.

"I never hear no speech from this child before. Is what he saying in truth, May?" Maw asked.

They both looked down at Daniel.

"Bye Maw," May said again testing him.

"Bye, Maw," Daniel echoed staring directly at Maw.

Maw stared back for a moment. "Bye, darling." She gave a little wave to him. Daniel watched her walk down the corridor until he didn't see her any more.

A week later, Mavis rang the doorbell of her childhood home with Daniel propped up on her narrow hip. Maw opened the door, and Mavis rushed in.

"Oooh, Maw I have to pee. Excuse me, sorry." She put Daniel down and ran to the bathroom. Maw and Daniel were left alone in the foyer.

"Hello, child," Maw cautiously greeted Daniel. Daniel reached into his jacket pocket and pulled out his red truck. "Oh, you bring red truck?" Maw bent down to him. He stepped closer to her and peered into her face. "You like when our eyes make four?" Maw stared back with her eyebrows knitted. Daniel smiled a closed-mouth grin and wrapped his small arms around Maw's neck. Maw, taken by surprise, laughed. "I think you want us to be friends." She patted his small back. "You know what, I have something for you. Come with Maw." She stood up and extended her hand to him, which he willingly latched on to.

Mavis returned from the bathroom. "Maw, is what they put in that lemonade down by the...Maw?" She entered the empty foyer. "Daniel?" she called out. Fearing that he had wandered into Maw's child-unfriendly home on his own, but she soon heard her mother's voice coming from the bedroom.

"Yes, this suit you good," Maw said. Mavis turned the corner to Maw's bedroom and saw Daniel facing the full-length mirror.

"Oh my gosh. How cute you look, Daniel!" He turned at the sound of his mother's voice. "Maw, where did you get this?" Mavis examined

Daniel.

"On sale in Caldor. You said the child need it for the party. I don't know what you were waiting for to see about it. The poor thing would be the only one without," Maw ranted.

Mavis just looked at her mother and smiled as her heart swelled. They both watched as Daniel checked out his reflection in a silver Hershey's kiss costume, complete with Hershey's banner hat.

Dinner Party

Mavis prepped each table setting one more time. Maw stood in the kitchen watching her.

"May, I don't know what all the fuss for."

"Maw, please. You said you would be here to support Hersh. Don't turn it into a war."

Maw held up her hands in surrender. "I never said anything that wasn't true. Who would give up they child, Mavis?"

"Maw!" Mavis steamed. "If she didn't ask me to raise Hersh, then what? Who would be sitting in the audience at your forty-nineteen senior center shows? Who would you play Pokeno with? Who would you bake Easter bun with, Maw?"

"Alright, Mavis. Please, I can't take you going on and on, chuh." Maw pulled out a chair and sat at the table.

"I know you love Hersh, Maw. But remember if it wasn't for her, we wouldn't have him in our lives."

Maw sucked her teeth. "When she coming? Didn't you tell her 7? It's 7:10. I hope she ain't bring none of her pickney with her." Maw arranged and rearranged the place setting. "What she presenting them for? To show she was able to raise children? Hmph, she might as well left them home," she said under her breath.

Daniel walked into the room stone-faced with two shot glasses. His stomach was upset, and he had a headache. He considered slipping out the side door twice, but he couldn't do that to his mother. She begged him to show up and pleaded with him to be pleasant during the ordeal. He had been nothing but pleasant his entire life. Maybe a little standoffish, but never much less than pleasant. That's how he was raised. Nothing to do with genetics. "Where are you going with that? Hersh, they will be here any minute," Mavis told him.

"It's for me and Maw," Daniel said while looking at the bar cart, rather than at his mother. Maw stood and followed him. He poured two shots of Abuelo Anejo, then he and Maw exchanged saluds and chugged. Mavis was about to tear into the both of them when the doorbell rang. Daniel retreated to the backroom. He'd be pleasant, but he certainly wasn't going to greet this woman at the door. He'd join the dinner when he felt like it. Just like she'd pop in on his life according to her own whims.

Mavis opened the door to see her oldest friend. The local pretty young thing in their younger years, Beverly, still maintained her looks and slim figure. Her nutmeg colored skin glowed in spite of age. Her smiling eyes twinkled and she wore her hair in a burgundy pixie cut.

Beverly extended her arms to Mavis. "Girlfriend!" Beverly exclaimed and hugged Mavis. She resumed the same fun and excitable spirit every time she saw her. As if they had only seen each other the week before, when in fact, it had been close to 5 years since laying eyes on one another. They swayed in a squealing embrace.

Mavis remembered Beverly's youngest daughter. "Don't tell me this is Jada," Mavis smiled at the young woman standing next to Beverly.

Jada was shapely and petite compared to Beverly's tall, modelesque frame. She wore her jet-black hair long and straight. Jada favored Beverly's people with full lips and dark eyes. And Mavis immediately saw Hersh in Jada but would never dare bring that thought to her lips.

Jada stepped forward and extended her hand. "Hi, it's so nice to meet you. My mom has said so many wonderful things about you. Thanks for inviting us. You have a beautiful home Ms. Mavis."

Mavis was taken aback at how much she reminded her of Beverly when they were young. Always the charmer. She was immediately endeared to her.

"Ms. Jacobs, how nice to see you," Beverly greeted Maw.

Maw nodded, "It's nice to see you as well." She struggled with the lie.

Beverly could see the indifference in Maw's eyes. She pulled Jada in front of her as if to shield her from Maw's evil rays of judgment. "Jada, this is Mavis's mother." "Hello, nice to meet you," Jada offered.

Maw replied with a weak, "Likewise."

Beverly complemented Mavis on her hair, clothes and the decor of her home. They made as much chit chat as they could until they ran out of small talk steam. Then a heavy silence crowded the dining room.

Jada finally broke the silence. "Ms. Mavis is..." She didn't know how to address him. She heard her mom refer to him as both Daniel and Hersh, but she wasn't sure what she should call him, if she should call him at all. She already felt out of place but promised her mother she would come along for support. Beverly confessed to visiting him before. And Jada was excited to know she had another sibling. She thought it would be cool to have a little brother to bond with. Karen, her older sister, refused outright to have anything to do with this so-called brother. Karen thought it absurd for Beverly to seek out a grown man-child she gave up so many years ago.

Jada struggled to complete her sentence. "Um, I mean is he here? Your, I mean my...um, Daniel?"

Beverly sat in silence. Mavis noticed the vein at the side of Beverly's head flash while Jada worked through her question.

"Yes he's here, Jada. He will be out in a few." Mavis said.

Jada, relieved by Mavis's comforting tone, continued, "I don't know what I should call him," she shrugged. "I've heard mom refer to him using different names. I just don't want to say the wrong thing."

"Daniel is fine," he said as he emerged from the backroom.

Jada turned around at the sound of his voice. She was surprised at how tall and handsome he was. He also looked familiar. Beverly refused to show them any pictures of him; she claimed she had none. Only saying that he favored her brother Travis. That was where the likeness came in. She was looking at a younger version of her recently passed uncle.

Beverly, already teary-eyed, looked at Mavis as she smiled reassuringly. Beverly got up from the table and turned so that she was face-to-face with Daniel. "Hello, Daniel," she said.

Daniel had taken the bottle of liquor to the den with him when he heard the doorbell ring. He felt his nerves on edge, his heart racing and his stomach bubbling. He hoped two more shots of the brown juice would relax him and carry him throughout the dinner. He heard them talking in the dining room about bullshit. *Is this what she came over here to do, make bullshit small talk?* he wondered. And she'd brought someone with her? How dare she? He didn't want to see her, what made her think he wanted to have dinner with whoever she brought along? When he overheard her guest ask about him, he made a decision to get the ball rolling on this circus hoping it would end soon.

Dinner was long and uncomfortable for Daniel. Beginning with the hug he allowed Beverly to give him when he walked into the room. Beverly and Mavis chatted it up, reminiscing about old times, laughing and even reciting some golden era hip-hop. Maw looked on in quiet disgust and Jada stole glances at Daniel. *Beverly didn't even have the decency to be uncomfortable*, he thought. She seemed completely at peace yucking it up at his mother's dinner table in his presence.

Side Bar

"Daniel?" Beverly called to him after helping Mavis clear the table. He looked up from his phone. "I'd like to talk to you in private." she said barely above a whisper.

Daniel blinked in return.

"You all can sit out on the deck if you want," Mavis told them.

Daniel flashed eyes at his mother who nodded toward the rear of the house. He sat on the single chair of the deck furniture, fearing she would try to sit next to him.

"You will never understand, nor do I expect you to understand why I did what I did." Beverly began.

"Ok then, we're clear." He got up to leave.

Beverly reached for his hand, "Please hear me out." Where she touched him on his hand sizzled. He sat back down. "I'm not here to be your mom or friend. I just felt that it was time, well overdue time, that I speak to you one-on-one as an adult. Not asking for your forgiveness because I have a feeling I won't get it. But I wanted to own up to what I did. I was young and stupid, but I feel I made the right decision. I don't know who else could have raised you better than Mavis. She was my best friend, and the closest thing I had to a sister. I knew I could trust her with you," she said in one breath.

"But you had other kids. I don't understand what one more kid would have done," he said to his feet.

"I was trying to get out of the hood. I met a man who I thought was my one-way ticket. I made a lot of mistakes prior to you and the girls," she confessed.

"Mistakes?"

Beverly sighed. "I did things I'm not proud of."

"Drugs?" he asked.

"No, I never did drugs. But I did surround myself with people who made money illegally."

"So you were a drug dealer's hoe?" Daniel's face didn't flinch.

Beverly looked out into the yard. "Again, I was young and foolish. And when the girls' father got locked up, that was one of the best things that ever happened to me. He was abusive, and I never thought I could escape him. He was arrested when I was at my wit's end. And three months into his jail time, he was killed. Jada had just been born..."

"Wait," Daniel paused, "we don't have the same father?"

"Well no," Beverly said matter of factly.

"My mother never mentioned that."

Beverly winced at his reference to Mavis.

"And," Daniel's face crumpled as if he smelled a foul odor, "Jada said we're barely a year apart."

"That's right. You're 11 months apart," Beverly confirmed.

Daniel looked into the face of the woman who birthed him. He couldn't believe what he was hearing. All these years, his mother painted a particular picture of Beverly. She never mentioned that she was the neighborhood good time girl who ran with drug dealers. Mavis always made it seem as though Beverly had too much on her plate and begged her to take Daniel off her hands. As if she were a poor welfare mother just struggling to make it by the skin of her teeth. When in fact, she was living high off the hog going from drug dealer to con artist to whatever man she could find to support her. He overheard Maw in conversation some years ago saying that the man Beverly ran off with was a con artist and was eventually sent to prison landing her back where she started. He knew nothing of his father, only that he died in a terrible accident. He assumed neither

136

Mavis or Maw knew any more details about him. He also assumed he shared the same father as Beverly's other children.

"Wooooooow." Hersh guffawed and ran his hand over his head.

Beverly exhaled, "I know it sounds crazy." Daniel stared straight ahead into the neighbor's yard. "Now your father, was the love of my life." Beverly's face lit up.

"You recovered quickly." His words stole her smile.

"I didn't realize it then, but in hindsight..." Beverly's voice trailed off and she began to cry. Daniel looked at her. The hairline fracture in his heart started to separate. He quickly turned his head away from her. "I don't expect you to understand, Daniel," she said in between sobs.

"Don't call my name," he instructed.

"You were named after him, you know?" Beverly sniffled and smiled at the memory. "We weren't together that long when he died."

"What happened to him?"

"Car accident."

Daniel's brows met. "I know that much," he said in a snarky tone. "That's it? No backstory, no details?"

Beverly hung her head and released another soft wave of tears. "He got mixed up with a bad crowd. I dated a certain type back then."

"Hustlers," Daniel added.

"They all pursued me the same way. But he was different than any man I'd ever met." Beverly reminisced.

Daniel imagined this phantom of a man vying for Beverly's expensive attention.

"He was making a drop for a local drug dealer, trying to get into the lifestyle. The cops were tailing him, he ran a stop sign, t-boned with another car," her shoulders heaved, "he thought he would be able to afford a family if he hustled. I threatened to leave him. So he was trying to make sure I didn't."

"You must sleep well at night," he added insult to injury.

"I deserve every hateful thought you can conjure up. Just don't let hate eat you alive like it almost did to me," Beverly advised her son.

Daniel looked into her face. "What are you talking about?"

"I'm a recovering alcoholic. I've been clean for one year, six months and four days."

"Is that why you didn't keep me?" Daniel's eyes began to well up against his will. He was a bag of mixed emotions. He needed another drink and laughed inside at the irony.

"I didn't keep you because I didn't think I deserved you. His family didn't even know he had a child. When I showed up to the funeral, they thought I was a co-worker or something." Beverly reminisced sadly.

"Mavis says you're seeing someone?" Beverly asked taking in his profile, so distant yet familiar to her.

Daniel stared straight ahead.

"If you find someone special and she tugs at your heart, don't drive her away. Don't be like me, Hersh."

He squinted hearing his childhood name fall out of her mouth.

"I could never be the type of person you are."

He took a mental picture of her face in his mind. He got up and left her sitting on the deck. He never wanted to see her again.

III

A to 207th Street

Firestick

Asha stood outside of the glass doors of Daniel's building. Just as she looked for a bell or a button to press, she heard a click and the automatic doors slid open.

She accepted his invitation for the quintessential movie and chill night. She figured it was to make up for the booty call/happy ending massage debacle at her place.

According to what Daniel told her, she was carried in the last time she entered this lobby. She laughed at herself; she was over being embarrassed. She didn't have an opportunity to take in the lobby's modern chic fixtures and marble floors when she left in a rush the morning after. She drove by this building several times before meeting Daniel and wondered what it looked like inside. The building, industrial in style, could have been mistaken for a warehouse or factory if not for the large glass windows that gave a view to the beautiful lobby. It was one of several new constructions by a foreign real estate developer who recently 'discovered' the area. AJ joked that the developer must have randomly spun a desktop globe and landed his finger on the Rockaway and Five Towns area.

She continued to the elevators when someone called to her, "Excuse me miss. Miss lady, excuse me." Asha turned around to see a short, dark-skinned man making his way around the lobby's desk.

"Oh, I'm sorry," she backtracked to the lobby's center.

"Good evening miss, who are you here to see?" he inquired in a heavy, Haitian accent. Asha was caught off guard by the question. "Um, I'm going to 5A."

The doorman's eyes lit up. "Ohh ok miss, and your name please?"

Asha's eyes darted from side to side. "Uh, I can call him to come down." She placed the bag she was carrying on the concierge desk and reached for her phone.

"Oh, no. No, miss. You have to be announced. Your name please?" he insisted.

Asha's head jerked back, "Asha Martin." The doorman reached for the phone on his command center, "Ok I announce you, thank you."

"Hello. Yes, Mr. Danny. Miss Ashay..." he spoke into the handset.

"Asha," she corrected him.

"Miss Asha Martin is here for you Mr. Danny." The doorman dramatically paused as if receiving detailed instructions. "Ok, ok yes Mr. Danny." He hung up the phone. "You can go now, Miss Asha. Mr. Danny accepts your announcement," he informed her.

"Thanks." Asha said sarcastically on the way to the elevator.

Daniel opened the door.

He stood in the threshold in a tank top and basketball shorts. His beard was fuller than she remembered, and he smelled of a mixture of good and gooder. Asha swallowed her mouth's excess water.

"Jean Claude finally let you up?" he greeted her.

Asha laughed, "Your doorman is a trip. I didn't know I needed security clearance to have Trini food and watch a movie."

Daniel surveyed her legs in the short sundress, "He's just doing his job."

"He's a gatekeeper. Humph, you must have a lot of traffic coming through here." She walked into his living room. "Here." She handed him the brown paper bag.

He opened it and pulled out a bottle of Jack Daniel's Honey. "Oh word, you tryna fast forward?" He smiled reviewing the bottle.

"I'm watching a movie. I don't know what you'll be doing." Her eyes narrowed at him, and her mouth smiled. "You reeked of Jack Daniel's when you came to my house. I figured you were all out."

"I did not reek," he denied.

"You reeked," she assured him. "That probably explains a lot of what happened that night." He hung his head in mock shame.

"Mmm, smells good," she said in response to the heavy aroma of the doubles with channa in his kitchen.

Daniel moved behind her to reach the takeout container on the counter. His body brushed up against hers. "There's bake and shark too, if you want."

"Yeah, there's shark alright." She laughed and turned around to face him. She held his eyes in hers for a moment and slid out of the small space between them.

"You came here trying to get me drunk. I'm just trying to watch a movie," he joked.

Asha was stuffed after dinner. When he asked her if she liked Trinidadian food, she threw a travel toothbrush in her bag. She loved the spicy cuisine, but it wasn't the type of food that was kissing friendly. There were also other side effects from dinner that weren't conducive to being bent over a chesterfield. So she popped a Gas-X. When she came back from the bathroom and sat next to him, he asked her, "Everything ok?"

Asha scooted closer to him, "Yeah everything's cool." She hadn't seen him since the massage, and all she had to go on was the memory of their night together after the rooftop party. His visit to her house took a weird turn. And his energy that night was off, but he seemed thankful to her for her comfort (for lack of a better term) and apologetic for what happened.

Oddly, Khalil had recently resurfaced in a flurry of confusing text messages. She pegged the first two as check-ins, despite the angry words they exchanged at the retirement party. Days later to her surprise, she received several Richard flicks. All of which were tempting with flattering angles and good lighting, but she never responded to his genital selfies. Strangely, what Khalil's photos did do was remind her that she was missing out on the mahogany goodness of Daniel's power. His invitation came as a welcomed relief, even if it was veiled in dinner and a movie.

She reached to touch his cheek, and his cologne slid up her nose. The warmth from his hand on her waist gave her goosebumps.

Sparrow's calypso pleas for Maggie to accept his lying excuses sang out from Daniel's phone. He reached for his phone to quickly answer and to stop the blaring music. Asha got a quick glance at his screen as the name *Maw* appeared. Asha saw a picture of a woman in an ostentatious tilted hat. "I'm sorry, I have to take this," he explained to Asha. She nodded and backed off of him.

"Hi, Maw," Daniel answered.

"Hello, my sweet kiss," Daniel's grandmother answered.

"I called you at home and on your cell phone. Where were you?"

"But you is fresh, asking a big woman where she was," Maw told him.

"Your foot hot, Maw?" Daniel teased as he pictured his grandmother's face.

"You want licks!" Maw laughed, "I went to dress rehearsal for the fashion show. You comin' right?"

"Yeah I'm coming. I was just checking on you."

"Awright, darling. Love you," Maw told him.

"Love you too, bye," Daniel ended the call.

Asha, intrigued by what she just heard, decided not to pretend she wasn't listening. "You're into Sparrow?" She laughed when he put his phone down.

"Sorry, that was my grandma," Daniel smiled. "You probably heard the whole conversation. She talks so loud. She's not hard of hearing. She's just Caribbean." He sat back on the couch, "She's in a fashion show at her senior center."

"Aww, that's adorable," Asha smiled.

Daniel laughed at her reaction. "Yeah she thinks she's hot shit."

Asha shoved his arm, which didn't budge, "How can you say that about your grandmother?"

"I guess she was it back in the day," Daniel shrugged.

"What about your grandfather?" she probed.

"Dead."

"Ok, well does she have a man friend or companion?" Asha continued.

"Nah." Daniel gave her a mean glance.

Asha played off his apparent opposition to the notion, "Are you sure? She could have a male suitor or gentleman caller if she's as hot as you're saying."

"Nah, that's not funny," Daniel said with the straightest face.

"Okay, then." Asha left it alone.

Daniel picked up his phone. "This is her on Mother's Day." He showed her the picture she got a peek of while his phone was ringing.

Asha got a good look at the blue-eyed, fair-skinned senior citizen in the oversized coral hat. She asked, "She's mixed?"

"Mixed?" Daniel asked.

"Yeah, this looks like a person of mixed heritage."

"Not to my knowledge."

"I mean," she pointed to the phone, "she basically looks like a well-tanned white person."

"No, she looks like my grandmother." Daniel took the phone from her.

"A well-tanned white person with a Caribbean accent?" Asha thought out loud.

"I guess," Daniel paused, "someone was white back there."

"Where's back there?"

"Uh…somewhere between Trinidad and Panama or something," he dismissed.

Asha knew all there was to know about her father's side of the family. Uncle Rand made sure she was well versed in the good, bad and ugly of the Martin family history. But her mother's family history was another story. She shook off the thought.

"You don't know which island your grandma is from?"

Daniel was beginning to feel uncomfortable about the line of questioning. "I don't know. It's one of the two, or maybe it's both." He shifted his body toward her, slipped his arm around her waist and lifted her onto his lap. "We gonna talk about my grandmother, or are we gonna make," he laughed, "I mean 'watch' this movie." He gave a coy smile.

She peered into his face and positioned herself onto his lap. "Oh, so that's what you do up in here? No wonder Jean Claude was acting funny about letting me up."

He laughed out loud. "I'll let him know that you're the talent, and you get all access," he said in response to her heat on his crotch. Then he held her face in his palms and kissed her full on the lips. The movie from his queue served as white noise to the action that took place on Daniel's couch.

Sushi & Salmon

Asha was enjoying the time they'd been spending together recently with street festivals, walks on the boardwalk and outdoor movie nights. It was mostly casual events that allowed them to learn each other. But the post-festival, boardwalk adjacent and moonlit sex connected them on physical and emotional levels. She picked the venue tonight in an effort to low-key impress Daniel. To nonchalantly show him that she didn't only eat Caribbean takeout and have relations under the stars.

She approached the hostess at Hewlett's Xaga Sushi, but before she could ask to wait at the bar, she recognized Daniel's frame. He was leaning on the bar and standing with one foot on the bar's foot rest. As she got closer to where he was, she heard his boisterous laughter and saw him lean back and bang his hand on the counter. She stood off to the side, waiting for a break in his conversation. The Asian bartender made eye-contact and smiled at her. Daniel followed the bartender's sightline and greeted her as well.

"Hey," he pulled her in for a kiss.
She was slightly embarrassed and a little excited at his public display of affection.
"Ken, I'll hollah." He gave the bartender a pound.
"D, good to see you. Let me know where you're staying for the convention," Ken replied never taking his eyes off Asha. She blushed at the bartender's blatant attention despite Daniel's greeting.

"I thought you said you'd never been here before," she asked as they were shown to their table.

"I haven't," he said, pulling out her chair for her.

An older white couple was also being seated at a table nearby. The man, chubby and balding, sat down and stared at Asha's jeans-- shredded denim with horizontal slits down the leg in a lycra blend that showcased her assets. The woman, oval-shaped with a salt and pepper bob, watched Asha and Daniel and smiled. She stepped over to their table. "What a lovely young man," she said and patted Daniel's arm. Her eyes lit up at the firmness of his biceps. "That's a rarity these days, honey. A gentleman seating his lady?" she gushed.

"Marian," the man called out to her. Marian ignored her companion.

"Thank you," Daniel said. "She likes when I seat her." He winked, and his knee brushed against hers under the table.

Asha contained her laugh. "Yes, ma'am. You're right. It is rare," she said.

"You two make a stunning couple." Marian clasped her hands together. "He might be a keeper," she fake-whispered to Asha behind her palm.

"Marian," the man called again. Asha and Daniel looked over to him, and he shook his head.

"Love calls." Marian shrugged before returning to her table.

Daniel hopped up, stepping over to Marian's table and pulled her seat out for her. "Oh my, thank you young man," Marian squealed and blushed.

"You're welcome," Daniel smiled.

"Don't go spoiling her, otherwise you'll have to take her with you," her companion laughed.

Asha snickered when Daniel returned to the table. "What a ladies' man," she exhaled.

"I already told you, I'm not a ladies' man." Daniel looked at the menu.

"Yeah, yeah. You connect on a familiar level." Asha teased.

"You're familiar with that level."

Her cheeks brightened, and her lashes fluttered. "Whatever." She stifled a smile and changed the subject. "If you've never been here, how do you know the bartender?"

"Why? Do you want his number?" he teased. "I saw you checking him out."

"What? No! Shut Up," she blurted. "He was looking at me!"

Daniel laughed.

"You're not funny," she smiled.

"We were in a training class together," Daniel said returning to the menu.

"Training?" Asha thought for a minute. "You went to bartending school?"

Daniel laughed, "Things are really one-dimensional in your eyes, huh?"

Asha was surprised at his answer. "Actually, no not at all." She briefly considered her hidden dimensions and decided to scan the menu instead.

"Ready to order?" the waitress inquired.

"Spicy tuna cracker to start. And I'll have the shrimp tempura and an avocado roll." Asha rattled off her order. "Ooh and a glass of plum wine."

The waitress turned to Daniel. "And for you sir?"

"Salmon Teriyaki."

"Salmon?" Asha asked as the waitress walked away. "You don't like sushi?" She was disappointed.

"Yeah, it's ok. But I love salmon," he told her. She sat back in her chair, deflated. "Why?" he asked.

"Nothing, I was just hoping you liked sushi." She put her elbows on the table and palmed her face. "And I kinda hate salmon," she told him flatly.

He unfolded the napkin on to his lap and feigned an appalled look,

"Salmon is the shit."

"I take it you don't read those Facebook posts about farm-raised fish," she teased.

Daniel leaned into the table. "Salmon by sea or by farm is no threat to this body." He pounded his chest.

Nothing is a threat to that body, Asha thought to herself.

"What did salmon ever do to you?" he asked jokingly.

Asha's spicy tuna and wine arrived at the table, "You wanna try some?"

He looked at the plate and declined. She sat staring at the food. He watched her eyes rove all over the plate, finally she swallowed.

"Is your mouth watering?" he laughed. She smiled embarrassed at her struggle to have some manners.

"You can eat. Go ahead." He released her to her food.

She dug into the plate. "I had a neighbor that made salmon. Canned salmon," she emphasized. Daniel wrinkled his nose. "Yeah, well she made this canned fish all the time," she told him in between bites of her food.

"So you don't like the smell of canned salmon," he confirmed.

"The smell, taste, even to see it on the shelves in the supermarket." She sipped her wine.

He watched her maneuver her chopsticks. "Why do you hate it so much?"

Asha shrugged. "The thing is, I ate at her apartment—a lot," she took another swig of wine, "because my dad wasn't much of a cook."

He looked confused. "I thought your uncle and aunt raised you?"

"This was before I went to live with them."

The remainder of Asha's order and Daniel's entrées arrived. He looked at her cautiously.

"It's fine," she laughed. "The teriyaki is masking the smell."

"Are you sure? I can change it." He looked around for the waitress.

Asha's heart lightened at his offer. "Thank you, but it's fine Daniel.

Eat eat." She shooed him on.

He cut into the steak of fish. "So you ate a lot of canned salmon. Why didn't you ask your dad to make you sandwiches or something?"

She watched him eat. Knife and fork, methodically cutting his food. Bringing the food to his mouth. Chewing with his mouth closed. Wiping his mouth with his napkin ever so often. He was definitely taught how to dine in public. He was also taught how to treat a lady. But Asha was no slouch though, thanks to Uncle and AJ. But what her life would have been like under different circumstances constantly floated around in her head.

"My dad was a crackhead," she said as she picked up the roll with her chopsticks.

Daniel looked up from his plate. "Wow. I'm sorry."

"Yeah, me too. But, thanks," she shrugged.

He put his knife and fork down. "So, he died...I mean, not to pry," Daniel continued.

"Speedball." Asha told him flatly, as if discussing the weather.

He watched her in silence. "What do you mean?"

"He died from the speedball." Daniel remained silent. "Do you know what that is?" He returned a blank stare. She leaned into the table. "Cocaine with heroin or morphine. In this case, heroin," she explained.

"Damn," was all Daniel had.

"He was busy cooking up drugs, not making lunch. My neighbor upstairs felt bad for me I guess. So she always saved me a plate. Of canned salmon," she laughed.

"Your dad... he never tried rehab?" His voice was careful.

"Tried? Ha!" she laughed out and startled him. "He was a pro at rehab. He promised to go to rehab just before he died. My uncle was pissed."

Daniel looked down at his plate a little embarrassed for himself, her, and the context of the conversation altogether. She finished her avocado roll while Daniel's food sat cold.

"Oh my gosh, I'm stuffed." She reclined in her chair and took a deep breath. Then she waved the waitress over and asked for the green tea ice cream.

He squinted and asked, "I thought you were stuffed?"

"Huh? Oh," she laughed. "It's not like real dessert dessert. It's just ice cream. But it's so good."

He pushed his unfinished plate to the side. "So you didn't have a babysitter or I don't know, something? Someone else besides your neighbor and your dad?" He looked into her eyes.

"No, just me and him until he died. I thought he was asleep."

Daniel's thick eyebrows raised, and his eyes were sad. "That's rough."

"I mean, I figured out he was dead once the coroner came. But my uncle was pissed, let me tell you."

He took a deep breath. "I'm not following."

It was then Asha realized that the story she was relaying was a lot. For anyone. Especially for her. Which explained why she was telling it in such a nonchalant manner. She regretted bringing up the subject of the salmon. Outside of her uncle and aunt, only Cleo knew her story.

She already told him she was raised by her uncle and aunt. Now here she was knee deep in the details of her bullshit. Her level of comfort with him allowed her to slip up into the mess of who she was. But she couldn't turn back now. He sat across from her listening. Waiting.

She took another sip of wine. "I thought he was asleep for two days. By the end of the second day, I got hungry and I refused to eat the salmon. So, I went to visit my uncle to see if I could get some money to buy something to eat."

Daniel's pensive eyes stayed fixed on her. "How old were you?" he asked.

"I was eight." She shifted around the remnants of her plate with a chopstick.

His eyes bore into her. A blanket of the restaurant's noise fell over their silence. She imagined his mind conjuring up images of a tiny, disheveled Asha. He probably pictured her walking along a cold, hard city street in search of a hot meal. He finally spoke. "You're strong. Resilient." His eyes stayed in hers. "That has to be," he looked up into the restaurants tray ceilings, "divine providence."

His words warmed her. She wasn't sure what his reaction would be. But she was relieved.

"Oh, I'm totally screwed up in the head but I wear it well," she joked to lighten up the moment. He smiled at her. "Thanks, though," she smiled back.

He watched her eat her ice cream, despite her claims of being stuffed. Her story floored him, but he didn't want to make the situation awkward. He thought of his own abandonment, not by death but by choice. Her dad, even in his crackhead stupor, chose to keep Asha. At least she knew her father wanted her in some way.

She scooped up a portion of the ice cream and held it up to him. "Please, at least try one spoon." He leaned in and opened his mouth. Her body warmed at the sight of his tongue. The warm, crunchy, sweet shell and cold smooth ice cream together brought a smile to his lips. "I know right?" she exclaimed.

He laughed, "Yeah gimme some more." He nodded toward the bowl.

"See? Dimensions." She winked at him as she fed him the last spoonful.

Hamptons

Asha stared at her phone. Her boss was out of town, and the small law office was dead. She considered calling in a personal day or doing paralegal work from home. However, she decided to go in and make use of the company's AC instead. She sipped her iced coffee and tried to explain to Cleo via text why Daniels' invite to the Hamptons wasn't a big deal.

Cleo: *Asha you know how you sound?*

Asha: *Cleo, it's not a big deal.*

Cleo: *You're bringing sand to the beach.*

Asha: *Sand? Have you seen him? He's not sand, girl.*

Cleo: *I'm just sayin'. It's gonna be dudes there and you invitin' this nigga.*

Asha: *He could say no. I don't know yet Cleo.*

Cleo: *It's gonna be mad chicks there too. Why you wanna invite him around a bunch of hoes?*

Asha: *There's always hoes around him. Anyway, this is my set.*

Cleo: *Ok, Ice Cube. I was just saying. I don't know if you know what you're signing up for.*

Asha: *I'm good.*

She hated when Cleo got this way. So adamant about her stance. It was a barbeque, big whoop. She wasn't even sure he would say yes. It was a summer weekend. He probably already had plans. What she wanted was for Uncle Rand and AJ to get a look at him. But very informally. Because it wasn't serious. It wasn't even dinner. It was people eating outside. She texted him.

Asha: *Hey*

That's a good informal start. If he answers right away, she'd tell him about the barbeque and let him decide if he wanted to come or not. If he took a long time to respond, she'd follow suit and delay her reply. Plain and simple text strategy 101.

Daniel: Hey Beautiful.

Asha blushed at her phone. His response never failed, always flattering. Now she had to figure out how to word the invitation super casually.

Asha: Hanging out in the Hamptons this weekend. My cousin is having a get together. If you're not busy, come through.

There, she said it. It was out in text universe now. She put her phone in her desk drawer. Just as she closed the drawer, it buzzed.

Daniel: The Hamptons? Not exactly a come through lol.

He was right. That was a ways out to invite someone at the last minute. He could drive out, but he'd probably have to spend the night. Kariem wouldn't care; the summer house he rented was big enough to sleep eight.

*Asha: My cuz has a big summer house. I can squeeze you in for the night *wink emoji**

Daniel: Cool.

Cool? That's it? She thought she was being flirtatious, and his response was *cool*. Maybe Cleo was right. Maybe it was a bad idea. Her phone buzzed.

Daniel: That squeeze tho.

Asha smiled at her phone. She couldn't wait for the weekend.

AJ prepared a plate for Uncle Rand and whispered to Asha, "So when is this friend coming? Does Rand know? Is he coming alone? Wait, is he staying the night?"

Asha shook her head, "AJ please."

"I'm just asking because you know how your uncle can get. At least give him a heads up. He's been throwing back those Heinekens. You might want to get to him before he's too far gone," AJ cautioned. She knew AJ was right. Uncle Rand rarely liked any guy she brought around. He half liked her cats because they were male.

Rand and AJ were staying at a swanky bed and breakfast a couple of miles from Kariem's place. They were only there for the day time BBQ. By the time the night time turn up began, they'd already be settled in Sag Harbor. Uncle Rand complained about coming out east every summer. It was AJ's people who summered here; they were "uppity negroes" as Rand called them. He suffered through a couple of weekends for AJ's sake, but couldn't wait to get back to the city where he felt more comfortable.

Asha caught Rand as he came out of the bathroom, "Uncle!"

"You scared the shit outta me." Rand held his hand to his heart dramatically.

"I'm sorry. I just wanted to talk to you in private real quick," Asha apologized.

"Well, what the hell is it?"

She could tell he was tipsy by his exaggeration. "Listen," Asha took a deep breath, "I have a friend coming out to the BBQ."

Rand looked confused. "Who?"

"A friend of mine." Asha blinked rapidly.

Rand tried to focus on Asha through his slightly inebriated vision. She only blinked rapidly like that when she was either confessing to something or trying to get over. "A friend?" Rand caught her drift. "Does this friend piss standing up or sitting down?"

"He's really nice. I just want you to not..." Asha pleaded. Rand folded his arms. "Unk, please be nice."

Rand growled, "And where's he staying?"

"Kariem has so much room here, you know that." She brushed imaginary lint from Rand's shirt. Another habit when she was nervous.

"Now Asha," Rand began in his police officer voice. Asha's head fell back in exasperation. "Don't be out here lookin' like no harlot."

"Unk, he's just somebody I'm hanging out with. A harlot, though?" Asha laughed. "I just thought it would be cool for him to come hang out this weekend. It's nothing serious," she assured him.

Rand's brows met. "Hmph, yeah ok. I see how you just spring this on me at the last minute. Well, where is he then? After this next drink, I may need a nap." Asha hugged and swayed her Uncle to which he laughed, "Yeah, you think you're slick."

Asha repeatedly checked her phone for a message from Daniel. She gave him the address and time frame two days ago. His reply was a simple: Got it, thanks. She hadn't heard from him since. She definitely wasn't going to call or text him again. If he showed, he showed. Whatever. She looked at her phone again.

"That negro ain't showin'," Cleo said from her lounge chair in between bites of her burger. Cleo's long, brown legs were stretched out to infinity on the chair. Her tangerine pedicure and matching bikini popped against her ebony skin. She was devouring a jerk turkey burger with no regard for etiquette or home training.

"Cleo, shut up," Asha told her.

Cleo licked her fingers and savored the flavor of her specialty burger. "Mmmm, I'm just sayin'." She wiped the burger juice from her mouth. "You looked at your phone four times in the last 20 minutes. It will vibrate if you get a message, boo." Asha sighed. "You might need that vibration later on if your precious bae don't show," Cleo continued. Asha picked up Cleo's plate from her lap and threw her half-eaten burger in the trash. "BIIITCH," Cleo shouted. Cleo stood up, and Asha ran off the deck laughing. *That'll teach her to keep quiet*, Asha thought.

The day was sunny and cloudless, which was perfect for this event. AJ's nephew Kariem had outdone himself, as he did every year. He had the money to blow on such extravagant entertainment as a music industry executive. No one was sure exactly what his position was, and no one really cared at this point. His friends and family just looked forward to his events. They were eager to get a taste of the good life and maybe spot a B-list celebrity or two. This annual BBQ offered prime meats, fresh seafood and delicious desserts prepared and served by a top-rated catering company. And there was no question as to who made the potato salad. She saw the purple majesty potatoes being prepared herself by one of the sous chefs that morning. Uncle Rand scoffed right in front of the catering staff. "I don't like all that shishi foofoo mess," he fussed. "Who the hell eat purple potatoes? That ain't natural." Asha tried to explain to him it was a specialty potato, popular in South America. "Yeah? Well guess where we are? North America! I ain't eatin' that," he said.

Asha was restless. She spent some time in the pool, ate two plates of food, sat in for Unk in a round of spades and chatted it up with some of AJ's relatives. They all called her their cousin, although there was no blood relation. Sabrina, an age-appropriate cousin, was one of those women who always had to one up the other women around her. If you got a promotion, she got a new job. If you moved into a new apartment, she was house-hunting. Asha always let her shine because she knew that deep down inside, Sabrina was miserable. A nice looking, well-educated girl with a chip on her shoulder, stemming from what Asha couldn't figure out.

"I haven't seen you since last year's event, Asha," Sabrina greeted her.

"Yeah, you know how it is. What have you been up to?" Asha asked her, already bored of her answer.

"Oh, you know. The regular. I'm getting ready to go to Paris next month," Sabrina said.

That's real regular, Asha thought to herself.

"Really? That's awesome Sabrina!" Asha faked.

"Yeah, my fiancé has never been, so I thought it would be cool for us to go." Sabrina popped a jalapeño popper in her mouth.

"Wow, I didn't know you were engaged. Congratulations." She scanned Sabrina's fingers and was surprised to see a ring on the fourth digit of her left hand.

Sabrina held up her hand. "We got engaged over the holidays. I didn't make a big deal about it though. Some people are such haters, you know?"

"Yeah, tell me about it. Well, I'm sure you'll have an amazing trip." Asha wanted to leave the conversation. She knew Sabrina was full of lies. She may be going to Paris but not with a proper fiancé, that's for certain. It was probably with that same lame dude she told her about last summer, and she most likely bought that stupid ring. She'd been known to pull off fantastical capers like this. Layers upon layers like a trifle dessert of imagined people, places and things.

"Where's your fiancé? Is he here?" Asha asked.

There was a flash of alarm in Sabrina's eyes, "Oh no, he couldn't make it. Yeah, he's traveling on business so I'm here by my lonesome," she shrugged. "Kariem always has the nicest friends though, so I doubt I'll be lonely for long." She winked and walked off towards the bar. *A liar and a whore*, Asha laughed to herself.

She looked over and saw Uncle Rand yawning, and the DJ setting up his station near the pool. She knew what that meant. Her uncle and aunt would be leaving and the turn up would begin soon.

Just as she was about to check her phone one more time, she looked over to the backyard's entrance and saw him. Her heart did a small leap. She attributed it to some type of indigestion. She tried to suppress her smile by fake coughing. Asha pretended not to notice him entering the backyard by focusing on her phone. She hoped her heart didn't beat out of her chest and prove her unbothered attitude a fraud. She hadn't felt this way in a long time. That thought alone made her a little sick to her stomach.

He walked right up to her chair but said nothing. A shadow fell over her screen. She could feel his magnetic pull and smell his cologne creeping up her nose like a cartoon scent.

"I came all this way for you to look at your phone," he smiled.

"Heeey," Asha looked up pretending to be caught off guard. She stood up into his chest and gave him a hug. His super soft brushed cotton t-shirt against his firm chest and arms was the perfect juxtaposition.

"You didn't get lost, did you?" She scanned his beautiful face that was becoming familiar.

"Nah, just ran into some traffic." He studied her face as well.

She changed her hair color from the last time he saw her. He smoothed back a stray honey blonde curl from her face. The sun had given her an amber complexion and highlighted the freckles she usually wore makeup to cover. Her neon green maxi dress made her body look like a bronze medal.

"You've been in the sun." He drank her in.

"Yeah, some of us are melanin deficient," she laughed. He looked summer casual in a white tee, khaki cargo shorts and navy leather boat shoes. He carried nothing in his hands. Not a hostess gift, overnight bag or anything. Asha thought it was in bad form to show up empty-handed to someone's home. Even if it was a rented summer home.

"I have a bottle of wine in the car. I wanted to find you first," he said as if reading her mind.

"Oh, don't worry about that now," she scolded and laughed at herself at the same time. She linked her arm in his, "Let me introduce you to some people."

She walked toward her uncle standing near the grill. He'd been supervising the catering staff all day. She was sure they couldn't wait for him to leave. "Uncle," she said. He looked up from the grill. "I want you to meet Daniel. Daniel, this is my uncle Detective Rand Martin."

Rand stepped back and looked Daniel up and down. Daniel offered his hand, "Good to meet you, sir."

Rand shook his hand. *Where the hell did she get this sasquatch?* Rand thought. "Retired Detective. But good to meet you, too," Rand replied. "Congratulations on your retirement. One of my mentors,

Lieutenant Grandison is also retiring soon," Daniel said.

Rand's eyes lit up. "Oh, you know Grandy?"

"I did some volunteer work with Lieutenant Grandison in the Man Up Mentoring Program within the 100 and 101 precincts. The last time I saw him was after his heart surgery earlier this year. He was doing great," Daniel told Rand.

Asha was floored. Her and Daniel briefly discussed her uncle retiring from the force, and from that conversation, she surmised that he was anti-law enforcement. She had no idea he did volunteer work with the NYPD.

Daniel spoke to Unk with both confidence and reverence. She even noticed a change in his body language. Other guys she introduced to Uncle Rand either cowered or were standoffish in his presence. But Daniel stepped right in and captured Rand's attention.

She was relieved, impressed and a little turned on. Actually, a lot turned on. She'd been turned on since she saw him walking into the yard.

Rand gave him a slow nod. "Grandy is a good man. That program means a lot to him. Good to see young men like you benefit from it."

Just then, AJ approached Rand from behind. "Excuse me," she said to Asha. "Rand, don't forget your hot sauce. You know Kariem will keep it."

Rand brushed AJ off, "Yeah, yeah. Now are you going to the golf outing..."

Asha cut Rand off, "Daniel this is my aunt AJ, I mean Jessie. I mean, I call her AJ, short for Aunt Jessie. Well, you get it. AJ, this is Daniel." Asha finally recovered from her fumbled introduction.

"Pleasure to meet you, Ms. Jessie." Daniel extended his right hand and covered AJ's hand with his left, making a hand-sandwich. He flashed a 100-watt smile and looked down into AJ's face.

AJ's cheeks brightened, and her eyelids fluttered. "Oh my, it's wonderful to meet you Daniel. Aren't you a tall drink of water?" AJ giggled.

Unk and Asha exchanged looks. Then Unk's eyebrows furrowed. Asha had never seen AJ like this. She had to pull her lips in to keep herself from laughing. "AJ, I'm gonna show Daniel over to the food," she linked her arm in his again, "I'm sure he's hungry after the long drive."

"Again, sir. My pleasure,"

"Ms. Jessie." Daniel gave a nod then a bashful smile.

Rand looked from his wife over to volunteer sasquatch boy and back again.

"Asha, make sure he gets some of the ribeye now. Oh and the lobster tail, too." AJ called out to them.

"Jessie, you should be embarrassed," Rand scolded.

"What are you talking about Rand?" AJ said.

"Falling over yourself at that young man," Rand tsked.

"Oh, please. He's a child!" AJ dismissed Rand's accusation. "He is a charmer though." AJ held her finger up to her chin.

"I knew it!" Rand said.

"Remember when you used to charm me, Rand?" AJ rubbed on his arm.

"Girl, ain't nobody used to charm you." Rand turned his head from her. In the same breath, he returned with, "But I got some charm for you tonight." He put his arm around her waist.

"Do you now?" AJ blushed.

"Let's get my hot sauce and get outta here." Rand nuzzled her neck, and AJ let out a squeal of delight.

Grandy was indeed good people. He'd given Rand a couple of those blue pills he couldn't use after his heart surgery. Good thing Rand packed them this weekend.

Afterparty

She was glad he was there. She felt silly second guessing whether he would show or not. Cleo was wrong in her prediction. He didn't crowd her at all. In fact, she had to keep herself from fawning after him. She was surprised that he knew several friends of Kariem's, including of course, some women. And the ones he didn't know certainly made their presence known. She stood back and watched his friendly, yet reserved interaction with them. Every time she saw some miscellaneous bitty in his face, she winked at him. He could feel her eyes on him and was barely able to keep his composure. Their little game was fun until she came across three plates of food in front of him. She sat next to him on the lanai.

"Isn't this the popular table? Who's sitting here?" she asked, looking at the food on the table.

"Just me," he told her.

"You're gonna eat all this food?" she was confused. She made sure he had ribeye and lobster tail per AJ's instruction. She couldn't imagine that he was hungry.

"No, but they kept bringing it to me," he smiled at her.

"I don't understand." She looked at the plates of food again.

"Three different people brought me food. I thought you were being funny." Asha gave him a blank stare. He leaned in while pointing out to her, "You see the girl in the blue one-piece by the DJ? The one in the striped sundress by the bar? And the one in the white mini skirt sitting by the pool?" he leaned back in his chair, "they all fixed me plates of food."

"Oh, really?" Asha's eyebrows raised.

"Each asked if I was hungry, and I told them I was good. They brought food over anyway," he shrugged.

Asha ceremoniously walked the three plates of food, untouched, to the nearest trash receptacle. Daniel laughed and covered his face with his hand. She dramatically clapped her hands clean over the trash. He saw the three culprits watch her with seething looks. She sauntered back to him and made a throne of his lap. His hand landed on her thigh and she said into his ear, "Whatever you're hungry for, I'll serve it to you."

She'd been really sweet the entire night while still giving him space. He didn't expect to meet her aunt and uncle, but it went well in spite of being caught off guard. He was lucky he remembered Lieutenant Grandison so quickly. Her uncle responded positively to that. And her aunt's reaction to him was commonplace. Older women usually returned a girlish blush or giggle, and then wanted to stuff him to the gills with food.

Her pledge and eyelashes blinking on the side of his face gave him goosebumps. He was enjoying himself but wondered when this party was gonna wind down. He wanted to peel that dress off of her.

The crowd started to disperse around 2 a.m. Daniel, Kariem and a couple other guests gathered under the pergola to smoke cigars. She pretended to be interested in a conversation about the best brunch in the city, while sneaking glances in the direction of the symposium of smoke puffs, low voices and occasional laughter. Daniel held the unusually large cigar between his fingers and stared right back at her. He blew a tuft of smoke out of his full lips and dropped his cigar between his wide legs.

Asha's eyes followed, and her mouth watered. She met his eyes once more, and this time he licked his lips. She swallowed and grinned.

He observed Asha in her comfort zone. She was beautiful, relaxed and flirtatious tonight. But not only with him. He noticed her light-hearted flirting with guests. He knew some of these men and their type. So any communication outside of common courtesy was an invitation to them. She danced with a couple of them but managed to avoid any direct physical contact. He didn't dance with her tonight though. He was saving his motion for the after party.

Bed & Breakfast

"So, this is where you'll be staying." Asha turned on the light. The room was cozy with a full-sized bed, nightstands, armchair, dresser and TV. Daniel dropped his Tumi duffle near the closet.

"And where are you sleeping?" He sat on the bed.

"Unfortunately, we have to share the sleeping quarters," she feigned disappointment.

"What about your uncle and aunt?" he asked.

"My aunt and uncle are long gone. Only a couple of the guests from the BBQ are spending the night."

"Oh. I wasn't sure if I'd have to cover your mouth," he smiled.

Asha walked into the space between his legs. It was becoming one of her favorite places. She wrapped her arms around his neck and kissed him. His lips were thick soft pillows that tasted of cognac and mint tobacco. His eyes were low; his lashes nearly met each other.

"Thanks for having me," he said.

"I haven't had you yet," she flirted.

He palmed her ass through the stretchy cotton material.

"Let me take a shower first." She backed up from him.

He pulled her back in, "Nah you good."

She laughed, "I've been running around all day, in the pool and whatnot."

He kissed the space between her neck and top of her dress. "You taste good to me." His voice was at an octave lower. He stood, finally getting his wish.

He peeled her out of her tube dress. The absence of tan lines made him salivate. She had laid out in the sun somewhere, topless. He continued to pull the dress down to reveal a yellow G-string. The tiny triangle shaped material barely covered her triangle. She favored yellow; he'd keep that in mind.

She stepped out of her dress and backed up. He smelled vanilla, suntan lotion and her heat.

"I'll be five minutes in the shower," she pleaded.

"Nah," he said. He stepped closer to her, and she fell back onto the armchair.

Asha was cornered. She really wanted to jump into a five-minute shower. She needed five minutes to brace herself. They'd been playing cat and mouse all night. The look he gave her every time their eyes met told her she was in for it. Now she was eye level with the bulge below his belt buckle. He steadied himself. Then Asha took her time unbuckling his belt.

Pushing his khaki shorts down, she smelled the familiar scent of peppermint soap and male musk. He struggled against the boxer brief material. Finally, she freed him.

She held him in her hands so close to her face. So close to her perfect mouth. Daniel watched her examine him and his heartbeat sped up. She cupped him below, and he almost swayed. Almost.

Regaining his composure, he took hold of himself, and her hands fell away from him. She looked up into his soul and opened her mouth.

Brunch

Daniel entered the room, his skin not quite dry from the shower. Asha looked up from her phone at the struggling towel. The two corners were trying their best to stay together against the pull of his waist.

"You just walked out of the bathroom like that?" she stared at the towel.

"I'm not naked," Daniel answered.

"I mean," Asha was distracted by his wet bare skin, "I thought you would get dressed in the bathroom."

"Nah, it's too hot in there," he told her, running his hands over his head.

"Did," she kept her eyes on the towel, "did anybody see you?" Asha wondered out loud.

Daniel grinned, "Anybody like who?"

"Never mind." She waved it off.

"I did see your cousin." He sat on the bed.

Asha's face went flat. "My cousin?"

"Yeah, Serena or something?" His head tilted.

"Sabrina." Asha crossed her arms.

"She was talking to me in the hallway," he told her, noting the shift in her body language.

"In your towel?!" She looked like she smelled something bad.

"I'm not naked," he repeated and laughed.

"What did she want?" Asha's marbles narrowed.

"She wanted to pick up where we left off," he shrugged

"Pick up?!" Her perfectly arched eyebrows faced off against each other.

"I was talking to her yesterday," he said. *Was this jealousy?* he thought. He didn't recognize it from her. She'd make snide remarks every now and then, but this vibe from her was foreign.

Asha thought back to the night's events. She saw him interacting with a lot of the women but didn't recall Sabrina. "So what was she talking about?" Asha tried to ask casually. She didn't want to seem territorial. She also didn't want Sabrina spewing any of her tall tales to Daniel.

"How I knew you. And she asked about us," Daniel said. He said "us" so casually and with such familiarity. Were they a couple or unit of some sort? Asha thought it best to tszuj over it, though the thought of them as an "us" made her smile inside. "She's super nosey and opinionated. That's why I asked. I didn't introduce you to her just for that reason," she said in a controlled tone.

Daniel noticed the underlying irritation in her voice. "I told her we have a lot of sex," he offered as innocently as he could, draped only in a towel.

Asha laughed, "I'm sure that's what she wanted to hear."

"I told her to ask you about us."

"Hmph, she won't." Asha pursed her lips.

"And if she does?" Daniel probed. He was curious as to how she would define them to her family.

"What do you mean?"

"What would you tell her if she asks you?" He sat on the bed wide-legged. His towel barely covered his thigh.

"I don't know," Asha shrugged. "I'd tell her...it was none of her business." Daniel's eyebrow raised and he nodded. "Because it isn't," Asha said while sitting on his lap.

He was surprised at her answer, especially because she'd introduced him to her family. She threw him for a loop, again. "True," was all he had to say. He thought back to the conversations they had and the ones they didn't – when they just enjoyed each other's silent company. Like last week, he watched SportsCenter while she roller set her hair. They were settling into comfortability. But there was no "us" to speak of. He had a good time when they were together. He figured that was mostly what mattered to her, too. But the issue of the connecting connections gnawed at him. Weren't they connecting? They connected, just last night. Her response to his touch was electric. But was that it?

"Get dressed. There's breakfast downstairs. Hopefully Sabrina's greedy ass didn't eat all the blueberry crepes." She got up and fixed her hair in the mirror.

Asha was a riddle wrapped in a mystery inside an enigma. With a fat ass. But he'd solve it eventually.

Seven Whole Days

Asha stepped out of Daniel's shower and looked at herself in the mirror. She had to get to the gym. She started to gain "lay up weight" since they'd been seeing each other. They went out often, but they also stayed in from time to time eating, watching TV, having sex and repeating the process. They were supposed to be going to dinner tonight but ended up in bed. After draining one another and falling asleep, she insisted on a quick shower before they attempted dinner again. Funny, he didn't seem to be gaining an inch. She knew he was a gym rat, but he would get his regimen in at home or in the park if necessary. She needed more structure, she wasn't that dedicated. She'd look into the 24-hour gym soon before she had to start buying her clothes in a bigger size.

She opened his medicine cabinet in search of Q-tips. She came across the caddy that held seven small glass vials of liquid again. *What the fuck is this?* her curiosity returned. She stretched over the vanity to get a better look. Some of the unlabeled vials were filled with clear liquid, others with amber liquid. She took a chance and picked one up. Bringing it to her face, she recognized a familiar smell. There were two quick knocks on the door.

"Let me get my brush," he said through the crack of the door. She was stuck. She didn't want to rush to put the vial back and mistakenly break or spill something. But then he opened the door, and she was busted.

He looked from the vial in her hand to the open medicine cabinet. "Taking inventory?" he asked her.

"What is this?" She wanted to know.

He grabbed his brush and leaned against the door jamb. "What do you think it is?"

"It smells like," she lifted it up to her nose, "it smells like you. It's cologne!" She grinned like a game show contestant.

"Correct. And I win first prize." He tried to undo the tuck of her towel across her chest. She swiftly grabbed the towel and rewrapped it.

"No, but why is it like this?" She sniffed it again.

"Like what?" he asked.

"Why do you have them all...generic and mysterious?" She put the first vial back and sniffed another one. "Mmmm, this is the one I liiiike," she swayed.

"Good, I'll keep that in mind." He tried her towel again, and it fell to the ground.

"What cologne is this?" she asked him, naked.

"Oh, that one?" He took the vial from her and held it up for a better look, "It's the one you like." He put the vial back in the cabinet. He took a backward glance out of the door, entered the bathroom and locked the door behind him.

"Why the mystery?" she laughed.

"If you like it, I'll wear it. No mystery," he said.

"You're sweet," she said suddenly aware of her nakedness. "So secretive, just tell me the name of it." She crossed her arms.

He moved in front of her and dropped the brush in the sink. "Why? So you could brag to your friends about how good it smells on me?" He lifted her onto the space between the two sinks of the large vanity.

"What? No, I just wanted to know, mmmm," she moaned into his kisses on her neck. "I just don't see why." She tried to continue as his beard brushed against her cheek.

"So you could ask for a sample at the counter at Saks?" he whispered in her ear.

She had fully intended to do just that. "No?!" she protested. "It's not that serious."

"So you could spray it on your pillow and squirt on your fingers at night?" He breathed into her other ear. His middle and ring fingers entered her warm slick, and he thumbed her swelling pearl. Eyes closed, her mouth transformed into a small O. She scooted back taking his fingers with her, legs lifted onto the vanity.

He continued to pet her while licking the nape of her neck as she let out barely audible moans. Daniel lowered his shorts and released himself. He reached into the drawer and handed her the condom. She slid it onto his thick, dark power. He steadied her with his hand on her waist and tunneled into her. Her head fell backward into her arched back supported by her forearms. He watched her as she continually received all of him. Her head bobbled with each stroke. Her breasts undulating with alert nipples pointed toward the ceiling.

"Señor Danny?" a female voice came through the door.

Asha's head perked up; her eyes were wide.

"Dígame Marta," he answered mid-stroke.

Asha's eyes were in panic. "Who the fuck is that?" she whispered loudly.

"Tienen Fabuloso?" the voice asked.

Daniel pushed Asha back into position and pounded into her. She let out a yelp that was quickly stifled by his hand.

"Bajo el fregadero de la cocina," he said, never losing his rhythm.

Asha wanted to protest, but she was quickly caught up in his cadence. She felt heat radiating through her body, and the ache building up to its peak. She released a hum. Daniel felt his ride coming to an end and held on to her waist to keep his balance. "Umphmmm," he finished into her. He placed his hands on the vanity on either sides of her legs. Beads of perspiration from his face dripped onto her thighs.

173

"So you could tell the next nigga," he huffed breathless, "what you like?" She held her head up, panting. He stood there between her legs for a moment. Finally he disengaged from her grip, pulled off the condom and threw it in the small trash receptacle.

"I know what you like, Asha," he told her. She watched him handle the power she'd just been smitten by, putting himself back in his shorts. "If you want it, come get it." He looked dead into her eyes. "Seven days a week." He pointed his chin toward the open medicine cabinet to the vials. Asha blinked slow, still sprawled atop his vanity.

"Get yourself together. My cleaning lady's here." He winked and stuck his fat tongue out at her before exiting and closing the bathroom door behind him.

"Psycho," she exhaled.

Go Maw, It's Your Birthday

A handful of relatives, neighbors and a couple of her senior center crew had already arrived at Maw's 70th birthday party. Daniel invited Asha at the last minute, and she said she'd try to make it. That's one of the things he both liked and hated about her. She was unbothered. Diamond would have killed to be at the party. That's why he would never invite her to something like this.

Asha and Cleo pulled up to the house.

"This is a nice area, Asha. If he lives here he had no business taking you to no corny coffee shop." Cleo said.

"I took him to the coffee shop. And he doesn't live here. This is his mother's house," Asha informed Cleo.

"I'm just sayin'—" Cleo stopped mid-sentence when she caught Asha's glare.

"Cleo, I asked you to come with me for support, but you're pissing me off."

"Ok, just relax. I'm sorry." Cleo checked her face in the visor mirror.

Asha took a deep breath, "Ok, come on. Wait, how's my makeup?"

Cleo didn't know why Asha even bothered with makeup. Any blemishes, aside from her freckles, were paled in comparison to those big ol' cat eye marbles in her head. "You look good girl," Cleo reassured.

Asha and Cleo heard music as they approached the rear gate to the backyard. Salsa music. "You sure we at the right house?"

Asha was about to answer when the gate opened and a middle-aged woman in a navy, sleeveless romper stood on the other side.

"Hello," the woman said taken aback.

"Hi, I'm Asha...a friend of Daniel's?" Asha said unsure.

"Oh yes, he mentioned that you would be coming. "I'm his mother, Mavis. Very nice to meet you." Mavis extended her hand.

She wasn't at all what Asha expected. Then again, neither was the picture of his near white, unbeknownst to him, grandmother. This woman had only been blessed with a teaspoon more of melanin.

"It's nice to meet you, too. This is my friend Cleo." Asha introduced them.

"Hello Cleo, welcome. You ladies come on in."

Mavis opened the gate wide enough to let them in. Asha and Cleo looked at each other with laughs in their eyes. The backyard was a well- manicured area with a large tent, seating, and a bar set up. Between the tent and deck was a gazebo with a gift table and decorated chair. A gaggle of women and a couple of men talked and laughed near the bar. A couple others sat on the deck edged with fuchsia colored balloons.

Asha turned to Mavis, "I hope your mom likes red wine." She handed her a gift-wrapped bottle of Port.

"Oh, yes," Mavis smiled, "the birthday queen will love this!"

Asha was relieved with her final choice of wine after spending close to an hour in the liquor store.

"Daniel should be around somewhere. In the meantime, help yourselves to food and drinks ladies." Mavis smiled and headed back toward the gate where they entered.

Cleo whispered in spite of the loud music, "Mother is giving me full Sade. You see that forehead and lips? About how old you think she is? She's pale, though. His daddy must be black as night. Does the daddy live here, too?" Cleo took in the landscaping and expensive patio furniture.

Asha ignored Cleo's questions and took a long sniff. "I smell roast pork. But I don't want to look greedy."

"But you are greedy," Cleo told her.

"She told us to eat and drink though." Asha's mouth watered.

"People say that, Asha. Then they watch to see if you have any home training." Asha looked longingly at the buffet spread.

"Let's get a drink first," Cleo offered.

"There's no home training regulation on that?" Asha asked.

"Yeah, only if you drink too much," Cleo laughed.

They walked over to the bar where a group of men were chatting.

"Good evening ladies," a short, chubby senior with a horrible jet-black dye job greeted them.

"Good evening," they returned in unison.

"How are you ladies doing tonight?" Jet Black continued in a Caribbean accent.

Asha hoped this old coot was being courteous and not trying to kick game. Cleo looked him up and down. He was dressed modern enough in cargo shorts and a polo styled shirt. The tell-tale sign was once Cleo got down to his feet. Uncle/grandpa sandals. The kind that only 2 to 5-year-olds or 70 to dead-year olds wore. Cleo sighed, his saving graces were his stylish sunglasses and expensive watch.

"We're fine," Asha answered growing annoyed with the old-timer.

"And how are you? My name is Cleo, and this is Asha." Cleo flashed her campaign trail smile. She loved attention from men: 2 to 5-year-olds, 70 to dead-year olds, and anyone in between.

Jet Black removed his shades and gave Cleo the once over. He extended his hand and stepped closer. "Very pleased to meet you.

My name is Clive."

Just as he was about to give his AARP pitch, Daniel walked up on the conversation. "Mr. Clive, thanks for keeping my guests company." He gave three swift pats to the elderly man's back, causing a bronchial eruption.

"Hey Cleo, what's good?" he gave her a friendly hug. He wrapped his arm around Asha's waist and kissed her on the lips.

Mr. Clive gave Daniel a snarl. "You ladies enjoy the party," he walked away clearing his throat in cough aftermath.

Cleo laughed, "Why'd you do Medicare like that? He was sugar daddy material." She looked in Clive's direction to see that he had moved on to another woman. She was not as young as Cleo, but much younger than himself.

Daniel chuckled, "I'm sure there are other prospects for you here."

Cleo tightened her ponytail and adjusted her skirt. "Let's see about that. You lovebirds enjoy. I'll be interviewing candidates." She winked at them and wandered into the growing crowd of guests.

Daniel gazed down at Asha. She was just short of disrespectful in her yellow midriff top and high-waisted silk joggers. The sliver of abdomen showing was the perfect amount of distraction.

"Your mom is gorgeous," Asha gushed.

"Thanks," he smiled.

It was difficult for people to hide their reaction when he presented his mother or when Mavis presented her son. He was sure there were women who gave birth to children who looked nothing like them. He assumed people were taken aback because Mavis looked great to be circling 50-years-old.

Mavis was surprised to hear he had invited someone to Maw's party. He didn't bring women around often. He was rarely with one woman long enough to bring her around. He was also wary about allowing casual acquaintances into his most safe space. Mavis surmised he was into this girl. Finally.

"What are you drinking?" Daniel turned to face the bar.

"Just water is cool," Asha told him. Daniel furrowed his eyebrows at her response. "Water," Asha insisted, "or a seltzer is fine," she added.

"You wanna be the only sober one here?" he teased her. "Papo, un agua de seltzer," Daniel called to the bartender.

"Thank you," she said as he handed her a plastic flute of sparkling water. She took a sip. "Nice Spanish." She was certain he blushed despite the absence of color in his cheeks.

"I mostly use it at the bar. And in the bathroom." His eyes smiled.

She almost spit out her seltzer water. "Funny. You sound pretty natural." Asha searched his face for a clue.

"My grandmother taught me as a kid." He watched her sip her drink while her eyes watched the party going on around them. He grabbed her hand, "Come with me."

They walked across the yard, through the crowd of guests, on to the deck, and into the kitchen's sliding doors. Asha stepped into the large chef's kitchen. Her eyes took in the gourmet appliances and large floating quartz island. The tastefully decorated kitchen was almost HGTV status, save for the large wooden spoon and fork hanging on the wall.

Maw stood near the island with her back to them refilling a utensil caddy.

"Maw." Daniel's hand went to her shoulder.

"Yes, sweet." She turned around, looked into Daniel's face and then over to Asha.

"Maw, this is Asha. This is my grandmother, Marguerite Jacobs."

Asha's words were momentarily stuck in her throat.

Marguerite Jacobs was even more stunning than the picture in Daniel's phone. She was petite. Asha was only slightly taller, barely able to see over Maw's head. Her platinum grey hair was styled in a close-cropped pixie cut. The short hair offered no shelter for her flat forehead. Focus was forced on the terrain of her high cheeks and piercing ocean blue eyes. Her skin was richer than in the picture Asha saw. It was like a perfectly toasted plain bagel, compliments of the summer's sun. Her nose declared prominence on her face with sharp nostrils that held a subtle but ever ready flare. Finally, her full lips struggled to reinforce the dab of melanin she owned. In the mathematics of Maw's features, Asha came to the conclusion that Daniel's grandmother was in fact a person of mixed heritage.

Asha cleared her vocabulary from her throat, "Happy Birthday Ms. Jacobs, it's a pleasure to meet you." Asha extended her hand to Maw.

Maw's royal blue, two-piece silk palazzo pant suit flowed with her movement as she graciously accepted Asha's handshake, "Thank you, dear. So you're a friend of my Hersh?"

"Maaw," Daniel whined.

"My Daniel, I'm sorry." Maw affectionately rubbed and squeezed his arm.

"Yes, we met...at the auto shop." Asha looked to Daniel for confirmation, although she knew it to be true.

One of the guests called to Maw, and she waved to them. "It was lovely meeting you Asha. Thank you for coming, and enjoy yourself darling." She went to her guests.

"Wow," she exhaled.

"What?" Daniel asked.

She would get to the bottom of this color divide later. "Your grandmother is fabulous," she told him.

"Thanks, she knows it," he laughed, looking over to Maw laughing with her friends.

"I see you got it honestly," she observed. Daniel smiled at the irony. "I couldn't pick up her accent. She sounds a little like my neighbor who's from Belize." Asha said.

"I never thought about it until you asked me." He leaned on the large island. "I know she was raised in Panama, which explains the Spanish. But her parents were from Trinidad and Jamaica. So, let's just say she has a lot of attitude problems," he explained.

"That's rude to say of your grandmother," Asha laughed.

"It's not, it's true," he told her. He ran his finger across the sliver of skin between the end of her shirt and top of her pants. "Can I help you?" She gave him a coy smile.

"Yeah, there's a guest bedroom just past that hallway." He nodded toward the hallway past the front of the kitchen.

"What?!" she whispered. "You're out of your mind." She turned to look in that direction.

"Hersh, there you are," Mavis said as she appeared in the hallway that led to the suggested boom boom room.

"You met Asha, right?" Daniel straightened up as his mother approached them.

"Yes, when she came in with..." Mavis looked around the kitchen, "where is your friend, honey?"

Daniel pointed toward the sliding door. "I think she made some new friends."

They all looked out to the paved area of the backyard. Cleo was dancing with a member of the Medicare crew while the others cheered them on.

Mavis let out a laugh, "Look at that child. She knows how to enjoy herself."

"Yeah, that's Cleo." Asha looked on, slightly embarrassed. But Cleo wasn't doing anything that was distasteful; she was just being Cleo. Anything she did with those long brown limbs would draw attention eventually. Luckily, Daniel's mother found it amusing and not offensive.

Mavis turned her attention to Asha. "So Asha, where did a beautiful young lady like you find this scoundrel?" She nodded in Daniel's direction.

"Her car was a wreck, and I fixed it." Daniel shrugged and bit into a cocktail patty.

Asha looked from Daniel to his mother and back. "He did an awesome job on my car for a great price, and I invited him out for coffee to thank him."

"To thank me." Daniel winked at her, and Asha's eyes widened in alarm.

"Hersh don't be fresh," Mavis warned him. "In fact, make yourself useful and take this tray of patties out to the buffet table. And don't eat another one," she admonished. "Asha, come with me dear, let's freshen your drink." Mavis looped her arm into Asha's and led her out of the kitchen, leaving Daniel behind.

Daniel saw Germ making his way down the buffet line as he placed the tray on an empty sterno. "Bout time, shit," Germ said as he took three patties out of the tray. "And I know you got some more hid in the kitchen, too," he added.

"I don't have nothing hid. You don't even have room on your plate, you savage." Daniel looked at Germ's plate which was weakening in the middle.

"My plate good," Germ mumbled through a mouthful of chicken wing. Daniel shook his head in disgust. "So where the chick you invited?" Germ asked. "This your girl, right? I mean you bringing her around the family and shit."

"She's a friend, relax," Daniel told him.

"I'm just saying. Wait, is that her? Talking to Tia May?" Germ wiped his mouth.

"Yeah that's her. Don't go breathin' on her either," Daniel advised.

Asha's back was to them and from that view, Germ gave her a thumbs up. While speaking to Mavis, her plump rear jiggled in her silk pants as she shifted her weight from one leg to the next. Mavis pointed toward her prized rose bushes, and Asha turned around facing Germ and Daniel's direction.

Germ choked on his chicken wing.

Daniel stood back. "You good?" he asked.

"A-yo!" Germ recovered. "Yo, she look like Maw, son," he declared.

Daniel looked in the direction of his mother and Asha. "What?! No, she doesn't."

"They from the same tribe, son."

"Germ, you're drunk." Daniel dismissed his theory.

"She cute, but she's givin' me Maw. Facts." Germ left Daniel standing at the buffet mulling over that nugget of info. Of course they were both fair-skinned and light-eyed. Petite. Independent. Quick witted. Reserved on the outside. A touch of crazy on the inside.

Shit, he said to himself.

The theory that Asha was an alternate version of Maw started to fill his mind. His thoughts were interrupted when he recognized a song playing that he'd been hearing since his childhood.

"Hersh," Mavis called to him and pointed toward Maw dancing with one of the guests. Her eyes lit up when she saw Daniel approaching the paved area. He politely cut her dance partner out and took the floor with Maw. The makeshift dance floor seemed to magically clear out, and only the two of them glided across the pavement.

Daniel, for his size, was incredibly agile and light on his feet. He guided and twirled Maw seamlessly to the salsa music. His movement was fluid and effortless. Maw's 70-year-old legs weren't too shabby either, as she kept up with his footwork. Their form was perfect as if participating in a dance competition. Yet relaxed enough to jam at a backyard party. Maw and Daniel's hips swayed rhythmically to the music while the crowd clapped and whistled. A few even sang along with the lead singer's smooth vocals atop the rich horns and percussions.

Asha was floored. His movement to the music ignited a small brush fire in her core. *He's dancing with his grandmother for crying out loud,* she thought. In an effort to stifle her inappropriate reaction, she glanced at Mavis who was looking on with glistening eyes.

Cleo sidled up to the other side of Asha. "I see why you always so preoccupied," she whispered in her ear.

"Cleo, shut it." Asha shooed her away.

"I mean, he fine and everything. Plus he can dance that Spanish shit? That's not a two-step, Asha. That nigga got rhythm and coordination. And them boat shoes, they're boats. What is he, like a size 11?

"Twelve," Asha corrected.

"Giiiiirl." Cleo went on.

"Cleo, if you don't shut up, I swear," Asha said through clenched teeth into her cup.

"He be rockin' yo ass to sleep," Cleo added.

Asha choked on her seltzer water.

"Are you ok?" Mavis rubbed Asha's back.

"I'm fine, thank you. Just went down the wrong pipe," she told Mavis, mortified.

"That's one of my mother's favorite songs. And Daniel is one of her favorite people, so..." Mavis told her as the song ended and Daniel embraced his grandmother.

Asha watched Maw beam up at Daniel and hug his waist. The crowd soon closed in on them and danced to the next song the DJ spun. His grandmother, along with mostly everyone else in his circle, seemed completely enamored with him. It was becoming easy for Asha to see why. But she'd been careful not to get caught up in that web of excessive admiration.

The Eyes Have It

Asha dried her hands on the finger towel. She looked in the mirror and attempted to smooth down her rowdy curls. Any hint of humidity would send her curls into a rage resulting in a frizz fest. She was getting ready to leave anyway. She'd finally stuffed her guts with Caribbean food, watched Daniel dance with his grandma, and saved Cleo not once, but twice, from being kidnapped by geriatric mack daddies. Seeing Daniel in his natural habitat was interesting. It was evident that he adored his mother and grandmother. While he was attentive to Asha and even Cleo at times in her AARP shark tank, he was at Ms. Mavis and Ms. Jacobs' beck and call. The way his grandmother's face lit up when they danced warmed Asha's heart. She saw now where he learned how to treat women. The Jacobs women explained his charm and charisma. But she'd have to get a gander at his daddy in order to explain his good looks and King Kong.

Asha exited the powder room just off the kitchen. "Ooh, I'm getting the light-skinned treatment, girl," Cleo joked. Daniel insisted they used the indoor restroom instead of the port-o-potties stationed in the backyard. Asha shot her a look.

Daniel laughed at Asha's reaction. "We got to look out for each other fam." Daniel offered his melanin rich fist to which Cleo bumped with her own chocolate clenched hand.

"Them old men can drink! That rum, is it called Seeco?" Cleo asked.

"Seco Herrerano," Daniel corrected her.

"Yeah, it's running right through me." She did a pee-pee dance and headed toward the bathroom.

Daniel stood against the farmhouse sink and pulled Asha toward him. She pushed away from him and looked around the kitchen. "Daniel, no," she protested.

He crossed his arms and grinned at her, "Oh, you're a good girl?"

"Yes, I am. You know that," she smirked.

"I know what you're good at," he laughed.

"Danny, trae un bolsa de hielo," one of the guests called out to him from the sliding door.

"Voy!" he answered the ice request. "You're lucky," he said as he walked past Asha and tried to grab a handful of her ass.

She slid past him just as Cleo came out of the bathroom. "Wooh! Ok, I'm ready for these grandpas. They not gonna show me up again," Cleo said. She adjusted her dress and stepped onto the deck.

Asha popped a tostone from a platter on the counter into her mouth just when Maw glided into the kitchen.

"Oh, hello darling," Maw greeted her once again.

Asha covered her mouth full of fried and smashed green plantain, "Hello Ms. Jacobs."

"It's Asha, right?" Maw leaned on the island with her forearms.

"Yes ma'am." Asha managed to speak after hurriedly chewing her mouthful.

"That's a beautiful name."

"Thank you," she answered finally recovered.

She was alone with Ms. Jacobs and it was an odd, surreal feeling. "Is your name African or Indian?" Maw scanned her like an airport security wand.

Asha was familiar with this optic play. She'd done it many times with her crystal greys. However, Daniel's grandmother was an expert with 70 years of practice under her belt.

She bravely approached the island and stood opposite Ms. Jacobs. "It's Swahili." She looked directly into Ms. Jacobs' eyes. They quietly assessed each other's ambiguous identities. "It's supposed to be a

186

variation of my dad's name Ashe," she explained.

"Oh. But Ashe is..." Ms. Jacobs paused.

"Yoruba," they both finished.

"Yeah, they didn't really think that through," Asha smiled.

"I see. Nevertheless, your father gave you a beautiful name. And your mother, did she gift you those eyes?" Ms. Jacobs inquired.

Daniel's grandmother was from the old school. She chose her words carefully, but Asha caught her drift.

"Yes, one of the few things given to me by my mother."

Ms. Jacobs nodded. "Well, mine are on a short list of gifts from my father. A gift and a curse really." Ms. Jacobs sighed and rearranged perfectly situated dishcloths. "But you know how that goes, my dear," she added. "Yes I do, Ms. Jacobs," a small part of Asha's heart was endeared to her in that instant.

Daniel opened the sliding door. Relief washed over Asha. Ms. Jacobs may have been a kindred spirit, but she had a boss ass bitch aura that could suck the air out of a room.

"To be a fly on the wall," Daniel said to them.

"Oh, Hersh. Nobody studying you boy," Maw dismissed him. "I had a nice talk with the lovely Ms. Asha. Come to find out, we have something in common," she told Daniel, eyes still on Asha.

"And what's that?" Daniel inquired. He couldn't imagine what they could have been talking about, besides him.

"That you are crazy about the both of us." She kissed at Daniel and gave a soft pat to Asha's hand. Maw took a tostone from the tray and returned to her guests while Asha exhaled.

Roundtable

Daniel smelled food and heard Soca music when he stepped into his mother's foyer. Long after Asha and Cleo left, he'd gotten drunk with some of the social security crew as a result of a peacock contest and dominos game. They'd beat his ass in dominos and threatened to take his girl and her long-limbed friend, too. He woke up to Germ's punches on the couch of his mother's den at 3 a.m. Germ drove him home, and he returned the next afternoon to retrieve his car.

He walked into the kitchen where Germ, Maw, Mavis and two men were gathered around the island.

"Sweet kiss," Maw got up to greet him.

"Morning Maw," he said, with his eyes on the men he vaguely remembered from last night.

"Morning? Child, it's after two o'clock." Maw and Mavis laughed.

Mavis stood up from her seat, "Daniel, I want you to meet someone." Germ coughed and cleared his throat at the microwave. When Mavis looked in his direction, Germ pretended to concentrate on the heat settings of the microwave. "This is my friend, George," Mavis said.

George, a cheap knock off of Beyoncé's stepfather, stood up and offered his palm to Daniel. "Good to meet you, Daniel," George said. Daniel's face was stern before his mind rewound to meeting Asha's uncle. Being caught off guard and having to meet the most important man in your woman or whatever's life, was an uncomfortable feeling.

"Same here," Daniel replied while accepting his handshake.

"I will be back later," Mavis told the room as George's key fob clicked in his hand.

"Where you going?" Daniel asked.

"I'm going out, Hersh." Mavis's eyes told him to stop right there. She walked past him and pinched what she could of Daniel's waist. He watched as they walked toward the front of the house.

"Well, since we're doing introductions..." Maw smiled at the silver fox seated at the island.

The older man stood up and Daniel's face went into a panic. Germ made himself busy in the silverware drawer, knocking about utensils.

"Hersh, this is my friend Bernard. Bernard is a retired criminal defense attorney and does work with the youth out in Long Island. Similar to your involvement with the ManUp program. See, you have something in common already," Maw shoved down his throat.

Daniel's brows lowered and met.

"Nice to finally meet you, young man," Bernard said. Bernard was a gray-haired ringer for the All State man. He reached for Daniel's hand and placed his other hand on his shoulder. "You're all your grandmother talks about. If you ever need anything or want to come and volunteer out in Nassau, you give me a call." He gave Daniel his business card after vigorously shaking his hand.

Daniel opened his mouth to speak. Before he knew what was happening, Maw said "Bernard, I will walk you out honey." The *honey* rang in his ear. Maw walked past Daniel and pinched him in the same place.

The microwave dinged, and Germ removed his plate. "Two for one, fam," he said.

"Wait, you knew all this was going on? Why didn't you text me or something?" Daniel confronted Germ.

Germ put a forkful of food in his mouth, "Not my business."

"You ain't shit, Germ." Daniel opened the fridge out of habit.

"Man, grow up. Why Tia May can't get hers? I mean, she still poppin' for her age and..." Germ started to explain.

"I don't care what Maw do." He cut Germ off.

Germ took a bite of his chicken. "A-yo, fam. You got problems. I wasn't even talking about Maw. You need help," Germ mumbled with a mouth full of food.

"Man, shut up." Daniel snarled and sat on a kitchen stool.

"You obsessed with her. What you call that shit?" Germ's face was deep in thought while he chewed.

Daniel could see and hear the masticated chicken tumbling around in Germ's mouth like a front-loading washing machine. "You're disgusting, yo," Daniel scowled.

"Oedipus, you on that Oedipus shit, son," Germ diagnosed.

Daniel sucked his teeth and hopped off the stool. He uncovered the foil pans of leftovers. "Where's the fritters?" he huffed. His eyes zoomed in on Germ's plate, which held several of the codfish appetizers stacked up atop of rice and pigeon peas.

Maw returned into the kitchen and said, "I have some fritters for you, my sweet. Sit down, love," she told him.

"Yeah, sit him down, Maw. He having a breakdown," Germ added.

"Yo, shut the fuck up," he yelled at Germ.

"Nah, you shut up, H. Shut up and grow the fuck up, nigga!" Germ stood up.

"Aye!" Maw shouted. "The two of you, enough!" She looked back and forth between her grandson and grandnephew. "Now you want the fritters or not?!" Maw's hands went to her hips.

Daniel exhaled and glared at Germ. Germ shoved a codfish ball in his mouth for spite. "Maw, that man was at the party?" Daniel stood over his grandmother.

"Yes, Hersh," Maw sighed.

"And he came back today?" Daniel continued. Germ made choking noises over his plate. "Yo, on everything I love, Germ," Daniel threatened.

"Maw, get your boyfriend," he nodded toward Daniel, "I mean, your ex-boyfriend."

Daniel reached over to Germ and Maw grabbed his hand. "What is wrong with you? You gone mad?" she yelled at him. Daniel stared at the wall. "Hersh, I talking to you," she reprimanded.

"No, Maw. I just asked a question."

Maw inhaled and exhaled slowly then looked into his eyes. "Listen, Bernard is a very nice man. We enjoy each other's company."

"I'm sorry, Maw. I just didn't expect all of this now. Today. Just, be careful." He'd hate to stomp out an old buzzard on account of Maw. But he would.

"Yes, love. I am careful. In fact, we both got tested for STDs the other day," Maw told him.

Germ's plate crashed into the sink. Daniel's face went blank. He closed his eyes, "Maw, my stomach."

"Get him some water, Jeremy," Maw called to Germ.

"Hersh, I turned 70 last week. I am not dead," she told him as she rubbed his back.

"Ok, Maw, I get it," he said, hoping the conversation would end.

"No, you think I am just a little old lady. I am young at heart and other places, too," Maw informed him.

"Oh my God." Daniel put his head down on the countertop.

"Jeremy the water, nuh?" Maw called to Germ.

Germ placed a bottle of water next to Daniel's head. "Water for the princess," he joked.

Maw swatted Germ away. "That girl you brought here, she seem like a nice girl. I saw how you were watching each other." She attempted to change the subject. Daniel sipped the water. "I assume you are being safe, too. You ain't breed no girl yet, right?"

Daniel's head resumed its place on the cool quartz. "Maw, please," Daniel begged.

191

"H, stop being a baby, yo! Maw, show him the stuff you gave me."
Germ cut the coddle session short.

"Hol' a minute," Maw said as she got up. "Drink your water, babes."
She patted Daniel's back and left the kitchen.

"You should be happy you have a grandma that's still fire. You
should be happy you still have your grandma, period," Germ pointed
out as he cut a piece of Maw's leftover birthday cake.

Daniel knew Germ had his own attachment to Maw. He developed a
close relationship with her after losing his own grandmother, Maw's
sister, several years ago. Germ was Maw's blood relation. But Daniel
also laid claim to Maw because one of his earliest memories was of
her loving him.

Maw came back to the kitchen with an oversized cosmetic bag and
set it on the counter. "These are some of the products they gave
out at the senior center. Now I know you are both virile young men
in your mid to late twenties, but I don't think these would hurt. If
anything, they enhance," she said with a dramatic wave of her hand.
She took out several varieties of condoms.

Daniel's head spun. Germ reached over and picked up one of the
packets and said, "These are the ones that heat up. I need more of
these Maw."

"Yes, love. I will see if they give more next month," she answered.

"Germ!" Daniel yelled.

"What? These are expensive." Germ said in defense.

"You have a federal job. You can buy a fucking pack of condoms,"
Daniel yelled. His face twisted.

"Cálmate!" Maw shouted.

"Maw, I'm glad you have a friend, ok? I don't need your condoms,"
he said not looking at the condoms spread out in front of him.

"You using protection though Hersh? Because that girl is pretty,
you know. Girls pretty like that have plenty men. You must protect
yourself," Maw advised.

"I'm not having this discussion. Where's my car keys? I come to get my car and get ambushed." Daniel got up and grabbed his keys from the key holder on the wall. "Don't leave, sweet. This is important," Maw called out to him.

"Bye, Maw. I'm gone." He glared at Germ going through the condom packets. He got into his car, turned the key and remembered the codfish fritters. He banged his hand on the steering wheel. There was no way he was going back in there.

Fuck those fritters.

Skull Island

Daniel's left leg began to cramp. The pain was worth the pleasure he received from Diamond on an old couch in the senior's lounge.

He hadn't heard from Diamond in several weeks. He'd only known of her whereabouts based on her social media accounts. And that was fine with him. He didn't want to cloud his mind with Diamond's antics once he started seeing Asha. Diamond was a bad bitch, but he just grew tired of her. She was beautiful and fun, but she didn't reach his core. Diamond was bad, fun, and also persistent. She tracked him down from one of his check-ins and posed as his fiancé. When she arrived at the front desk of the YMCA, Ms. Carmen, the security guard, called down to the basement's extension and Daniel picked up.

"This is Daniel."

"Daaahhhnyyy, mira es un lady here say she jur fansay? She say her name is... wha ju name?"

"It's Diamond. He only has one fiancé," Diamond scoffed at Ms. Carmen.

"*Diemun*. Ju know a Diemun, Danny?"

Daniel was annoyed. "Ms. Carmen, I'll come up. Thank you."

As he appeared at the double doors near the entrance to the gym, he saw Diamond's perfect rear end. She was bent down looking for something in her tote bag on the floor. She was wearing a hot pink lycra unitard and running sneakers bedazzled in reflective gemstones.

"Daaahnyyy, ju finish de counting downstairs?" Before he could answer, Ms. Carmen continued. "Por que I want to go home now. I no wanna miss my novella."

Danny approached the security desk where Diamond planted a juicy kiss on his lips right in front of Ms. Carmen. "Go, Doña. I'll lock up with Mr. Willie when he's done cleaning," he said. As much as he hated closing with Mr. Willie, the Y's creepy, old crotchety janitor, he'd give Ms. Carmen a break. She was his friend's grandmother who worked security at the Y to pass time and avoid boredom. The staff and kids loved her, in spite of her tendency to tell people off in Spanish whether they knew the language or not. Although he was her superior in the staff tier of authority, he made it a point to address her as Ms. Carmen or Doña out of respect. Plus, she usually came to work with goodies for the staff, including some banging arroz con pollo. So he couldn't bite the hand that fed him.

Ms. Carmen grabbed her handbag and marched her five-foot frame draped in a baggy security uniform around to the front of the security desk. She tiptoed and reached up high to air kiss each of Daniel's cheeks. She made the sign of the cross in front of his chest and said, "Dios te bendiga joven." She pivoted on her heel and cut her eyes at Diamond before she walked out the door. "Dique diemun fansay, mira la gran puta cabron..." Ms. Carmen was heard mumbling as she pushed the doors open and walked into the night air.

Diamond kept up with his long strides as she followed him down to the basement. "What can I do for you, Diamond? I have to finish this inventory," he told her.

"Mmmm, you can't call nobody but whatever." she quipped as they entered the senior lounge where he was unpacking math and science materials.

"I didn't hear from you either, Diamond." He sat down on the couch to arrange the boxes in small stacks nearby. Diamond stepped over the boxes and stood in front of him; his face level to her crotch. He looked up at her, and she pushed his back onto the couch and straddled him. She kissed his neck and ears and felt the expanse of his arousal. Daniel shoved her off of him. He didn't want to get caught up with her, but her magnetism was pulling him in. She quickly positioned herself in front of him, fell to her knees and pulled down his basketball shorts. Daniel gave in.

He enjoyed periodically glancing down as her bobbed-weave bobbed and weaved. He exhaled and closed his eyes as he escalated to the brink of eruption. Just then, she detached herself from his manhood. "Lemme ask you something," she said as she licked her lips.

"Ask me later," Daniel whispered hurriedly and grabbed the back of her head.

"No, for real," Diamond snaked her head away.

"Why didn't you invite me to your grandmother's party? Don't you think that was fucked up?" She tilted her head to the side.

He sighed and looked up to the ceiling. He looked at her glistening lips, and then straight into her eyes. "Finish," Daniel demanded.

Diamond opened her mouth to give him a few choice words. He swiftly handled the back of her head, ensuring that his essence chased the words she was forced to swallow. Diamond took it like a champ, wiped her mouth and hopped up from her knees. Daniel opened his eyes. Diamond was still there. "You know, you're something else," she told him.

"How's that?" He popped himself back into his underwear.

"You act like we haven't been going out for like... almost a year," she said.

Six months, he said in his mind. "I haven't seen you in weeks. You get wind of my grandmother's party, and you pop up," he said to her.

"Actually, I came to talk to you about something." She sat down next to him.

"Good talk," he said as he got up to leave.

"Daniel, for real."

He sat back down, "What is it, Diamond?"

"So, I met someone."

Daniel laughed. "You just said we were dating for a year."

"Well, it's not like that. He wants me to marry him. He'll pay me," Diamond said.

Daniel inhaled the smell of him on her lips as she told him about her impending nuptials.

"You know, like for papers. He's Nigerian," she continued.

"Diamond, you're telling me this why?" He grew impatient.

"Because I'll be moving for a little while, and I don't want to give up my place. Do you think your cousin would sublet from me?"

"Germ?" Daniel asked.

"Yeah, I mean it's a nice apartment." She lived in a huge pre-war one bedroom apartment she inherited from a dead relative. Well, dead to her, but not to the management company. Hence her insanely low monthly rent.

"I'll ask him." He wondered why Diamond was marrying some stranger for money, but he didn't have the mindspace to inquire further. She wasn't a horrible person. She just wasn't what he needed in his life anymore. Well, up until a couple minutes ago.

"Plus I wanted to see if there was still anything between us before I agreed to do this. And I don't really think there is. I mean, besides your big dick." She squinted at him and smiled.

He shook his head, "It's all good, Diamond. I wish you the best."

"Thanks, Daniel," she said picking up her bag. "You can give Germ my number."

She walked past the janitor's closet on her way to the stairs. Mr. Willie exhaled as he watched her fat ass jiggle by. He wiped his sticky hands on a nearby cleaning towel. Quietly, he closed the slightly ajar door to the janitor's closet – which was premium seating for Daniel and Diamond's private performance.

Blackout

Daniel was deep in the thralls of Call of Duty Black Ops when his lights and TV shut off. He felt for his phone on the couch and checked the time and his battery supply. It was 9:47 p.m. and he had 72 percent battery life. He used the flashlight app on his phone to walk over to the window. The entire block was dark. "Shit," he said. His first reaction was to call his mother.

"Yes, Hersh," Mavis answered.

"My block is out. You ok?"

"Mine is out too, but I have my flashlight and my phone is charged. George already alerted the power company."

"Who?"

"George, Hersh."

Daniel paused for a minute. He already forgot, or rather blocked out, that his mother was seeing some lame. At least she wasn't by herself in the dark. But she was in the dark, with George. Daniel shook the thought from his head. Still, he offered to check on his mother. "Ok, I'll be there in a couple minutes."

"Hersh no, I'm fine. Plus you don't need to be driving in this blackout."

"Ok. Imma call Maw." Just as he said that, Mavis's phone beeped.

"That's Maw now. Let me conference her in. Maw, it's me and Hersh. You ok?"

"Yes, I was just calling to check on you. George there?" Daniel's grandmother said.

"Yes, we're ok," Mavis said.

"Ok, good. I am here with Bernard. Hersh, you alright?"

"Maw, you got a man there with you too?!" Daniel barked. He couldn't believe the two of them were holed up in the dark with strange men.

"Hersh, watch yourself," Maw warned.

"Maw, that old man can't drive home in the dark. What if this blackout last 'til the morning?" Daniel's mind reeled.

"Who said he was driving home?" Maw yelled.

"You really got that old man up in..." Daniel continued.

"Hersh, now you stop it," Mavis interjected.

"But..." Daniel began.

"Daniel," Mavis warned.

"Mavis, get your child." Maw's blood pressure rose.

"Maw, calm down," Mavis sucked her teeth. "Ok, you and Mr. Bernard be safe."

"Safe?! Safe for what?! I can't listen to this." Daniel became flustered on the phone.

"Mavis, your child want licks!" Maw screamed into the phone.

"Maw and Daniel!" Mavis yelled to quiet them both. She played referee when they disagreed with each other which wasn't often. But when it did happen, they grated her nerves. Daniel would dangle on the precipice of disrespectful, and Maw would stop at the curb of cussing him like a stranger.

Mavis took a deep breath. "Alright, everybody is ok. Hopefully the lights will come back on soon. I will call you both in the morning. If you get power, text me." Mavis heard nothing but breathing. "Hello!" she spoke into the phone.

"Ok," Daniel said weakly.

"Alright May, I'm gone," Maw said and everyone hung up.

Daniel sat in the dark feeling lost. He always helped or was at least welcomed at his mother's or grandmother's during times like this. The image of them loved up with their dumb boyfriends irked his nerve. His mind went to Asha. His phone buzzed.

*Asha: I like it dark, but this tew much *black moon emoji* lol. You ok?*

Daniel laughed at his phone screen.

Daniel: Yeah I'm good. What about you? You have flashlights?

*Asha: I'm good, my landlord has a generator so it's about to be poppin' over here. *party hat emoji**

Daniel took that as an invite.

Daniel: Let a brother get some...

*Daniel: *lightbulb emoji**

*Asha: come thru *kissy face emoji**

Daniel: Be there in an hour.

He'd one upped Mavis and Maw. He'd be holed up with someone, too. *Only thing is, we'd choose to be in the dark,* he smiled at his jealous thought.

Asha, as usual, was excited to spend time with Daniel. She found out from her timeline that most of the peninsula lost power. She barely had time to scroll before her phone rang.

"Cupcake," Rand said.

"Hi Unk, I'm ok," she answered.

"You come on over here. I'm finally getting my monies worth from that generator."

"That thing is so loud. I rather be in the dark," AJ yelled out.

"Hush, Jessie," Rand said, his mouth away from the phone.

"Unk, I'm ok. My landlord has a generator, remember?" Asha reminded him.

"Oh, ok now. What about Cleo? Is she there with you?" Rand asked.

"Cleo's out of town, Unk."

"You sure you don't want to come over? I'll send a squad car over there to pick you up," Rand tried again.

"Unk, you can't send a car. You're retired, remember?" She laughed into the phone. "Let me talk to AJ. We might need to get you some help."

"Watch your mouth. Ain't nobody getting senile over here," Rand warned.

"He be forgettin', Asha," AJ yelled through the phone.

"I'm good, Unk. I'll call you in the morning."

Just as Asha ended the call, her electricity resumed. She got a text from her landlord that read: *Tenants, please be mindful of the electricity used during this time. Unplug unnecessary appliances and use lights as needed.*

She decided cooking would be necessary. She assumed Daniel would be hungry, so she'd make something quick to eat. AJ nearly fainted when she asked her for a portion of the fish uncle brought home from his hook at the docks. "Did you say salmon?!" AJ asked.

"Yeah, just like two steaks," Asha's voice was quiet.

"Is this for Cleo? I gave some to her mother last week," AJ asked confused.

"No, it's for me," Asha sighed.

"What you need salmon for?" AJ squinted. Asha rolled her eyes. "Set them slot machines straight when you talk to me, girl," AJ joked about Asha's large rolling eyes.

"It's for my friend," she blushed.

"Ohhh, tall, dark and handsome? Mmmmm," AJ teased. "Here, take four of them. You can't give that strapping thing no two pieces, chile." AJ packed up the salmon steaks for Asha.

She planned to invite him over for a surprise dinner, but now was a good time as any. She turned on the gas range and grabbed a skillet from the lower cabinet.

Asha did unplug her newly fixed washing machine. Rand and Cleo always poked fun about how often her appliances broke. They were convinced she was cursed with appliance black thumb. Last week, she tried to send Cleo packing before Uncle Rand showed up to take a look at her washer. But she decided to entertain Cleo because she came bearing gifts. Cleo's connect at the free clinic blessed her with a shitload of condoms. And being a true friend, she arrived at Asha's door with a shopping bag full of latex goodies.

She placed the bag on Asha's couch. "I'm sure the person who gave you this is well on their way to being fired," Asha said as she looked into the bag.

"Nah, he's still there. He just made supervisor," Cleo laughed.

"Pilfering from a non-profit? That's nice."

"Are you criticizing, complaining or what?" Cleo barked. "And it's no pilfer. This is full on stealing."

They both cracked up. She dug into the bag and pulled out three wholesale boxes of condoms. At the bottom of the bag were lubricants and other adult accessories. "What's all of this?" Asha asked, holding up a tube of swelling cream and a small box. She opened the box to reveal a male enhancing sex toy.

"Oh, that's some stuff I won at one of those sex parties," Cleo said.

"And what makes you think I want this freak shit?"

"Because you're a freak," Cleo answered as she plopped down on Asha's couch. "And before you become a choosy-ass beggar, that's all they had. You lucky you got that one box of Magnums."

"I didn't say anything. I'm good," Asha replied to Cleo's reprimand.

"I don't know where you be finding them horse dicks anyway," Cleo continued.

Asha ignored Cleo's statement. "I hope you don't be sucking on them things. It ain't good for your fillings, and you know you need some dental work done." Cleo put her feet up on Asha's cocktail ottoman as the doorbell rang.

"That's my uncle." Asha went to open the door.

Upon the mention of Rand, Cleo had the quick presence of mind to stuff the goodie bag into the storage compartment of Asha's ottoman. "Lord, what did you break now?" Cleo, asked.

"Shut up!" Asha called from the hallway.

Daniel parked across the street from Asha's place. There were more drivers on the road than he anticipated. He reached into the back seat to grab the bottle of wine. She liked red wine, and he noted her preferred brand the last time he was there. The shopping plaza where the liquor store was located hadn't lost power and was buzzing with shoppers. It had only been an hour or so since the loss of power, but the public already went into an apocalyptic frenzy.

"Hi!" Asha reached up and kissed him when she opened the door. He handed her the bottle of wine. "Oooh! Thank you. I already started sipping," she confessed. "I'm just making something quick to eat. Are you hungry?" she said pointing toward the kitchen.

He followed her watching the sway of her ass under her terry cloth dress. "Yeah, I could eat." Upon entering her kitchen, his mind tried to register what his eyes were seeing. Salmon on her countertop. She was preparing it just for him. He opened his mouth, but the words got stuck in emotional traffic between his heart and mouth.

"What are these?" he decided to ask her while picking up a square container amid her dinner ingredients.

"Ooh, those are my fave!" she informed him. Asha opened the box and popped a creme puff in her mouth. "Mmmm," she beamed. Her enthusiasm made him curious as to how good they really were. He put one in his mouth and bit down. His face contorted, and he ran over to the garbage can to spit it out. "You don't like them?" she said as she ate another. "But the filling is so sweet and fluffy! Maybe you got a soggy one. Here try this one." She offered him a second creme puff.

He held up his hand and declined. "No, I'm good."

She looked at the container, "Wow, everyone I know likes these."

"Everyone?" he asked her.

"Well, yeah." she said.

"Men?"

She stopped to think, "I guess, I never really..."

"Straight men?" he folded his arms.

"Straight men? What does that have to do with it?" She gave him a confused look. He waited for the lightbulb to appear above her head. Her eyes lit up, and she let out a huge laugh. He laughed at her laughing. "Wooow, that's funny. I never thought of it that way," she said.

"Well, you seem to enjoy them." He gave her a chin nod and lowered his eyes.

Asha felt the heat of his eyes on her. She closed the space between them, pinning him against the refrigerator – as much as her small frame against his could.

"Facts," she smiled a naughty grin. He smiled down at her.

"Especially the chocolate ones." Her eyes flashed, she reached up and kissed his clavicle working her way up to his neck. While she grazed on him, Daniel looked over at the food prepped on the counter. He was hungry, but decided that dinner would have to wait. Her galley styled kitchen didn't offer a lot of space to cook together, much less to do anything else. He wouldn't let that deter him. He turned her around to face away from him, and she leaned her body over the kitchen sink. His hands slid up the soft skin of her thighs. Asha positioned herself on her tiptoes. She let out a pre-emptive moan while gathering up her dress, revealing her bare ass. Daniel quickly freed himself from his shorts with one hand and palmed her largest muscle with the other.

"Fuck, you got condoms?" he said barely audible.

Asha stood upright and led him by the hand to her living room which was dark, except for the kitchen light. He was barely seated on the couch before she straddled him kissing him hard on the lips and probing his mouth with her tongue. The hem of her hiked up dress brushed against his erection. She slid off of him, and he heard something fall on to the floor. Before he could look to see what it was, he felt her warm, soft hands on him. His head fell back as he enjoyed her touch. Next, was the texture of her taste buds diligently sliding from his base all the way up to his tip. She took her time and savored each inch like a rocket pop on a hot summer day. The kitchen light provided a soft silhouette of her maneuvering around his crotch. He let out a grunt amidst the symphony of her suction, licks and kisses.

He heard the familiar sound of the tear of the condom wrapper and anticipated the tight fit of latex. Instead, he was ensconced in the warm, wet, passage of her mouth that ended in the deep recesses of her throat. "Ssssss," he exhaled.

Cleo's caution of damaged dental work came to her at the most inopportune moment. She almost laughed and choked herself, knowing that she would have to avoid him after her upcoming oral surgery.

She was this close to saying "fuck it" in the kitchen. She was relieved at his request, but she also wondered what it would feel like to envelope him without the condom. Tipsy from the wine and high off his pheromones, she almost threw caution to the wind. Her IUD and the contraceptive foam she used immediately after texting him provided her with backup safety. She considered the horse dick as Cleo called it, a work of art. Perfect in color, shape, texture, and of course, size. She was mesmerized. Dick whipped was the diagnosis. She held it flush against her cheek, certain that electric current ran through it.

Daniel moaned. She worked his nerve endings with a salacious rhythm that left him nearly breathless. He had plenty of mic checks that ran the gamut from gravity defying positions to sweet, salty and spicy condiments. But the way she was completely caught up in her own ecstasy while pleasuring him, set his mind and body ablaze. He was almost at the end of his rope when she finally slipped the condom on. The pinch-pop of the reservoir brought him back to reality, if only temporarily. As she mounted him, the light in the kitchen flashed, and the generator failed. They were left in pitch darkness with only their remaining four senses to guide them.

Daniel stirred when he heard the zoom of the power resume. He didn't realize he fell asleep until he woke up. More like passed out from heat exhaustion and overexertion. He felt good as fuck and worn out at the same time. He turned on the lamp. Asha was curled up next to him on the couch in a fetal position with a thumb in her mouth, the ends of her hair tickling his shoulder.

He stretched his long legs and cracked his neck. Daniel looked to retrieve his underwear only to find that her cats had made use of his clothes. The fat black one was resting comfortably on a pallet of his shorts. The tawny one had tunneled himself through one leg of his underwear and wore the elastic band around his neck. Her cats slipped him dirty looks every now and then, but for the most part, they stayed out of the way when he was there. He looked around for something to use to rescue his clothing. He saw the ripped open case of condoms on the floor next to his feet. *What the fuck*, he thought. The storage compartment to the ottoman was ajar, and he opened it further discovering 2 more boxes of condoms and an assortment of lubes and adult accessories. He looked back at Asha, still sound asleep, and then quietly rummaged through the loot.

They always had safe sex. At his apartment, at hers, on the beach at night, in his car, in the back office of the auto shop and any other place in between. In most instances, he provided protection, meanwhile she was sitting on a lifetime supply. Why did she have a lifetime supply? Why in her living room ottoman? Why wasn't she using them all on him? These were questions that needed answers. He grabbed a handful of assorted lubes and a tube of swelling cream. He sneered; he had no use for any magic creams. This was a lot of ammunition. Even he didn't have this much artillery. And he certainly didn't keep it in his living room. And he had sex on a regular basis. The thought had only now occurred to him. He'd only been with her for the past...however many weeks?

He had to dismiss everything he just saw. Shame on him for going through a chick's belongings. This certainly wasn't big dick behavior. He looked over at his clothes still being held hostage by the cats. He looked back at the condom filled compartment. He looked over at her again. Her mouth was slack, and her thumb was loose inside. She was knocked out and buckid nekkid, as his Uncle Vince would say. His chest swelled in post coital posturing. Now *that* was big dick behavior.

Her eyes fluttered open and she smiled, "Hi."

"Well rested?" he asked her.

"Yeah, but I'm starving. We never got to dinner." He watched her flex her ankles and wiggle her toes. "I guess I could finish cooking," she offered. Asha followed his eyes to the pile of latex supplies on the floor. "Oh, I see you found my stash." His eyes searched hers for an explanation that wasn't there. "Safety first!" she joked.

"Just seems like a lot," he said.

She stared at him, not sure what his point was. She decided to play along, "It *is* a lot right?"

They sat in silence.

He quickly glanced at her, and then back to the stash. "Let me get some, you don't need all of that," he tested her.

Initially, his request stunned her. Their "us" conversation in the Hamptons defined them as undefined, just the way Asha wanted. It was one of the ways she protected herself. That and the abundance of prophylactics. So she called his bluff.

"Ok, let's see," she said. She opened a multi-pack and made a presentation of her assortment. "Ribbed, extra sensitive, glow in the dark." She placed several condoms on his naked lap. She dramatically swept them all off his thigh. "Wait, no. These are all regular sized, never mind." She looked at his face anticipating one of his big laughs.

His face sat still. She dug into the box she'd torn open just a few hours ago. "Here you go." She offered two handfuls of oversized condoms to him. He stared at her, and she stared back. She was seconds from busting out laughing until he broke their stare down.

Daniel got up in a huff and walked to the bathroom in all his natural naked glory. *God, he was beautiful*, she thought. And fun. And delicious. And now a little jealous, she noticed. She was determined to keep what they had casual. But it was becoming extremely difficult.

All The Pretty Girls

"Hersh come, nuh?" Mavis yelled from the living room.

"I'm eating," he answered.

"Just come for a minute."

Daniel didn't want to get up from his mother's dining room table. He didn't want to see her getting ready for her date. He noticed she was increasingly busy and secretive ever since he walked in on her afternoon delight episode. Finally, she introduced him to her corny boyfriend the day after Maw's party. Now everything was George this and George that. "Fuck George," Daniel said under his breath and over his bowl of cow foot soup.

"You know how a relationship progresses. I don't have to explain that to you," she told him a couple days ago while he was fixing a collapsed shelf in her closet. When he sarcastically inquired about why her *boyfriend* couldn't fix the shelf, she matter-of-factly told him that George was away on a business trip. Daniel would not get used to the role of second fiddle.

"Relationship?!" he inquired with a twisted face.

"Yes, relationship," she confirmed.

He huffed as he drilled the brackets into the wall. He laid the drill on the ground and turned to Mavis seated on the bed. "How you go from 'friend,'" he air quoted, "to relationship?"

"Well, with sex," Mavis told him straight-faced.

"I'm going to be sick." He hunched over and heaved.

"Daniel, don't you vomit in this closet boy!" Mavis threatened.

He wanted his mother to be happy. He just didn't want to know about it. For so long, he had been the focus of her attention. Even when she dated Crane, he never felt second best. Whenever she went on dates or out of town, Maw was there to pick up the slack. He'd spend the night at Maw's, and then he'd be the focus of *her* attention. Time with Maw meant staying up late and dancing to calypso or salsa (depending on her mood). He loved watching her TV programs with her, playing cards, drinking hot toddies and finally falling asleep on her La-Z-Boy recliner. Maw swore him to secrecy about the hot toddies.

Now even Maw had some loser baby boomer beau sniffing around her. She introduced them as *friends*, and then went on to inform him about their STD status. He didn't know why the women in his life insisted on lying.

Mavis looked at herself in the full-length mirror. She was petite like Maw with skin the color of graham cracker crust. She usually wore her jet-black hair in a ponytail, which added to her youthful appearance. Tonight, her hair was out in soft curls. Daniel found safety and love in her bright, doe-shaped eyes. Now she had this clown peering into them and basking in their light. He burned his mouth with the soup while thinking about it.

"Zip this up for me, Hersh," she requested.

Annoyed, he got up and zipped her dress. The low-cut dress cinched her barely-there waist and hugged her hips. Mavis was pressed down, shaken together and running over in her cocktail-length little black dress.

"You gonna wear one of them shawl things or something?" Daniel asked.

"What? Boy, move." Mavis shoved him out the way.

"You need to…" He began while trying to pull her dress up by the shoulder straps to decrease the cleavage show.

She slapped his hand away and yelled, "Stop that!"

"Why you have to have all that out?" He pointed to her bosom area.

"Excuse me?"

"I'm just saying."

"Daniel, I am grown. Or did you forget?" she asked with her eyebrow raised.

Daniel sulked back to his unfinished dinner at the table.

She went back into her bedroom to put the finishing touches on her makeup. Daniel was always so sensitive to her dating, which is why she mostly hid it from him. But she'd had enough of sneaking around. George was such a nice man, and she wanted to fully let him into her life. Her life, up until now, was mostly Daniel.

Mavis knew her boy was genuinely bothered. She returned to the dining room and stood behind his seat. She hugged his head. "You know you're still my number one," she reassured Daniel. She lightly swayed his head while he chewed the dumplings in his soup.

"I'm eating," he repeated. This time when he said it, his heart felt a little lighter.

Don't Get Gassed

Cleo looked back at her friend in the back seat of her car. She was tangled in her seat belt reciting her own gangsta rap.

"Asha, are you ready to go inside?" Cleo asked.

"Fuck these niggas. I'll bust these niggas," Asha slurred.

Cleo looked at the time on her dashboard and sighed. She didn't think Asha's reaction to the laughing gas at the oral surgeon's would be this bad. How the hell was she going to manage setting Asha up at home safely and make it in time for work? She heard buzzing and reached in Asha's bag in the passenger seat.

"Hello?" Cleo answered.

"Asha?" Daniel said.

"Hi, Daniel. No, this is Cleo."

"Oh, is Asha alright?"

"I wouldn't say alright. I mean she's ok, just loopy. Actually, she's a mess. It took me 20 minutes to get her in the car, and another 20 to drive home because she kept taking off her seatbelt and opening the window."

"Damn."

"Yeah, I know. I'm supposed to be at work in an hour. I think I'm gonna call in." Cleo sighed.

"I'll bust a cap in your motherfuckin' dome piece," Asha yelled out.

"You see what I'm dealing with?" Cleo looked at Asha in the rearview mirror.

"What the hell is she saying?" Daniel laughed.

"It's not funny," Cleo chuckled, "she's fucked up."

"You're at her house now? I'll meet you there," he offered.

"No, that's ok. I don't think she'd want you to see her like this," Cleo told him.

"She's gone like that?" he asked.

"Asha, leave the window alone, please." Cleo yelled at her from the front seat like a mother disciplining a child. "You know what? Just come. She won't remember either way."

"Ok, I'm leaving in 10," Daniel said.

"Wait, can you bring her like a milkshake or ice cream or something? She has to drink something cold." Cleo added.

"Ok, cool."

"Thanks Daniel."

Cleo ended the call.

"My mouth!" Asha yelled from the couch after Cleo finally got her inside.

"What is it?" Cleo stood over her.

"It's gone. My mouth, it's not there," Asha cried.

Cleo tried not to laugh. "Asha you're tripping. It's ok, your mouth is still there. But you have to stop yelling and bite down on your gauze." Cleo was relieved to hear the doorbell ring. "Thank God," she said when she saw Daniel.

Daniel stepped in the door with a drink tray that held an ice cream cone, milkshake, lemonade slushy and caramel mocha frappe.

"I said bring something cold to drink, and you bring the whole store," Cleo took the tray from him.

"I must tell Jesus all of my troubles," Asha sang. She was sprawled out on the couch. Her eyes fluttered and then closed.

"She fell asleep," Daniel said standing over her.

Cleo set the tray down on the ottoman. "No, she didn't," she took a sip of the frappe, "she'll doze off and pop back up. You'll see."

Daniel peered down into Asha's face.

"Mmmmmmm," Asha moaned. "I'll smoke that bitch, my nine

214

got the clip," she slurred.

Daniel looked at Cleo with alarm. "What's wrong with her? Should we take her to St. John's?"

"No need to take her to the hospital," Cleo shrugged. "She's been going on like that since we left the surgeon."

"Cleeeeeeeee," she said through clenched teeth.

"Yes, Asha? Look, your boo bought you some ice cream." She picked up Asha's limp hand and dropped it.

Asha's eyes opened. They were glassy and dilated. "Boo? I'm a free agent, BITCH. Hashtag free mafuck..." Her eyes fluttered again, and her head fell back.

Daniel's face read horrified. Cleo laughed, "I told you she was bugging out."

"My faaaaaace," she cried.

"Asha, it's ok." Daniel sat next to her.

She opened her eyes wide and tried to focus on Daniel. She touched his face. "Mmmmmm. It's him, Cle," Asha attempted to whisper.

"Daniel bought you something cold for your mouth."

Daniel looked at her in wonderment. Asha squinted and zoomed in on Daniel. "Did you bring your King Kong dick?" Asha asked. Her bloody gauze visible in her mouth.

"What?!" Daniel barked. She'd embarrassed him. He'd never been embarrassed about his dick before.

Cleo stifled her laugh. "Asha, stop it now, and eat your ice cream. I'm sorry, Daniel. I'm gonna call in. Thanks for bringing the ice cream and stuff."

"No, it's fine. I can stay with her." He watched Asha curiously. "I'm not going back to the shop. You can go ahead." He got up from the couch.

Cleo wavered about leaving Asha in his care. "Listen, this is not her. You know that," she told him.

"I know, it's fine," he assured her.

"Don't take anything she says seriously, it's the medicine. They said it'll wear off gradually."

"It's cool, Cleo. I got her." They both looked at Asha, now eating her ice cream cone. She caught Daniel's eyes and began licking the cone provocatively.

"Asha! Ugh, she's gonna be single by tomorrow." Daniel pretended to ignore Cleo's statement. "And don't try to fuck her either," Cleo added.

He couldn't ignore that one. "What?!" he shouted and turned to Cleo.

"I'm just letting YOU know that if you try some slick shit..." Cleo's neck went into overdrive.

"You dead ass," he said.

Her reference to Asha returning to singlehood followed by banning them from sex made him laugh.

"I'm not playing," Cleo warned.

"Cleo, we good. Let's not be otherwise," Daniel issued his own warning.

She looked from Asha who'd made a mess of the ice cream, to Daniel who watched Asha with curiosity and a little fright in his eyes. Cleo patted her weave, finally knocking a decision into her brain. "Ok. Alright. I'm gonna go." She picked up her handbag. She shot him one last look and said, "I'll call her on my break."

"We'll be here." Daniel gave a sarcastic smile.

Asha stretched and squinted at the numbers on the cable box. When she turned her head on the unusually hard pillow, she recognized a familiar scent. She popped up and her head spun. She held her head and winced.

"Hey, hey, calm down. You're ok." She turned and looked into Daniel's face. His eyes were low as if he'd been sleeping.

"What? What are you doing here?" She looked around her apartment.

"I think you'd be used to passing out and waking up with me by now." His warm eyes smiled. "You had your teeth pulled. Do you remember that?" He looked at her quizzically.

She threw off the chenille throw and stood up. Her head spun again. He stood up just in time to catch her. He eased her back down onto the couch.

"But Cleo, Cleo is supposed to be here," she panicked.

"Cleo was here. She took you to your appointment and brought you back. She had to go to work. She called twice, but you were sleeping." He looked into her eyes. "Asha, it's ok. You're ok," he reassured her.

She looked at him and took a deep breath. He was so calming, but she was still unsure. She remembered sitting in the dentist's chair and flashes of the drive home. Everything after that was a blur. He picked up her phone and said, "Call Cleo." She saw that the last two calls were in fact from Cleo. She hit the tiny image of Cleo on her screen. Cleo answered on the second ring.

"Asha? You're ok?"

"I'm good. Just a little sore."

"I called twice, and he said you were sleeping."

Asha looked at him only to find him staring into her face. "Yeah, I, I guess I was."

"Oh ok, cuz I told him I'd fuck him up."

"What?!" Asha laughed and held her jaw.

"I'm just saying, if he tried any funny business."

She could hear Cleo's eyes roll through the phone. "No, I'm fine."

"Ok girl, let me go. I'll call you later. Get some more rest." Cleo ended the call.

Asha put her phone down and sat back on the couch.

"You good?" Daniel asked her.

"Yeah, I just... I just freaked out, I guess," she said and exhaled.

"Dramatic." He shook his head.

She smiled and held her jaw.

"As long as you good, you might want to rinse out your mouth," he said.

"What?!" Asha looked him up and down.

"Your gums," he paused, "I think they're still..." His brows met. "They may still be bleeding a little."

"Oh. Oh, um, ok," Asha said slightly embarrassed.

"Really? That's what you think..." Daniel scoffed at her insinuation.

"I'm sorry. I just... I mean... They said the medicine may make me paranoid."

"Right." He gave her a short nod.

She looked so pitiful, he thought to himself. "Call me tomorrow," he said as he got up from the couch.

"Ok, um. Thank you," she said, still tired and dazed.

He gave her one last look and walked out the door.

Rock Bar & Lounge

Daniel and Germ stood outside of Rock Bar & Lounge bullshitting with the bouncer.

"I'm telling you. That big one, she's laying down," Germ insisted.

The bouncer looked from Germ to Daniel. "Yo, get your mans," he said to Daniel.

Daniel laughed, "You wild disrespectful, Germ."

"How old is she? Like 17 or 18? At 17, I was getting it in. I don't know about y'all," Germ told them.

"Get the fuck outta here, Germ," Daniel said.

The bouncer agreed, "Man, shut up. You was wacking off at 17."

Germ looked hurt by the accusation. "I'm dead ass," Germ countered.

"Nigga, even if you was smashing, you wasn't smashing no chick like Malia Obama. Fuck outta here. This nigga crazy," the bouncer fussed.

The bouncer and Daniel gave each other dap.

"She ain't all that anyway. She mad boring in the face," Germ defended.

Daniel laughed at his cousin. He'd been known to say dumb shit often. Daniel was beginning to think Germ actually believed himself. His point of view was heavily influenced by popular trends, media spins and big booty hoes.

"Yo, you reckless right now," Daniel told him.

"She's not fire, B," Germ continued.

"Check this out fam, she's a child, you fucking pervert," the

219

bouncer told Germ. "And why ain't she cute? Cuz she ain't no plastic ass attention hoe like them reality star bitches?" The bouncer got in Germ's face.

Germ was either too dumb or too afraid to step out of harm's way. The bouncer was well over six-foot tall and past 250 pounds and towered over Germ's five-foot-nine height and average frame.

"She's the first daughter! Have some motherfucking respect." The bouncer knocked Germ's hat off his head.

"Whatever, man." Germ waved the bouncer off with a shaky hand and picked his hat up off the ground.

Daniel just watched. He had no interest in defending Germ tonight. People usually put up with Germ based on their relationship with Daniel. But to let Germ tell it, he was the man. Daniel's phone buzzed.

Asha: We just parked.

"Good looking on the section." Daniel gave the bouncer an Andrew Jackson filled dap and pulled Germ to the side. "Listen, they're about to come through. Just chill out, ok?"

"Hersh, go 'head with that man." Germ placed a mint-flavored toothpick in his mouth.

Daniel was always trying to prep or coach him. Germ was doing him a favor by agreeing to this last minute non-double date. Not that he had much else going on this Saturday night. What it really was, was a single date with two plus ones. Daniel was lucky that Germ got a good preview of Cleo at Maw's party. She was definitely a banger. Not that he was guaranteed to smash, but still. He enjoyed being in the presence of beautiful women. Mostly because they made him look more attractive. Also for social media purposes, of course.

"I should have worn flats," Cleo complained as they got out the car.

"I told you Cleo, it's just Rock Lounge. I don't know what you got all glammed up for," Asha scolded her. Asha wore a red romper short with flat gladiator sandals. The lounge's AC was known to be intermittent, so the less clothing she wore the better. When she showed up at Cleo's apartment, she was surprised at her getup. She was wearing an animal print that was either leopard or cheetah (Asha could never tell the difference), tube dress and corkscrew heels.

"Wait, are you trying to get boo'd up with Jeremy?" Asha teased her as they crossed the parking lot.

"Bitch, whet?! Hell no," Cleo protested. "I mean he's cool, but he ain't my type."

"Why? Because he has a real job with benefits and a 401k?" Asha shaded.

Cleo shot her a look. "See how bitches act when they gettin' steady dick?" Cleo answered.

Asha laughed, "You know I'm just playing with you, boo." She slipped her arm around Cleo. She knew Cleo was one that could dish it but couldn't take it. She could be sensitive at times, and even a little jealous, but she was loyal to Asha to a fault.

"Whatever, I mean he' s not the ugliest thing. A little on the short side," Cleo considered. "But we all the same height horizontally, girl."

Asha shuddered at the thought and paused as they approached the strip mall where the bar was located. "Cle, please don't sink your claws into his cousin." Asha clasped her hands together.

"Let me remind you that you and I were supposed to hang out tonight. Then at the last minute, you turn it into a four-seater. Now you telling me what I can and cannot do?" Cleo fired off.

Asha raised her prayer hands to her chin. "You can do whatever you want. It's your vagina," Asha busted out laughing.

Cleo's face went flat. "You know I hate when you say that word." She took a deep breath as they arrived within earshot of Daniel and Germ.

"I've never known Rock Lounge to have such a handsome welcome committee." Cleo flashed her megawatt smile.

Daniel's smile expanded with every step Asha took toward him. Her insides fluttered. She walked right into his chest and put her arms around his neck. His palms landed on her hips, and he leaned in to meet her lips.

"Hi," Asha smiled after his plush lips left hers.

"Ahem," Cleo interrupted.

"Hey, Cleo. You remember my cousin Jeremy?" Daniel introduced them. Germ eyeballed Cleo like he was a castaway on a deserted island, and she was a rotisserie chicken.

"Of course I remember him." Cleo batted her expensive lashes. "Good to see you again." She flirted and gave him a Hollywood kiss on the cheek.

Germ's toothpick fell out of his mouth. "Yeah, yeah. You're definitely good to see again," he answered.

"Ready to go in?" Daniel asked before Germ could embarrass him any further.

The crowd at Rock Bar & Lounge was made up of urban professionals mostly born in the late '80s and early '90s. The bar was one of the most recent leaseholders in the newly renovated strip mall. Abandoned and dilapidated for decades, the shopping center had recently undergone a revitalization much like many other pockets of the small beach neighborhood. The owner and life-long resident of the peninsula decided that revitalization meant that gentrification was around the corner. The owner staked his claim in the neighborhood that shaped him by opening the bar lounge. The venue filled the void for a sophisticated and intimate space to enjoy drinks, small plates, listen to music and get your dance on. For the sixth-borough millennials, it was a night out, without leaving home.

Tonight the place was packed and the A/C was pumping, much to Asha's relief. Daniel led them through the crowd with Asha's hand clasped in his. Asha's other hand kept Cleo close behind. Germ brought up the rear struggling to keep up as they snaked through the crowd. Daniel walked up to a banquette that faced a small stage. He unlatched the velvet rope that cordoned it off, stepped back and motioned for Asha and Cleo to enter. Asha looked around the crowded space. Patrons who arrived too late for bar seating and failed to make booth reservations watched their party of four with envy. A tightly packed Latina dressed in all black rushed the space and banged on the table. "Excuse me, this space is reserved. You can't just let yourself in," she said with an attitude.

Cleo was about to give the barmaid a piece of her mind when Daniel stepped forward, "Juanita, they're with me."

Juanita's disposition instantly changed. "Oh God, Danny. I didn't see you, my bad. I gotta guard these booths because people be bugging up in here." She looked up and down the bar. "The manager will have my head for a mess up like that, plus it's my first night hosting. And the bouncer never said who the section was for," she exhaled.

"It's cool, 'Nita," he said to her. Daniel took out his money clip and handed her his credit card. He whispered something in her ear and then asked, "Can you start us with a tapas platter and a pitcher of Rock Rum punch?"

Cleo nudged Asha under the table. "This nigga finna run a tab. He just be running tabs all over town, huh?" she whispered in Asha's ear.

Asha nudged her back, "Talk to your company." She nodded in Germ's direction. Germ was busy taking a pseudo selfie, pretending to look off into the distance. "Ugh. This is going to be a long night," Cleo said.

Two pitchers of rum punch and a couple shots of tequila later, Cleo and Germ had settled into flirtatious conversation and even took a couple usies together. Asha was enjoying herself but wasn't keeping up with everyone else's drinking pace. Daniel, on the other hand, was tipsy. He was extra affectionate and kept his hands on her all night. As was the case during most social outings with him, he ran into several people he knew. Guests repeatedly stopped by the table greeting him with variations of his names: Big D, Danny, D-bo, Hersh, H-town along with a couple others. He introduced her every time. The men were happy to meet her, the women, not so much.

The music lowered, and the lights on the small stage came up. Juanita appeared on the stage and adjusted the too tall mic. "How y'all doing tonight?" The crowd gave a mediocre response. "Oh, y'all ain't turnt tonight." The crowd responded with increased volume. "I'm Juanita, they call me Juicy J." She pivoted and gave the crowd a view of her apple shaped bottom - the crowd whooped and hollered. Juanita laughed and continued, "I'm your host tonight at Rock Bar & Lounge." She removed the cordless mic from the stand and walked across the stage, "Who's ready for Rock's Lip Sync Challenge?"

The crowd erupted. Asha and Cleo looked at each other. "Wait, what?" Cleo said.

"Niggas be twisted up there ma," Germ told her. "They wait 'til you toe up then they start with this shit. Won't catch the kid up there." Germ popped a fresh toothpick in his mouth.

"Oh, this is gonna be funny. You should get up there, Asha," Cleo teased.

"You wish," Asha replied. "I'm gonna have a good laugh myself." She settled into the nook of Daniel's arm.

"Our first challenger is gonna start the night off with a throwback. DJ cue his music," Juanita instructed the DJ. "Y'all give it up for my good friend, Danny!"

Daniel got up just as the intro to Carl Thomas' "I Wish" came through the speakers. The crowd cheered and whistled as he stepped on stage.

Cleo grabbed Asha's arm and shook it, "Girl WHAT is going on?"

"Cle, "I don't knooooow. I didn't know he was getting up there. Oh my God," Asha laughed and her head fell onto Cleo's shoulder.

Germ looked on and shook his head, "This nigga drunk."

The first verse began. One woman in the crowd yelled out, "I love you too, baby!" Daniel looked over to the banquette and winked at Asha. The women in the lounge rushed the front of the stage. Asha couldn't believe what she was seeing, but she couldn't take her eyes off him. He continued to lip sync his lovelorn ballad, and the women of Rock Bar & Lounge showered him with adoration.

"These bitches is thirsty," Cleo declared. "Look how they just drooling over your man."

"He's not my man," Asha quickly corrected.

"Keep playin' around, and one of these hungry hoes will take his ass home tonight." Cleo sipped her punch. "Right from under your unbothered ass."

Daniel fell to his knees, and the front row of women clamored to touch him. He laughed and quickly backed up from the edge of the stage. He looked over at Asha, who continued to laugh at his antics. By the end of his number, the crowd was singing and swaying along with him. He received a standing ovation complete with kisses blown, offers of love, money and sexual favors. Winded and out of breath, he returned to his seat next to Asha. Cleo greeted him with a high-five.

Asha's cheeks hurt from laughing. "You're crazy," she smiled into his face.

Juanita returned to the stage. "Well, alright. I don't know who can follow that act, but I'm sure somebody's drunk enough to try."

A waitress came to the table with their final bill. Germ made a fake reach for his wallet, "You got it fam?" he asked.

Daniel didn't even bother to look at his cousin. He signed the slip and whispered to Asha, "You ready?"

"So Cleo, what you doing after this?" Germ asked.

"I'm going home, thank you. What you doing?" she quipped.

"I was thinking we could get into something." He looked her up and down.

"Well, yeah," she smiled. "I'm gonna *get into* Asha's car and drive my ass home. She gotta drive Carl Thomas Jr. home cause he's bent," she said.

Germ looked at Daniel and Asha who were interlocked in each other's reckless eyeballing. "A-yo H," he called to Daniel. He slid his eyes off Asha and on to Germ. "Yo, what's good? You know I didn't drive," Germ said as his toothpick dangled in his mouth.

"Man, you live up the block," Daniel snarled.

Germ sucked his teeth and looked at his phone. Daniel pleaded to Cleo, "Can you please drop him off? Asha has to take me home," his eyes returned to hers. "I got something to give her," he slurred and blinked slowly.

Uber

Daniel feigned sleep. He watched her maneuver through lowered eyelids in the limited early morning light. She was fully dressed, and her hand went to her ear. She searched the sheets. He couldn't suppress his smile and sat up.

"I'm sorry," she said. "I can't find my earring." He looked at his phone on the nightstand, it read 7:10am. She lifted a pillow, "Ooh I found it." Asha put the hoop in her ear and sat on the edge of the bed next to Daniel.

He ran his hand up her leg. "Getting an early start today?" he asked careful not to sound too interested.

"Yeah," her hand glided across his bare chest.

Where could she be going this early on a Sunday morning? He certainly didn't feel like driving her home at this hour. But maybe he would get more info out of her during the ride. He made a motion to get out of bed, and her phone buzzed. She gave him a quick peck and stood up, "Ok I'll text you later. Maybe sushi on Thursday." She walked backward out of the bedroom.

"What?" he answered. "Where are you going?" He was confused.

"My," she pointed toward the window, "Uber." She stared at him blankly.

"You called a car?!" His eyebrows raised causing lines in his forehead.

"Yeah?" She stopped at the threshold. "We came here in your car, remember?" She questioned him. "Or those tequila shots still have your head messed up?"

Her calling a car was genius, convenient and Sunday morning friendly. But it upset him. She laughed and headed toward the door. "Sushi Thursday," she called behind her.

He got out of bed. "Asha," he barked. A chill ran through her when she heard her name. She turned around and felt a wave of déjà vu from the first time she spent the night.

He stood in front of her in his boxer briefs. The rising sun illuminated his form through the half-opened blinds. "Cancel your car." His voice was firm.

"What?" she laughed. "No, you think I'm made out of elastic." She rubbed her right hip, sore from last night. She turned to open his front door, and he pushed it closed before she realized he was standing behind her. "Excuse me," she laughed at his insistence.

He went to his kitchen and opened the window. He looked up and down the street and saw the Uber car service plaque in the window of a black Honda Accord. Daniel leaned out the window, and he whistled. The driver stuck his head out the car window and looked up to where Daniel was yelling. He made a neck cutting motion and yelled, "Cancel that fare, we good."

"Oh my God," Asha called out from behind him. "You're gonna have me caught up in the church lady rush," she stomped. She tried to look out the window, but his frame took up the entire space.

The driver got out the car and called up, "Ju gotta cancel on ju phone, papa." He spoke with a heavy Spanish accent. Daniel pulled his torso back in from the window, and his chin nodded toward the phone in Asha's hand.

"You're a maniac," she declared canceling the request on her phone. "I need an ice pack though for my hip." She put her phone in her pocket and pulled him down to kiss her. He grabbed her wrists. His reaction took her by surprise.

"Don't ever call a car here." He looked dead into her eyes. She couldn't figure his reasoning. He should have been relieved. She would have been gone and out of his way before the day began. Uber was a morning-after godsend. A booty-call blessing. "I," she was frozen in his scowl, "I mean, it's early. I didn't drive and..." Her eyes fluttered.

"That's not how I operate." He dropped her wrists. He used a car service for women plenty of times. Usually in the dark of night. Especially if he had the inkling that they wanted to get comfortable until daybreak. He went back to the bedroom and sat on the bed. She stood in the doorway. "You have errands at 7:00am on a Sunday morning?" he blurted out. He didn't mean for it to spill out that way, sounding weak and needy.

Did he really desire her company? Maybe he just wanted to get his morning nut off. Or was he being controlling just for controlling's sake? The questions rolled around in her head. "A girl has to keep busy," she smiled.

He laughed because it was all he could do. He'd almost lost it. He felt emotional, and emotional was not allowed on a Sunday morning with a beautiful girl in your bedroom. She sensed he was embarrassed. She never took privilege when it came to the "morning after" scenario. Never wanting to be asked to leave in a subtle or not so subtle manner.

"Look," she laid across the bed on her good side, "we have a good time together, right?" His eyes narrowed and his head tilted to the right. "I mean, we good," she continued.

"Wait," he stopped her, "you giving me the 'we good' speech?" His ears ran hot.

"No, no, no," she waved her hands. "I mean, you know who you are." Her heart raced. She didn't want to have this conversation with him. She wanted them to be what they were. Which was a casual, undefined, fun, sexy, comfortable, funny, sweet, summer thing. Kinda.

"And who is that?" he challenged her.

"Well for one, you're offensively good looking." She began to count on her fingers.

He shot her a look, "Don't give me that."

"I'm serious. You have mirrors, so don't bullshit me either, Danny."

She never called him that before. He liked that his name was comfortable in her mouth. "You're fine as fuck. Gainfully employed. You have no kids. You're...sweet," she swooned and her cheeks subconsciously colored. "Your body is sick," she continued. He gave her a bored look. "You have a King Kong dick and a devil's tongue," she shrugged. A smile crept across his face against his will. She smiled too. "You're hot shit. You know it, and I know it," she shrugged again. She made his attributes sound like disadvantages. He'd never heard it spun like that before. He refused to accept the mindfuck from her though.

"What does that have to do with you breaking out like that? Calling cars and shit like some kind of..." He stopped short.

"I'm never going to monopolize your time and space, Daniel," she announced. "I mean, but we're cool with what we do, right?" As soon as the words left her mouth, she felt a pang of remorse.

Monopolizing his time and space didn't seem like a bad way to spend the day. In spite of all that she stated, she did feel that most times he was into her. She was completely caught off guard by the invitation to his family event. Meeting his mother and grandmother gave her a window to who he was. And she liked what she saw through that window. But she stood firm in her decision that it couldn't be more than a summer thing. The sun was hot, the drinks were cold, the titties and asses were out. He couldn't possibly be interested in only her at this time. Hell, at any time. She distinctly remembered his words to her that night in the parking lot. He was never at a loss for ass. That information stayed in the front of her mind. Besides, her duty was to protect her heart, not to appease his whims. Regardless of how good his whim felt just a couple of hours ago.

Most women would have welcomed the day with his dick in their mouths. Followed by domesticated role play including bacon and possibly grits. Most would have stalled around to absorb his time and space as much as they could. Instead, she made a dash for the door before daybreak.

She did all the things a girlfriend would – and things some girlfriends wouldn't. Yet, she refused to hold any claim to him. What did he want from her? Or was it that he wanted what wasn't being offered to him? In spite of the laundry list she rattled off, maybe he wasn't enough for her. An ugly, familiar feeling he couldn't shake.

"Yeah, we good," he lied. "But you don't have to run outta here like you stole something."

Her response was a bashful smile.

"Hungry?" he asked.

She took a peek at the lump in his underwear. She raised an eyebrow, "Why? you got something for me?"

He laughed. "I was gonna offer you breakfast." His sleepy eyes twinkled.

"I could eat but," she yawned, "I'm more tired than anything."

He laid back in the bed and extended his arm to her. Asha looked around as if expecting a hidden camera crew to appear. "You acting funny." His lowered eyes still held remnants of their twinkle. His bare chest was so inviting. She pulled her romper off and removed her sandals. She slipped under the sheets and rested her head on his chest. His body was warm and firm; it would be easy to get used to this time and space. She momentarily sighed her hang-ups away and settled in for a Sunday morning snooze.

Blast

Cleo: Girl

Asha: Sup?

Cleo: Guess who I saw in the mall today?

Asha: Today? You're not at work?

Cleo: Asha! Pay attention.

Asha: Ok who?

Cleo: That's not a guess

Asha wasn't in the mood for one of Cleo's hood sightings. She tapped Cleo's name on her phone and placed the call.

"You always do that when I'm in the middle of texting you!" Cleo answered.

"Yeah because you'll go on forever. And why aren't you at work?" Asha said.

"Do you wanna know or not?!" Cleo was frustrated already.

"Well, who was it?" Asha's frustration wasn't far behind.

"Again, not a guess?"

"Cleo, I will hang up this phone."

"Ok, I saw Blast."

"Excuse me?"

"You heard me, Asha. Don't play dumb."

"Blast, who?!"

"How many Blasts were you madly in love with when you should've been getting slayed by all them fine ass..." Cleo began.

"That's enough," Asha sighed. "Did you speak to him?"

"Hell yeah, I spoke. In fact, he called out to me. He said he was home for a little bit, and he's sponsoring the Wavecrest tourney. He invited us to the afterparty."

"Us?! He didn't ask about me, did he?" Asha's eyes went wide.

"Of course he did. He said what's up with my flower?" Cleo poked fun at Asha.

Asha briefly let her mind wander to when Cameron "Blast" Miles was the most important person in her life. He was an all-American small forward for his college team. His dreams of making it to the NBA were crushed when he didn't get picked for the draft two years in a row. She was more than prepared for a long-distance relationship if he went to the ABA league. She would have settled down in a heartbeat had he gotten an assistant coaching spot in a college athletic program. But he called her two days before he left to play overseas and never looked back.

She hadn't let another man into her heartspace since. Against her own will it seemed, she caught herself looking through her heart's screen door at Daniel.

"His flower? Hmph," Asha pursed her lips.

"His flower done bloomed, chile. Been pollinated and errthang," Cleo added.

"Cleo, I will hang up," Asha's mood instantly darkened.

"I'm just sayin'. He still look good though. He might bring light skin back."

"Excuse you?" She could tell Cleo was in a playful mood, in spite of her obvious annoyance.

"I mean, y'all was cute together. But it was too much light skin and light eyes. That ain't good for future generations."

"Whatever." Asha's annoyance increased when her mind's reel flashed back to the way Blast's light amber eyes would look into hers when he was lying.

"Your kids woulda been lookin' all jaundice and whatnot," Cleo went on.

"Are you done or are you finished?"

"These are facts, Asha."

She wanted to see him just to show him that she was doing great. Still cute, employed, no kids and getting dicked down on a regular basis. Then again, what did she have to prove to him? He broke her heart and kept it moving. He was a distant thought, until now.

"I don't think I want to go to that. I don't want to see him," Asha said.

"Girl, please. Let's just go. It'll be fun," Cleo persuaded.

"You just tryna see some fake ass passport ballers."

"Shiiiit, they get paid enough for me. What time you want me to come get you? It's at Backstage in Woodmere."

"I'm not going," Asha said.

"I'm comin' for you at 11. Good and BYE," Cleo disconnected the call.

Asha sipped her drink and perused the party. Cleo drove her to the party but if she decided not to linger around, she would leave the night club/bowling alley on her own. Dressed in casual thot wear: a wife beater, pum pum shorts, knee socks and converse. She wanted to gently remind Blast of what had been his. What he'd thrown away. Show him what someone else was currently partaking. Her mind went to Daniel.

The morning after Rock Bar & Lounge, she was unsure of his motives. She wasn't sure whether it was control or genuine interest. She was flattered but cautiously accepted his invitation to chill in bed that Sunday morning. Having a good time with him was easy. He was fine, sweet and considerate. His staying with her after her oral surgery was an unexpected gesture of kindness. She was so surprised by it that she didn't know how to properly receive it.

Maybe she'd call him after this party. She might need to if Blast looked as good as Cleo claimed.

She felt a hand on her arm and turned right into her past.

"Hey, Flower," Blast said into her ear above and beneath the music.

"Oh hey," she said acting surprised to see him.

Cleo was right. He did look good. He had gained a couple pounds since she'd seen him last, but he wore it well. His fair skin was tanned, and his eyes were a little bloodshot but the same beautiful light brown she remembered. Blast gave her a long hug and kissed her on the forehead. He reeked of Hennessy. He held her hand and walked her out to the corridor. They stood in the small vestibule that led to the exit doors.

"How's your uncle and aunt?" he asked.

"They're good. My uncle retired," she said.

"Oh, wow. That's cool." Blast drank in her tight shorts and thighs.

"How's your grandma?" she asked aware of his sightline to her legs.

"She's ok. She's in a nursing home now." His eyes made its way back up to hers.

"Aw, I'm sorry."

"No, it's fine. She's made friends there, and my mom visits her a lot."

"You look good, Asha," he told her after a moment of uncomfortable silence.

"Thanks. You too, Cameron."

"Wooow, you're one of the only people that still call me Cameron."

Asha smiled back. She could tell he was drunk by his eyes and from the scent of liquor that seeped out his pores. She felt young and dumb in his presence. She knew it was mostly nostalgia. That there was no real connection left. Just the memory of being carefree and in love. Young, dumb and full of cum, as Uncle Rand would say.

"So, what you doin' later on?" he asked.

Asha had just looked at her phone when she ordered her drink. It was 12:15 a.m. then. Later on was tomorrow. Surely he wasn't asking about tomorrow. "Well, I'm here with Cleo," she answered.

"Oh, ok. Wait, is that why you came? She told you she saw me earlier?" His "earlier' slurred.

"She has a friend that played in the tournament. We were coming anyway," Asha lied. How dare he think that she would show up somewhere just to see him. She laughed at herself.

"Oh," Blast said somewhat deflated. "So, she's your ride?"

"Yeah?" Asha answered without sounding concrete.

"I can drop you off, if you want," Blast smiled. "I'm staying at the Fairfield on the Turnpike." He closed in on her and said in her ear, "I've missed you. I want to spend time with you." He remembered exactly where to kiss her on her neck. She almost spilled her drink.

Asha contemplated it for a split second. It might be fun, just for old time's sake.

He grabbed her left leg and lifted it to his waist. The pressure of his body against hers took her back momentarily. He tried to slip his hand into her shorts right there near the exit.

She snapped out of it. She hadn't laid eyes on him in years and now he missed her? Fact was, he was drunk and wanted some familiar leg. She caught her breath and pushed him away. "I'm gonna go find Cleo." She patted herself on the back. That was a train wreck avoided. A pretty looking wreck, but a wreck all the same.

Birthday Observed

Asha re-entered her bathroom to find Daniel sitting perfectly still, staring straight ahead, palms on his thigh. "Are you ok?" she asked. He turned his whole body toward her, causing her to laugh. "You can turn your neck. It's not stone. It's just a mask," she laughed.

They were full of pizza, crime dramas and each other. Somehow they'd settled into a Tuesday routine of ordering in and binge-watching TV. Then screwing each other's brains out. The increasing comfort level between them excited Daniel and made Asha nervous. This Tuesday evening he came across her opening her monthly beauty club shipment and ended up being a participant in her test lab.

"What does it do?" he asked examining the toothpaste-sized tube.

"It makes your skin radiant," she told him about the organic mask. She examined his face, "Your skin is flawless. You wouldn't know anything about masks." She took the tube from him and stole a second look. She decided to fuck with him. "Oh, wow," she said.

"What?" he asked.

"You have like...a blackhead."

His eyebrows knitted. "What?! Nah," he dismissed her.

"Yes!" she said in victory.

He went to the mirror in her bathroom and leaned in. "I don't see anything."

"You should use this." She held up the tube.

He didn't give much thought to his appearance because it was a given. Even when he needed a shape-up or was sick or hungover, his looks were never questioned. It was a constant in his life. His ace, his sure-thing, never failing him. *She wouldn't lie to him, would she?* he wondered. He played it off and played it safe.

"There's nothing on my face. You just wanna use me as a guinea pig. You're not slick." Asha was busted, so she laughed. "But you're cute, so I'll let you do it." He smacked her ass.

About thirty minutes later, he murmured, "It feels tight." His lips were barely moving.

"You like tight, don't you?" She winked and stuck out her tongue.

He struggled to laugh, "Stop. Take it off now." The stiff white mask left only his eyes, lips and beard uncovered. He looked like a mix between an African tribal mask and a horror movie serial killer.

Asha stood between his legs and bent down to check the mask, "Ok, it's gonna feel a little pully."

"What?!" he leaned back, "you didn't say that before!"

"It's a peel-off mask, what did you think it was gonna feel like?" She laughed at the fright in his eyes. "It won't hurt. It'll be a tugging feeling. You like to be tugged," she teased. His eyes remained serious. She straddled him on the toilet seat. "You feel better now?" she asked. He held her by the waist and nodded. "You're such a baby." She teased him.

He relaxed as she peeled the mask from his face. Her touch was so soft and relaxing. How silly he must have looked holding her on his lap while she peeled his face off. She was right, it did feel "pully". However, the air on his face was refreshing.

"What's good for this weekend?" he asked her.

She reached for the green tea wipes. "I'm out east on Saturday morning, then I'm having dinner with Unk and AJ Saturday night. On Sunday, I have a spa day with Cleo."

"You're booked," he said.

"Yeah," she wiped his forehead, "I've done the same thing for my birthday for the past couple of years."

"Your birthday?" he squinted. His mind raced. He thought back to their conversations. *Had she told him and he forgot? No, she never mentioned her birthday.* "When is your birthday?" he asked.

"Saturday," she told him. "Now look at your face." She got up and directed him to the mirror. She stood next to him. "You see how your skin looks refreshed?"

Daniel stared into her mirror. He didn't see a big difference in his skin. In fact, he appeared ashy, which was a big no-no for a dark-skinned brother. What he did see was their reflection together in the mirror. He towered over her, but her presence was larger than she physically appeared. It was then he realized that Germ might be right. She did remind him of Maw. He unwittingly added her to the short roster of women who could wrap him around their finger.

He spoke to her reflection, "So, you were never gonna say anything about your birthday?"

"I'm not Martin Luther King Jr. It's not a holiday," she joked.

Her reaction stumped him. He thought back to how Diamond insisted that he celebrate her. And he obliged her just to get her off his back.

"How about dinner?" he turned to her.

"Sunday may be tough, not sure what time I'll be back from the spa," she replied.

"Friday?"

"Oh, that's bad luck celebrating your birthday before the actual day." Her eyes widened.

"You're superstitious?" he laughed.

She shrugged, "A little."

"You can knock on wood later," he winked.

"Ooh, we can try that Thai truck in the food truck park. I've been meaning to go. Have you been?" she said excitedly.

Daniel sneered, "Food truck park?"

"Yeah, you've never been? It's near the Beach 28th Street boardwalk every Friday night in the summer."

He shook his refreshed face. "I'm not taking you to a food truck for your birthday."

"But, it's for me. Don't I get to choose?" she asked innocently.

"I know a cool spot, don't worry about it."

"Ok, don't forget to text me the address." She removed a stubborn piece of the mask from his cheek.

"For what?"

"Soooo, I can get there?"

"I'm gonna pick you up."

"What? Why? Is it far? If it's in the city, that'll be a bitch to find parking. Or an arm and a leg to park in a garage," she thought out loud. "I said the food truck park because it's close, cheap, and..." she went on.

Daniel stopped her by holding up his palm. "Why are you making distance or cost an issue?"

"I was just saying."

"I've never treated you less than, Asha." His arms were folded, and he stared into her face.

She noted the change in his body language. "I'm not saying that. I was just making a suggestion." Her voice was soft.

"I got this," he declared in finality. He then reviewed his face the mirror. A loud silence hung over them. He turned back to face her. "And wear something tight." His eyes twinkled as he looked her up and down.

"If I'm going somewhere far and expensive, I'm gonna eat. I'm gonna wear my fat pants," she laughed. She looked forward to going out with him as always but dreaded him making a big deal of her birthday. That was a boyfriend thing.

"Fucking food truck for your birthday." He turned back to the mirror in disgust.

"Technically, it won't be my birthday yet," she said. Daniel shot her a look. "I'm joking! You can't take a joke now?" She pressed against him. She gathered up the neckline of his t-shirt into her fist. "Stop being so sensitive," she warned him through clenched teeth.

He laughed. Her delicate hands could only gather but so much of his shirt. She was the furthest thing from a threat. "Or else what?" He palmed her ass.

"Or else you'll get dealt with," she snarled. She was adorable, sexy and wannabe thuggish at the same time. His heart leapt at her silly threat. At her body's proximity to his. At her modesty about her birthday. He felt the words on the tip of his tongue. They'd developed so naturally and were ready to be birthed. Instead, he aborted them and put his mouth on hers.

"We good?" he asked after their kiss.

"Yeah," she managed to whisper. The kiss left her with a recurring giddy emotion she'd been ignoring for the past couple of weeks.

As soon as Daniel's car pulled off, Asha dialed Cleo.

"Hey, boo," Cleo answered.

"Girl, Daniel just left here," Asha breathed into the phone.

"You should be sleep then."

"Cleo!"

"Well, what is it?"

"He wants to take me out for my birthday. On Friday."

"Ok, and?"

"I mean like out out. I suggested the food cart, and he flipped."

"Girl, let that man celebrate you."

241

"No Cle, I don't want him to get the wrong idea."

"Bitch, bye."

"I mean, I don't want him thinking that's what I want."

"You didn't ask him for shit. He offered."

"You're the one who told me to just have fun for the summer, now I feel like it's getting serious. More serious than I intended."

"Food, Asha? That's not serious."

Asha sighed, "He looked at me funny." She thought back to when they were standing in the bathroom.

"What the hell are you talking about?"

"He had a look in his eye, Cleo, I'm telling you."

"Like what? Like he wanted to try anal? Just tell him no," Cleo said matter of factly.

"I swear I don't know why I call you."

"Asha, I don't know what you mean. I'm trying to find out."

"Like," she closed her eyes tight, "like he's really into me."

"Like, in love?" Cleo whispered.

"YES!" Asha exhaled.

"Girl, he just liking that good good."

Asha sighed.

"Seriously, you think so though? That he's falling in love with you? You're so modest," Cleo laughed.

"He wants to know what I'm doing. He acts funny in the mornings when I'm leaving."

"You still runnin' outta there? You gotta at least stay around for the morning wood, girl. That's a freebie," Cleo advised.

Asha remained silent.

"But what do you feel? Do you love him?" Cleo heard Asha's TV in the background. "Asha?"

"I don't want to, Cle. This is supposed to be a summer thing. That's it," Asha stated.

"I personally don't think you should blow this. This summer thing you're insisting on is gonna turn into the autumn blues. Don't let your bullshit from the past fuck this up for you," Cleo told her.

"I know but," she sighed, "I have to think about this."

That Friday, Asha sat in the stylist chair distracting herself with nearby pocket monsters in her phone.

"Mami, you need a trim," the stylist told her.

She hadn't been to the Dominican salon in almost three months. She'd been handling her own hair in an effort to save up for Unk's golf clubs. "Um, ok but not too much please," she instructed the stylist.

"I know mami, ju like a nice long hair." The stylist jerked her head to the left, and then to the right examining her roots. "Ju put a color?"

Any time she stayed away from the salon, they'd grill her upon her return. The Spanish inquisition began.

"Aye, ju damage ju hair like dah. Wha color ju put?" the stylist asked.

"I don't remember," Asha huffed.

"Next time I make a nice color for ju, mami. I make un sexy blonde, como un blanquita." The stylist winked at her in the mirror.

"Yeah, next time," Asha lied. She had no intentions of returning to the salon any time soon. She was only there today because of Daniel and his mystery dinner. He still hadn't revealed the location despite her numerous requests for information. Part of her wanted to sit back and enjoy it like Cleo suggested. The other part was nervous about what this date would imply.

Daniel pulled a shirt and a pair of slacks from his closet and listened to the ringing of his speaker phone. Crane's deep, gravelly voice filled the room when he picked up on the third ring.

"Crane."

"Crane, it's Hersh."

"Weh yu deh pon?"

"I'm good, listen..."

"Yeah mi know, yu need a faaa-vaaah."

Daniel laughed, "Crane you act like I don't look out for you."

"Look (h)out?" Crane repeated. "Mi nuh tief nor child. Mi nuh use lookout."

"Crane, I detailed your car myself. For free," Hersh reminded him.

"How much schew chicken and (h)oxtail you eat from den? Fi freeee," Crane returned.

Daniel was stumped.

"But you bright," Crane replied to Daniel's silence.

He remembered Crane's annual charity event that sponsored barrels of canned goods and clothing to be sent throughout the Caribbean diaspora. "When is the Barrel Bounce?" Daniel asked.

"September. Me have yu dung ahreday."

"You have me down? You mean to host?"

"To stuff barrel!" Crane yelled. "Yu stocious to bloodclot," Crane cursed.

Hersh laughed, "I'm just messing with you Crane."

"Is what yu want, Hersh? Mi have a business to run, my yout. Mi nuh idle like you." Crane was getting irritated.

"I need a reservation," Daniel said.

"How much time mi tell yu fi call di reservation desk fi dat?" Crane said.

"I need the Lover's Rock Booth." Daniel shut his eyes tight in anticipation of the oncoming tongue-lashing.

Crane was quiet. "Mi nuh like your style yu know."

"Crane, I'll rotate your tires and change your oil." Daniel offered.

"My (h)oil good, bredren."

"Crane, please."

"When?" Crane barked.

"Friday." Daniel held his breath.

"Mi nuh like your style atall. A nuh di way me run my business."

"You need a timing belt," Daniel offered. He was running out of bartering options.

"Hol' on," Crane growled.

Daniel pulled the shoe box from the top shelf of his closet. He'd drop off his favorite pair of Paul Evans for a shine at the shoe cobbler on his way to the cleaners.

Crane came back on the line. "9:00. If you come two minutes later, watch me and you."

Daniel sighed a wave of relief. "Thanks Crane. Good looking out."

"Stacy Ann coming next Sunday. Mek sure yu tell yu (h)ol' country bush uncle."

"Yeah, yeah, I got it. Thank you, thank you," Daniel repeated.

"Seen," was all Crane said before disconnecting the call.

Daniel knew he would spend all day next Sunday with Stacy Ann, Crane's vintage Bad Man Wagon (BMW). But this favor was worth it.

VIP Reservation

Daniel walked around to the back of the restaurant. He was sure that the service door would be propped open by one of the workers. The smell of stew peas welcomed him in as he slipped into the kitchen. He snuck up behind the head chef and pinched more than an inch of her broad waist. "I thought you were cutting out carbs," he teased.

The chef grabbed a kitchen utensil and swatted at him, "Facety!" she laughed. "What you doing here boy?" she pulled him into a hug. Anna Bleu was the head chef at Crane's. She used no measurements and had no written recipes. She cooked everything from the memories her mother placed in her mind's recipe book. She trained her assistant chefs verbally by using grand hand gestures and terms mostly known to people of Caribbean descent. New and American assistants would have to use Google for clarification.

"I'm just passing through. Is Rasta here?"

"Yeah he fixin' up out on the main floor. How is your mother and grandmother?" she asked.

"They're good Bleu, thanks."

"Lord, if I knew you was coming I woulda make some bakes." Her hands went to her hips.

"It's ok, Bleu. I'll be back tonight," he told her.

"Oh, you have a hot date? Is that long weave girl again? Lord, she weave did long. Who need all them heap o' hair?" Bleu scrunched up her nose. She kept her hair in a short, platinum blonde buzz cut. Hair was the least of her worries.

Daniel laughed. It seemed the whole restaurant knew when he came with a date. Bleu rarely came out on the floor, but she knew the length of Diamond's weave. "You never call me back. Otherwise, it would be you," Daniel teased.

Bleu let out a hearty laugh, "Boy, go and scratch. You wish you could handle Bleu in her prime." Bleu twirled and gave her bottom a slap.

Daniel laughed, "I bet. Lemme go and find Rasta."

"Alright, love. Walk good," she told him and turned her attention back to her assistant.

Daniel approached the restaurant's aesthetic director, Royce Valley. Everyone called him Rasta, despite the absence of locs. It was because of his laid back, no problem attitude. He never seemed to rush but got more done in one day than most general contractors could do in a week. Rasta could paint, reupholster chairs, hang drapery, repair floors and even clean windows. Crane gave him the title of aesthetic director. Handyman just didn't suffice, especially when relaying the tales of his New York life to his family back home over their Digicel connection.

"Rasta, what's good?"

"Coco man, wha gwan?"

"I'm good, can't complain."

"Yu come fi check we or yu come fi check yu set up fi dis evenin'?"

"Word gets around fast in here."

"Big wager a gwan."

"Wager?" Daniel asked.

"Dem a bet pon the toroughbred, my yout." Rasta patted Daniel on the back. Daniel held the ladder steady while Rasta climbed up to a non-working light fixture.

"What's the bet?" Daniel asked, unsure he really wanted to hear the answer.

"Bleu say is a new ting," Rasta informed him as he adjusted the wires to the sconce on the wall. "Petal say is the magazine ting weh yu did bring with the see tru blouse."

Daniel laughed. "Crane know about this illegal betting?" He handed Rasta a Phillips head screwdriver from his toolbox.

"Well," Rasta paused, "Crane say new ting, fi $100 U.S."

"What?!" Daniel exclaimed. Rasta laughed. He shouldn't have been surprised. Crane was probably the bookmaker, too.

"Come mek ah show yu the space." Rasta closed his ladder and moved his toolbox to the side.

They walked across the restaurant floor. The prep for dinner service had begun. Chairs and tables were being set up and fresh linens were being spread. Rasta led Daniel to a corner of the restaurant sectioned off by heavy drapes. He pulled the curtains back and pulled a pocket door to reveal a small private booth. A tufted bench sat behind a table and faced a large picture window that looked out to Jamaica Bay. Daniel stood in front of the window viewing the water that separated the peninsula from the city. The view looked like shit. Choppy, murky waters with a couple of brave fishing boats and a hint of civilization in the distance. By 9 p.m. tonight, the view would receive a makeover. Similar to a hoodrat with a MAC make-up palette and a Peruvian bundle, compliments of the illuminated New York City skyline.

Asha pivoted and examined her reflection in her bedroom mirror. She ran her hands from her torso down to her knees to make certain that her assets were secure and free of bump or lump. The yellow dress hugged and molded her hourglass shape. He wanted tight, this was as tight as it was going to get. She recently began working out and could see slight results. She definitely felt a difference in her clothes. The handful of inches she'd put on kept her out of several pieces in her closet. But she took a chance and pulled the dress from the back of her closet. She had it for almost a year and didn't dare put it on for fear it wouldn't fit.

She leaned into the mirror and smoothed down a flyaway hair near her left ear. The trip to the salon was worth it. The stylist gave her soft, bouncy waves. She decided on a side sweep that cascaded down her left shoulder. The length of her straightened hair always surprised her because she was so used to her shoulder–length coils. The last time she wore her hair straightened was at the gallery event. He seemed so intent on impressing her that night. She figured it was to get in her pants. That mission had been accomplished. Now with this mystery birthday dinner, she didn't know what his goal was. But she was impressed by his effort and insistence alone. Almost to the point of reconsidering her summer fling ordinance. She took one final look in the mirror before jumping at the sound of the doorbell.

Friday Night Lights

Daniel caught his breath when she opened the door. He was used to her summer, casual, carefree look: sun dresses, rompers, tanks, shorts, flat sandals and the occasional wedge. His eyes roamed her body from head to toe. Tonight she was breathtaking in her skintight dress and nude heels. Her hair framed the left side of her face and stopped just short of her nipple, if his guess was accurate. If Crane hadn't promised to kill him, he'd cancel dinner altogether and spend the night devouring her.

"Hey," he managed to verbalize.

"Hi," she blushed.

The pull of the door opening sent a whiff of his cologne straight up her nose. He'd cut his hair lower than usual into a sharp Caesar. The fluff of beard he was developing had been tamed into a silky, smooth frame for his face. The precise line up defined the dickens out of his cheekbones, making her want to reach out and cradle his face. His black linen shirt fit his frame like a store window mannequin. The flat front slacks he wore were long and lean like him. The cuffs barely kissed his footlong cognac, wholecut oxfords. If she weren't so curious as to where they were going, she'd work him over right there in her hallway.

"Let me grab my pocketbook." She turned around to grab her bag off the bookshelf.

His face crumpled upon sight of her ass presented to him in yellow lycra. "Goddamn, girl," he exclaimed.

"What?" she answered, wide-eyed and alarmed. She worked so

hard at this total look: hair, makeup, dress, shoes. She prayed that nothing was wrong.

"That ass though," he answered. His face was still contorted.

She sucked her teeth, and he laughed as she locked her door. But inside she smiled; she was very satisfied that he approved.

"You could have just called me to come out," she said as they exited her apartment.

"You're starting already?" he asked guiding her to the inside of the sidewalk.

"No, I mean," she began. He looked at her. "Nevermind," she finished. She wasn't used to this alpha male behavior from him. He was usually easy-going and rarely reprimanded her. She didn't want to like it, but she did.

She prayed he didn't park far because her shoes weren't made for more than five minutes of concrete sidewalk. She looked up and down the street for his SUV when she heard the toot of a car alarm.

He approached a silver luxury sportscar and opened the passenger door.

"You're kidding," she said.

"Are you gonna get in?" he asked.

She eased herself into the seat, and he closed the door. It was a Mercedes Benz; she recognized the emblem on the steering wheel. The interior was immaculate in a combination of smooth leather and wood grain. And it smelled good. Like him.

"Daniel, you rented a car? You didn't have to go through all that trouble, seriously. I'm just happy to be going to dinner with you." She turned to his profile and placed her hand on his thigh. He started the car, and the engine hummed.

Her words, *I'm happy to be with you* made him aware of his heart beating in his chest. Her hand on his leg made him aware of another body part.

"Don't worry about it," he said and hit the gas.

They pulled up to the restaurant's circular entrance. Daniel stepped out the car and was greeted by a young man in a white polo styled shirt with VALET written across the back. A second valet approached the car.

"Aaaayo!" the second valet said. "This shit clean, son." He made a loud whistling sound. "CL63?"

"2011," Daniel told him.

"That interior though." The valet bent down and peeked into the pearl beige leather interior of the car where he saw Asha sitting. "Daaaaaamn," he mouthed to the other valet.

Daniel came around to the passenger side of the car and opened the door for Asha. He held her hand as she made her way out of the car and guided her to the curb. The first valet extended his hand for Daniel's key, "Per Management, your car will be parked next to the executive spot, sir."

"Good looking," Daniel told the valet.

Asha heard the valets fighting over who would park the car. "Imma be like the big homie when I get mine, bruh. Facts," the second valet declared.

"You ain't getting no coupe or bad chick like that. This the closest you gettin' to it, B," the first valet joked.

She looked up at the entrance of the restaurant. Flanked by two large expensive looking faux palm trees, the illuminated signage above the entrance was in a Pirates of the Caribbean-esque font. So this was Crane's. There'd been nothing but rave reviews about the food, service and decor in the local newspapers. There'd also been some celebrity spottings recently. Mostly B-list celebrities looking for an authentic tail of ox or jerk of chicken on the outskirts of New York City. It was the it-place for people who were too low-key or honestly too lazy to go into Manhattan. The waitlist for reservations was insane during the summer months because of its location near the water. She was satisfied with his choice of venue. And excited to be there. Tonight. With him.

She felt his hand on the small of her back as a greeter opened the front door. "Welcome to Crane's. Enjoy your experience," she said.

Asha smiled in return. They stepped up to the podium, and the Maître D' looked up from his reservation tablet. "Welcome to...Hershington, weh yu ah deal wit?" The Maître D' came around from behind the podium to give Daniel a brotherman hug. Then the Maître D' turned to Asha and returned to his Yankee voice. "Good evening, miss. Welcome to Crane's." He hit the Bluetooth in his ear, "Concierge for Lover's Rock to the Maître D', please." He turned to Daniel, "You come tru in the silver bullet, bloodclaaat. Dat ting dust off nice, bredren," he stated while holding a fist to his mouth.

"Thanks," Daniel said dryly in response to the Maître D''s excitement about the immaculate condition of his luxury vehicle. "You want to wait at the bar? You have a couple minutes?" he asked Daniel reviewing the reservation.

"No," Daniel answered sternly. He didn't want to wait anywhere. He was ready to get this night started. As he was about to ask for Crane, he appeared behind him.

"Good (h)evening and welcome," Crane extended his hand to Asha. If Daniel heard another welcome, he was gonna flip over the podium.

"Hi, thank you," Asha said.

"I am Samuel Crane, and I'm so pleased that you could join us this (h)evening." His gold tooth shone. Daniel was over the spiel before it began. "Daniel is a very good friend of mine. You are in incredible company, my dear." Crane held and shook Daniel's hand in a vice grip. Daniel winced and smiled at the same time. Crane's old man strength fortified his grip. "This is Petal, and she will be curating your dining experience this evening."

Petal, a tall lanky young lady, supermodel material if not for her badly bleached skin, stepped up and nodded in their direction. "I hope to see you again, soon," Crane said to Asha as Petal motioned for them to follow her.

Daniel hung back a few steps and whispered to Crane, "Raise up off your winnings for that timing belt." Crane laughed his signature baritone Count von Count laugh.

Asha was having a surreal experience. She'd never get used to how Daniel was received anywhere they went. The amount of people he knew. The type of people he knew. He was a social darling. The people's champ it seemed. In the beginning, she was put off by it because it seemed as if she was always the plus one to his celebrity. But the more time they spent together, the more she saw what pulled her to him (aside from his good looks and large appendage) was his kind charm and sincere disposition. Tonight, she was receiving the red-carpet treatment at his insistence. And she didn't feel like a plus one at all.

Petal pressed her finger to her Bluetooth as she led them to the rear of the restaurant. "Rasta, gimme a final on the LR." Daniel knew that was the final check on the private booth. Petal opened the pocket door to reveal the space. He looked at Asha as the door slid open.

Asha stood frozen with her mouth open. She peered in beyond the opened drapes. She felt Daniel's hand on her back once more, urging her to step in. The private booth was dimly lit by a Swarovski crystal laden chandelier. The ivory booth was filled with oversized gray and yellow pillows. She took a deep breath and inhaled the smell of the dozens of yellow calla lilies that flanked either side of the booth. The sight of them caused a knot in her throat. The table was intimately set for two. It had large square ivory dinnerware, various barware, including oversized Olivia Pope-esque wine glasses and flatware that was shined within an inch of its life. A bottle of Veuve Clicquot chilled on the left side of the table, while a bottle Concho y Toro Merlot held down the right side in its own chilling station.

Her eye caught sight of the picture window's view. The city's lights were clear and twinkling as Jamaica Bay swayed beneath as if dancing to a reggae beat.

She detached herself from the view's spell. Turning into Daniel's chest, her mouth opened but nothing came out.

Petal interrupted the magical moment. "The Lover's Rock suite is pleased to have you, Mr. Daniel and Ms. Asha. Tonight's menu has been customized to your palate's preference. Please be seated, and enjoy our chilled libations. Should you need anything, I can be reached with a press of this button." She handed Daniel a pager device. "Your first course will be served momentarily."

Petal exited the suite and closed the pocket door behind her.

"Daniel," Asha finally exhaled.

"You ok? The flowers, are they too strong?" He held up the pager to summon Petal.

"No, it's not that." Asha placed her hand on Daniel's chest. She tried to compose herself. She was near tears. This was nothing she expected. She was overwhelmed. She hadn't prepared for this. There was no way that she could have. "Thank you," she managed to get out.

"Happy Birthday, almost," he whispered in her ear while wrapping his arms around her.

The Push In

She never smoked weed before, but she imagined this is how it felt. Maybe she was feeling the effects from the champagne mixed with the intoxicating scent of Daniel's cologne. That coupled with the incredible food and romantic ambiance. Dinner at Crane's was definitely an experience, as the staff told her repeatedly. When Daniel excused himself to go to the private restroom, Asha pulled out her phone. First she Googled *Crane's Lover's Rock* but nothing came up. She tried again and searched *private seating at Crane's*. Zero results. She knew he had pull, but didn't fathom anything like this. When he came back into the suite, she asked, "How did you pull this off?"

He grinned at her with her chin in her palm. She was beautiful. Naturally, effortlessly and most times completely unbothered. But tonight, she was bothered. Hot and bothered, and he could tell. The way her crystal eyes burned hot into his face while he ate. The way she snuggled under his arm and ran her hand up his leg after her slice of rum-infused pound cake.

"You like when I pull things off," he answered her with his eyes low. She wanted to mount him right then and there, but she thought better of it. Petal and the wait staff seemed to appear out of nowhere, but eerily just as they were needed. She suspected there may have been cameras in the suite because she never saw Daniel touch the pager device. "You had a good time?" he asked her.

"I had the best time. This is one of the nicest things anyone has ever done for me," she told him.

"Let's get you home." He kissed her lips and goosebumps covered her skin.

The ride back to her place was quiet. She was ultra-relaxed but hoped the Blue Mountain coffee she had with dessert would kick in soon. She could not fall asleep. She laughed at the memory of the night of the rooftop party. Asha searched her small bag for her keys. Daniel leaned on the door, "You good?" he asked her while she struggled to focus her vision.

"I'm gonna be good in a minute," she said as she finally got her door open. She entered and held the door open for him.

"I'll call you tomorrow night," he said.

She looked back at him in the doorway. "Huh?" She assumed maybe she hadn't heard correctly.

"I know you have an early start," he told her.

"You're not coming in?" She couldn't have been more confused.

"Nah, you have a lot going on tomorrow." He looked down at his car key in his hand.

She was dumbstruck. She looked at her phone. "It's not that late."

"I'll call you."

"Wait, but what happened?" she said with audible hurt in her voice.

"Nothing Asha," he smiled. "Go in, get some rest."

"Rest?" She pressed her body against his. "You're gonna make me beg on my birthday?"

"It's not your birthday yet."

Her eyes bore into his. "You don't want to come," she paused, "inside for a little bit?" She tugged at his belt loop. He looked down at her hand near his crotch then back up at her.

Independent strands of her soft, perfectly coiffed waves started to break free from their form. Her eyes were glazed over and cheeks flushed. She held her bottom lip in between her teeth, with quickened breath. Her shoulders were dewy, and her nipple imprints called for his attention through the fabric of her dress. He pulled her in for a deep, long kiss. "Goodnight Asha." He looked at his watch, and it was 12:02am. "Happy Birthday," he said. He gave her a sealant kiss and left her standing at her door.

She watched him walk away, baffled as his car pulled off. *What in all the fucks had just happened?* she wondered. She closed the door. She had an incredible night. He'd been so sweet and attentive. She had plans for him once they got back to her apartment. She scanned her memory for what could have gone wrong. She barely spoke; she was so taken aback. She was certain she didn't say anything to upset him. Her bedroom mirror revealed the answer. Her hair had begun its descent into frizz city, her eyes were glassy, her cheeks were red and she was sweating. She looked a mess. *No wonder he bolted outta here*, she thought. Asha pulled down the straps of her dress and stepped out of it. She couldn't decide whether she would use her waterproof massager or showerhead. Or both. She'd never get to bed if she didn't undo what he'd done to her. She turned on the shower, now to think where she'd last seen her massager. Hopefully it still had a charge. She opened the cabinet of her bathroom vanity and looked in.

Her doorbell rang. She froze in her nakedness. Unk said there'd been a series of push-ins in her neighborhood. She decided not to answer the door. Asha removed a couple bottles of hair products and an old blow dryer from the cabinet. Still no massager. The doorbell rang again. She was freaked out and wished Daniel had stayed. She grabbed her robe off the hook of the bathroom door. Tiptoeing to the door, her heart beat out of her chest. Maybe she would get her gun license like Unk had been urging her to. Holding her breath, she looked through the peephole. Hand to her chest, she sighed in relief at the sight of Daniel's forehead. He was looking down at the ground, maybe he'd forgotten or lost something.

She opened the door, "Oh my God, Daniel. You scared the..." He grabbed her waist with one hand, pushed his way in and slammed the door shut behind him with his other hand. He held her against the wall and drove his tongue into her mouth. Her only response to his ambush were muffled whimpers spoken into his mouth and down into his core.

IV

Q22

Diamond Discovery

She and Uncle Rand hit mega traffic on the way back from Pinelawn Cemetery. She tried to tell him that taking the Northern State would be easier. But he insisted on the Southern, and they crawled through the exits for an hour and a half. Only Unk, AJ and Cleo knew what she did every year for the birthday that she shared with her father. People would probably think it odd to visit the dead on your birthday, but it was a time to reflect on her life. The choices that both her dad and uncle made had a direct effect on the person she was today. Ashe's submission to crack cocaine, and Unk's submission to honor his older brother by raising her.

Asha approached the gravesite first. She carried a bouquet of calla lilies and a tiny wine of Johnny Walker Black, her dad's favorite. She spoke to the plaque about her life, work, friends, AJ and Uncle Rand. She also told her dad's memorial photo image that she thought she was in love again, for the first time in a long time. She closed by telling him that she loved him and would always remember him. Asha kissed her hand and placed it on the plaque, her face wet with tears. She walked toward the car and Uncle Rand got out. "You ok, Cupcake?" He hugged her.

"Yeah, Unk," she inhaled in his embrace. She got into her uncle's SUV and watched him walk toward his brother's resting place.

Later that day, Asha got up from the couch and put on her tea kettle. Tea and Advil were in order. She still felt the effects from last night's pre-birthday dinner and after party.

She reached for a mug out her cabinet and experienced a residual aftershock from last night's session. They had their fair share of sex. It was always fun and satisfying. He allowed her freedom to lose herself in him. He seemed to get off on her getting off. That was definitely a plus. He always gave her what she wanted, but last night was different. Last night was intense. His movements were slow and deliberate, and the air was thick with an emotion she refused to place. He was serious and quiet the entire time, much different from their usual m.o. of playful dirty talk. Last night, Daniel's ardent gaze was fixed on her as he systematically stroked her into nirvana.

Her phone buzzed.

*Cleo: Happy Birthday Hoe! *heart eyes, birthday cakes, birthday hats and kissy face emojis* Cleo* followed up by sending a couple shots of the two of them at the Rooftop party.

*Cleo: We look good *kissy face emoji* There's more pics of us with the other girls too.*

Cleo included the link to the photo website.

She forgot all about the photographer snapping a photo of her, Cleo, and their friends at the party. Asha perused the page filled with pictures of partygoers. She was pleasantly surprised to see a random photo of her and Daniel dancing. It was a crowd shot, but she recognized them immediately. She was leaned into him as he spoke into her ear. She kept scrolling. There were also two other shots of him, one with a group of guys and another of him with Germ who was making a hideous gorilla face. She screenshot the photo of her and Daniel.

After skimming through photos of different events on the club photographer's page, she clicked on one last event, a white party. Something caught her eye. As she scrolled back up, her eyes zoomed in. It was Daniel and a chick. An overly made-up, weaved-down, glamazon chick. Asha peered into her phone's screen. She checked the date of the event and rummaged through her mind's calendar. The event was some time after the art gallery and before the rooftop party. She wore a skin-tight white dress. It was strategically cut out on the sides, covering only the necessary. She was tall and shapely with undeniable sex appeal that oozed through the screen. Unk would have called the woman a brickhouse. Brickhouse faced Daniel with her tongue licked out while Daniel stared at the camera with a bored look. Asha scrolled down to the comments. There were over 200 comments from men and women objectifying both Daniel and Brickhouse.

This doesn't mean anything, Asha rationalized. A picture is a picture. She may have been a model-skank the promoter hired to come to the event. Asha did not screen shot that image, but against her better judgement, she kept scrolling.

There were other pictures of Daniel and this Brickhouse bitch. One was from a side angle in front of a club banner. Brickhouse stood in front of him slightly bent over with her ass pressed up against his groin. Daniel bit his bottom lip with a scowl while his paws gripped her hips, and his eyes were focused on her ass. Asha seethed. She didn't realize she was seething until the third photo in which Brickhouse was seated on Daniel's lap whispering into his ear. Daniel wore a glazed over grin.

The pictures of him with that bitch made her stomach turn.

Three pictures of him and the same hoe. He seemed pretty comfortable with her body and vice versa. But he was comfortable with everyone's body. That was his fucking problem. *Maybe she was a model,* Asha returned to her first thought. The poses were staged, but there was a natural ease with which they handled each other. She knew women were all over him because she'd seen it firsthand. But something about these photos got to her. Perhaps because she had her own photo with him floating around cyberspace. In spite of the chemistry she felt with him at the moment the picture was taken, it exuded none of the chemistry these photos did.

She didn't want to care. But she had just let her guard down. Literally hours ago, she opened up to the possibility of something real with him.

She looked at the date of the event again. It was earlier in the summer, and they hadn't known each other that long. Hell, they still didn't know each other long. But last night, she protested. Another aftershock ran through her core. Asha put her face in her palms.

"Snap out of it," she said out loud to no one. She reminded herself it was the summer. And it was a summer thing. A good summer thing. She couldn't discount her experience with him because of a couple of pictures. She didn't want to feel that burning feeling that he was out there with dozens of women. That nagging burn of insufficiency that begged to know if she was just another place for him to park his penis.

They

"Another one," Daniel said to himself. He glanced at the newspaper at the customer service desk in the shop. He had developed a callous to the trending current event. He purposefully didn't follow the protests or pundit weigh-ins on the news shows. But he couldn't escape it. He didn't join in on discussions or debates at work or with his friends and family. But it followed him. The photograph of the heartbroken mother holding her son's framed picture. The photograph of the daughter holding her father's photo. The photograph of the lifeless body abandoned on the street. They all sent chills up his spine.

The hashtag chants, virtual rallies and baited breath with which social media waited for the verdicts unnerved him. He was that teenager several years ago. He is that unarmed man today. The thought of having to bury a teenage son shook him. The thought of his mother and grandmother burying him rattled his soul. Sure, he'd lost friends to violence. Innocent friends who he'd promise to *hit you back tomorrow*, for which tomorrow never came. Not so innocent friends he distanced himself from for fear of a tragic end. His teenage mind's tragic end was imagining his mother stripping his room of all its technological amenities. His wayward friends' tragic end: a jail cell or cemetery.

The verdicts didn't surprise him but they hurt. He dealt with hurt by numbing himself with distractions. Work, women, alcohol, women. But this was different. The legally justified killings told him that the lives lost weren't worth anything. His own worth was a personal struggle. That an entire public opinion considered he was worthless too? Too much to deal with. Crane and his Uncle Vincent, the two most influential men in his life, taught him to be independent and observant. Make your own money. Have your own things. Be of service. Mind your company. Keep an eye out for trouble. These warnings proved futile in today's hunting season.

"Ah nuh, nuttin' new," Daniel heard Crane say as he worked under the hood of his prized vintage BMW.

"Sho' ain't," Uncle Vince chimed in.

"The Spanish man wha play football in front him yaad, Vince," Crane began.

"That was some years back now. Yeah, Christmas time, round '94. Choked the life outta that boy. They said that one liked to choke. He was full of complaints." Vince popped a pork rind in his mouth.

"And what about the one they made a bitch out of with the baton?" Uncle Vince remembered.

"Yes, star. Inna de precinct. A Haitian dat. Me never know battyman ting come with them shield."

Daniel felt his stomach tighten.

"An de (h)African wha reach fi 'im wallet," Crane added.

"Yep. Yep, that was a mess. Right on his door step," Vince agreed.

"Dem kill di man wha deh pon him bachelor party, yu memba dat?"

"Yeah, that was a shame. Poor girl lost her husband. Pretty girl, too."

"Woman nuh lef' out Vince," Crane folded his arms.

"Now that wasn't about shit. A fucking lane change. I ain't never heard no tired shit like that in my life." Vince said.

"A maama man ting dat. Either dat or him nah get nuh slam," Crane hypothesized.

Daniel spoke up. "Y'all gotta talk about this right now?"

"Ah trut, my yout." Crane took a swig of his Guinness.

"Some of these cops, they been killed in the line of duty too, now. We can't be so biased," Vincent offered.

"Ah dem job dat, Vince. Mi no sorry fi dat," Crane informed.

"These is still young black men. Some of them with families and whatnot," Vincent told him.

Crane sucked his teeth. "If me sell cigarette inna di street, me nah (h)expect fi die, bredren. When me sign up fi uniform and shield, me know say me coulda dead pon the job," he huffed.

"Now that young officer the other day was from the islands, Crane. They shipped his body back home. His momma, poor thing." Vince tsked. "And the black fella and oriental sitting in their cop car, a little while back, they was minding they own business."

"Asian," Daniel corrected.

"What?" Vince asked.

"Asian. The cop was Asian, Uncle V. No one says oriental anymore."

"Well he was from the Orient, wasn't he? I ain't teaching no geography class. I'm talking real shit here boy. Shut your mouth," Vincent dismissed him.

"Dats what they want, for you to mind a heap of foolishness. Chiny, (h)oriental, wha di rass?" Crane chimed in.

"Yeah, all that politically correct bullshit," Vince said.

Daniel went back under the hood.

Both men were adamant purveyors of the ideology of *they*. Regarding the election and re-election of the big-eared, Harvard law grad from Chi-town: he's there because they want him there. Regarding the price of gas and the weapons debate: they control the oil and distribution of weapons. Regarding the recent weather events: they concoct all these so-called natural disasters. The seemingly omnipotent "they". Though never directly identified, Daniel knew who "they" weren't. "They" weren't anyone who had any fraternity, allegiance or empathy toward him. "They" were the opposite of him. And that made him angry, determined, aware and hurt.

"Like I said, these are fairly young men doing their job. They got families, and it's a shame that their lives got taken like that," Vince resumed his stance.

"The law is meant to be my servant and not my master, still less my torturer and my murderer," Crane recited in his best Yankee voice.

Vince smirked, "What you know 'bout that, boy? You was still climbing coconut trees when Baldwin said that."

"Climbing yu mumah to bumboclaat," Crane laughed.

"Yeah, for a green card," Vincent answered.

They cracked up at their corny insults. The conversation turned to their usual offensive banter, and Daniel's stomach began to relax. He wasn't interested in hearing the list of his dead peers. Or slain police officers. He thought back to Asha and how she defended her uncle. Her eyes were so serious and her tone was hard, despite her soft, beautiful appearance. It seemed like so long ago when she threw him for a loop that night in the parking lot. They'd come far since then, yet a part of her remained distant. But he was working on it. Similar to Crane's car, an ongoing project he didn't mind spending time on.

21 Questions

Asha struggled to sit up in the bed. Daniel shifted and reached for her. She moaned, but she was drained.

"Comere," he said in a morning growl two octaves lower than his usual voice. She laid back down, and he stretched his arm across her body. He lifted her tank top. "I gotta go to my spin class," she protested. "No," he answered.

She almost gave in until she ran her hand down his stomach. His body was near perfect. She had to stay up on her workout regimen if she was going to continue to, whatever they were doing. She'd be damned if he was going to look at her and compare her to some surgically snatched big booty hoe.

"What time is your class? Lemme know how much time I got." He moved close to her, and she felt him growing on her hip. "10 o'clock, and I can't miss another one," she said.

"Another one?" he sat up.

"Yeah, I'm not messing with you." She searched for her underwear in the sheets.

"When did I cause you to miss class?" he asked.

"Last Sunday when I was here," she hopped off the bed, "No more Saturday night innings with you."

His eyes darted from her face to her landing strip as she walked to the bathroom. He got up from the bed and followed her. "You ran out of here practically before daybreak the last time. How could you miss a 10 o'clock class?" He stood in the threshold of the bathroom.

271

Asha turned and looked at him, "Excuse me?"

Daniel caught himself. Regardless of the fact that he made her cancel her Uber that time, she still had a habit of running out at dawn's early light. How is it that she didn't make it to her class hours later?

"I'm just sayin'." He shrugged it off. "Wherever you have to be at 10 a.m.," he sidled up to her, "it's only 8 now." He entered the bathroom and kissed her neck.

She pushed him away. "I have a stop to make before class." She gave a sarcastic smile, "If that's alright with you." Daniel jerked his head back and lifted his hands in surrender. "You seriously have nerve." Asha stated while her hand went to her hip. Daniel left the bathroom and walked to the kitchen. She followed behind him. "To question where I'm going, and what I'm doing?" Her hand went to her chest while her mind retrieved the images of him and Brickhouse, which was still unspoken between them.

He turned to face her. "I'm not questioning you, Asha. Sorry if you think that I was."

"No, I don't *think*," she huffed. "Don't try to pull that bullshit with me." Her eyes burned into him.

"Woah." Daniel raised his brows and folded his arms. "Wait, you're arguing with me? With no pants on?" he laughed. "You win, you win," he looked her up and down, "I can't go up against you bottomless. I mean, I could but...you have somewhere to be," he grinned.

Asha remembered she was half-naked. She sashay-stomped her way back to the bathroom.

Workout Plan

Daniel collapsed on the bed with sweat coating his skin. This was the third time for the night. Well, the day that turned into night. But that was it. That was all he had to give her. She'd been steadily clawing at him lately, and he was happy to oblige. He noticed that she was developing a leaner, tighter body. The soft area around her midsection was becoming flat and taut. Her ass was lifted and developing into a mostly muscular bubble. Her cheekbones and jawline began to peek out giving her face a more defined, sculpted look. Together with her killer eyes, the combination made her downright breathtaking. She mentioned working out, but he was now seeing the results. She tossed a hand towel to him.

"Damn girl," he wiped his face.

"That was light work," Asha grinned and climbed on the bed next to him. "But look what you did to my dresser." She directed his attention to the makeup and beauty products scattered on the floor as a result of their tussling episode.

"You been going pretty hard with your workouts," he said winded.

"You see it?" she asked excitedly. "Yeah, sometimes five days a week!"

He slapped her ass, "Hell yeah, I see it."

She blushed, "I have all this energy, too." Her blush melted something inside of him.

"I see that too. Where's your gym?" he asked her.

"I go to 24/7 Fit. My trainers are crazy. At first, I was like, no this is too much. I mean, they just went hardcore from the beginning,

273

and I was like—"

Daniel interrupted, "24/7 where?"

"On the turnpike. So the first week, they—"

"You have trainers, *plural*?" he asked.

"Well yeah, you know they're part-time. So I have one guy a couple days a week and another guy on the other days. It's a new training package they're promoting for new members. So the first dude I trained with, his name is Chris. He had me so sore…" she blabbered.

Something in Daniel darkened. He knew the caliber of personal trainers at that gym. Most of them used personal training as an in, and then worked their way up to bedding their clients.

"So, you need two men, huh?" fell out of his mouth.

She was momentarily stumped. *He is being slick*, she thought. She'd been super horny lately. She didn't know if it was the clean eating, natural supplements or the workouts. Or the fact that she had a point to prove after discovering the club photos. He was being slick, but she was slicker. "My trainers are great! They really know how to work my body," she said. "Especially my core." She winked at him.

"The trainers there are scumbags." He gave her a hard squint.

"No, they know what I need. And when I think I'm done, they know how to work my body to the last drop." She popped the "p" in *drop* and leaned in to kiss him. He got up, and she fell face down on to the bed. She let out a raucous laugh.

"What's up with you? I'm just playin' around," she said to him, laying on her stomach with her legs crossed and bent at the knees.

"You think they're about fitness, but they're not," Daniel told her. He was annoyed by her antics. She usually had a sarcastic comment to which he would return with something equally as clever. That was their way, and he liked that she was witty and quick on her feet. But this time, he was bothered. Bothered by the idea of those clowns at that rinky dink gym pawing at her and watching her body transform. Her spin class wasn't enough? The definition in her legs and tone in her abdomen was something he could have helped her with. But she chose to seek help from tag team so-called trainers. She was just another woman in his life with outside interests. *Fuck this shit*, he thought.

"If you wanted training, you could have told me. I would've helped you." He regretted those words as soon as he said it. He'd caught feelings; that horrible, viral illness. He'd been infected with the virus for some time now, but tried to keep the symptoms at bay. But it was too late now because he had already exposed himself. "Fuck this shit," he thought again, but out loud this time.

She watched him buckle his belt and reach for his shirt. She got off the bed and reached up to put her arms around his neck, "You're already helping me to keep the weight off." He removed her hands from his body.

"Daniel," she called to him as he walked out of her bedroom. She stood there naked, not quite sure of how their fun night took such a drastic turn.

Hey Stranger

Daniel lay in bed awake. He wanted to go back to sleep, but his mind was heavy. He had a couple more hours before Bulldog's celebration brunch.

His phone buzzed.

Asha: hey stranger, *kissy face emoji*

He put the phone back down. He didn't know how to address her without seeming like a lunatic.

He avoided her after blowing up about her multiple trainers. He was full of emotions that kept his stomach on fire. He laid in bed and thought back to his appointment last week with his therapist. He hadn't been to see Dr. Parsons in almost a year. He felt good, especially when he was with Asha. No need to rehash negative feelings, but this recent resurgence of emotion made him curious.

Mavis signed him up for therapy when he was 10-years-old, after the first time Beverly visited. He had been going on and off ever since. He'd been through seven therapists already. All women, which probably furthered his issues. This last one, Dr. Parsons, was pretty straightforward but insightful. He didn't feel like a basket case when he spoke to her.

Dr. Parsons asked him what he'd been up to recently. He didn't tell her about Beverly's visit. Instead, he recounted his regular going-ons. He remembered installing his mother's closet shelves. Then he remembered the day after Maw's party. The night of the blackout also came to mind. The recollections squeezed his innards.

"My mother and grandmother have boyfriends," he blurted out.

"And what does that mean for you?" she asked.

"Nothing," Daniel shrugged.

Dr. Parsons remained quiet.

"It means they have boyfriends. Someone to spend time with," he said.

"Anything else?"

"Share interests," he added.

"Is that it?"

"Someone to love them." Daniel's eyes rolled.

"Do they need love?"

"Everyone needs love."

"Do they love you?"

"Of course they do."

"And you love them?"

"What do you think?" Daniel was annoyed with the conversation.

"So what's the use of them having companions?"

He took a deep breath. "I know that it's a different type of love, and they couldn't love me more if they tried."

"Have you met their companions?"

"Yeah."

"And how was that for you?"

"It was aight," he said tight-lipped.

"Did you have an issue with your mother's previous boyfriend?" Dr. Parsons asked.

"I was a child. And Crane is family." Daniel looked out the window into the traffic.

"How do you feel about sharing your family now? With these men?"

Daniel's head whipped around to the therapist, "I know they love me. I believe they would never abandon me."

"You remember your affirmations," Dr. Parsons nodded.

"Yeah," Daniel sighed.

"And you repeat them daily?"

"No." Daniel looked at his feet.

"Are you dating?"

His mind flashed to Asha. His eyes went back toward the window. "Yeah."

"The same woman from the last time we met?"

"No, not her." Daniel fidgeted with his watch.

Dr. Parsons paused. "Are you having multiple casual encounters again?"

"Just one person, now," Daniel admitted.

"And how do you feel when you're with this one woman?"

Daniel blew imaginary smoke out of puffed cheeks.

"Daniel?"

"Most of the time, I feel like I'm enough."

"You can repeat that if you need to."

"I feel like I'm...enough."

He picked up the phone. He was ready to text her back.

Daniel: hey. dinner next week?

*Asha: yes *kissy lips emoji**

Ghetto News Network

The scantily clad bottle service girl crowded Daniel's space. She set up the bottles of champagne and carafes of orange juice with her ass propped up and poked out in Daniel's direction.

"I can't get no play when this mothafucka come through," Bulldog approached Daniel in the VIP section.

"That's how you treat your guests, yo?" Daniel gave him a dap. "Congrats on the salon, fam."

"Thank you, thank you. Shout to my sister, but I had to do my own thing. But I ain't seen you in a minute. I thought I'd see you at the Y's block party."

"Nah, I was out east that weekend." Daniel poured champagne into the flute.

"Oh word? This nigga stay in some exclusive shit," Bulldog teased him.

Daniel laughed at Bulldog's assumptions. He either pegged Daniel as a pimp or some type of socialite. "Nah, just a lil somethin' in the Hamptons," he told him.

"Oh, that nigga Kariem shit?" Bulldog asked.

"Yeah, my first time out there. Shorty invited me. Kariem is her cousin."

"Oh, lil dime with the cat eyes? She be with that wannabe modeling chick. Dark skin, cute in the face. Carmen or some shit."

"Uh, yeah her friend Cleo." Daniel corrected him.

"Yeah, I seen them at Backstage. My man had an after party for the tourney."

"Oh word? Small world." Daniel's stomach jumped.

"Yeah, shorty was with my man, Blast."

"Cleo?"

"Nah cat eye shorty. Nigga had her hemmed up in the vestibule, son." Bulldog laughed.

"Word?" Daniel laughed in spite of himself.

"Facts. Some of us gotta get in where we fit in, my G."

Daniel nodded, but his mind was reeling. Backstage. Afterparty. Blast. Hemmed up. Vestibule. So on top of the multiple trainers pawing at her every week, she was fucking some bootleg small forward?

"Shorty aight, though. I know she be killin' niggas with them eyes son." Bulldog went on.

"She aight," Daniel murmured.

He often wondered what she was doing when they weren't together. On the rare occasion when he broached the subject, it blew up in his face. But they were together a lot. At least, in his mind. Twice during the week and usually some part of the weekend. They had a natural chemistry and a good time together. That should have been all that mattered. But it wasn't. Of course the sex was a big part of it. But he could pretty much get sex anywhere and at any time really.

He didn't know Blast personally. He knew he was an up-and-coming basketball phenom who ended up overseas. Theirs was a small town, of course he would run into someone she knew. Or was currently knowing. She insisted they didn't have a definition, and he didn't have a right to be upset.

"I see you finally made it to flyer status, Lemuel," Cleo said. She crept into the section seemingly out of nowhere.

"Speak of the devil, the she-devil that is," Bulldog teased. He gave a sly grin and looked Cleo's long, brown physique up and down.

"Hey Daniel," Cleo cooed.

"Sup, Cleo," Daniel returned weakly.

He quickly scanned the area for Asha. He hoped not to see her and hoped she would be there at the same time. His emotional jambalaya made his stomach queasy. If she was here, he would deal with it. If she wasn't, he would get a message to her.

Mimosas & Messages

"Hey Cle, what's up?" Asha picked up her phone on the first ring.

"So guess who I saw at Milled Out Mimosas?" Cleo dove right in without a greeting.

"At what now?"

"At Milled Out Mimosas' Hustle Hard Heavyweights and Boss Bitches Brunch." Cleo rattled off.

"Why would you go to something called that?" Asha laughed.

"The entrepreneurs brunch, Asha."

"Ugh, who names these events?"

"Asha!"

"Ok, ok. Who did you see now? You're always seeing somebody," Asha sighed.

"You'd want to know about this somebody."

"Don't tell me Blast again."

"Guess again."

"Khalil?" Asha guessed.

"Now you know Khalil ain't no entrepreneur. He ain't got no business." They both laughed. "Poor thing, it's not his fault," Asha said.

"He better start slanging that eggplant. That might be all he got goin' for him. Find him a cougar that want some of that young..." Cleo waxed on.

"CLEO!" Asha yelled.

"I'm just sayin' girl."

Cleo always took it further than it needed to go. Especially when it came to men and sex. If they weren't best friends, Asha would have told her having sex with lots of different men makes you a couple of things. It certainly didn't make you an expert though.

"Who was it then?" Asha asked.

"Your ol' chocolate bar boo," Cleo said.

Asha paused, "Daniel?"

"Yes girl, unless you got another one I don't know about."

"Oh," Asha stuttered," ok."

"Ok? I thought you guys were going steady," Cleo teased.

"Nah, we're cool," Asha lied.

"What does that mean?" Cleo inquired.

"It means we're cool, Cleo." Asha answered.

She was relieved Daniel finally responded to her text. She was still uneasy about the status between them but felt hope in their impending date.

"Mmmmm, that's not what he said," Cleo told her.

"Wait, what?" Asha panicked. She'd just text him yesterday, and all seemed right with the world.

She still didn't know why he blew up about her gym, but she gave him space to be upset. She used the time away from him to catch her breath. She'd be sexing him down like crazy and felt herself drowning in the chocolate chasm. It was becoming increasingly difficult to keep a safe emotional distance from him in spite of Brickhouse.

Brickhouse didn't exist when they walked the boardwalk late at night. Brickhouse meant nothing when they bet oral favors on the killer's identity in a crime drama. Brickhouse's pictures were the last thing on her mind when he let her win in Halo. Brickhouse was a non-factor when he bought ice cream for her and all the kids they skipped on line at Johnny's Good Humor ice cream truck. Brickhouse was nonexistent when he cooked braised oxtails shirtless in her kitchen.

Quipped with the knowledge of Brickhouse and other imagined whores of that ilk, she should have been more careful with her heart. Now, this.

"He was talkin' to that old dogface, Lemuel."

"Bulldog?"

"Yeah, that fool done opened a beauty salon. He was one of the honorees. Not sure why Daniel was there. What does he do again?" Cleo asked.

Asha grew annoyed. "What were YOU doing there, Cleo? You're one step above Khalil. Now what did he say?"

Cleo held the phone away from her face. "Ooh girl, you tried it. You on your period or something? Anyways, I asked him what's up with you and my girl?"

"Why would you ask that?" Asha yelled into the phone.

"I wanted to see what he was gonna say. Especially after your fancy birthday dinner. And in front of company. You don't say nothing in front of Bulldog unless you want the whole Peninsula to know. So he was all like, you need to ask your girl that. So I says, 'Well I'm asking you, Special Dark.'"

"You did not say that." Asha covered her face with her hand.

"I sure the hell did," Cleo said.

"And?" Asha pressed.

"So his black ass says, 'Tell your girl to call me when her gym membership expires, and her draft picks are over.' Then he just walks away. What the hell is that about?"

Asha's armpits started to sweat. That goddamn ghetto roving reporter, Bulldog. Always running his mouth. No wonder he opened a salon; it's right up his gossiping alley. She remembered seeing him at the afterparty but only briefly. She cursed to herself. She should've stayed her ass home. She collected herself.

"Girl, I don't know what he's talking about. I'll catch up with him later. As a matter of fact, let me go. I have some errands to run." She hurried Cleo off the phone.

"Mmm hmmm, handle your scandal," Cleo told her.

The Pop-In

She put her car in park. She hadn't heard from him since the day of the entrepreneur's brunch, which was over a week ago. She went through his social media accounts. Nothing out of the ordinary. No sickness or travels. He was definitely avoiding her. She looked at the clock; an hour had passed. She had only expected to wait for about 15 minutes. She was stalling. She assumed he was home by now. It was a Wednesday. He didn't check in at the gym or anywhere else. She crossed her fingers that he would be there. She crossed her toes that he would let her in.

Daniel checked on the lasagna. He waited all day to come home and stuff his craw with his mother's recipe. Her lasagna was only second best to her linguine with clam sauce. Daniel thought back to the night Asha sat at his breakfast bar eating linguine. She seemed so genuine that night. And every other night up until he discovered the truth about her. He didn't want to rehash the events in his mind. Lately, it seemed as if he had no control over his mind or emotions when it came to her. Was he being jerked all this time? He was reminded they never had a definition. And that was at her request.

He struggled to remember a time in his adult life when a woman did not want to claim him. She never attempted. The closest to an attempt was meeting her family in the Hamptons. He usually found a way out of meeting women's families. He was surprised to meet hers that day, but it also made him feel—well, he didn't have a name for that feeling.

The timer on his oven went off, and his mouth watered. As he set the pan on the stove, his phone buzzed.

Jennifer: Hey zaddy.

He'd been distant with Jennifer. All this time, he could have been sampling what she was desperately trying to feed him. He replied to her.

Daniel: What's good? Where you been?

He knew exactly where she'd been. At Neiman Marcus waiting for him to accept her invitation. He grabbed a bottle of water out the fridge and sat down to his plate of lasagna. No veggies or salad. His tastebud's only focus would be the pleasure of the pasta, cheese and meat sauce. His phone buzzed again.

Asha: Hey.

He dropped his fork and looked at his plate of food as his stomach knotted. *Great*, he thought.

Jennifer: I should ask you that question. What's up for Friday night?

He switched back to Asha's text and stared at it.

He switched back to Jennifer.

Daniel: You tell me.

His stomach was still irritated, but he pressed on with his lasagna. He'd deal with the consequences in the bathroom later. He managed to finish his meal and dragged his stuffed stomach over to the couch. He considered Jennifer. Blowing off some steam with her might do him some good. He settled in to watch a 90's sitcom rerun though he doubted he would stay awake long enough to make it to the end. A notification from the lobby appeared on his screen, and his phone rang. He wasn't expecting any packages or company, but he picked up anyway. He was prepared to tell the doorman to keep the delivery in the office until tomorrow.

Daniel was learning a little bit of Kreyol thanks to the Haitian doorman. They frequently exchanged common phrases in their respective languages. They were up to women's body parts and what to do with them. Jean Claude was a fast learner.

"Mr. Daniel, Ms. Ashay is here for you. I send her up, yes?" Jean Claude announced.

Daniel's already troublesome stomach flipped. "What?" He couldn't have heard correctly.

"Ehhh, your fwend," Jean Claude whispered into the handset. "The young lady with the eyes like the cats."

"Fuck!" Daniel yelled.

"I send her up fast fast!" Jean Claude grinned into the phone. They'd covered that term last week. Before Daniel could reply, the doorman hung up.

A wave of relief washed over her when she heard the doorman emphatically agree to send her upstairs. Asha stepped into the elevator. She was pissed about the Blast situation, but that was really her own fault. She should've sat her ass down instead of showing up at the party.

She took a deep breath and rang the doorbell. She fidgeted with her nails and inspected her sandals while she waited. She leaned into the door to see if she heard anything. Nothing. She rang the bell again. She looked up and down the hallway, then leaned on the doorjamb. She heard movement and backed off the door.

Daniel opened the door in his usual chill mode uniform of basketball shorts and a wife beater. Her heart still fluttered upon the initial sight of him. She had to get that checked. His eyes were low, and the hallway behind him was dark and smelled of food. Pasta, if her greedy Spidey senses served her right. His chest heaved as he inhaled before speaking to her. She almost got lost in the rise and fall of his pecs.

"What's up?" he said and stood firmly in the doorway.

A cacophony of alarms went off in Asha's head. 'What's up?' He'd never greeted her like that before. The dim lights, smell of food and his stance in the threshold like she was a religious sect crusader. She didn't like it one bit, but he wasn't going to get away from her that fast.

"Hey, I just figured I'd stop by. I hadn't heard from you in a minute. We were supposed to hang out the other day, remember?" she offered as if she never got the message he sent to her via Cleo.

"Oh yeah, my bad," he answered. His face void of remorse. He was unmoved in the doorway, and she could barely see behind him.

Her mind immediately went to Brickhouse. She couldn't help herself, "Is there an issue between us?"

"An issue?" His eyebrow raised, and he held his head back and laughed.

"I'm just asking because I noticed... well... I feel like you've been ignoring me, and I want to know why." She folded her arms in hopes her pseudo ignorance would fly.

He stepped back, halfway opening his apartment door. Asha stepped forward to enter his apartment when he stepped out and closed the door behind him. They almost bumped into each other. He'd only stepped back in to release the slam lock on his door. She struggled to register what had just happened.

"Oh, it's like that?" she asked him.

"You noticed? I thought you were too busy to notice." He looked her up and down ever so quickly, she almost missed it.

"You're kidding right? You don't even know what happened or what didn't happen and you're jumping to conclusions."

"Nah, I don't think I'm jumping to anything."

"Somebody told you what they thought they saw, and you shut down? No call back, text or anything?"

"They thought they saw you dry humping in a doorway? How do you mistake dry humping?"

"What?! I was not...you know what? Nevermind. You made the decision about us before you even spoke to me."

Daniel paused. She was right. He didn't confront her because he felt like a punk. He just wanted to ignore the emotion that was building up inside him. But he was furious and wanted to let her know. "About us?" he gave her a confused look.

She blinked rapidly and stepped back into the wall. She recovered quickly. "Right, I forgot. No such thing," she stated sarcastically. "Bye, Daniel." She walked toward the elevator.

"That was your choice," he yelled to her back.

He watched her from down the hall as she waited for the elevator. She looked down the hall. She was too far away for him to see the tears welling up in her eyes. The elevator door opened, and she gave him the finger. Daniel ran his hand down his face and went back inside his apartment. His stomach burned, and he knew it wasn't the lasagna.

Blast's Reprise

Asha closed, locked and wall-slid down the door.

"Fuck!" she sighed.

"Meooow," Biggie sounded and strolled over to her.

"Biggie, why didn't you stop me?" She pet her large maine coon.

"Meoooow," Biggie answered. Biggie cared nothing about her problems. He made his warm, furry body comfortable on her feet.

"Get off me, fatso." She scooted him away and got up. He shot her a look of feline judgment. "Oh shut up," she answered his haughty glare. Asha tried a cleansing breath as she opened a can of cat food. Tupac appeared behind Biggie in answer to the can opener's call.

She leaned against the kitchen counter and watched her cats devour the food. She was having another bout of whore's remorse.

Blast's pop-in caught her off guard. Why did she open the door? Why did she let him in? Why did she let him in, again? She could have said she was wallowing in self-pity after the break-up. But since they weren't an item, she didn't have a definition for why she did what she did. She didn't dare reach out to him, for fear of rejection and the notion of having been replaced.

She just wanted to snuggle up on her couch and watch TV. She was knee deep into chips and dip and a "CSI Miami" marathon when the doorbell rang. When she looked out the peephole, her first thought was to walk right back to the couch and pretend she wasn't at home. She should've followed her first mind, as AJ always told her. For whatever reason, she opened the door. She opened the door to a lot of things that night. Mixed emotions, familiar feelings and sentimental memories. It was only after she opened herself up to Blast that she realized she should have known better.

Miraculously, he remembered where she lived. Funny, he couldn't recall her address for the last year and a half. She banged her hand on the counter in frustration. Tupac jumped. Biggie continued eating. "Sorry 'Pac," she apologized. She headed to the bathroom to wash off last night's memory. The bathroom mirror told the story of her frazzled hair, puffy eyes, sad mouth and two love marks on her neck and upper chest. "FUCK!" she screamed.

Asha stepped into the hottest shower she could stand. She hoped to scald away last night's event.

Magic Wok

"Ayo, H, you wanna get in on this order?" Junior Tech yelled to Daniel.

"Nah," Daniel mumbled.

"Oh, I forgot you be eatin' that gourmet shit for lunch," Junior Tech teased.

He always had a comment when Daniel bought lunch to the shop. Sometimes he would stop by Crane's and pick up an order of cocktail patties or codfish fritters for the staff. Other times, he would show up with a three-course meal just for himself.

"Why you ain't bring me none?" Junior Tech would quip in the breakroom as he mowed down his giant hero or pizza slices.

"Cuz your mouth is used to garbage," Daniel would answer. He was not in the mood for Junior Tech's antics. He wasn't in the mood for much of anything these days. He just went through the motions.

He missed her. That was the long and the short of it. He'd been fighting the urge to look at her social media all day but lost the battle after a couple of hours. He told himself he'd delete and block her altogether but hadn't worked up the nerve to do so. He stared at a picture she posted of them a couple weeks ago, surprised she hadn't taken it down.

The one time she dragged him to the beach for a picnic. His insistence that he was black enough without the sun's help didn't suit her. He showed up in a wide brimmed Tilley hat with vodka slushies in hand. She set up their camp with a tent, umbrella, beach chairs and a picnic lunch. She worked hard to make him as comfortable as possible, and he enjoyed a day at the beach for the first time in a long time. The picture showed their legs only. The sun's rays highlighting the butter pecan and chocolate contrast. He didn't remember her snapping a pic. She snuck in a candid. He stared at the pic until Junior Tech jolted him back to reality.

"Yo you got change for a five?" Junior Tech interrupted.

"A five?!" Daniel wasn't sure he heard right.

"Yeah, the Chinese delivery is here."

Daniel walked to the front of the shop where the other mechanics were in a food bill cypher, arguing about who ordered what. Daniel busted up the circle. He approached the delivery man, a young chubby Asian who looked to be barely out of his teens. "How much is the bill?" Daniel asked.

He fumbled with the receipt, "Uh, your total $69.50."

Daniel pulled four $20 bills from his money clip. Delivery Man began to make change with the money in his pocket. "Nah, you good." Daniel handed him the money.

"Thank you, thank you." The delivery man repeated as he walked backwards out of the shop and jumped into his double-parked car.

Daniel snatched the monies out of each of the mechanics' hands. A chorus of *hey*'s and *wait a minute*'s followed. "Cheap motherfuckers, with cheap nigga arithmetic," he barked as he made his rounds. He collected the last of the monies and walked to the back office with his fist full of dollars and slammed the door.

Junior Tech peeked his head around the corner to make sure Daniel was gone. He scurried to Vincent's office. "Mr. Vince." He hung on to the sides of the doorway.

"Yeah, what is it?" Vincent answered, his head buried in his keyboard. "H took everybody's money. He got an attitude problem, yo!" Junior Tech said.

Vincent looked up. "What's that now?"

"H took our money for the food delivery."

"And did what with it?"

"He paid, but he took our money."

Vince stared blankly.

"I mean, we didn't get a chance to count it out or nothin'."

Vincent leaned back in his chair. "I'll talk to him." His face went back to the computer.

"And get our change?"

Vince looked up again. "I pay you enough not to be a pussy about a couple dollars boy." He went back to his keyboard. Junior Tech huffed and left the office.

Vincent walked into the back office where Daniel sat at the desk staring at his phone. The money was on the desk in front of him. "What got stuck in your pisshole?" he asked Daniel.

"Tell Junior Tech to stop being a pussy."

"I did," Vincent said as he sat down. "Now what's going on with you? You been stomping around here all week, yelling at the guys and banging on shit. I don't need your big ass tearing up the shop."

"Nothing, Uncle V. I'm good," Daniel informed him, his face still in his phone.

"I know you not good, boy." Vincent put his feet up on the desk. "Or you don't want to talk to me about it?" Vincent gave his grandnephew a once over, "What your momma say?"

"She said nothing because there's nothing wrong with me." Daniel put the phone down and concentrated on counting the money.

"You still seeing that shrink?" Vincent asked.

Daniel sighed, "Vince I'm fine. I told you."

"Talk to somebody, son. Call up that coconut, Crane. He got to be good for something besides them spicy patties," Vince pressed on before getting up to leave.

"I broke up with Asha," Daniel blurted out.

Vincent sat back down. "So?"

"So?! You ask me what's wrong with me. I tell you and you say 'so'," Daniel exhaled.

"You break up with a girl every week. Usually after they parade through here with their piece of shit cars talking 'bout *Daniel told me to bring my car in*," Vince said in a high-pitched voice and wobbled his head.

"I wasn't serious with them," he said.

"Serious? You just knowing this girl when? June?" Vince asked.

"May," Daniel said.

"Same difference. That ain't shit," Vince told him. Daniel looked down at his work boots. "Ohhh, you was falling for her? She put the hoodoo on you, huh? Hmph," Vince laughed. "That's why I don't trust no light-skin, light-eyed wimmens." Vincent made a face like he smelled something foul. "'Cept your Maw. Now, she alright with me. My brother, God rest his soul, he knew she was a solid woman, just came out on the bright side is all. Now this Aza," Vince asked.

"Asha," Daniel corrected.

"Oh, Asha. She one of them swamp girls? Where her people from?" Vince asked. Daniel remained quiet. "She cute though. I'll give her that." Vincent clasped his fingers behind his head. "But she ain't the baddest thing you ever did bring in here. Memba that one you said she used to pose for them magazines?" Vincent grinned, revealing his huge false teeth. "Ooh wee, that girl was bad," he reminisced.

"Uncle Vincent," Daniel interrupted the walk down memory lane.

Vincent saw the stress in Daniel's face. "Listen boy, maybe she wasn't it. You're young. You got plenty of women still to run through." Vincent's speech wasn't reaching Daniel the way he hoped it would. He took a different approach. "You wanna go to Titties on the Bay with me tonight?"

Daniel laughed, "That's not the name of the club."

"Well, that's what they call it." Vincent thought for a minute, "What's it called then?"

"Bombshell Bay, Uncle Vince." Daniel shook his head.

"Whatever, what the hell do I care." Vincent waved at him in dismissal. "They got a girl there, Trudy. She'll treat you real nice," he offered Daniel.

"Nah, I'm good. But thanks."

"Ok, Youngblood suit yourself. But don't keep wallowing now because it ain't no good for your soul." Vince advised and offered a fist bump before leaving the office.

The visual of Vincent getting a lap dance from one of the skanky strippers at the run-down strip club made Daniel laugh.

Blast Off

Asha pulled into Uncle Rand's driveway behind a strange car. She spoke to AJ just a couple hours earlier, but she didn't mention anything about company. She opened the kitchen door and saw AJ preparing one of her hors d'oeuvre platters. "Hey Asha, you're just in time."

Asha heard chatter coming from the den. "Just in time for what?" she asked.

"Come with me." AJ told her and Asha followed her and the hors d'oeuvre tray.

"I knew they wouldn't make the championship," Rand shouted. Asha stepped into the den to see her uncle, two beer bottles and Blast. She stopped dead in her tracks. "Heeeeey Cupcake, look who's here!" Uncle hugged her. "You didn't tell me Cameron was in town."

If she could've slapped the smug look off of Blast's face, she would've.

"I did ask about you, Mr. Rand. I thought Asha would have passed on the message." Blast took a sip of his beer.

"Um, yeah. It slipped my mind." Asha gave him the evil eye.

"Look at this," Rand showed off a set of golf clubs. "These are Callaways, girl!"

She shot a look at AJ and AJ shrugged. They were both saving up to buy Rand a set of clubs for his birthday.

"You bought my uncle a set of golf clubs?! Why?" Asha was steaming. How dare he pop up at her family's home with an expensive gift at that. AJ tried to diffuse the moment by asking Asha to come with her into the kitchen.

"Actually I won them in a raffle. I already had a set, and I knew Mr. Rand would like them," Blast offered to Asha's back.

"What's the matter with you?" AJ demanded in the kitchen.

"He's a creep, AJ," Asha said.

"That's a beautiful set of clubs. Don't you embarrass your uncle like that," AJ reprimanded.

Asha sat at the kitchen table. She didn't want to discuss this with AJ, but her aunt wouldn't understand her stance if she didn't. "So I ran into him at a party a couple weeks ago and he tried to get at me, but I turned him down," she said.

"Well, he certainly hasn't given up. Coming by here with expensive gifts," AJ noted.

"I ended up giving him some." Asha's head fell back, and she stared up at the ceiling fan.

AJ's left brow raised.

"But it was a one-time deal. I told him it was a mistake. I told him it would never happen again. And, that I would appreciate it if he kept his mouth shut. He's only here now to spite me," Asha exhaled.

"What happened to that nice young man from the BBQ?" AJ asked.

"Nothing happened to him." Asha fidgeted with the paper towel holder.

"Now, Asha." AJ gave her a stern look.

"AJ, nothing happened to him," Asha lied. She prayed this was the last she would see of Blast and slid down into the chair.

Timeline

"Girl."

"What, Cleo?" Asha snapped.

"I need you to get your life."

"Whatever, Cle."

"Like, a case from Costco. The whole thing in its entirety," Cleo continued.

Asha continued to scroll through her phone.

"See, that's what I'm saying. You have an attitude with me. I'm not the one who took the dick out your mouth." Cleo made a pop noise with her lips. "You better call Big Black and snap at *him*." Cleo's neck waved back and forth.

Asha was tired of hearing Cleo's mouth. Truth of the matter was, she was miserable. She lowered her sun hat to cover her face and block Cleo out. They were on Cleo's rooftop sundeck sunning and sipping their Sunday afternoon away. Asha busied herself by painstakingly trolling Daniel's timelines. She didn't find much information as to what or who he was doing lately. He posted the regular fare of car stuff, workouts, food and reposts of his swim class from the Y's page. A couple of posts with his family. His mom and grandmother at brunch. With Germ playing soccer. He didn't even have the courtesy to look miserable in the posts. She guessed he was doing just fine. She came across a recent post of him in the gym. He looked incredible as usual. It was a shot from his lips and beard down to his navel. The angle of the photo told her that it wasn't a selfie. Asha only imagined what thot volunteered to take that pic.

The caption read: *Gettin' the pecs right. Cuffing season around the corner.*

Careful not to double tap, she screenshot the image and poured over its every detail. The mouth that shared with her, laughed with her and electrified her body. The under beard and neck she found comfort in sniffing every time they embraced. The perfect chest she became accustomed to laying her head on. The oblique and abs with nary an ounce of fat to be found. The photo stopped at the end of his Adonis belt, just short of his groin. She felt gypped.

She read the caption again, as if he could improve anything. He basically maintained perfection, while others strived for him on his worst day. *How fucking annoying*, she thought. The longer she looked at it, the more she fumed. She switched back to the app. She hit the comment button: "Maybe you should get a trainer." Post.

She chuckled after she sent it. She looked over at Cleo who was immersed in her own timeline review. "I'm coming off of social media," she declared.

"No, you're not," Cleo answered, not bothering to look up from her phone.

"I'm just tired of people's bullshit."

"Including your own?" Cleo challenged her.

Asha was quiet.

"What happened, now?" Cleo put her phone down and turned in Asha's direction.

"Nothing," Asha pouted.

"I know you ain't trolling. I taught you better than that."

"Please, I ain't thinking about..." Asha's phone lit up and a fire alarm ringtone sounded. She dropped it like a hot potato and jumped out of her lounge chair. "Oh my God. Oh my God," Asha cried out.

"What?? What is it?" Cleo looked at the phone's screen that read *King Kong.* "Who the fuck is...Ohhh," Cleo's eyes widened. "Well answer the damn thing." She reached for the phone.

Asha slapped Cleo's hand away. "No, don't answer it." The

phone finally stopped ringing. Asha's antics caused the other sun worshippers on the roof to look in their direction.

"Girl, don't you go alarming these white people. I paid good money to live here," Cleo scolded.

Asha laughed at herself. "I commented on one of his posts," she confessed. Asha then proceeded to show Cleo the post on her phone.

Cleo gasped, "Oooh bitch, you petty."

"Me?" Asha recoiled.

"He's the one posting about cuffing season. Fuck him!" Asha's phone went off again. They looked at each other, then at the phone and back at each other again.

"Just answer it, Asha. Don't be a punk ass," Cleo dared her.

"Hello?" she answered as nonchalantly as she could.

"You got jokes," Daniel said.

"I'm sorry?" she asked innocently. Cleo snickered in her chair and sipped her drink.

"You real funny," Daniel told her.

"Who is this?" she inquired sincerely.

Cleo put her hand over her mouth and laughed into her palm.

Daniel laughed so loudly that Asha had to pull the phone away from ear.

"Oh, your contacts is lit?" he asked her.

"Daniel?" she pretended to be unsure.

"Nah," he paused. "This is King Kong."

Asha's mouth fell open, and she tried not to laugh.

"Yeah," he said as if he could see her face. "Meet me at Applebee's at 5 o'clock."

"Excuse me?" she sneered. Meet him somewhere? How dare he! He wouldn't even let her into his apartment a couple weeks ago.

"You heard me," he told her. She expected to be cursed out. His demand for her to meet him turned her on just a little.

"I'm...I mean, I'm busy," she lied.

"No you're not. I'll see you at 5," he said and hung up.

Asha gasped and looked at her phone in disbelief. "Ugh! This nig—" She looked around her. "This dude got nerve," she told Cleo.

"What did he say?"

"He tells me... didn't ask me, to meet him at Applebee's in like two hours," Asha explained.

"Ok?" Cleo said, reaching for her bag of kettle chips.

"Ok, nothing. He's got balls."

"You should know." Cleo crunched her chips.

Asha resumed her position on her lounge chair. She popped back out of her chair. "How dare he. If I hadn't commented on his post, he wouldn't be calling. He just assumes," she waved her hands in the air, "that I'm not doing anything."

"Weellll." Cleo looked at her manicure.

"Well, what?" Asha asked nervously.

"I kinda checked you in with me," Cleo said quickly.

"Oh fuck, Cleo," Asha sighed.

"I thought you saw it. You've been on your phone all day." Cleo showed Asha the caption. It was the collage of their drinks with Asha's sun hat covering most of her face and Cleo only showing her legs: *Lazy Sunday with my chica.*

"Are you gonna go?" Cleo asked.

"Fuck him," Asha said.

"Yeah, you should," Cleo told her.

She turned to Cleo and asked, "You think I should go?"

"Yeah, go. And fuck him, too." Cleo took a sip of her drink.

Asha sighed and looked at the time on her phone. She had two and a half hours to decide whether she would show up at Applebee's.

Summer Clearance

Asha pulled into the parking lot of the Five Towns' Applebee's at 4:50 p.m. She hoped she would hit traffic and be fashionably late. She looked at her phone. Cleo had text her.

*Cleo: *bomb emojis**

Asha: wth?

Cleo: you get summoned to Applebee's on a Sunday evening. It's about to go down LOL

Asha put her phone to sleep and threw it in her bag. She pulled down the sun visor and checked herself out in the mirror. She looked ok, just a little sunburnt from falling asleep on Cleo's roofdeck. She piled her hair up in a sloppy bun atop of her head. "Fuck it," she sighed and got out the car. She didn't know what would become of this meeting. Maybe he'd apologize. Maybe he'd try to get one last romp in. Whatever the outcome, she wanted to get it over with.

She saw him stand up from his seat at a booth as she arrived at the hostess podium.

"What's up?" she greeted him dryly.

He wore a loose-fitting muscle tank, summer sweats and slides with socks. The open sides of the white tank was a window to the chocolate wonderland of his torso and back. The sweatpants were a whole other level of unfairness. With the slightest motion or arbitrary breeze, the fluid heather gray fabric would show her what she'd been missing. Thank goodness he was standing still. She fought to keep her eyes on his face.

"Sup," he returned. They sat across from each other and looked out the window to the parking lot. She was the first to turn her attention to their table and speak.

"So?" she raised her eyebrow.

"So," he answered flatly.

His intestines cornrowed themselves together since her comment on his post. He didn't expect something like that from her. Then again, he didn't expect her to be making out in public with another man either. But still, he took the chance and called her. And since she eventually answered the phone and subsequently didn't hang up on him, he was confident she would show. Nigga logic, is what Uncle Vincent would call his presumption.

"You're the one who invited me here. Well summoned me, actually. Behind a picture comment at that," she huffed.

He leaned back in the booth and stretched his legs out. His knee accidentally brushed up against hers. He saw a familiar flicker in her eyes when their bodies momentarily touched. "You got jokes," he said to her.

"You said that already." She looked at her nails.

He never saw this flippant and dismissive side of her. "I'm surprised you showed," he lied. "I didn't think your boyfriend would let you out."

She looked up from her nails. He couldn't have known about her encounter with Blast. The real encounter, not his imagined faux pas. *Could he? No,* she thought, *he was here to play games.*

A busboy approached their table with two glasses of water.

She leaned in and smiled at him, "Now you know I don't have a boyfriend."

"Right, right. I forgot you were out there," he nodded.

Embarrassed and hoping the busboy didn't overhear their exchange she recoiled, "What does that mean?"

His eyes under thick luxurious eyebrows went dark.

During their time together, she'd become familiar with the seasonal language of his ebony eyes. Summer when they were smiling with laughter or surprise. Spring when they were bright with interest in what she was saying. And fall when their lids were low and focused on responding to what her body's language was saying to him. She'd only seen a glimpse of winter, which was during the Uber ordeal. She'd hope to never experience that season again. But here it was.

"If you had a man, you should have just told me. I wouldn't have been crowding you like that," he told her.

"I just told you I don't have a man. Never said I wanted one." Her mind flashed to the pictures of him and Brickhouse. He had nerve asking about whether she had a man when he never mentioned that amazon bitch.

"True, you never tried to make me your man. We never labeled whatever this was, and that's cool."

Asha squinted. "Listen, we spent almost the entire summer together. We had fun. But it seems like you want a label. What would you label it then?"

The label bullshit and showing up at the tourney party was her fault really. If not for her bad decisions, they could have been laid up on this Sunday evening. But what was done was done. He wasn't going to get away with badgering her about it.

"Nah, I don't need a label." He said. "We weren't exclusive, that's cool," he repeated. Although he kept saying it was cool, his energy was saying different.

"For the record, I wasn't with anybody else while I was with you," he told her. That had to count for something.

"Oh, really? That's news." She couldn't believe he was pulling this mess.

"Excuse me?" His thick brows met, and he leaned into the table.

"I never asked who all those women were that we ran into every time we went out. Every single time we went out." Her eyes widened. She looked around the restaurant. "Shit, I'm surprised you haven't run into anybody here yet."

"You're mad because I know a lot of people?" he laughed.

She took her phone out of her bag. "I never asked who this bitch was." She showed him the picture of him ogling Brickhouse's ass at the white party. She purposely went back and found the picture after he called her today. Just in case he tried to play the fool.

He looked closely at the picture. He was wasted, and Diamond took that opportunity to put on a production at the party.

"You're kidding, right?" he asked her.

"No, I'm pretty serious. And you never volunteered the info, either," Asha added for effect.

His eyes got small, and his voice took a tone she never heard before. "Diamond is nothing to me. We dated, and then we broke up."

"Oh, Diiiiamond," she motorboated. "You look like you would date a Diamond." She threw up exaggerated air quotes. "When? When was this break up?" Her lips pursed to the side in disbelief.

Daniel's memory queued up the session in the YMCA basement. He blinked it out of his head.

"Diamond and I went our separate ways shortly after I met you. In fact, she's engaged now."

"How convenient." She gave a smug smile.

Daniel put his clasped hands on the table, just then, the waitress came over to their table. "Hi, I'm Lisa. I'll be your server."

"Can you give us a minute?" Daniel said sharply without taking his eyes off Asha. Lisa disappeared.

"So, because you find an old picture of me drunk at a party, you let a washed overseas baller fingerfuck you in the doorway?" he hissed. "If that's what you were about, you shoulda told me." He reclined in the booth, "I wouldn't have wasted your time with formalities like dates and shit."

His candor and vulgar language sent a chill through her. He never spoke to her that way before. Her jaw dropped, and she fought back

307

the wetness in her eyes. She stared back at him. "I already told you he didn't fingerfuck me in the doorway, Daniel."

His eyes searched hers. "He fucked me with his dick in my bedroom." She took an unbothered sip of her water.

He was just going through the motions with her but praying for a glimmer of hope between them. He'd fallen prey to Diamond's wiles during he and Asha's...whatever this was. But he was successful in eluding Jennifer's grasp. He found that all his mindspace was occupied with Asha.

She was right. They'd been together practically all summer. He scanned his mental calendar. In spite of his accusation, he couldn't figure out when she would have had time to be with someone else. He reflected to the condoms he found at her place the night of the blackout. The early morning departures she insisted on. Then there were the trainers she raved about. Maybe she wasn't just messing with his mind when she talked about how they handled her body. His mind ran its adding machine, and his stomach turned. He regretted calling her here to meet him.

Asha looked at him over the rim of her water glass. His eyes were vacant, and the muscles in his jaw flexed. Finally, he blinked.

Daniel snatched the glass from her hand and threw it across the restaurant, and Asha screamed. The glass shattered against a wall, sending neighborhood memorabilia crashing to the ground. Other customers looked in their direction. Daniel swept his massive arm across the table and sent the condiment basket and menus flying. He slid out the booth and stood over her. His eyes reduced to slits, and his chest heaved.

Asha cowered, and his eyes held her frozen in her seat.

Lisa, their phantom server, signaled for the hostess to dial 911. The pale overweight manager and the tall thin assistant manager both pushed each other over to where Daniel stood. Neither one of them wanted to go up against this large, obviously upset man.

"Sir!" the manager called to Daniel from three feet away. "Sir, we're gonna have to ask you to leave."

Daniel heard nothing and saw nothing else but Asha as she sat below him crying. He shook his head ever so slightly. The restaurant fell quiet from its initial gasps and *Oh my God*'s.

"Sir!" the manager yelled again, snapping Daniel out of his blind fury. He looked up to see the entire restaurant looking at him. Two Nassau County Police Department officers entered the restaurant with firearms drawn. Daniel suddenly became aware of what was happening. He raised his hands in the air and looked straight ahead. The middle-aged officer of Indian descent whispered to the young white officer. He then yelled to Daniel, "Keep your hands up!"

The Indian officer slowly approached Daniel while his service revolver was still drawn. Daniel watched as the gun's muzzle got closer and closer to him. His mind whirled with images of Maw, Mavis and Beverly. "Oh my God, no!" he heard Asha's voice. Daniel inhaled what he believed to be his last breath.

The officer stood arm's-length from Daniel. "Sir, I'm going to cuff you, and we're going to talk outside." Daniel nodded and the officer moved behind him, pulled his arms behind his back and secured the handcuffs. As Daniel was led out of the restaurant, the crowd cheered and hissed.

Asha was still frozen in her seat with tears rolling down her face. The manager, hostess and Lisa, the server, came over to the booth. "Miss, are you ok?" the manager asked her, his face coated with sweat.

"Yeah, I'm fine," she said as she exhaled.

"This officer is going to assist you with pressing charges," he told her, referring to the second officer that remained in the restaurant.

"No," Asha said. "I don't want to press charges."

The waitress and hostess exchanged a look. "Miss, it's ok. It's not right for him to treat you that way," the manager offered.

"Thank you, but I'm fine," she exhaled shakily.

"The officer can give you a ride to a safe place," he told Asha.

"No, I'm ok." She wiped her face. The hostess and server walked away but not before Asha overheard their conversation.

"These niggas is crazy nowadays girl," the hostess said.

"Yeah, I know. But did you see him? He fine as fuck," the server added.

The officer walked Daniel to the squad car in the rear of the parking lot and instructed him to stand next to the driver's side door. He stood in front of him and crossed his arms. "You is Ms. Jacob's grandson," he said to Daniel in a Guyanese lilt. Daniel thought his stomach would fall out of his ass at the mention of Maw's name. "She was my dean in high school," the officer continued. Daniel's legs were weak from the thought of Maw getting wind of this. He leaned his weight on the squad car to avoid his legs giving from under him. "What happened in there?" the officer asked him.

"I lost it," Daniel said. "I didn't hit her though. I swear."

The officer nodded. "No gul ent worth it, buddy."

"I know," Daniel agreed, his limbs limp as spaghetti.

"My partner in there have the potential to be a good cop. But he scared, yuh hear what I say? And that fear does turn into men like us DEAD," the officer yelled into Daniel's face. Daniel blinked. "I know Ms. Jacobs ent raise you to tun fool in the street. But yu bruk up the people ting," he nodded back toward the restaurant, "is a desk appearance. Charges coulda be worse."

"Thank you," Daniel said. Relief washed over his face.

"You have somebody to come and pick up your car?" the officer asked.

The first person that came to mind for him to call was Germ, so he replied, "Yes."

"You have a lawyer?" the officer asked him.

Daniel's mind immediately dismissed their family attorney. He couldn't possibly call him. He remembered Mr. Bernard. *Fuck*, he thought. "Yeah," he said.

The officer guided Daniel's head into the squad car.

His stomach was on fire and head spinning. He'd gotten himself arrested. As if that wasn't enough, his inability to control himself ran him the risk of getting killed by a nervous rookie. In spite of all of what just had happened, he scanned the parking lot for her car as the squad car pulled off.

VS Auto Collision Group Revisited

Asha wasn't able to eat or sleep properly in the days since the Applebee's incident. She was either laid up in bed or camped out on her couch when she wasn't at work. Both AJ and Cleo stopped by with food to try and get her to eat, but the containers only ended up in the refrigerator. She'd avoided social media and binged on crime dramas. She received notifications but ignored them until Cleo tagged her in a sentimental post about sisterhood. Even the simple task of liking the post took a lot out of her. She put her phone on the floor next to the couch, and immediately picked it up again. Against her better judgment, she went to his timeline. Surprisingly and fortunately, he hadn't deleted her yet. His most recent post was a check in at a hotel in South Beach with the hashtag #NATES2016. She couldn't believe her eyes. Here she was wallowing, and he was chilling in Miami. Talk about speedy recovery, or maybe he had nothing to recover from.

Business my ass, she thought. She recalled him mentioning a business trip earlier in the summer. She laughed at Cleo's reaction to his business trip. "Business? In Miami? What business he got in Miami?" Cleo scoffed.

"I don't know, Cleo. I don't get in his affairs like that." Asha blew it off.

"What is it like a motor oil meeting? Fuck they gonna be doing? Changing tires all day?" Cleo guffawed.

Out of curiosity, Asha clicked on the hashtag. The hashtag resulted in over 2,500 posts. It looked to be a convention. A pretty large one at that. She poked around the pictures and gathered that it was in fact an automotive event. She Googled the convention name and discovered it was one of the nation's largest automotive technicians and engineer societies. *Well, good for him*, she thought.

She told him she was feeling stuck in her current position at work during one of the few weekend mornings she spent in bed with him. He encouraged her and told her to do something about it sooner than later, but never did he mention anything about advancing his own career. *The convention showed initiative*, she thought. Perhaps his uncle would give him more responsibilities at the shop. In spite of what happened between them, she was happy to see that he was taking steps to improve himself.

She went back to the hashtag results and scrolled through posts. Mostly men at convention booths showing off swag like pens, bags and hats. A couple of business suits posed in front of promotional banners showing off awards. Lots of pictures of auto part demonstrations and products. She kept scrolling until something caught her eye. Something big, dark and handsome. She clicked on the post. It was a photo of Daniel surrounded by a group of men of varying ages and ethnicities. She read the caption: *Great technical session on fuel injection and thrust lubrication strategies with co-chair, Daniel Jacobs, of VS Auto, Lawrence, NY.*

Asha almost fell off the couch. She was too stunned to dwell on the title of the session; she'd save that for bedtime. He was the co-chair of a workshop of a national society's convention? She kept scrolling and found that the picture had been reposted by several profiles:

BMW of Freeport: Congrats to former lube tech Daniel Jacobs at NATES2016
Mercedes Benz of Rockville Centre: Benz Alum Diesel DJ at NATES2016
Paragon Acura: NATES2016 Acura Fellow Diesel Daniel Jacobs

Co-chair? When did he have time to be involved in such a thing?

She once co-chaired a Police Athletic League Arts and Crafts event for 7-year-olds at the insistence of her uncle. She almost died, and all she had to do was make a Michael's run for crayons and glue. She stared at the picture. He towered over most of the men, smiling that smile through the eye of cellphone camera lens and into her face. *Beautiful Daniel.* She didn't know if he looked different or if she was seeing him in a different light. But he'd never shared anything about his work with her. Other than *I'm going to work, I'm at work* or *coming from work.* And he worked two jobs, so she never knew whether he was referring to the auto shop or the Y.

She opened her search engine and entered *Daniel Jacobs, Lawrence NY.* She took a deep breath before clicking the magnifying glass icon.

The first result was his LinkedIn. LinkedIn was the furthest site from her mind when she thought of Daniel.

Daniel Jacobs

VS Auto Collision Group, Partner.

Her marble eyes almost fell out of her head.

Partner? He told her it was his uncle's shop. The sign said VS Auto. There was no D, nor J. She kept scrolling.

Education:

Masters of Science in Automotive Engineering

Bachelor of Business Administration in Automotive Technology

Wayment, she thought out loud.

Certifications:

Industrial Technology and Management

ASE Master Certified Technician

Certified Mercedes Benz Master Technician

"Is he serious?" she said to her phone.

Memberships/Organizations:

National Automotive Technician and Engineer Society
USA AAU Swimming Instructor
American Red Cross Certified Lifeguard
YMCA Rockaway STEM Kidz Mentor

He said he taught swimming at the Y to stay in shape. And worked the STEM program as a favor.

Shore Art Gallery Trustee
NYPD Man Up Mentoring Program Alumni

Asha poured over his accomplishments. He never mentioned a word about any of it. Just as she began to feel cheated, she paused when the thought came to her. Did she ask? Did she ever ask him anything about his interests, goals and accomplishments? She never asked him how he knew what he knew. Her memory of their conversation on the boardwalk slapped her in the face.

V

Dollar Van

Bye Beverly

Daniel walked into his mother's home.

"Mavis Ann, they didn't have grated coconut. You gonna have to mess up your manicure," he yelled into the foyer.

Mavis had everything set up on her dining room table for them to make Maw's famous gizzadas. They made the Caribbean coconut pastry together since he could remember.

He found Mavis sitting at the kitchen table with her face in her hands. She removed her hands when she heard Daniel's footsteps. Her eye makeup slid down her face.

"What happened?!" he said in a panic.

Mavis shook her head. He knelt down next to his mom.

"Beverly," she whimpered.

"What now? I'm not sitting through another dinner. Especially now that I know..." he went on.

"Daniel," Mavis said.

He stopped talking when she said his name.

"She died this morning," Mavis said.

Daniel's bent knees gave from under him and landed him on the floor.

That was the last thing he expected to hear. Today or ever. He told himself he never wanted to see her again, but he wanted to make that decision. Now it had been made for him.

"What, what happened?" he asked.

"Complications from cirrhosis," Mavis told him.

"But, she told me she stopped drinking." Daniel recalled her declaration of sobriety.

"She recently stopped, but she drank for a long time, Hersh. She was hard on herself and never really learned how to work through things until it was too late." Mavis heaved and tears fell from her eyes. Daniel watched his mother cry for her friend. He didn't know what he felt. Grief, guilt, relief, shock. Maybe all. He moved closer and hugged her.

"I'm so glad you got to see her, Hershey," Mavis spoke into their embrace.

He'd been so mean to Beverly that night. "Mom, I..." his voice trailed off. He rarely ever addressed her as mom. She never objected to being called by her name when he was a child; she was just so happy to have him. *Mom* was usually reserved for crisis. When his goldfish died. When Maw had heart surgery. The first time Beverly visited.

Mavis looked into her son's eyes. "I know, honey. She told me." He hung his head in shame. "It's ok, love. She was just glad to have the chance to talk to you."

"Did you know? Did you know she was dying?" he remembered Mavis's insistence and extra preparation for the dinner party.

"I knew she wasn't well. I didn't think she would go this quickly." Mavis eyes watered again.

"Why didn't you tell me? If I knew she was dying..." Daniel started down the road of regret.

"She asked me not to tell you. She begged me. I had to keep her trust," Mavis confessed.

"You've always done that for her." He looked at his mother under a saint's halo. Mavis smiled through her tears, "Yes. I'm blessed to have helped my friend."

Stop & Shop

When Asha finally resumed eating, she continued eating clean. Her only complaint was how expensive this lifestyle was. And how often she found herself at the farmer's market or supermarket. She picked up a cantaloupe and sniffed it. She shook it, then squeezed the top to check its firmness. Satisfied with its ripeness, she placed it in the cart and moved on to the vegetables. She gathered a medley of greens and made her way to the checkout line. The woman in front of her was digging frantically in her bag and mumbling to herself. "Dammit," the woman exclaimed and stomped her foot. She turned to walk off the checkout line and bumped right into Asha, whose face was buried in her phone. "Oh, I'm so sorry! Excuse me," the woman said.

Asha looked up from her phone into Mavis's face. "Ms. Mavis?" Asha asked caught off guard.

"Asha, how are you?" She offered her a hug. "I apologize, honey. Looks like I forgot my wallet in my other bag." She tried to squeeze by Asha to get off the line. The conveyor belt held about twenty dollars worth of items.

"That's ok, I can cover it for you" she motioned for the cashier to ring up Mavis's things.

Mavis didn't seem like the well put together woman she'd previously met. This time, she was dressed in a t-shirt, leggings and flip flops.

"Oh, Asha! Thank you so much. I'll have Hersh pay you back. I don't know where my head is these days," Mavis exhaled.

"Don't worry about it. It's my pleasure," Asha handed the cashier her card, "besides Daniel and I... well let's just say he's not accepting my phone calls." Asha gave a weak smile.

Mavis grabbed her bag from the carousel. "Oh? He hadn't mentioned that to me," Mavis' eyebrows raised. "And I asked for you just recently. We had a small barbeque, just a few family and friends. He said you were *otherwise engaged*." Mavis made air quotes.

Asha's cheeks flushed as they exited the store. "Daniel meant a lot to me. I know it was only a short time." She threw her reusable shopping bag over her shoulder.

"I can tell you were important to him, too. He doesn't bring many women around." Mavis looked out into the parking lot where Maw was waiting in the car. That nugget of info made Asha feel both better and worse.

"Ms. Mavis," Asha blinked rapidly, "I was with another guy." Mavis' eyes widened. "I'm sorry. I don't even know why I'm telling you this. It was a mistake, but I think I was falling too hard and too fast for Daniel. I just tried to counter it. I know it sounds dumb." She looked at her feet.

Mavis put her hand on Asha's shoulder. "We all have been caught up in situations we never thought we'd be in." Mavis thought of her own botched abortion and the severe consequences that followed— a mistake that stopped her from having children of her own. Asha hung her head, grateful for Mavis' understanding.

"We had a death in the family," Mavis said. Asha's eyes widened and immediately went to Daniel's grandmother. "A close relative and Daniel is not dealing well with it. My mother and I are doing the best we can, but I think it would be good for him to see you," Mavis said.

"Oh no, I doubt seeing me would help." Asha shook her head.

"Asha, I know my son. Seeing you would do him good." Mavis

hoped her interference wouldn't backfire on her.

Asha felt a beam of hope, "When is the service? I'll try to be there Ms. Mavis."

Mavis gave her another hug. Asha felt a familiar warmness in her embrace.

She watched as Mavis walked to her car. Asha felt a mustard seed of hope at the thought of seeing Daniel, despite the circumstances.

Mavis flopped down into the driver's seat. "What happened? They had to grow the yams in the back?" Maw joked.

"Oh, Maw," Mavis looked up and out of the sunroof, "I went in that store without a stitch of money."

"What? But I see you put bags in the trunk? They give you for free? You know that store manager is damn fresh. Don't take nothing from his ass. Watch me and him." Maw unbuckled her seat belt.

"Maw," Mavis stretched her hand across Maw's chest, "it's ok."

"You know I don't fool with Raul. I don't trust that long pinky nail," Maw declared. They both laughed.

Maw was always ready to defend her loved ones. Even in her 70s, she had no problem approaching the sleazy supermarket manager and telling him a thing or two in both English and Spanish.

"I ran into Asha," Mavis said.

"Who?"

"Asha, Maw. You know the girl Hersh brought around?" Mavis started the car. "Well thank God she was in the store, she paid for the stuff I was buying." Mavis stole a glance at her mother before saying, "I told her about Beverly. I said we had a death in the family. She's going to come to the service."

Maw turned to her daughter, "Now May, I don't know if that was a good idea. You know how he sensitive. Something happened why he and the girl ain't tie up like before."

"I know, but," Mavis remembered what Asha told her in the store,

"I think it will help him."

"Well he extra sensitive now."

"Yes, Maw, but we can't keep coddling him." Mavis' frustration reared its head.

"Is a time of death, May. What other time than now to help him?" Maw's voice rose.

"I didn't say not to help him. I said we can't coddle, Maw. He used to us spoiling and doting on him. And these women ain't no help. They just clamor to him. Ever since he could pee straight, Lord," Mavis exhaled.

"Me? I ain't spoil Hersh." Maw turned away from her daughter and looked out the passenger side window.

"Don't start." She said to the back of her mother's head. "I don't know who spoiled him worse, but it's time for him to be a man. None of us can blame Beverly anymore."

Purple Ties

Daniel looked at his black suit hanging on the closet door. He didn't want to put it on. He didn't want to go. Twice he got out of bed and twice sat back down. Jada called him three days ago.

"Hi, um Daniel?"

"Yes?"

"This is Jada. Ms. Mavis gave me your number?"

Daniel's hand squeezed the phone. "Hi. I'm sorry 'bout your... I mean...um, Beverly."

"Thank you," Jada sighed. "Listen, I know this is awkward and I understand if you decline," Jada paused. "Hello?" Jada spoke into the silence.

"Yeah, I'm here." Daniel started to sweat.

"Would you... I mean...my mom never said it directly. But I feel she would have wanted it." Jada stammered. Daniel breathed into the phone. "Would you be a pallbearer for my mom? Please?" Jada's voice went faint.

He could barely hear her. A wave of anxiety washed over him. He was being asked to carry the dead body of the woman who birthed him. Daniel's stomach started to bubble. There was no way he could bring himself to do that. He shut his eyes tight.

"I'm sorry, but I can't. No. I can't do that," his *mind* said.

"Ok," his *mouth* said.

He heard Jada's tears through the phone. "Thank you, Daniel. Thank you so much. She would be so honored. Thank you, thank you."

"Ok," was all he could muster before he disconnected the call.

He sat on the edge of the bed and fumbled with the purple bowtie Mavis gave him yesterday. Being a friend to Beverly, she knew all about Jada's request. She asked him to wear the purple tie since it was Beverly's favorite color. Everyone was asking him to honor this woman. He couldn't bring himself to call her his mother. He didn't know why he found it hard to believe she was gone. She'd been gone all his life. He had a mind to get back into bed and dream this whole day away. But he couldn't because his mother asked him to pick her up, to wear the tie and to not be late. He got off the bed and reached for his suit.

The service was a daze. Daniel sat in between Maw and Mavis and stared straight ahead. Germ, Crane and Uncle Vincent sat behind them. The casket was beautifully draped with a rich velvet purple pall. The powerful scent from the dozens of floral arrangements arrested his sense of smell. Daniel silently thanked God that the casket was closed. He did not want to see her again, and he definitely did not want to see her lifeless body. He would remember her jovial and lively personality from their last encounter. It was only when she spoke to him privately that he sensed her pain. During the dinner, she was indeed the life of the party and Mavis was swept up in her charisma. He'd never seen his mother laugh like a schoolgirl or hear her tell such silly stories. Beverly was the ying to his mother's yang. It was then that he saw the bond between them was more like sisters than of friends.

The service ended, and Daniel began to sweat. Maw tilted her head up, in spite of her dramatic wide brimmed black hat, and looked at her grandson. "May, tell that girl Hersh not feeling good. Look how he sweating."

"Maw, I'm fine," he told her.

"If you don't feel well, it's ok, you know?" Maw gave a stern look over to Jada's direction with her nostril flared.

"I'm ok." He hugged her shoulder and walked over to where Jada was standing.

"Hey." He rubbed Jada's arm.

"Hi," she turned to him and said. He saw that her eyes were small, and she lost weight since the dinner. She gave him a hug and held on tight.

"These are my two cousins, these are brothers from our church and these are my neighbors. This is Daniel," she said to the group of men decked out in purple ties. They all looked at him with unabashed wonderment. Exactly what he wanted to avoid coming to this funeral: being the Bigfoot, Loch Ness Monster and Abominable Snowman of the hour. Daniel gave a nod to them. Just then, the funeral director came in and instructed them in regards to exiting the funeral home.

The actual lifting and carrying of the casket to the hearse was a blur. Daniel checked out and blindly followed the man in front of him. Once his hands were free from carrying Beverly's remains, he took a deep breath and looked into the crowd of mourners for Mavis and Maw. He scanned the crowd twice and couldn't find them. On his third try, he saw Maw in an embrace. He looked closer to make sure it was in fact his grandmother. *Who the hell would she be hugging at this service?* he thought. Once Maw released from the embrace, he met a wave of wild, honey-blond curls and solemn grey eyes.

Apology Repast

Daniel's heart leapt against his will. "The fuck is she doing here," he mouthed. He made his way through the crowd as several people patted his back and shook his hand. They all seemed to know who he was. Maybe he wasn't Beverly's dark little secret after all. The thought gave him conflicting feelings. But he had enough emotions going on. He had to deal with the most disturbing emotion at hand; the one he felt building in his chest as he got closer to where she stood.

Maw saw the determination in her grandson's gait, so she quickly met him halfway. "You alright, my sweet?" She put her hand to his chest.

"I'm fine." His eyes were fixed on Asha in conversation with Mavis.

"Look Hersh, don't be an ass," Maw said. His eyes darted to Maw. "The girl came because May asked her to," she informed him.

"What?!" Daniel exclaimed.

The people around them turned in their direction.

"Mind how you yelling, boy!" She put her finger to his face.

He guided Maw to a less crowded area of the sidewalk. "Why would she do that?" Beads of sweat formed on his head. He undid his tie.

"We saw her at the market a couple days back." Maw took a monogrammed kerchief from her designer clutch and motioned for Daniel to bend down. She patted his forehead and the sides of his face. "May told her that Beverly passed," she said. Daniel opened his mouth to speak and Maw cut him off. "She tell the girl Beverly was a relative. She ain't tell all your business." Daniel exhaled. "That girl

328

care for you, Hersh," she told him.

"Maw, you don't know what she did," Daniel started.

"Look, I don't engage in all you young people nastiness," Maw's voice began to rise. Daniel looked up into the sky. "Just have some broughtupsy when you greet her," she demanded. He looked past Maw into the distance. "You hear?!" Maw warned.

"Yes, Maw," he obliged.

Once they maneuvered through the crowd, they found Mavis, Asha, Jada and Karen in conversation. Jada hugged Daniel. She quickly became attached to him. Staring at him, holding his hand and hugging him before and after the service. She, more than Karen, knew how her mom loved and pined for him. Beverly shared with Jada on her deathbed that while she never regretted asking Mavis to raise him, she wished she would have formed a better relationship with him.

Karen was initially standoffish. She was certain that Jada's request would be denied. However, her heart softened when he showed up in his purple tie. She stood by silently as Jada presented him with a purple gift box before the service began. They both watched his face as he opened it to reveal a funeral program and memorial card. Also in the box was a small hospital wristband that looked even smaller in his hands. They watched as he squinted to read the blurry name on the band. He looked at them both and croaked out a *thank you*. The last item in the box was a photograph they found in Beverly's things. The photo showed the four of them sitting on a stoop. Beverly had Jada on one knee, Daniel on the other and Karen seated on the step above them hugging her mother's neck. Daniel was still in diapers and wore those hard-ass baby shoes that helped toddlers stabilize when preparing to walk.

"I was just thanking Asha for coming," Jada expressed as she smiled into his face.

Daniel nodded. "Excuse us," he said to the group and signaled for Asha to follow him away from the area.

Asha walked behind him as he removed his blazer. He leaned against one of the cars in the parking lot. Her mind flashed to their date at the gallery. His proposition to drive her home in the morning seemed like such a distant memory, considering all that had taken place since then. His eyes were tired and lacked the twinkle it usually gave. He was clean-cut and sported a sharp goatee instead of the beard she was used to. He gingerly laid his blazer on the hood of the car, folded his arms and looked into her. Even in this instance, she couldn't help but to get swept up in the masculinity he exuded. The open first button and untied bowtie catapulted her mind into thoughts of him being further unclothed.

She shook the imagery from her mind and began with, "Hi." He only blinked in response. "Um, my condolences. This... this is for you." She offered him a card out of her envelope pocketbook.

He reached for it, and his fingers brushed hers. They both flinched. "Thanks," he said dryly.

"Listen, I know this isn't the most appropriate time or place..." she started.

"Yeah, it isn't," he countered.

"Well, I just want to let you know I'm sorry." Her eyes were genuine. She looked down at the pavement and shifted her weight from left to right foot.

"Yeah, me too." She looked up, not sure of how to interpret his statement. "Sorry it didn't work out between us," his mouth said, but his body language showed no remorse.

She took a deep breath. "I admit that I fucked up." She fidgeted with her pearl necklace. His eyes were steady on her. "I didn't think it would be a big deal to someone like you," she confessed. He tilted his head. "I mean, I know you have your choice of women. We never said we were exclusive...I don't want to get back into that discussion again." She sighed, "I just didn't want to be more into you than you were into me. It may have been a defense mechanism more than anything else." She thought she saw his eyes soften, but he said nothing.

To lighten the mood, she changed the topic of conversation. "I saw pics from your convention." He gave her a puzzled look. "I mean, I'm not a stalker or anything," she joked.

"You like looking at pictures of me online." He looked down at his shoes and back up at her with a small smile. She blushed.

"I didn't know you were so," she searched for the word, "accomplished."

"What does that mean?"

"I mean, you never said anything about being part owner of the shop. Your experience, education and whatnot," she sheepishly told him.

"Would that have changed anything?"

"Well, no. I mean...not like that. I... I don't know," she bumbled.

He examined her face. She was apologetic and embarrassed. "My mom and grandmother are degree freaks. They wouldn't let me fix cars without a post-graduate degree. But, I'm really just a grease monkey with an impressive vocabulary," he smiled.

His reference warmed her heart. "Well, I have good news for you, grease monkey. You're eligible for another massage. I'm definitely going to get certified, and I need the practice," she announced. His eyes brightened, and his left eyebrow went up. "A clean and dry massage!" she laughed. He finally broke into a smile, and she felt a weight lifted off her shoulders. "I hope we can at least be cordial." Her voice broke, and she faked it into a cough. "Maybe we can build that into a friendship? I really liked you, Daniel. I was just afraid."

He wasn't sure how to respond to her. He wanted to believe her, but he was drained from everything that occurred between them and today's events. And then seeing her again. It took balls for her to show up here. Even to speak to his mom and grandmother took courage. She's lucky they didn't know the full story.

"Beverly was my birth mother," he blurted out.

Her jaw dropped. "What?! I mean, oh my God. But? Oh no, I'm so sorry." She rushed into the space between his legs and wrapped her arms around his neck. He was taken aback at first but returned her embrace. "Oh, Daniel," she said into his neck. His heart melted at her touch and kind words. She pulled away from him but kept her hands linked around his neck. Her eyes were glassed over. "I didn't know. Your mom, well Ms. Mavis, told me it was a relative. But, she didn't say. Well, of course not. How horrible. I'm so sorry." He watched her mouth deliver the sympathetic rant. He missed the plump pout of her lips.

"They were best friends," he spoke into her face.

She hugged him again and abruptly let go. "Sorry. I mean for just bum-rushing your personal space like that. I'm sorry about a lot of things today." She brushed nonexistent lint off his shoulder and chest.

"I appreciate you coming," he told her.

"I assume they're waiting for you." She saw Mavis and Maw looking in their direction.

"Yeah." He stood up off the car.

"Well, um, I'm around. You can call, text, whatever. You have my um…everything," the words fell out of her mouth.

Daniel didn't know what he felt. He pulled her close and kissed her forehead. Asha received his kiss and filed it into a reserved space in her heart.

Wave Your Flag

His phone buzzed.

Germ: Yo, you comin'?

Daniel: Nah

Germ bugged him about going to Jouvert for the last couple of days, in an effort to pull him out of his funk. Daniel reached for the bottle of whiskey and poured another shot. It was the same bottle Asha had given him. He took the bottle and shot glass over to the couch. He promised Maw he would play Mas in the band she'd played in for years. That was the only reason he was going tomorrow. Plus he already paid a shit load of money for his costume.

He put his legs up on the couch hoping for sleep to come. He hadn't been able to sleep without the help of Jack since the funeral. When he did sleep, he had reoccurring nightmares. The dreams usually involved Asha and Beverly travelling together. In one version, Asha and Beverly were riding on a bus that he couldn't catch. Another version of the dream involved Beverly picking Asha up in his Benz, despite the fact that he held the keys in his hands. Maw always told him that dreams don't walk straight, but he was certain about the theme of these nightmares. Beverly's unsolicited advice on his mother's deck that night played over and over in his head: *If you find someone special and she tugs at your heart, don't drive her away.* The one piece of advice he'd ever gotten from her, he wasn't able to follow.

Bored and agitated, he scrolled through his phone and came across a text from Jennifer. It happened to be an almost nude of her in her bathtub. She'd been coming at him hardcore ever since he finally

333

took her up on her offer of discounted designer footwear. She was a quick lay and had no qualms about cocking up her legs on a step ladder in the store's stock room. When he was done, he walked away with a pair of Allen Edmonds and a proposal for a threesome. She served the immediate purpose of shoes and a hard-on, but he had no other use for her. No conversation or connection on any other level.

He felt the effects of the shots creeping up on him. He went through his timelines until he came across a post from Jada. She found him online shortly after the funeral, and he returned her follow. He was cordial but somewhat distant with her and Karen. There was uncertainty about whether he wanted to open himself up to his remaining bloodline. Jada posted several pictures from the service. There were pictures of her and Karen, some guests and floral arrangements. His stomach tightened at the post that followed; it was a group picture of Jada, Karen, Mavis, Maw and Asha. The summation of his female relationships stared at him through the screen. Jada and Karen link to a pre-historic foundation that reached out to embrace him despite their now broken bond. Mavis and Maw were his collective backbone. Their love and support shaped him into who he was. And finally, Asha. He knew he wanted to build with her. He thought he gave it his best, albeit territorial and overbearing. There were only two women in his life that ever held back their feelings for him. And one of them was now gone. He decided he loved Asha and wanted her to love him back.

Asha slept most of Labor Day away. When she was awake, she thought of Daniel. She was tired and chalked it up to overdoing it at her spin class yesterday. Although she initially dismissed Daniel's warnings about the trainers, she'd come to see that there was truth to his cautions. Once she'd peaked and was super close to her goal weight, her trainer became a little too friendly. Hinting at taking her out and asking about her personal life. She decided to end the sessions and transferred her paid sessions to Cleo.

Her kitchen clock read a quarter past five. Hungry but too lazy to cook, she opened her drawer of takeout menus. She pulled out the sushi menu and a wave of depression fell over her. She recalled their dinner at Xaga when she spilled her guts to him. In hindsight, he treated her differently after that dinner. It was a turning point in their...relationship. He became more attentive to her. Attentive and present. She recalled his eyes in the parking lot at the funeral. They looked lost, sad and tired. But she was just glad to see him again and relieved he accepted her presence.

Her doorbell rang, and the cats meowed. She wasn't expecting anyone, so she ignored it. It rang again. Déjà vu of the night of her pre-birthday dinner. She crept to the door and peeped out the peephole. Her heart did a somersault. "Oh my God," she whispered.

She ran to the bathroom and checked her hair and face. She looked sullen and tired, which is exactly how she felt. She came back to the door, took a deep breath and slowly opened it.

A carnival warrior stood on the other side of the door. An elaborate breastplate in shades of turquoise, blue and green hung from his shoulders and broad chest. Matching medallion arm cuffs hung onto his biceps for dear life. Blue shorts with a feathered and fringed apron in similar hues covered his muscular thighs. Hints of the costume leg cuffs peeked out from the top of his construction Timberlands.

"Hey," he said weakly.

"Hi," she answered while her thirsty eyes drank him in. "What are you doing..." she stopped herself. "I mean, is everything ok with your mom and Ms. Jacobs?" she asked first.

"They're fine," he told her.

She stepped aside and invited him to come in. As he crossed her threshold, she got a whiff of one of his seven scents mixed with outside, sweat, grilled food and a hint of liquor.

"I hope you're coming from the parkway," she laughed.

He smiled, "I forgot I was wearing this shit."

"I saw some of it online," she said. "Looks like a LOT."

"Yeah, it is," his eyes were tired, "but I promised my grand-mother."

"Ms. Jacobs?" Asha gasped.

Daniel removed his phone from a hidden pocket in the costume. He showed her a picture of himself and Germ in their warrior getups; flanking Maw in her similarly colored sparkly costume complete with headpiece.

"She is something else," Asha laughed.

Daniel laughed, too. Neither said anything for a moment. Finally, Daniel spoke. "I...um," he looked down at the floor, "I want to apologize for what happened at Applebee's. I couldn't get an apology together at the service. My mind wasn't in the right place."

"No. Please, you don't have to apologize. Considering what all happened." Asha looked away from him.

"I shouldn't have lost my temper. My grandmother's friend," he paused and blinked hard, "is helping me with the desk appearance."

"Desk appearance? I didn't press any charges. I told them no. I told them several times I didn't want to press charges," Asha recalled frantically.

"Public disturbance and destruction of property. Big, angry, black guy tearing shit up," he half-smiled.

She hugged herself and leaned against the back of her couch. "I'll call my uncle. He knows some people in Nassau County."

"It's ok, I got it," he told her. His breastplate lifted and fell. "Maybe, we could try again." His eyes were intense and glassy. She hoped it was her hallway lighting. "The summer was crazy," he continued. "We kinda dove into it. I don't know if it was the heat, solstice or what," he laughed.

"Danny," she said to him and paused. She tried to get her mind to stop racing in order to formulate a sentence. Her hesitation was enough for him.

He held up his hand. "You don't have to say it. It's cool. Had to shoot my shot." He opened her door, stepped out and the door closed behind him.

Fuck, she thought to herself. She opened the door to call him and collided into his chest.

"Sorry." He held her waist, out of habit, to steady her. "I almost forgot. Your book." He pulled the book out from another pocket in the costume. "You can call me a lot of things, but you can't call me a thief." He stepped back and handed her the book.

She thumbed through the book. "Well, this book is overdue," she teased while raising her eyebrow.

"Yeah, sorry about that." He turned to walk away.

"Daniel," she called to him. He turned around to her, dreading the oncoming *we're better off as friends* speech. Instead, she tiptoed up and cradled his face in her hands. Her lips met his in a kiss he'd been missing. "I'm sorry. And I want us to try again. I love you." She felt her pulse in her eyelids.

His heart expanded into his throat, making speech almost impossible. "I love you too, Asha," he exhaled. His declaration left him winded.

She smiled into his weary face. "Now," she led him back into her apartment, "to figure out how you're gonna work off this overdue fine." Her eyes sparkled.

"What? I thought you loved me?" he laughed once on the other side of the door.